THE OCCUPYING POWER

By the same author

BY THE NORTH GATE
SOMETHING OF AN ACHIEVEMENT
MASTER OF THIS VESSEL
FREEDOM OBSERVED
A SIGNIFICANT EXPERIENCE
A LAST LAMP BURNING
AN OPERATIONAL NECESSITY
THE OCCUPYING POWER

Short Stories
A SCORPION ON A STONE

Gwyn Griffin

THE
OCCUPYING
POWER

G. P. Putnam's Sons
New York

c. 2

FIRST AMERICAN EDITION 1968

Copyright 1956 by Gwyn Griffin
Copyright © 1968 by Patricia V. Griffin

*Library of Congress Catalog
Card Number: 68-26797*

THE OCCUPYING POWER

During World War II, British soldiers
take over an island, but cut off from
the mainstream of the conflict, they
proceed to go native with happy abandon.

I

By three o'clock, the hour of mid-siesta, the house was asleep. Drugged by the heavy heat, it lay silent and white under the glare of the afternoon sun. The wide gardens in front with their neatly spaced hibiscus, oleander, and jasmine bushes, the wide, treed lawns behind that stretched in terraced slopes up the hill, lay empty and still beneath the blazing sky. Even the tiny sparkling lizards sought the shade at this hour and crouched, motionless except for their quickly pulsing throats, in the nooks and crannies of the rockery whose gray boulders shimmered in the heat zenith of the day.

The interior of the big house was filled with a green gloom and the soft swish of electric fans. An occasional chink in the heavy wooden shutters let in a glint of bright light, a thin shaft of gold down which the dust motes swam lazily, emphasizing the dim cool dusk within. The coolness was only comparative to the blazing heat outside; it was not really cool, but mostly an illusion caused by the green twilight of the shuttered house and the artificial draft of the whirring fans. Without the fans the siesta would have been quite impossible—as had been proved on more than one occasion when the power plant broke down.

Colonel Giordano, lying in an unnaturally strained position on the double bed he shared with his wife, had only just gone to sleep. For an hour he had tossed and turned irritably and, despite the four fans that depended from the high painted ceiling, the sweat dripped off his half-naked torso and dampened the sheet beneath him. He was still feeling the effects of the attack of food poisoning he had brought upon himself three days before. It had been caused by a surfeit—the Colonel ate surfeits of all his favorite dishes with unwholesome regularity—of slightly dubious oysters, and for nearly twenty-four hours he had lain doubled up

7

with pain on this very bed. He had received scant sympathy from anyone except Dr. Valdonetti, who admired the dogged way in which the Governor continually disregarded his professional advice despite the unpleasant effects of so doing, and this had induced a fit of depression that had not yet worn off.

The hum of a motorcycle coming up the hill throbbed faintly in the dim air of the bedroom, swelled to a stuttering roar as the machine approached the house, and ended in a series of crashing little explosions as the engine was revved up and switched off in the courtyard outside. The Colonel groaned and sat up, pressing the tips of his fingers into his eyes. His brown face, weary, lined and a little dissipated, had the look of a melancholy, rather sly monkey.

There came the sound of hurried steps below and then ascending the stairs. The soft pitter-pat of the barefoot native servants and the tramp of booted feet on the tiled mosaic floors. A rattle at the ornate double doors of the bedroom—urgent voices:

"*Eccellenza!*"

"*Signor Colonnello—per favore!*"

"They've come," muttered the Governor to himself, and was surprised and faintly pleased at the calmness of his tone. "A moment!" He swung his short legs to the floor and felt with his toes for the leopard-skin slippers on the mat. Then he rose with a sigh and walked over to the door, his heedless shoes slapping and clapping on the colored tiles. His wife, he noticed as he turned the handle, was still asleep.

Outside the native servants flew about like agitated, brightly plumaged birds. "What is it?" they called to each other. "Quick, quick—come here! Oh, Mahmud, come here—and Abdulrahman —at once! *Allah karim!*"

A tall, plump young man, sweating and out of breath and wearing a limp khaki drill uniform with an automatic pistol sagging from his belt, clicked to overemphasized attention and saluted as the Colonel appeared.

"*Eccellenza,* they have come!" He shot curious glances into the Colonel's bedroom until Giordano shut the door. So they *did* sleep in a double bed after all! And Commino had said—but Commino was probably inventing in his usual malicious way. There was so much scandal about governors on this island.

8

"What has come, Amerigo?" The Colonel frowned and scratched his chest.

"It is a big warship—a battleship or perhaps a cruiser. It is standing off the harbor and they are training their guns on the town. Commino rang through from the docks about——"

"English?"

"Yes, Excellency." Carabiniere Amerigo was excited and rather frightened—excited because it was fun to be the bearer of really bad news and frightened because he would have to go down to the town again and he thought the English might start shelling it at any moment. Both emotions showed plainly on this young sunburnt face, as the Colonel noticed with a certain amount of annoyance. There was nothing for anyone to fear.

"Where is the *Maresciallo*?"

"He was asleep—he is coming."

"And Captain Diaz?"

"He has been sent for."

"The Port Pilot?"

"Also."

"Good! And don't look so scared, boy. There's nothing to be frightened about."

The young policeman flushed and scowled. Silly old bastard, he thought, I bet he's scared all right! "I'm not in the least afraid, Excellency," he said, trying, as he always did when talking with superiors, to keep the strong Sicilian accent out of his voice. "But it's very humiliating, after all," he added sulkily.

The Colonel, in his turn, scowled. "It's much worse for me, isn't it?" He turned to a tall African in a fantastic livery of green and orange. "Abdulrahman! Go and see if the children are awake. If they are they can get up. If not, don't disturb them. Understand?'

"Excellency!" The Negro bowed and pattered off.

"Wait while I dress," said the Colonel to Amerigo and slip-slapped back to the bedroom.

"Anna! Wake up!"

Signora Giordano turned over, sighed, and raised herself on her pillow. Her husband stood at the side of the bed, struggling with his tight white drill trousers. The fans whirred, but he was sweating profusely.

9

"The English have come, Anna." A button snapped off and rattled across the floor. *"Madonna mia!"* swore the Colonel under his breath.

Signora Giordano regarded her husband with large brown eyes, unintelligent and apprehensive. "Oh, Mario! At this of all times! It's not half past three!"

"The English," remarked the Colonel dryly, "do not observe the siesta." Then his tone changed. "Look, Anna," he said kindly, "you are not frightened, are you? There's nothing to be frightened about, I promise you. There will be no fighting and everything will be quiet and orderly."

"The children——" began his wife.

"Are perfectly safe," interrupted the Colonel confidently. He pulled on his tunic, heavy with gold ornamentation. "Now my belt and I must be off. I'll put some of the Banda around the house." He smiled wanly, still dripping with sweat and, wiping his face, he turned to go.

"Mario! You're not well! Can't Diaz——" But the Colonel was already out of the room.

The big white and blue reception room was full of people, mostly in uniform and all chattering and gesticulating twenty to the dozen while the native servants flew about with glasses of iced water and orangeade. The atmosphere was like that of a successful cocktail party.

When Giordano entered, gleaming and resplendent, the talk died away and ceased. The Governor glanced quickly around the room at the assembled officials. All appeared to be present, even Signor Alivetti the Sanitary Inspector, whose low social standing did not generally permit of his visiting the Villa.

Standing at the end of the room under the picture of "Il Re" and opposite that of "Il Duce," the Governor cleared his throat.

"Gentlemen, I think most of you are aware of the present situation and also of the orders from Rome concerning such an eventuality which I circulated to departments a month ago. Nothing now remains but to put them into practice. The English have arrived and we shall surrender to them. I said 'surrender', but I should, perhaps, say 'hand over'. Surrender denotes a military defeat and there has been no military defeat—nor will there be one. There are barely forty soldiers on this island and San Pietro

10

is an open town. We are a purely civil administration and as such will hand over peaceably to the English who land. Many of you, I expect, will be retained in your positions—in which case you will carry on your duties to the best of your abilities in the knowledge that within a few months at the most the armed forces of our country, together with those of our great German ally, will have broken England on land, sea, and in the air, and you will be relieved. The present position and the outlook for the immediate future are galling to us all, but we must be strong and patient. Italy will soon triumph and we shall not be forgotten because we have not been in the firing line. I have here"—the Governor unfolded a sheet of paper which he had been holding tightly in his left hand—"a message from Il Duce which I shall now communicate to you all." He cleared his throat. "Italians! Comrades! Colonial citizens on the Island of Baressa! . . ."

The Island of Baressa—an irregular oval ninety-five miles long and some fifty miles broad at its widest point, nearly a third of which was desert—was one of Italy's earliest and most disappointing colonial acquisitions. It lay, edged by a rocky, and in places, palm-fringed coast, in shark-infested waters six hundred miles off the northeast coast of Italian Somaliland between Socotra and the Laccadive Islands. For years it had been the stronghold of pirates—Arabian, Indian, and African. Dhows chased each other through the intricate passages among the reefs and small rocky islets along its northeastern coast. Sometimes they fished halfheartedly for pearls and fought bloody little marine battles for the pearling grounds among the rocky promontories and barren capes. What Tortuga was to the buccaneers of the West Indies, Baressa and its bleak satellites were to the marauders of the Arabian Sea.

In 1860 the island had become the base of a loose confederacy of polyglot privateers under the still looser control of a cashiered officer of King Charles Albert's Sardinian Grenadiers. This cheerful, bibulous brigand was a certain Captain Count Giulio Brocca, a man whose lurid escapades had proved too much even for the colorful insurgent commanders of the Risorgimento. Brocca had had to fly from Italy with a price on his head, though the biography published in 1936, with a laudatory preface by H.E. the Head of the Government, conveniently ignores this fact.

11

The splendid idea of hoisting the newly victorious tricolor over his island came to Brocca when gold was accidentally discovered on the arid northwest coast. He needed some official standing, some protection, before he could start mining properly, and he saw no reason why his native land should not provide it. So the green, white, and red banner bearing the Cross of Savoy was hauled to the top of a lopped palm tree above the squalid clutter of palm-thatched huts that comprised Baressa's only "town" and Brocca became "His Excellency The Governor."

For adding to the territories of his country Brocca's crimes were all discreetly forgotten; he was presented with the coveted 'Collar', and Victor Emmanuel sent out a young lawyer, a Signor Gasparo Da Ponte, to advise and assist his new 'cousin'.

It was regrettable that Brocca should have died almost before he had received a chance to profit from the advice of his young assistant. A mysterious complaint, which to a modern doctor might have seemed to display all the symptoms of powdered glass administered in a cup of coffee, killed him only two months after the arrival of the advocate. Da Ponte had no difficulty in getting himself made the new governor and swore, with tears in his eyes, to carry on the good work of colonial administration where the ex-Sardinian Grenadier had so abruptly left off. He started by interring the remains of his genial and wicked old predecessor under a particularly heavy marble tomb and then settled down to a life of efficient, if rather corrupt, government.

It was during Da Ponte's long rule that the island became really populated. Arabs, Indians, Levantines, and members of the oppressed minorities of the Balkans came, attracted by the lure of gold, and, not finding any, stayed to eke out precarious livings as best they could. An exiled Abyssinian Dejazmach, banished by the Emperor Menelik, arrived with a large retinue and founded the monastery and little supporting village of Addi Jesus on the inland plateau. A few years later the remains of a Sudanese tribe from Kordofan, who had offended the Khalifa Abdullahi, landed and built themselves a straw-thatched village—Agamo, they called it—on the coast. They made a happy little community, unenterprising, lazy, and intensely polygamous.

By the end of the century the little town in the bay where Brocca had first hoisted Italy's flag had acquired the name of San Pietro and the status of a capital city. It had more than a dozen roads, some offices, a native market, and a low rambling bungalow of a building glorified with the name of Governor's Palace.

Little by little as the years went by the town expanded. Roads pushed out farther into the dusty coastal scrubland; native huts sprang up along them, decayed, and were replaced by low mud-brick houses. Then these in their turn were pulled down and small, pretty European bungalows with white walls and little flower-filled gardens took their place. Government offices became less uninspiring; avenues of scarlet Golden Mohurs, blue jacarandas, and pink and white oleander bushes lined the principal streets. Prosperity, in the form of dhows from Yeman, Oman, Aden, and Somalia, arrived increasingly as the years went by. A customs tariff was introduced, and the coffers of the Administration began to fill.

Though the gold mine found by Brocca proved to be quite small and soon ran out, the Italian public had somehow become convinced that minerals, at least in small quantities, abounded on Baressa. During the early years of the new century an influx of more or less undesirable prospectors arrived on the island. They were invariably unsuccessful, returning after a few months from the interior, empty-handed and penniless, to lounge about the waterfront of San Pietro and make themselves a general nuisance to the authorities. Only two of them—an astute Jew called Saccomani and a clever but unfortunate young geologist named Balla —had the sense to cut their losses and buy fruit plantations on the plateau.

In the early 1930s Mussolini sent naval, military, and air force personnel to report on the strategical possibilities of the island, and after three months they returned to Rome and reported very adversely. The harbor of San Pietro was too small and shallow to berth anything larger than a light cruiser; the dock facilities, good enough for tramps and small freighters, were entirely unsuited for naval craft, and the construction of a dry dock was out of the question. With its long, exposed coastline the island, from a military point of view, was indefensible, and the air force representative said that the only possible site for a landing ground was on the low, arid northern plain, and the making of one would mean clearing a forest of dense though stunted trees. So, beyond the retention of one battalion of African infantry— whose officers regarded the island in the light of a punishment

13

station and consequently spent their tours in sullen idleness—
Baressa escaped the militarization that was being pressed forward
in the rest of the expanding New Roman Empire.

During the early months of 1940 all the African troops except
one depleted company were shipped unostentatiously to Somalia.
Several of the more important senior government officials went
with them. Some minor trouble in Abyssinia was given as the reason for the troop movements, and it was not until war was declared in June that the inhabitants of sleepy, out-of-date Baressa
woke up to the fact that they were undefended. Even then confusion and dejection were confined to the small class of government officials. No one else was very perturbed. The war was, after all, a long way off and nothing to do with them. Even Captain
Antonio Diaz, the extremely unwarlike commander of the tiny
garrison, could hardly be bothered to take any active measures.
He spent practically all his time absorbed in his hobby of con-
chology. "The King," he was wont to say with what he considered
to be unanswerable logic, "is a gentleman. He does not work. He
spends his time collecting coins. I, Diaz, am also a gentleman. I
will spend mine collecting shells." And he did. The forty-odd
native troops, left to themselves, grew slacker and dirtier every
day and indulged in petty pilfering in the bazaars. Their private
lives caused a continual series of minor scandals.

Thus on the hot afternoon of 29th August, 1940, when Carabiniere Aldo Commino, who was on dock duty, sitting at the end
of the Dhow Control Point, looked drowsily out to sea and saw a
warship steaming rapidly toward the coast, he realized, as he
reached for the telephone, that a new phase of life had begun for
Baressa.

2

ANOTHER afternoon a fortnight later. Fortunato Malema, sitting in a window seat of the long, lofty reception hall in the
ex-Governor's villa, twanged softly on his cheap guitar and gazed
out between the pillars of the loggia over the silent, heat-still

garden, empty and shadowless beneath the blazing sky. He thought with a detached interest over the events of the past two weeks. The arrival of the English cruiser, the landing of the soldiers by lighter—they had been decorously formed up on the docks and marched in sections to different points of vantage throughout the town—and then the landing of the armored cars. One of the cars had refused to start on its journey up the planks from the lighter's deck to the dockside, and after a good deal of fussing on the part of an English corporal it had backfired twice and shot in reverse over the stern of the lighter and into the sea. The driver had come spluttering to the surface to receive volleys of abuse from a young red-haired lieutenant and shouts of derision from his comrades. That had been the only untoward scene in the short, efficient course of the occupation. It had all seemed very unwarlike, somehow, and the English soldiers, though they got drunk in a dull unostentatious sort of way each evening, behaved very well. A week ago they had all left, handing over to a company of black troops from Africa, in appearance very much like Diaz's neglected soldiery, who had taken over the old barracks and did sentry duty outside the Palace in the town in the same way as their colored predecessors.

When the English soldiers left, embarking by lighter on an ugly black transport that stood outside on the roads, they took with them the Governor, his family and entourage, several of the higher officials, and Captain Diaz. Fortu had driven the Giordanos down to the docks on their last journey, a sad and distrait little family. Shorn of the prestige and dignity of their position, they rapidly reverted to the humble attitudes of the bourgeois stock from which they came. Sitting in front beside Fortu the Colonel had muttered worriedly to himself as he clasped an unwieldy brown-paper parcel and two Thermos flasks of cold water on his knees. Behind him Signora Giordano alternated between fits of red-eyed weeping at having to leave her house and furniture and attempts to console the children, who wept noisily in sympathy with their mother. Their luggage—leather bags, tin boxes, fiber suitcases, and wicker hampers—was piled all over the car, lashed with rope to the back and running boards until the springs were strained to breaking point. Fortu had had to drive very slowly and carefully. On the docks they found the Colonel's secretary, the Port Commandant, the schoolmaster, and three acting heads of local Fascist organizations, all standing about gloomily and surrounded by piles of luggage. Some distance away Captain Diaz was sitting on a bulging broken suitcase, blinking uncomfortably through his steel-rimmed spectacles. Some English soldiers walked slowly about with awkwardly held rifles as if uncertain whether or not they were on duty.

Fortu had never liked the Giordanos. They had only been on Baressa three years, but they had adopted a patronizing and condescending attitude to the island and its inhabitants—an assumption of complete superiority over everything and everybody—that had, to a greater or lesser degree, alienated most of the members of the older colonial population. The Colonel's pompous announcements in the Press and his wife's intense pride in his position—she had once, in a moment of condescension, told Fortu how lucky the island had been to receive her husband as Governor, and what a great career he had unselfishly given up by leaving the Royal Army—had done nothing to mitigate their growing unpopularity. But now, as they stood forlorn and unhappy on the dockside under the glaring sky, trying to comfort their children with cups of cold water from their Thermos flasks, even Fortu's hostile indifference was changed momentarily to half-contemptuous pity by their obvious and undignified misery.

Later, after much fretting and vexation about the baggage, the lighter had cast off. The last Fortu had seen of the Giordanos had been a small, dejected group—a fat small man, a fat tall woman, two pale thin children—staring back to shore from the stern of the lighter as it passed the Dhow Control Point.

The docks had seemed strangely empty when his erstwhile employers had gone. Fortu sat down on the hot running board of the big blue car and gazed out across the glittering sea to the British transport that shimmered in the heat radiated from its own iron hull and upperworks.

"This is the Governor's car, isn't it?" asked a pleasant musical voice beside him. Looking up, Fortu saw one of the two English officers who had come by plane a few days after the arrival of the cruiser. He had seen them ferried from the flying boat to the dockside and taken in a small staff car to the British Headquarters at the Municipio. He got up.

"Yes, *signore.*"

The officer was tall and very thin and carefully dressed. He

16

wore the three gold stars of a captain on each shoulder. He gazed down at Fortu from black eyes of an almost birdlike brightness —self-assured, arrogant, yet not unkindly.

"And who might you be?"

"I'm the Governor's driver—I was."

The Captain smiled and Fortu smiled back, and there was a sudden bond between them—a knowledge that neither regretted the departure of the Giordanos.

"I don't think he'll be needing a driver where he's going. I suppose that means you're out of a job?"

"Yes—but it doesn't really matter."

"Well, we're having this car. You can drive for us if you like."

"For you?"

"For the Senior Civil Affairs Officer—the English Governor—and for me, too, sometimes."

"Thank you."

"I hope you drive carefully. The Senior Civil Affairs Officer insists on careful driving. You're rather young. How old are you?"

"Sixteen. I've been driving this car for a year. Colonel Giordano thought——"

"Very seldom, if ever," interrupted the Captain dryly, "and then to no effect. If you want to keep this job I advise you never to mention Giordano's name, let alone his thoughts, to the Senior Civil Affairs Officer. He's fed up with Giordano."

"Oh!"

"Yes." The Captain smiled. "Well, now you can take me up to the Villa of the Unmentionable Personage—for that's where we are going to live."

So Fortu had been taken on and had become the first of the islanders to be employed by the British Military Administration.

A butterfly with great pointed wings of scarlet and yellow hovered for a moment above the hot gravel under the window and then landed on a pebble where it sleepily shut and opened its brilliant papery wings. Fortu watched it absently while his fingers softly picked out the notes of "La Paloma" on his guitar—notes which fell slowly, lazily, one by one into the intense still afternoon like leaves floating down a dim well.

Major Euan Lemonfield, coming in at the far end of the lofty rooms, paused under the recent site of the picture of Victor Emmanuel III—now, by his orders, reposing in the lumber shed behind the garage—arrested by the delicate haunting music of Yradier's "Mexican Serenade." Softly, sadly, the throbbing nostalgic notes hovered and fainted in the hot, sleepy timelessness of the long afternoon. Mexican music. Fortu was almost dark enough to be a Mexican; his somber Southern face and bare arms and legs had been burned a coppery gold, a deep glowing amber, by the tropical sun. Sitting there in the window seat, the guitar across his knees and against the background of blue sky and white sunlit pillars covered with glowing purple bougainvillea, he made a picture of dreamlike serenity. A picture, thought the Major idly as he stood, half under his spell, motionless in the doorway, that should be called "Afternoon on the Island." It would make an excellent subject for Naughton-Muirhead—he must remember to mention it at dinner that evening.

The last lingering notes of 'Paloma' faded into the hot air and Euan Lemonfield, Senior Civil Affairs Officer and Baressa's first British Governor, stepped forward into the long room.

"Good afternoon, Fortu. Are you going to drive me down to the Palace?" The Major never gave orders or issued instructions; he only requested, suggested, or advised.

Fortu put down his guitar and got up, smiling. He liked and admired the pale, delicate little Major with his quick, neat movements, quiet voice, and well-fitting, unostentatious uniforms. His small frame held a will of iron that was awe-inspiring in its strength, and in place of Giordano's windy bluster he possessed a searing sarcasm which had already been painfully felt by quite a number of the late Governor's officials at the Palace. He was everything that Giordano had not been, in fact, and consequently met with the unqualified approval of his young driver.

Together, side by side, they went out into the blinding heat of the afternoon. Fortu, at sixteen, was already a good two inches taller than the thirty-eight-year-old Major and considerably broader and stronger in build. Like many small men the Major carried himself very erect and dressed always with impeccable neatness. Somehow his short stature seemed to add to, rather than detract from, his dignity. In his presence bigger men often felt ill-proportioned and unwieldy. But then few people ever felt completely at ease in Lemonfield's presence. He was altogether too shrewd and too clever to make a comfortable companion.

When Fortu had backed the shining blue tourer out of the garage and the Major had got into the back they rolled smoothly down the white concrete drive lined with flowering shrubs and emerged at the top of the semi-private road that twisted and looped down the escarpment between banks of sisal and prickly pear to join the Via Umberto I at the end of the town.

The Governor's Villa was built on a broad shelf of the escarpment eight hundred feet above sea level, a shelf which undulated for a quarter of a mile behind the house before merging again into the southern slopes of the upland plateau. From the Villa, set in its large terraced gardens, it was possible to look down over the white roofs and dusty squares of San Pietro, less than two miles away, and to gaze far out over the glittering blue sea. A vast panorama of sunlit waters and pale sky passed Ras Godron, forming the east side of the harbor, and the native quarter of Daldacara with its high particolored lighthouse on the west. It was this all-embracing view which had induced a former Governor to build the Villa on the shelf of the mid-escarpment rather than at the top, two thousand feet farther up but nearly two and a half miles back. It was this view that consoled him for the fact that the eight-hundred-foot rise between the town and the Villa made little difference to the climate of the latter, whereas, had he built at the escarpment's top, he would have lived all the year round in a cooler, mosquitoless world.

The journey from the Villa to the Palazzo Firenze—built by Da Ponte sixty years ago as a gubernatorial residence but long since given over to the Headquarters of the Administration—took fifteen minutes, though the distance between them was less than two miles as the crow flies. While the car dropped, looping and twisting down the continual bends in the road, Major Lemonfield lay back on the uncomfortably hot upholstery and gave himself over to thought, becoming in a moment totally unaware of the heat of the blue and gold afternoon or the dust and bumps in the rough road.

Six months before, he had temporarily, and decidedly against his will, given up a particularly promising career at the Bar to join the small military organization that was later to supply the governments of the occupied enemy territories. He spoke good Italian, though not with the easy fluency and mastery of idiom of his second-in-command, and his outstanding personal qualities

19

were so obvious that he had been selected from among many older and more experienced men to rule this first piece of Italian territory to fall into British hands. Among the officers at the training school he had from the first been the star pupil. Had he possessed any actual experience of colonial government he would almost certainly have been retained as one of the senior staff instructors with the rank of colonel. As it was, he was given Baressa and a strong hint of bigger things to come.

It was not of himself he was thinking, however, as Fortu drove down the mountain road, but of the other Englishmen who were to work under him and the work they would have to do. And this work would be vast. It was, one might say, a parting legacy from Colonel Giordano. For a week Colonel Giordano had, in accordance with his instructions, attempted to hand over to the English officers. His idea of handing over had been to tabulate at great length and in sextuplicate all the furniture and equipment in all the offices down to the very nibs, drawing pins and typewriter erasers, and then to get the Englishmen to sign for them. He explained that this was the way Italian government departments always handed over. It was the way he would have handed over to another Italian Governor. He had been told to hand over and he didn't know how to do it in any other way. When asked questions about the population, trade, agriculture, revenue, native customs—in fact, about anything pertaining to the island or its inhabitants—he became confused and evasive and later rather indignant. Lemonfield had tried the subordinates, but they all shrugged their shoulders, wilted under the lash of his tongue, and cringingly passed him on to their equally ignorant fellows. No one seemed to know anything at all about the island save San Pietro, and they knew little enough about that.

"But surely the Governor goes on tour?"

"No. He is too busy here."

"But he's been on the island three years! He must have been on tour at some time?"

"Not as yet, *signore*. He had not been able to find the time."

"Then what has he been doing?"

"Working, Excellency."

"And how!"

It soon became clear that Giordano and his staff had done nothing save receive their salaries. As far as they were concerned it had been money for old rope.

"The whole of the Administration will have to be completely overhauled," Lemonfield had said at the end of the first week. He was actually quite pleased at this. Everything would be gone into, cleared up, straightened out, and arranged on new lines dictated by himself. It was really far better to start afresh. He and Sergeant Brinsmead—thank God for Brinsmead, he was really excellent —had done fourteen hours a day ever since Giordano had left and looked like having to continue in this way for some time yet. The Major, who was undoubtedly happiest in his office, was secretly glad of this. Hour by hour he sat through the torrid day examining files, account books, and regulations, sometimes getting up to study the great map that hung on the wall behind him and that he had found rolled up and dusty behind one of the office filing cabinets. Beside him most of the time would be Brinsmead. Brinsmead, clever, energetic, tactless, and brimming over with righteous indignation as each past scandal and racket was revealed. Brinsmead standing always at his elbow to discuss, consider, and wholeheartedly acquiesce as the new form of government slowly took shape among the multitude of papers on the great desk.

"The Customs Department is really in a ghastly state, Brinsmead. Simply frightful! We'll have to get cracking on them as soon as we've got a moment."

"That's so. All the Guardie di Finanza must go, sir. They're crooks, every one of them! Look at this! And these as well!"

"I know, I know. But I can't see how we can do without them at the moment. It's not as if——"

"Bloody lot of twisters—sack them all!"

"We can't do that *yet*, Brinsmead, but I think we can keep a fairly strict eye on them like this. Now take these dutiable goods accounts for the last month. . . ."

It would mean unceasing work for himself and Brinsmead, and for Naughton-Muirhead if he chose to do it—the Major secretly hoped he would not—for months to come. And then there was the personnel side, work that Brinsmead must not be allowed to touch because of his terrifying lack of tact. Firm coercion would be the answer where the Italians were concerned.

They would be given, and must learn to cooperate with, what they had never known before—a firm, efficient, and uncorrupt administration. The Major never doubted that before long he would get their cooperation. He liked Italians; they were a civilized and gentle people—perhaps a little childish. All the more reason then, for governing them in a kindly and paternal manner. Not for one moment would he have allowed his judgment of them to be impaired by the popular emotion of hatred generated three months ago by their sudden leap upon the backs of the reeling French. Toward the native islanders the Government would be still more paternal and cautiously progressive. Their rights would be safeguarded, but there must be no silly talk of "liberation" or "throwing off the hated Italian yoke" such as had characterized the British Press two weeks ago. As far as Lemonfield had discovered, there was no national feeling among the heterogeneous native population, who appeared to be reasonably contented and enjoyed a modest prosperity.

The real trouble at the moment was the lack of reliable officials. Several of the senior government officers had left before the occupation and Giordano's lazily chaotic Administration had been running on a skeleton staff during the last month of Italian rule. Now there were no heads of departments for the Public Works, Treasury, or Trade. Lemonfield was doing the work of all three. There were no Chief Officers for the Police or Customs—Lemonfield held those posts as well.

Until two days ago there had been no senior Port personnel. Lemonfield, not being nautically qualified, had felt unable to assume the roles of Harbor Master and Port Pilot, but he often spent an hour on the docks allocating berths to the big dhows and little steamers that still plied their uncertain trade across the Arabian Sea. Then, the day before yesterday, the mail boat *Emperor Napoleon* had docked and a tousled, elderly Hungarian naval man—an improbable red-bearded relic of the Austrian Imperial Navy with a past still more lurid and romantic than that of the original Count Brocca—had stepped ashore in a condition which, if not actually drunk, could neither be said to be factually sober. To a stiff and disapproving Lemonfield he had explained in vile English that he was Captain Baron Franz Ferdinand Zvengetzov, the erstwhile lord of large estates near Kluj in Transylvania, that he had been sent to take over the docks as Chief Port Pilot and Harbor Master and that he was to be paid thirty-two pounds a month. Dismissed with difficulty from the Major's office, he had spent the rest of the afternoon badgering Brinsmead for an advance of salary by showing him a packet of crumpled but laudatory references from the Port Offices of Callao, Foochow, Chittagong, and Cadiz.

As an acquisition to the Administration Captain Zvengetzov was a disappointment, but at least, felt Lemonfield, the technical aspects of harbor management might be left in his charge—and that was something.

He had already urgently requested the dispatch from Headquarters of officers able to undertake some of the other duties and lift at least a part of the great burden of work from his shoulders. Some time, he supposed, they would come. At present the only British personnel under his direct command were Captain Naughton-Muirhead—who made a charming companion but unfortunately little else—the invaluable Brinsmead, and the signal section who ran the radio station. There was the Commandant of the colored garrison, of course, but he was nothing to do with the Administration, having, at least in theory, the only other separate command on the island. This position of an independent military command in the midst of his kingdom was a sore point with the Major. It was due to the hardly concealed feelings of distrust and dislike with which the Army proper viewed the Occupied Enemy Territories Administration—in their eyes a new upstart organization staffed by unsoldierly intellectuals. It meant that in the event of an emergency the garrison commander would take over the responsibility for the island from the Senior Civil Affairs Officer, whose position in such a case would be as unhappy as it would be vague. Though the chances of such an emergency arising on Baressa were negligible it was irksome for an officer of Major Lemonfield's energetic and dominating nature to tolerate the bare idea of such a usurpation. Altogether the situation with regard to the garrison was unsatisfactory, and though Lemonfield had nothing whatsoever against Captain Kellermann, who seemed a quiet, deferential young man, eager to please, it would, in the Major's opinion, have been a far better arrangement if the Army had seen fit to place the garrison under the authority of the Administration. But of course it was too much to expect the Army to use the meager amount of common sense it possessed when it came to an issue in which O.E.T.A. were involved. During his short service the Major had been by turns amused, incredulous, enraged, and lastly appalled at the manner in which the Army functioned. To his sharp legal mind the very word "army" had become synonymous with chaotic bureaucracy, loose thinking, and the dully malignant frustration of the orderly and logical. Ah well, on Baressa at any rate the military mind would not entangle itself like an old bluebottle in the smooth, complex radiations of the web of government. If only, thought the Major for the hundredth time, he could be sent a few—a very few—useful subordinates.

He sighed and looked up, noting with surprise that they were already in the Piazza President Wilson. The Via Mazzini was up for repairs in two places, though no work was in progress. A deep irregular trench, heaps of pale gravel, some dented bitumen barrels, and an abandoned steamroller were untidily disposed about the dusty, deserted street and effectually blocked it. Fortu turned around the back of the Greek Orthodox Church into the Piazza del Re and glided to a stop before the Palace steps. Taking a pace forward from their ornate stone boxes, two great Negro sentries from the garrison company clashed and rattled through the motions of presenting arms. The multiple rows of brass buttons on their tight white tunics glittered, the ostrich plumes surmounting their tall turbans quivered, and their polished bayonets flashed blindingly back the afternoon sun. Under the great portico at the top of the sweeping marble steps two gaily uniformed Palace footmen flung open the vast double doors and stood bowing low at either side. Major Euan Lemonfield, Baressa's new ruler, entered his Palace.

3

THE heat at four o'clock was still intense, though the hard white glare of early afternoon was changing gently to a mellower golden light from the sun falling slowly westward. It filtered through the broad leaves of banyan, papaw, and banana trees, of crowded orange and guava and hibiscus, into an over-grown dell that lay, a luxuriant green pocket, in the escarpment half a mile down the white road from the Villa. A narrow lane hemmed in between tangled branches led from the road into the heart of the dell, and Major Lemonfield had passed it unnoticing on his way down to the town an hour before. Had he seen it— which would not have been likely, for it was little more than a gap in the overgrown bank at the roadside—he might have in-quired from Fortu where it led. And Fortu would have told him that it led to the strangest house on the island; the Casa dei Fiori —the House of the Flowers.

The Casa dei Fiori had been built in 1917 by a not entirely sane young nobleman, a neurotic inbred member of the once great Venetian family of Loredano, who, fleeing from the boom of Austrian guns along the Piave, had made in Italy's farthest colonial possession this refuge from the bloody turmoil that was Europe. Here, around a grotesquely ornate and rambling bunga-low—a place full of courtyards and pillars, fountains that seldom worked, and heavy semiclassical marble sculpture—he planted a large garden, an imitation Garden of Eden. In it he made to grow every tree that is pleasant to the sight and good for food. The whole fifteen acres of ground were devoted to as close an imitation as possible of the estate of Adam. Fruit trees of every sort he planted and mixed among them tropical flowering bushes —frangipani, jasmine, oleander. In the middle there was a pond where exotic lilies of every size and color flourished in the steamy atmosphere. Count Elio Faustino Loredano employed fifteen gardeners and lived shyly, remotely, in his strange estate for six years. He seldom left his grounds and only on the rarest occasions was he seen at any official function or festival in San Pietro. He never invited anyone to visit him and, surrounding his estate with a massive hedge of prickly pear, he remained shut in with his four Indian servants and his Swiss medical attendant, Beck-mann. In 1923 he died—quite suddenly and, according to Beck-mann, of heart failure. His heart had never—again according to Beckmann—been good.

A local doctor signed the death certificate, not without some misgiving. Beckmann, who had inherited most of the Count's money, sailed for Europe. The gardeners and servants were all dismissed and the Casa was shut up pending sale.

But no one bought it.

So the great garden had reverted, quickly as gardens do in the tropics, to an unpruned rioting shrubbery, then to a tangled wilderness, and eventually to a dense forest of luxuriant vegetation through which a man could hardly have cut his way. Great mango trees jostled thick-leaved banyans and between them the slender boles of coconut and date palms and papaws shot up their emerald heads to the sun. Below the sunny treetop roof the garden was in perpetual green gloom. Huge rotting fruits lay half buried under the thick creepers that trailed among the pulpy undergrowth on the dank, rich ground. The fruit and flower trees reverted to a semiwild condition, sometimes changing or mating to produce queer freaks and exotic unsymmetrical flowers that budded, blossomed, fell, and rotted unseen in the impenetrable depths of the man-made forest. The pond became a stagnant pool, overgrown and full of decaying vegetation. Out of its teeming humid mud sprang lilies of strange twisted shapes and angry colors, orchids of brilliant sheens and horrible scents, and sickly fungi that leaped to life in a night and decayed soon after dawn.

When man moved out the animals moved in. The treetops chattered with monkeys and shrieked with parrots all day, and at sunset and dawn the whole flower forest echoed their voices. The lean, flexible shapes of rodents glimmered about in the undergrowth, and a colony of mongoose waged perpetual war against the many species of snake that writhed over the roots and along the branches of the trees. Bright birds chased broad-winged butterflies between the intricate stems and lived in crowded squalor among the fronds and branchy thickets. Several of them made melancholy, unpleasant noises at night. The pond, of course, was full of life; a myriad reptiles, amphibious and leathery, lived amongst the thick twisted stems of its exotic lilies and under its sluggish bubbling surface. No fish swam there.

The air around the low house with its overgrown patios and loggias, its cracked steps and leaning marbles, was perennially heavy with the mixed scents of the flower forest—a thick, sweet, rich smell, sleepy and languorous, reminiscent of an overstocked hothouse. Attractive, unhealthy, and queer.

In August 1940 the Casa dei Fiori found a tenant at last. He lay now, at four o'clock on this hot afternoon, uneasily asleep on

26

a low bed in one of the big, empty, shuttered rooms, a place gloomy with pillars and great panels of high-relief sculpture let into the marble walls. A young man whose rounded boy's face was marked with a broad scar that swept in an ugly red curve across the left cheekbone and up into the thick dull-gold hair. There were no fans in the Casa dei Fiori, and he lay wearing only pajama trousers, with the sweat gleaming on his chest and his scarred face creased and puckered into a strained frown. Low down on his left shoulder, just below the clavicle, the damp, glistening skin was purplish and uneven around a healed bullet wound. His left hand was clenched tightly on the pillow beside his head and he panted and muttered in the hot greenish gloom.

The door of the big room opened noiselessly, letting in a shaft of filtered yellow sunlight, and in the doorway stood a slender native in a faded blue shirt and khaki trousers. For a moment he remained motionless, silently watching. Then he crossed to the bed and sank down on his heels beside it.

"Capitano," he said, gently laying a brown hand on his master's hot damp arm. "Capitano!"

The boy on the bed groaned, shivered, and opened his eyes. Green and oddly slanted, they stared at the servant for a second in blank terror, and then as consciousness returned he sighed deeply and sat up.

"Capitano—you dream again, yes? Bad dreams?" The native spoke softly in Italian, his big dark eyes full of questioning pity.

"Yes—bad dreams, Zeki. What time is it?" The boy's voice was low and distressed; he stared glumly around the room, frowning, rubbing his forehead, not yet free from the world of his dreams.

"Four o'clock. Your bath is ready."

"Good." With an effort he got to his feet and walked slowly to the door, Zeki following obsequiously behind. Down a long corridor filled with diffused green light from narrow windows high up in the wall they walked to a high, circular, domed room in which a great bath, almost a tank of green marble, was let deeply into the floor.

"All right, Zeki. I'll be going out at five. Tell Murad I'll want Achille—and tell him to see that the harness is clean. It wasn't yesterday."

"Si, Capitano." Zeki bowed, shut the door and walked softly

back along the passage, perplexed and sad. This was the fourth time in the last ten days that he had woken the Captain from panting, groaning sleep. There was some dark spirit that entered him while he slept and held him in a black suffocating grip of pain, only grudgingly to release him on awakening. Evil spirits. Zeki understood and sympathized. He was fond of his young master, whose morose and taciturn nature seldom obtruded uncomfortably into the peaceful lives of his servants. There were old men and women up on the plateau who understood these things and knew how to deal with them. But Europeans were blind and bigoted in these matters. The Captain, he knew, would never consent to see one of the old wise people. Turning out of the long, silent corridor, Zeki shivered slightly. This old house was full of ghosts.

Lying in the cool green water of the great marble bath, Christopher began to feel better. The horror ebbed slowly away, leaving only the dull lowering depression at the back of his mind that would remain for hours like heavy purple storm clouds low down over distant hills, threatening yet static.

He gazed up at the high domed ceiling pierced by six circular windows, latticed against the larger birds but unglazed. Upon some of them the foliage of the great banyan in the court outside pressed close, bright green and shot through with gold fingers of light from the falling sun, but the others framed circles of blue sky, pure, soft blue, infinitely peaceful. All was quiet with the lazy stillness of late afternoon. In the banyan outside a pigeon cooed, gently content, and Christopher rippled the flat green water with one hand—then again complete silence.

It had been the same dream again with minor variations in the smaller incidents. Corporal Hands had brought him the last radio signal, but he knew it had really been red-haired Signalman Culverstone, who was only attached to the platoon. Little things like that—one noticed them carefully even in the dream, but it didn't make any difference somehow. It didn't make one feel, "Because this is wrong I know I'm dreaming. I know I'll soon wake up in the Casa dei Fiori. This is not reality now, even if it was once." But that didn't matter, because it had been. Six months ago. Every detail of those livid, flaming days stood out in his mind like silhouettes sharply defined against the hot glare of

28

some burning building—and there had been many burning buildings.

Nineteen-year-old Second Lieutenant Christopher Kellermann had arrived in France a few days before the Germans launched their great attack. The strong social aspirations of his family, combined with the contacts which their wealth enabled them to acquire, had made him a subaltern in one of the most famous and expensive regiments of the Army, where his good looks and deferential manners had done a certain amount to reconcile the Colonel to the fact that his newest officer was the son of a half-Dutch businessman who had made his money in sausages and cooked meat. Christopher himself was frightened of the Colonel, frightened of his company commander, and of his own tall, hard men. He hid this fear behind a smiling face and an overpolite, subservient manner to his superiors, which was beginning to gain him the condescending approval of the more elderly officers when battle started.

Then Christopher's fears were all swallowed up in the one overriding fear of action. The regiment took up its usual time-honored role of shock troops—the first in and the last out. The enemy armor swept down on them. They fought, lost heavily, and retired grimly, still fighting. To any soldier unused to battle the experience would have been shocking. To Christopher, upon whose highly nervous temperament the sights and sounds of battle struck like vicious dazing blows, it was a time of nightmare horror and torturing fear. He stumbled back with the regiment across the hot summer fields, still smiling with terror-filled eyes in the sunlight. The other officers were far too preoccupied with the complexities of rearguard actions to notice the state of one young subaltern, but his men looked, cocked smoke-grimed eyebrows—understood.

They hated him for it. In their direct, half-illiterate minds, intensely impregnated with fiercely proud regimental tradition, they had always viewed him with suspicion. He was not the type of officer to whom they were accustomed. Too diffident when he issued orders to the N.C.O.s, too willing to pass the buck, too obvious in his avoidance of having anything more to do with them than was strictly necessary. And now at last the test had come and he had failed them. He was not a proper officer at all, just a scared boy of doubtful class with a star on his shoulder. To their resentment was added a sullen, self-righteous contempt.

Then came the day on the wooded hill. The regiment retreating somewhere on the left, a battalion of French *chasseurs-à-pied* supposed to be advancing to counterattack on the other side. The signal brought by Culverstone—the platoon was to hold on at all costs in their present positions. They were to fight to the last man and last round. To Christopher it was plainly a sentence of death. The crashing reverberations of enemy shells filled the wood and the bitter smell of cordite drifted through the trees and stung his nostrils. There was no sign of the French and he had every reason to believe that he was already outflanked by hostile armor, cut off and alone in the path of the juggernaut of flame and steel that was the German advance.

Then, mistakenly, he showed the signal to Booker, the big red-faced crop-haired platoon sergeant.

"Yes, that's what it means," Booker had said slowly, insolently. "Last man, last round. That's all of us, I reckon—and you, my boy, too."

"What d'you mean?" Christopher's voice was hoarse and unsteady. "You speak to me like that! You—anyway, we can't obey this signal, it's suicide!" His voice rose as terror mastered him. "Booker! Tell the men to lay down their arms. And find something white—we're surrendering. It's over—finished! I'm not going on anymore!"

Then horror. Booker getting slowly to his feet, towering over him, some of the other men crowding around.

"So that's your game, is it, my young friend? You're going to surrender, eh?" They crowded closer, grinning; at last they'd got him. Booker's sneering, harsh voice breaking suddenly into a roar of rage. "Why, you dirty little bastard! You'd give up, would you? We'll deal with you now. We could take you back and have you shot proper if we wanted, but we're staying here to fight, see—lousy little yellow-guts—see!"

The sweep of a rifle butt, a crashing blow on the side of his face, falling, silence. A voice saying, "That'll spoil his beauty!" Then, frightened, "You'd better not, Sarge." A sharp explosion, a blow on the chest, a curious spreading numbness, and then nothing.

30

Walking back to his bedroom along the passage filled now with a soft golden light from the narrow, deep-set windows, Christopher wondered once again what had happened while he had lain bloody and unconscious on the wooded hill. He could only dimly remember the French soldiers who had found him. It was sunset and a strange quiet filled the woods, broken only by excited French voices. His men, they told him, were all dead. The sergeant? "He, too. Only, Lieutenant, does one live—one corporal. But he, too——" The *chasseur* Major had shrugged significantly, and when they loaded Christopher onto the ambulance he found beside him Corporal Hands, with no legs below the knee. The corporal had died in the ambulance and there had been no living witnesses of the scene on the wooded hill.

Dressed in a white shirt—it was one of his last, and Zeki was supposed to be seeing about getting him some more—white breeches, and polished riding boots, Christopher walked out to the wide pillared loggia where his servant had laid tea. The floor was composed of intricate and indecent mosaic pictures representing the peculiar lusts of gods and goddesses from classical mythology. Beyond the stained and broken marble steps with their sweeping, grotesquely sculptured balustrades the jungly garden rose up in a solid green wall, splashed here and there with scarlet hibiscus and sickly sweet masses of white frangipani flowers. Christopher drew the heavy scented air into his lungs with deep pleasure. He loved this fantastic house and its tangled grounds and had done so ever since, two days after he arrived on the island, he had discovered it on a lonely evening walk, silent and decaying in the sunset. He had stood then on the loggia as he did now while the birds called and piped among the trees and a bright green serpent slid rustling into the gathering shadows beyond the long line of pillars. He had decided at once that the house must be his. A letter couched in the politest terms had been dispatched by the hand of one of his great black corporals to the little Major in the Palace, and his request had been granted. So now and for as long as he stayed on the island the Casa dei Fiori was his—and he was determined with a passionate intensity to stay on the island as long as the war lasted. He would live in this silent, dreaming house of dim leaf-filtered green light, with the haunting sense of timeless peace, and the past would slide

31

away, vanishing into the distance, separated from him by count-less long hot island days and warm island nights. More than two decades ago a young man had built this house to shut out an earlier war; now after years of emptiness and neglect it would once more fulfill the same purpose for another.

Half an hour later Christopher rode slowly down the white twisting road toward the barracks on the outskirts of San Pietro. He was to dine with Major Lemonfield at half past eight and the prospect filled him with foreboding. He had met the Major only once, but he had been even more impressed by that compel-ling personality than its owner had intended. Tonight, he felt sure, the Major would be summing him up, judging whether he was the sort of commandant suitable for the island. Perhaps the Major—surely those piercing eyes missed nothing—would some-how discover his fears and indecisions, his complete lack of self-confidence. He would decide that here was no fit officer for an in-dependent command and, reporting to the mainland, would sug-gest, unofficially but nonetheless with the authority of his posi-tion, that O.E.T.A. headquarters should approach the military command for a replacement. Then he would be recalled to Africa. And from there perhaps to—— In his unhappy mind the war took on the shape of a great whirlpool centered on Europe. Here on Baressa he was on the outer fringe of the swinging, swaying circle, as safe as in his circumstances it was possible to be. But let him once leave the island, veer inward toward the orbit of the stronger suction, and he would be dragged helplessly, hopelessly into the black roaring vortex of the center.

It had been only by the merest chance that he had gotten to Baressa at all. On his emergence from the hospital he had re-turned to the shattered remnants of his regiment, and while wait-ing outside the adjutant's office to report he had seen a request for applications to join colonial units in Africa. His application was granted—in view of his reputation for personal courage and devotion to duty through his supposed conduct in France he had been promoted and was particularly in the favor of the Colo-nel—and he had thankfully shaken the dust of war-racked Eng-land from his feet. And as a last incredible stroke of luck, just two months after war broke out in Africa, came the request for his new unit to supply a company of troops for conquered Baressa. Christopher, the only company commander with battle experience and consequently the only one thought fit to act independently in an emergency, was offered, and at once accepted, the post. Now, whatever happened, he must stay.

The sun was falling toward the purple rim of the ocean horizon and the cooling air was a magic web of orange-gold light when Christopher, with the habitual sinking in the pit of his stomach that occurred whenever he had to take up any direct contact with the Army, rode toward the barracks. The tall Negro sentries at the great arched gateway slammed into the "present," the bugles sang out as the guard hastily fell in and all over the barrack square the guttural Arabic commands of the N.C.O.s jerked men to attention. Into the taut expectant stillness rode the Captain, a resplendent figure on a white horse. The sunset light glinted golden on the buttons and badges of his uniform where the ribbons of the Military Cross and the Croix de Guerre glowed against the white starched drill, and flashed and shone on the polished buckles and gleaming leather of the horse's harness. Thirty feet above him on top of the gateway a Union Jack drooped its motionless folds over the stone head of a great Italian eagle.

4

" AND SO, merely because neither you nor this major or whoever he is could be bothered to visit the prison, I—not to speak of my wife and our infant daughter—were obliged to undergo a further quite needless sixteen days' imprisonment! I must say I consider it quite outrageous! I shall report it to our Bishop, I shall tell him——"

"My good Mr. Morle"—James Naughton-Muirhead sighed and shifted the papers on the desk in front of him wearily—"I have already told you twice that the responsibility for your imprisonment rests solely with the Italian Governor. I don't know why he did it—it seems unusual to arrest missionaries, even of an enemy nationality, but perhaps you had been engaging in some form of hostility——"

"I had not!" The tall, heavily built clergyman at the other side of the desk glared from reddish angry eyes at the Civil Affairs Officer. The thin lips of his hard mouth were pressed whitely together and a nervous spasm caused the left corner to twitch continuously. "I had done nothing more than was the duty of any patriotic Englishman!"

James gave a short burst of half-exasperated laughter. "What *does* that mean? Did you try to blow up the docks, or something?"

"I did not come here to be funny!" Mr. Morle's saturnine face paled with anger and his voice grated. "Nor did I come here to complain of Colonel Giordano—he was, in any case, a degenerate and unpleasant man—but of your treatment of myself, my wife and our infant daughter. We were left lying in a most insanitary prison amongst native criminals for days after the British occupation of this island. I want to know why. I am entitled to an explanation and I mean to have one!" He paused and fixed James with a basilisk glare.

"The reason we did not release you"—James explained patiently and for the third time—"is that we knew nothing about you—or your wife and infant daughter. No mention was made of you by Colonel Giordano or his staff or by anyone else until late yesterday evening when Dr. Valdonetti informed us of your presence on this island. This morning I phoned the prison and, after discovering that you did not appear to have committed any felony, I had you released at once."

"That was most kind of you—most thoughtful, I'm sure!" Mr. Roden Morle's voice quivered with sarcasm and suppressed rage. "After finding out that we had not committed felonies you decided—most graciously—to let us out! I see—yes!" His lips twitched convulsively and his anger, heated white-hot by the memory of sixteen days' needless confinement in Fort Brocca, broke through his control. He stood up. "I would have you know, young man," he almost shouted, "that by your cynical neglect—unless, as I think quite probable, you did it on purpose—you have kept an English family illegally in prison for over a fortnight! I shall make it my business to see that it has severe consequences for you! To start with, I shall see your major!" He flung out of the room, slamming the door behind him.

"Good God!" exclaimed James, at once amused and angry. He

34

lay back in his swivel chair and, picking up the telephone, got through to Lemonfield's office.

"Hullo! Naughton-Muirhead speaking. I've just had a rather shocking scene with this missionary the doctor told you about. I told the Fort Brocca people to let him out half an hour ago and within fifteen minutes of putting down the phone he was storming into my office in *the* most ungodly rage. He's a vast man with a huge red face and black hair—rather bull-like—and he's absolutely livid. I thought at one moment he was going to hurl himself upon me. Most disagreeable! Anyway, he says we've illegally imprisoned himself and his wife and infant daughter for a fortnight and he's coming to see you—in fact he's probably charging up the stairs at this moment."

"He sounds extremely unpleasant."

"He is. I expect that's really why Giordano locked him up. I tried to find out from our Police Chief, but all I could elicit were her views on missionaries in general, which are distinctly unsympathetic. She was having a dress fitted when I went to her office—a dreadful affair of golden taffeta all over flounces—so of course she was too preoccupied to be very informative."

"Confound the woman! She has absolutely no right to turn Police Headquarters into her private boudoir! Just because she's the widow of a Carabinieri commandant and badgered Giordano into letting her inherit his job she thinks she can do exactly what she likes. Well, she's mistaken. And by the by, James, I would like you to go back to Police H.Q., if you will, and get her to tell us why police vehicles use such an extraordinary amount of gasoline."

"Oh—couldn't Brinsmead go?"

"Brinsmead's busy. And in any case he and Mrs. Tamminetto are at daggers drawn."

"Very well."

James resignedly replaced the receiver and looked at his watch. Ten o'clock. Four more hours to go before they officially finished work for the day. He would go to Police Headquarters and then visit the docks and see what the Port Pilot was up to. He picked up his cap and the ivory-handled fly whisk of scarlet horsehair which he invariably carried and was about to leave the office when Brinsmead came in. Sergeant Brinsmead was short and rather fat. He had thick, vivid red hair, a large fiery moustache, and heavy-lensed steel-rimmed glasses. He looked pale and bad-tempered and he slapped two heavy files into the wire "in" tray on the desk.

"Commercial Taxes," he said distastefully, "and something to do with Inland Revenue."

"But I know nothing at all about Commercial Taxes," protested James with the air of languid flippancy which he knew annoyed Brinsmead to the point of exasperation, "and I never could discover what was meant by Inland Revenue."

"Major Lemonfield said you were to have them."

"But they only clutter up the office, and as I don't know anything about them it would be sheer folly to take any action. Don't you think it would be sheer folly to take any action, Brinsmead?"

"I don't know. Probably. Anyway, it's no use asking me. I'm only the Chief Clerk."

"I'm only the Civil Affairs Officer."

"Well, there you are!"

"True, true." James shrugged his shoulders and moved toward the door. *"C'est la guerre, Brinsmead, mon vieux,"* he said and went out, leaving the sergeant clerk staring after him indignantly.

In his large, handsome office on the third floor of the Palazzo Firenze Euan Lemonfield was confronting a furious Mr. Morle. Small and delicate in his highly starched uniform, he sat upright and composed behind the enormous bow-fronted walnut desk, glass-topped, gilded, and inlaid with ivory and mother-of-pearl, that had belonged to Giordano. His thin hand with the heavy gold signet ring tapped crossly on the head of a baroque angel which composed one of the arms of his high-backed brocaded chair.

"You can hardly blame us for not knowing of your presence, since we were not informed of it. It is not one of the functions of military government to search prisons for incarcerated priests. I cannot understand why your colleagues of the Roman Catholic Church did not inform us."

"Please don't refer to them as my colleagues," snapped Mr. Morle. "I have had no dealings with them since I have been on

36

this island. I am quite prepared to believe it was they who insti-
gated my arrest."

"I doubt it," retorted Lemonfield coldly. "But if, as it appears
to me, you have managed during your stay on this island to
antagonize both the priests of the Roman Catholic Church and
also the Italian Administration I can only consider that you have
yourself to blame for your arrest on the outbreak of hostilities."

"Thank you! Thank you very much!" Mr. Morle felt his self-
control once again leaving him. "I understand you to say that I
was responsible for my own arrest in the first place—that I have
myself to thank for it, in fact—and I suppose"—his voice shook
with bitter sarcasm—"that I might be allowed to thank you for
my continued imprisonment after the occupation!"

"Mr. Morle, I am not accustomed to being spoken to like that,"
said Lemonfield dangerously.

"Well, this will be a new experience for you then, won't it?"
The missionary got up. "If you think you can take this high-
handed attitude with an Englishman and his family you are mistaken. I will write to my Bishop and you will probably lose your
job!" He started to go.

"One minute, Mr. Morle!" The missionary turned back, half
expecting an apology. "You appear to be suffering under a mis-
apprehension." The Major's voice was icy. "*I* am the Governor
of this island, not *you*—as from your attitude one might expect
to be the case. You are merely an ordinary private citizen, and
under the Italian penal code which remains in force here you
could be sent to prison for anything up to five years for the remarks you have made to myself and Captain Naughton-Muirhead
this morning. If anyone writes to your Bishop it will be I—and
I shall be requesting your removal. That would, I may say, be
nothing more than formal courtesy on my part, for if I wished I
could send you straight back to Fort Brocca and deport you on
the next ship. I shall most certainly do just that if I have any more
trouble from you." There was a pause; Mr. Morle was speechless.

"I mean what I say, remember! Very well, you may go." Euan
picked up a pencil and drew a heavy file toward him. For a second
Mr. Morle gazed at him, too full for words. But he was beaten;
he turned on his heel and strode furiously from the room.

An hour later, as the increasing heat of the sun beat down on
the glaring white walls of the Palazzo Firenze and the long iron

roofs of the customs sheds on the east docks shimmered in the heat, Euan was drafting proclamations.

> WHEREAS the Island of Baressa is occupied by the Armed Forces of His Britannic Majesty King George VI.
>
> AND WHEREAS I, Euan Oliver Lemonfield, Major, have been empowered by warrant given by the Authority of the Commander-in-Chief to exercise all functions of Military Government in the Occupied Territory as Senior Civil Affairs Officer in accordance with the Laws and Usages of War and the International Conventions relating thereto, and subject to any directions which may be issued to me by the Chief Civil Affairs Officer.
>
> NOW THEREFORE I hereby proclaim as follows:
>
> ITALIAN LAWS (1) That the Gubernatorial Decree of . . .

The door opened and Brinsmead said, "Corporal Summerson to see you, sir."

"All right." Euan put down his pen resignedly as a very young corporal of the Royal Signals came in and saluted.

"Well, Summerson?"

"Sergeant Hope wants to know where we are to get our gasoline from in future, sir. The police won't let us have gasoline from their garage anymore. Sergeant Hope sent the truck just now and they sent it back. There was a note from the Italian lady saying that they were short of gasoline themselves and that we must get ours somewhere else in future. We've always got our gasoline from the police garage, sir, ever since we've been here."

"I see. I'll talk to them about it," said the Major grimly.

"And—sir——" Summerson hesitated.

"Well?"

"There's an old motorboat beached by our place. We thought —if no one wanted it—that is, that perhaps we could use it for fishing and so on—if you don't mind." Summerson, looking rather doubtful, added, "Sergeant Brinsmead said I must ask you."

"I see." Euan frowned. "Since the Signal section has been here I've had nothing but requests for articles of various sorts. I've supplied you with furniture, crockery, bicycles, and heaven knows what besides. Yesterday it was a refrigerator, wasn't it?"

"Yes, sir."

"And the day before that a radiogram. And now its a motorboat. All right, you can have it, I suppose, but kindly inform

38

Sergeant Hope that I and my staff are not here to play Father Christmas with the property of the Italian Government."

"Yes, sir." Summerson grinned and the Major smiled back.

"Very well, then, you may go."

But no sooner had the young corporal saluted and left the office than Brinsmead put his head around the door again.

"There's an English Fascist to see you, sir."

"A what?"

"An English Fascist, sir," repeated Brinsmead unemotionally, "and also an official from the Public Works Office, the Assistant Sanitary Inspector, the Chief of the Fire Brigade, and—I'm sorry to say—all the Guardie di Finanza."

"Blast! I thought you were dealing with them, Brinsmead?"

"I did my best, sir."

"Well?"

"Now it seems they've gone on strike or something."

"The devil they have! Well, send them down to the Captain —let him try his hand at them."

"I'm sorry, sir; he's out."

"Not back yet? He's been gone rather a long time."

"He's on the main dock at the moment, sir, with the Port Pilot and three Roman Catholic Fathers from the cathedral who followed him there." Brinsmead's mouth twitched beneath his heavy moustache. "They all appear to be importuning him."

"How do you know all this?" Euan was mystified.

"I have a pair of binoculars in my office, sir."

"I see. Very useful. Well, I'll see the English Fascist first, Brinsmead."

"Very good, sir." Brinsmead turned and held the door open. "Mr. Lillywhite!" he called. "You can come in now, please."

A tall, thin man with scanty reddish hair, a clipped moustache, and misty spectacles walked nervously into the room. He was wearing a black shirt and tie with a shield-shaped badge of some silver insignia on his left breast, a pair of old gray flannel trousers and cracked black shoes with no socks. In one hand he carried a brown hat.

"Mr. Lillywhite, sir," announced Brinsmead unhelpfully and closed the door.

Mr. Lillywhite took a few uncertain steps forward, dropped his hat, blushed hotly, and picked it up.

39

"Good morning," said Euan. "I take it you wished to see me about something?"

"Yes. I do, if I may," replied Mr. Lillywhite in a rather high voice in which an attempt at genteel refinement failed to conceal the distinct traces of an east London accent.

"Please sit down." Euan indicated the very uncomfortable chair, specially placed there by Brinsmead to discourage visitors from taking up too much time, that stood stiff and uncompromising at the other side of the desk. Mr. Lillywhite sat down carefully on its edge, put his hat on his knees, and gazed with pale watery eyes at Euan's ormolu inkstand. There was a long pause.

"Ah—I have—er—come about my salary," Mr. Lillywhite brought out at last, blushing faintly as if he felt the mention of financial matters to be impolite.

"Your salary?"

"My wages—yes."

"Oh, I see. What about them?"

Mr. Lillywhite coughed discreetly, shielding his mouth with his hand. "They have not been paid."

"No? I was unaware that you were on the government payroll. What is your job?"

Mr. Lillywhite hesitated, raised his eyebrows, lowered them again, smiled with what he presumably hoped was disarming frankness and said, "I teach the Avanguardisti English. Twice a week."

"Oh, really?" Euan looked at him coldly. "I am afraid that you will have to stop doing that. All the Fascist organizations have been suppressed by my orders. Also, I must say that I strongly disapprove of you wearing that shirt! I consider it unpardonable insolence for anyone—especially an Englishman—to walk into my office wearing the uniform of an enemy political organization!"

Mr. Lillywhite fell at once into the deepest confusion and despair. He blushed to the roots of his sandy hair and his spectacles slipped down his thin nose. He shook his head energetically and screwed up the brim of the brown hat in both hands.

"No, no, Major! I assure you, most sincerely, that I had no intention of being insolent. You see I am a poor man. I—well"— his eyes drooped—"this is my best shirt and I thought—as I was coming to see you . . . I am very sorry; perhaps I should have worn my other though it is somewhat threadbare. . . ."

Euan was both touched and annoyed by this confession of poverty. Poor Mr. Lillywhite! He was so genteel that to admit to possessing only two shirts must have been as gall and wormwood to his soul. But it was a great nuisance to have a "poor white" as an added burden to be dealt with, and particularly when he happened to be an Englishman. Something, Euan supposed, would have to be done for him.

"I see. Well, under the circumstances you will have to consider your last job to be at an end, so now we must try to find you something else. How long have you been on this island?"

"Twelve years. I came in nineteen twenty-eight. You see," explained Mr. Lillywhite confidingly, "I had a little money then and I had been ill in England and I wanted somewhere hot to live, where it was very cheap, and a friend—a sailor—told me of this island. So I came—and I stayed," he added dejectedly, as if he wished he hadn't.

"But your money—your own money, that is—you have it still?"

Mr. Lillywhite coughed again. "It was never very much. In fact, I may say it was very little—a legacy from my auntie—and now that I am a married man with eight children to support, you see. . . ."

"How many children?"

"Eight."

"Good Lord!"

"Yes, it is rather a lot, is it not?" agreed Mr. Lillywhite, smirking sickeningly.

"Well, look here, what can you do? If I'm going to find you a job I must know what qualifications you have got."

"I really don't know that I have any qualifications, really."

"Well, you apparently teach English. Can anybody vouch for that?"

"I don't know."

Euan sighed deeply. "Somebody must have *some* idea whether you can teach English or not—someone you taught. My driver, Fortu Malema, for instance. He was in the Avanguardisti. Did you teach him?"

"Yes," replied Mr. Lillywhite faintly.

41

Euan pressed the bell button on his desk. A uniformed native messenger, one of the score employed by the Palace, entered and bowed.

"My driver."

"Excellency!" The man bowed again and went out.

"I suppose," said Euan doubtfully, "you could teach English in the Italian school?"

Mr. Lillywhite didn't seem too sure of this; he hemmed and hawed. "Well, yes—if you say so I suppose I could."

"Don't you want to?"

"Oh, yes."

The door opened and Fortu came in.

"Ah, Fortu! You know Mr. Lillywhite?"

Fortu shot a look of surprise and dislike at the unfortunate Mr. Lillywhite, who met his gaze, lowered his eyes to the floor, and squirmed in his seat.

"Yes, I know him," said Fortu sourly.

"He taught you English, didn't he?" asked Euan, looking at Fortu, but watching Mr. Lillywhite from the corner of his eye.

"Yes."

"I didn't know you knew English, Fortu," remarked the Major, speaking in that language.

"*Signore?*" queried Fortu doubtfully.

The sentence was repeated in Italian.

"I don't speak it. None of us did. He taught it very badly."

"I gave of my best," ventured Mr. Lillywhite in a despairing voice.

"There's no reason to be rude, Fortu!" said Euan sharply. The boy's dislike of the man in front of him was glaringly apparent. But probably all the Italians hated him. "Well, Mr. Lillywhite, that doesn't help us much, I'm afraid. However, perhaps you can find some other work. I really don't think I can help you much at present. Perhaps your wife would like to try her hand at teaching very elementary subjects to the smaller children at school?"

"I'm not sure my wife——" mumbled the unhappy Mr. Lillywhite, and paused.

"She's a black woman off the streets," explained Fortu brutally, "and he's got eight half-caste children by her."

Mr. Lillywhite winced and blushed crimson, cowering, shabby and rather dirty, in his chair, while a few feet away his ex-pupil,

42

hands in pockets, stared down at him, his dark young face hard with derisive contempt. Euan, for once at a loss for words, looked from one to the other and Fortu's relentless voice went on. "She had them in a native hut in Daldacara and he used to fill her with arrack to help the pain rather than get a doctor. She got a taste for arrack after a bit, and now she's never sober; he seldom is either. One of the children's mad and blind. He was a spy for Colonel Giordano and he used to get native women for him and——"

"That will do, Fortu!" said the Major in a tone of voice that stopped his driver abruptly. "You have forgotten where you are. I will deal with you later. Now get out!"

Throwing one more malign look at the semiprostrated Mr. Lillywhite, Fortu left the office.

"We can't," Euan told James decidedly as they sat at lunch two hours later in the long, cool dining room of the Villa, "employ people like that in any government position. It's extremely unpleasant to have him on the island at all in the circumstances, very lowering for British prestige."

James agreed. "Yes. Our two compatriots seem to have contrived to make themselves extraordinarily unpopular with the locals—Lillywhite by being pro-Fascist, working secretly for Giordano, and leading a more than tolerably revolting life; Morle by being anti-Fascist, continually fighting with the Administration, and being a militant puritan. Odd, that, when you come to think of it."

"I wish I could expel them both—but I don't see how I can," said Euan bitterly.

"It would be pleasant to expel all the Guardie di Finanza as well. I fear they are valueless. I'm not," remarked James, helping himself to more wine, "a military man myself, but I do deprecate their habit of saluting while lounging in deck chairs outside the dock gates. I call it slovenly and unsoldierly."

"I've got to see them this afternoon. They're on strike at the moment."

"Indeed! Then I suppose they won't salute me, sitting down or standing up. By the way, Mrs. Tamminetto is getting very temperamental over the gasoline problem. I left her in tears."

"Good!" snarled Euan savagely.

43

"She should be on your list for expulsion—and I think perhaps the Hungarian, too."

The Major smiled reluctantly. "James, you won't take anything seriously. I'm afraid you're incurably frivolous. What, may I ask, were you doing on the docks this morning, surrounded by priests? Who were they?"

"Since you ask, they were Fathers Gregorio, Anselmo, and Innocento respectively—from the cathedral."

"What did they want?"

"For a long time I was unable to discover that, but after quantities of irrelevant circumlocution—in which Zvengetzov gratuitously involved himself—it appeared that they wanted to increase the cathedral's Fire Insurance Policy."

Euan was mystified. "But why come to you? It's nothing to do with the Administration."

"Not now, perhaps. But it will interest you to know that Giordano was the agent of a large insurance company, and anybody on this island who didn't want to fall out with him had to insure with that company and that company only."

From its cage in a corner of the room Mrs. Giordano's parrot, waking liverishly, swore softly to itself in Urdu—the Giordanos had once had an Indian butler—and slept again. Outside the long windows the light was a white glare over the silent, heat-still garden.

"I think," remarked Euan, "that I shall lie down this afternoon rather than go to the office. I have had a rather trying morning."

5

AT half past four on a chill, gloomy afternoon in late January 1941 a small convoy drove slowly southward along the broken potholed road on the northwest coast of Baressa. In front three Carabinieri on motorcycles bounced over the uneven surface, their goggled faces brown with the dust that a recent squall of rain had turned to mud. Immediately behind them a thirty-hundredweight troop carrier constructed in the manner of a fire engine with seats along each side held fourteen khaki-uniformed Negro soldiers and a mounted machine gun whose grim black muzzle pointed upward to the hurrying dun clouds low overhead. Behind this came a large blue sedan, swaying and rolling on its soft springs over the potholes and stones, and followed by another troop carrier and a small truck laden with wooden crates. Three more police motorcycles brought up the rear. Major Lemonfield was returning from his first tour of the island.

It had begun three days before when, to the thunder of the saluting cannons in the harbor bastions of old Fort Brocca, the Governor's motor yacht *Italia* had moved gracefully past the Dhow Control Point and taken a southeasterly course for the town of Cascio. Strolling the deck, occasionally going up to the bridge to chat with the deferential Captain Dibaldi, Euan had watched the long sandy coastline slip by while the great sweep of the escarpment, dropping almost sheer to the sea at San Pietro, receded farther and farther inland behind miles of scrub and low ranges of dusty foothills.

At Cascio he had been met by Captain Kellermann and the two truckloads of soldiers who were to escort him during the rest of the tour, and the round of inspections, speeches, and visits began. Most of one day had been spent touring the important pearling, shell, and fish-processing factories of the Arabian Sea Shell Company under the guidance of big bluff Signor Bertini, the resident manager and uncrowned king of Cascio. A short drive had been undertaken to the far smaller village of Agamo where, in the employ of a family of immigrant Czechoslovak Jews, almost the entire population were engaged in manufacturing buttons from the hard nuts of the dom palm, which flourished prolifically in the immediate vicinity. Next day the Major had driven westward up into the plateau to be shown the extensive pig farms and bacon-curing plant of Signor Calgarini, one of the larger concession owners, and had returned in time to take his place as guest of honor at a banquet given by the chief of the native notable in Cascio. On the following morning the convoy had set out for Dinghité, the last small fishing village on the very northernmost tip of the island, the farthest point from San Pietro. The country had changed as they lurched northward along a continually worsening track and it had soon become apparent to Euan that the northern half of Baressa was an arid desert of

45

scrub and rock, harsh, inhospitable, almost lifeless. So this was the reason—and quite a good one, too—why Giordano had never gone on tour. Nothing could have differed more greatly from the lush green fertility of the southern portion of the island than this bleakly barren, interminable expanse of baked earth and wiry gray-spiked thornbushes, broken here and there by towering anthills that rose, rugged primordial monoliths, from the flat plain.

When at last they reached Dinghité, a broken-down cluster of huts on a rocky promontory that smelled disgustingly of drying fish, they were caught by one of the freak storms that at this time of the year appeared suddenly over the northern part of the island. When it broke Euan had been engaged in a discouraging effort to carry on a conversation with the local sheikh, senile, blind, dribbling, and given to ineffectual gestures of a dim bygone Arab courtesy. The interpreter had also been unsatisfactory, a thin, lanky brown man in a tattered khaki suit who called himself Manoah and explained with a caustic dryness unusual in a native that he was an Anglican Mission scholar appointed by Mr. Morle as resident deacon to the tiny mission church of King Charles the Martyr. It was in this church, the only building, save an Indian store, which had a leakproof corrugated iron roof, that the Major and his entourage had sheltered during the brief storm. It had been a weird experience, standing in that dusty building of old weather-stained boards and rusting iron at the remotest end of a tropical island, to see a large and carefully framed reproduction of Van Dyck's famous picture of Charles Stuart hanging high up on the wall behind the altar. The sad, beautiful face, gazing down the short aisle and out over the rock-broken surf of the shore with a mild indifference to its strange surroundings, gave the whole church an air of dreamy unreality. Manoah, with a slight superior smile, informed the Major that the local inhabitants believed the picture to be a portrait of Christ, done from the life by Mr. Morle. Christopher, standing behind the Major, had burst out laughing, and in a rather strained silence they had left the building and, the storm being over, continued their journey.

Euan had originally intended to stay the night at Dinghité, having been informed that there was a large bungalow of stone, originally built for a resident officer who was never appointed, and now used as a government rest house. But, unused and untenanted for years, it had proved so derelict that rather than spend a night beneath its sagging and rat-ridden roof the Major had decided to push on and reach the escarpment by nightfall. He would stop the night at the northernmost concession, that of Signor Giacomo Balla, and return to San Pietro along the main road next day.

"What sort of people are the Ballas, Fortu?" he asked abruptly.

"There's only one, sir—Signor Balla. His wife died years ago and he has no children."

"He is like Commendatore Saccomani in that respect then?"

"He's not like the Commendatore in any other way, sir." Fortu's tone was quite definite. "The Commendatore is rich and a good man."

"And Balla is poor and a bad one?"

"He is poor, certainly, for a concession owner. But his estate is the last one on the plateau and not high enough for good fruit farming—the land is bad. He came here looking for gold at first. Years ago, that must have been. He didn't find any, of course. They say that he tried copper next and nickel, too, and that he was really a geologist or something and knows nothing of farming. They say if he tried he could do better than he does, but since his wife died he does not worry. He lives alone and practically never comes to San Pietro."

"He sounds rather a recluse. I hope he will not find our visit too inconvenient."

Beside the Major Christopher sat primly with his hat on his knees, gazing out of the window at the gray sea that broke on a wilderness of rocks along the jagged shore. The sun was falling in the west through a mass of broken cloud and from time to time thin slanting beams of yellow light filtered across the dismal seascape. It was during one of these short periods of wan sunlight that Christopher sat forward with sudden intentness.

"Look, sir! There's a boat out there! It looks like Fortu's seaplane float—silver."

At the mention of his name the driver turned his head inquiringly and the car lurched.

"Keep your eyes on the road, Fortu!" snapped his master. "A

47

boat? Probably a fisherman, though I'm told they consider these waters too dangerous to visit often." He peered past Christopher. "Yes, you're right. And it does look silver in this light."

"I think there's a white man in it, too. I—oh, the sun's gone in again! But I thought it was a white man."

"I shouldn't think it very likely," remarked the Major, settling himself in his seat again. "Perhaps it was a half-caste, though I haven't seen any of them about in these parts."

Christopher, too, sat back and resumed his contemplation of his present circumstances. He was worried and unsure. He had been five months on Baressa and had almost come to believe, in his more sanguine moments, that he might really manage to secure his position here indefinitely. It all depended on the little Major at his side. Everything he did must be done with the intention of pleasing Lemonfield, for continually he would be weighed in the balance against the possible qualities of other company commanders. He had, in the past months, learned much about the Major, for there was nothing concerning this man, upon whose whim he was firmly convinced his fate depended, that was too small to be of interest. He weighed up his store of knowledge, sifting facts from assumptions and guessing, with an eager acuteness borne of the peril in which he felt himself to stand, what words and actions of his were likely to propitiate the arbiter of his life.

Firstly, then, Lemonfield was no soldier and possessed an uncompromising dislike and contempt for things military. Yet at the same time he expected immaculate turnout, faultless ceremonial drill, and rigid discipline from the garrison company. While he lost no opportunity to ridicule the Army and assert the civilian character of O.E.T.A., no Guards R.S.M. had a keener eye for an unpolished brass button on a sentry's tunic or a slovenly "present arms." Christopher had found the right answer to this contradiction in the Major's character—what Lemonfield wished was to turn the garrison company into a subservient band of brilliantly uniformed, beautifully drilled janissaries for his own special use. If that was what he wanted he should have it. The biggest Negroes of the company were selected and put through hours of extra drill on the barrack square, the stores were ransacked for the newest full-dress white uniforms, and the result was a glittering show of stamping and clashing before the Palace steps at every arrival and departure of the Major. Not only that, but Christopher himself, wearing his best uniform, came at least once a day to supervise the changing of the guard and often, to his gratification, saw from the corner of his eye the Major appear on the balcony outside his office to watch it, too.

Then Lemonfield liked to know everything that went on in the barracks. To this end Christopher reported to him every other day with lists of defaulters, drill schedules, reports, and many other things with which the Major had no business whatsoever.

Lastly, his own services were required as a sort of unofficial A.D.C. The Major liked to have him, smart and deferential, walking behind him at any of the minor public functions he chose to order or attend.

All these things he had done, and they were appreciated. Lemonfield well knew that most garrison commanders would have taken an infinitely more independent line. Minding their own business, they would have expected him to mind his. Guards on sentry go before the Palace he might have got, though only as a favor, not as a right. But as to running the garrison from his office or using the company commander as an orderly officer—such a thing would have been out of the question.

Though the only reward that Christopher wanted was the Major's approbation he received many other tokens of Lemonfield's regard. With entire control over the previous Government's possessions, the Major did his best to see that the young Captain who seemed so eager to cooperate fully with O.E.T.A. should lack for nothing. Five truckloads of furniture had been sent to replace the few old gloomy pieces that were all the Casa dei Fiori contained when Christopher arrived. A shining new Alfa Romeo sports car—the pride and joy of the ex-Chief of Fascist Militia—had shortly followed and, best of all from Christopher's point of view, Giordano's two beautiful Arab horses complete with saddlery, stable gear, and even grooms.

There could be no doubt of the Major's approval—at present. Why, then, had he been so stupid as to get entangled with Toki? If there was one thing more likely than another to annoy the immaculate, impeccable little Major it would be the discovery that his garrison commander had taken a half-caste dressmaker as his mistress. Christopher had often heard Lemonfield deploring in the strongest terms the conduct of Mr. Lillywhite, who lived with

49

a native wife. How much more would he, one of the Major's officers, be blamed for an offense of that nature? He understood Lemonfield well enough to realize the view he would take of such conduct. It would not be a prudish one, a condemnation of loose morals—the Major was far too broad-minded and practical for such a narrow outlook. It would be worse, far worse. He would consider such behavior lowering to the prestige of the British Administration—to his Administration, and thus by implication a slur on himself. And that, above all else, he would not stand for. Christopher perspired slightly as he thought of the cold rebuke followed by the inevitable, "In the circumstances I will have to request your posting," that would follow discovery.

Discovery, that was what he must avoid. Toki had promised to be discreet—and so she should! In a sudden spurt of anger he realized that it was mainly her fault; she had seduced him, not he her. He had been unwilling from the first to get entangled—from the first evening when she had come to the Casa dei Fiori with some shirts she had made for him on Zeki's instructions. Attracted he had certainly been, amused, charmed by her small golden face and her seriocomic ways, and flattered, too, by her obvious admiration. But always he had tried to avoid the ultimate and dangerous relationship. As well might he have tried to avoid sunburn in the summer. Desiring him, sensing his own reluctant desire for her, Toki had been merely amused by his excuses, sent through Zeki, that he was ill or busy. Had he been an older man she might have been annoyed and drawn off, but Christopher's youth—he was three years younger than herself—made her believe that he was only embarrassed, unversed in the arts of love and unwilling to acknowledge it. So in the end it had been she who had suggested the obvious step—it had never happened that way with Toki before—and she had found to her surprise that he was not such a novice as she had taken him for.

He did not love her. He was not even certain that he liked her very much. But he was attracted by her quaint, quick manner, charmed and intrigued by her small, strong, beautiful body. But if the Major found out—Christopher sighed and unostentatiously wiped the sweat from his forehead. Having at last secured some measure of peace and quietness and safety, what must he do but deliberately start to destroy his hopes of retaining it? He must be mad! Hopelessly, for he knew he would not, he formed for the hundredth time a resolution to dismiss Toki once and for all.

Major Lemonfield's thoughts were also bent upon Christopher's relationship with the half-caste Japanese. He had actually been informed of it by Dr. Valdonetti, from the roof of whose house it was possible to see the entrance to the little lane that led to the Casa dei Fiori. At first he had been slightly annoyed, but, after reflection, on the whole approving. From all that he could learn about her Toki seemed a sensible and discreet young woman who, if not particularly virtuous, at least possessed no police record and catered in her professional capacity to a well-paying clientele whose susceptibilities she could not afford to shock too violently. All the young Italians of Kellermann's age had mistresses, and there was no reason why the garrison commander should not comply with local custom so long as he did not flaunt the fact openly. It was understandable that, particularly amongst the young on a tropical island, sex was bound to rear its discredited but not necessarily vicious head sooner or later. In many ways it was a decidedly good thing that the young man at his side should have chosen a half-caste woman of respectable profession and independent means for the satisfaction of those natural desires which might so easily otherwise have taken a shady and furtive turn. A decorously domestic life of chaste sin with a good, sober, hard-working half-caste was infinitely preferable to surreptitious nocturnal visits to Negresses in the native quarters or the scandal and ill feeling aroused by affairs with the females of respectable Italian families.

Whether this eminently practical point of view was in accordance with the official attitude of the British Army Major Lemonfield knew not and cared less. That it was not the view of the Church had been brought home to him by a letter—anonymous, but almost certainly originating from Mr. Morle—deploring the lapse from virtue of his young compatriot. Had he been able to prove the origin of that letter—the Major's thin lips tightened ominously. Unwarrantable, unheard-of interference!

Looking from the window at his side, he noted that the convoy, turning inland, had begun to ascend the low scrubby foothills that led upward to the plateau ten miles away. Dusk was falling rapidly over the dreary plain that stretched for miles behind and below them under the darkening sky. Low down in the west the storm clouds had parted near the horizon in a ragged gap through which the sky gleamed red and fierce—a lurid ember among the gloomy masses of black and gray. As the darkness increased a chill wind blew from the north. Beside the ascending track thorny bushes of mimosa lashed the swaying sides of the car with wet branches, and from time to time the long spiked twigs of a camel thorn tree scraped and rattled across the metal.

"And that," remarked the Major suddenly, "was where they hoped to find gold."

"Sir?" Christopher, jerked from a daydream in which the war was over and he lived a farmer forever on the island, looked at him questioningly.

"This plain we've just left," explained Euan. "For years the Italians hoped it was going to turn out to possess rich gold mines."

"And there weren't any?"

"No, only a little gold-bearing rock—very poor, really. But I suppose they felt it held a promise of better things. Then there was some nickel. Do you know anything about geology, Kellermann?"

"No, sir."

"Our host for tonight is, I am told, a geologist. He will doubtless explain the reasons for the early belief in large gold deposits to us. I shall inquire at dinner."

As they neared the top of the long, twisting track the hard, stunted, narrow-leafed vegetation of the plain began to give way to the softer, thicker foliage of the uplands, and after a further fifteen minutes of lurching and bumping they emerged onto a metaled road, narrow and rough in places but infinitely better than the potholed track along which they had jolted all the way from Dinghité.

"We shall not be long now, *signori*." Fortu voiced the thoughts of both his passengers as he pressed down on the accelerator and the convoy gathered new speed, its multiple headlights flashing out and cutting long white paths through the night.

When, half an hour later, they drove into the main courtyard of the Balla concession they found the place in complete darkness. But if the inhabitants had already retired for the night the noise of the vehicles awoke them, for in a few minutes lights appeared here and there and native voices exclaimed in accents of shrill surprise and apprehension. The Major and Christopher, climbing stiffly from the car, were approached by a large figure looming toward them in the glow of a storm lantern. It was Balla himself, a tall, heavy man in dirty khaki shirt and trousers, whose big head was covered with an unruly mass of snow-white hair. He towered over the Major, holding up the lantern, by whose light Euan made out a strong but fleshy face with a thick nose and a drooping, heavy moustache. The stubble of a two days' beard gleamed silver-gray over the heavy jowls.

"Good evening, Signor Balla. I am Major Lemonfield, the British Governor, and this is Captain Kellermann. I must apologize for this intrusion, but . . ." Euan explained matters with a brusque civility that he considered suitable to the occasion and requested that accommodation be placed at his disposal and food and shelter found for his escort. The big farmer heard him out silently, still holding the lantern high in one hand.

"I am afraid, *signori,* that you will not be comfortable here. I am a poor man and this farm is not likely to be a convenient stopping place for you."

His voice was that of an educated man, despite the grudging evasion of his tone. Euan was surprised and annoyed. Most of the local landowners would have regarded such a visit both as an honor and a heaven-sent opportunity to propitiate their new master, lavishing on him all the best that they had.

"I fear nonetheless that we must impose upon you," he replied impatiently. "We can hardly go farther tonight."

At the tone of the Major's voice Balla flushed and scowled; obviously the autocrat of his estate, he was used to having his own way.

"I am sorry, gentlemen," he said, taking a step back and lowering the lantern, "I regret I cannot offer you accommodation. I advise——" but he was allowed to proceed no further. Euan was tired and not prepared for argument; indignant at this surprising lack of the invariable servile courtesy that he had come to expect as his right, he abandoned any further attempt at politeness. His voice when he spoke was as harsh as any German *Feldwebel.*

"Balla, I have twenty-eight armed soldiers here. I will immediately order them to find the accommodation and food I have requested in your house and outbuildings—unless you prefer to do it yourself!"

In the face of this threat Balla could do nothing; he turned sullenly and, followed by the two officers and their personal servants, led the way into the house.

The *Italia* was pitching and tossing a mile off the rocky coast of Dinghité. All around her the water spouted and foamed among jagged reefs of razor-edged rocks that gleamed in the baleful light of a red dawn. Her engines were broken and at every swoop of her bows masses of suffocating black water poured over her shattered bulwarks. Struggling, battered from side to side, up the companionway from the flooded main saloon he saw that she was sinking fast. Behind him the inky water swirled up the stairs, tossing floating files against his ankles—"Public Works Department—City Drainage," "Financial Dues on Coffee," "Pearl Fisheries," "Police Vehicles—Gasoline Consumption." Then he was on deck climbing the iron ladder to the bridge. Where was Captain Dibaldi? Where were the crew? The bows were under now and the stern tilting high in the air against a paling sky. On the impossibly sloping bridge, solitary, thin, and windswept, the Reverend Manoah pointed with one long tattered arm to the huge moon blazing whitely above the high-poised stern. "I am appointed," he said bleakly, "by Mr. Morle." The ship plunged.

Euan woke up, shivering and sweating. The moon, vast and white as in his dream, glared down at him through the high French windows of the long room. For a moment he wondered where he was, and then the recollection of the previous day's events crowded upon him. The abortive visit to Dinghité, the long slow journey to the plateau, Balla's reluctant reception. Later he and Kellermann had dined together by candlelight— the farm did not appear to have an electric generating plant— and retired at an early hour. The fatigues of the day had been such that Euan had hardly climbed into the large old-fashioned bed before he was asleep. He glanced at his watch; the small glowing green hands pointed to one o'clock. He felt on the bedside table for the glass of water that Omar had orders to put there every night before his master retired, but it was not there, so, cursing his valet, Euan climbed out of bed and by the vivid white moonlight walked to the washstand.

On his way back he paused at the French windows for a moment and gazed out at the peaceful garden. A broad splash of light, at the angle of a long building to his left, fell bright and golden across the trees and bushes outside. It must be the light thrown from a window—a long French window, probably, like the one at which he stood. And the light was strong, almost vivid, even in the moonlight—too strong for oil lamps or candles. Balla had said there was no electric light in the house, but here was one blazing out from a room at one o'clock in the morning. It was odd. Euan opened the glass doors carefully and slipped out onto a cement path. The night air struck chill against the silk pajamas that still clung damply to his body. He walked gingerly along the path and found his way blocked by a thick bushy creeper that crawled heavily up the wall and interposed itself between him and the lighted window. Suppressing his fears of snakes among the foliage, Euan pushed his way silently through the leaves and stems and suddenly came upon the window.

It was wide open, and he found himself staring into a long, brilliantly lit room that had about it the air of a decayed and out-of-date and very cluttered laboratory. There were benches and tables and packing cases and straw and implements of glass and steel mixed in dusty confusion on the stone floor. One or two big presses of a nineteenth-century design with cracked and dirty glass doors and numberless tabulated little compartments reared their massive shapes against the walls. There were three men in the room and they were in the act of leaving it. One of them, half seen behind a pile of glass boxes, had passed out of the door before Euan had more than the briefest glimpse of him—barely enough to say whether he was a native or a white man, though he thought the latter. The second was Balla; scowling and gloomy, he strode out of the room with heavy steps, and behind him, meek and humble and not forgetting as he shut the door to switch out the lights, was Mr. Lillywhite.

So the ex-English master to the Avanguardisti was in Balla's employ—or was he merely a friend staying as a guest on the estate? And that other man—who was he? A native? A half-caste more likely, perhaps a servant. And yet he had preceded Balla out of the room—a servant or a half-caste steward would hardly do that. Musing on these questions, Euan made his way slowly back to his room and, climbing into bed, rubbed the itching spots on his unprotected ankles where the garden mosquitoes had attacked them. Well, if Mr. Lillywhite had got a job at last, and one so far from San Pietro, it would be a good thing, a good riddance. One o'clock was a late hour to work, though. And why had Balla said nothing about the man's presence the evening before? Admittedly the surly creature had hardly been in the mood to be informative, but even so . . . and who was the third man? And the electric light? Balla had said . . . The whole thing looked distinctly odd—looked furtive. He would look into it in the morning. Euan, slowly dozing, made vain, vague guesses until sleep overtook him. But next day he felt surprisingly unwell and departed without further inquiries into what he had seen. It was all probably quite harmless, anyway. Balla was nowhere about when the convoy left, and by the time it arrived in San Pietro the Major was shivering and sweating in the first throes of a bout of malarial fever.

6

THE spring came and the heat increased day by day. The life of Baressa sank slowly back into patient lethargy, waiting for the rains. Every year this happened. Every year as March gave way to April and April to May and the sun glared ever more fiercely from a sky that had turned from blue to brassy white, tempers shortened, livers swelled, and the citizens of San Pietro waited wearily for the great bulbous blue thunderclouds of the monsoon to swing up out of the sea and mask that intolerable fiery sky.

Half past twelve on a morning in early May. The town was empty and lifeless. By noon the last stall had been packed up in the bazaars and the last idler had left the cluttered native coffee shops. The long siesta was about to begin, draining the shadowless streets of passers-by, leaving only a stray cat, a slowly sauntering mongrel, or a strutting pigeon to throw little blots of moving shade on the baked dusty ground.

The Signals section lived in a house on the eastern shore of Ras Godron, the long jutting spur of land that enclosed the harbor like a curving arm and on the end of which the thick bastioned walls of old Fort Brocca Prison fell sheer to the sea. Most of the buildings on Ras Godron were of an official nature. Port offices, government warehouses, and customs sheds on the harbor side, and small wooden bungalows for the port officers on the eastern shore. It was in one of these, slightly larger than the rest and close to the radio station, that the four English signalers lived, and at half past twelve they were sitting down to their lunch, which they referred to as dinner, despite Sergeant Hope's pedantic corrections. It was typical of Hope to insist on the correct terminology for meals. A tall, lanky, colorless young man of twenty-six with a narrow head and steel-rimmed spectacles, he was a competent and conscientious N.C.O., but his stern and humorless sense of duty did not endear him to his subordinates. Of these there were three. Lance Sergeant Whyton, a leathery little regular soldier with a thin line of moustache above a sardonic mouth which he seldom opened for fear of letting fall some pungent military obscenity that would make his Nonconformist superior blush to the roots of his tow-colored hair. Then there were the two juniors, acting unpaid Corporal William Summerson, a thin, fair-haired youth of eighteen, and the section's dispatch rider, Dawson, a great hulking lad of the same age. As a section they did not get on very well together, but considering what a mixed bag they were it was surprising that they got on at all.

"Corporal, will you please pass the salt spoon to Signalman Dawson," remarked Sergeant Hope, without looking up from the joint he was carving. "I notice that he is using his knife again in lieu."

Silence save for the slither of meat as Hope's sharp knife sliced it. William passed the salt spoon across the table to Texas, whose ruddy face went a deeper red as he mumbled some incoherent thanks.

Whyton said, "Remember you've got the four o'clock call this afternoon, Summerson. Don't you go running off to that boat of yours and forgetting it, now."

"I shan't be going down to the beach till five."

"And not then either, I shouldn't think," cut in Hope dryly. "The four o'clock call will most likely take an hour, and then there's the ciphering to do, and—and there are a lot of batteries to be charged. I suppose Dawson had better see to that, though, since that's about all he's good for. Still, you'll have to deliver any signals on the bike."

"There are only two batteries to charge," remarked William patiently. "I did all the others yesterday." It was just like Hope to go trying to think up jobs for them when he knew they wanted to get on with the boat.

"Thank you, Summerson, I am quite aware of the position *in re* batteries. And, by the way, I want you to teach Dawson how to do the ciphers. Since he's disabled himself it's about the only thing he's likely to be any use for." He shot a venomous look at his dispatch rider, who, walking barefoot about the shore—which was forbidden—had trodden on a sea urchin and not reported it at the time—which was an offense—in consequence of which his foot was swollen and he could not ride his motorcycle —which reduced the efficiency of the section, thus amounting to a personal affront to Sergeant Hope. "So I don't think that either of you two will have time to play with that boat today," he concluded.

"There may not be any messages coming in."

"There *may* not, but there probably will be. Pass the potatoes, please." Hope gave a dry chuckle at his successful routing of William and was turning back to his food when he noticed Texas, who had been listening openmouthed as was his habit, pushing some peas onto his knife with a piece of bread. "Dawson!" he said dangerously. "Dawson, what are you doing?"

"Nothin', Sarg," mumbled Texas guiltily, stuffing the bread into his mouth.

"Well, I think you were. I think you were going to eat some peas with your knife—wasn't he, Whyton?"

"Looked ruddy like it," confirmed Whyton. He added gloomily, "With *my* peas I always eat honey. I've done it all my life. It may look kind of funny, but it keeps them on the knife!"

William laughed and Texas gave a sort of muted bellow that passed with him as a sign of amusement. Hope, however, was no more amused than Queen Victoria.

"Well, you won't do that here," he said, "*if* you please!"

After lunch Sergeant Hope retired to rest. A lunch of boiled mutton and peas and potatoes—for despite the climate Hope insisted on having plain English food, as he termed it—had a formidably soporific effect when eaten in a temperature of over a hundred degrees. Whyton, thin and wiry and used to the tropics, went off to the radio office to prepare for the two o'clock call and the two juniors were left to themselves. They took off their shirts —Hope insisted on proper dress at meals—and, slumping into two of the shabby old deck chairs that stood angularly about on the gray cement floor of the veranda, prepared to doze and read away the remaining hours of the siesta. Texas, the sweat gleaming on his burly shoulders, was soon immersed in *The Mystery of Red Gulch Ranch,* one of the invariable Westerns to which he was so addicted and to which he owed his nickname. William, sprawling panting nearby, wondered why they so often had alliterative titles. Texas must have read at least forty since they'd been on the island—and he read very slowly. It wouldn't be long before they'd been here a year, but it seemed much longer, somehow—a long, long time. How many Westerns would Texas read before they left? A hundred? Two hundred? One couldn't guess. They might leave in a week, the next time the *Emperor Napoleon,* their one link with the mainland, docked, or next month or next year or when the war was over. Half dozing in the stifling heat while the old electric fan clanked slowly around above him, William saw a vast panorama of sunlit island days stretching out endlessly before him, long hot mornings, longer hotter afternoons, slow calm evenings, deep calm nights. There was a queer peaceful pleasure in contemplating this prolonged exile; he hoped dreamily that it would continue. His eyes closed slowly until he could see only the craggy outline of Red Gulch Ranch on the back of Texas' book, until he could hardly see that, until he slept.

At a quarter to four Idris pattered onto the veranda with two chipped enamel mugs of tea. He woke William and, with some difficulty, Texas, and then with more reverence went off to wake Sergeant Hope.

Sergeant Whyton came across from the Signal office with two orange envelopes. "Here you are," he said, tossing them to William. "Only two. One for the Palace and one for Baines—and there won't be no call at four today, 'cos that's the lot, so you'll be able to get on with that boat okay."

"Oh, good!" William finished his tea and, picking up his shirt and the messages, wandered into the house. He always felt dreamy and rather melancholy when he awoke in the late afternoon; it was an effort to resume life again after the hot still deadness of the siesta, a gulf separating afternoon from morning, as deep and wide as the night that separated day from day. Hope was always irritated and bad-tempered at this time and so was Texas, in a surly, mumbling sort of way. Whyton, who never slept in the afternoons, was the only one who remained unaffected.

Putting on a clean khaki shirt before the mirror in the small bare room he shared with Texas, William sighed. Reflected back at him he saw a short, slender boy with pale hair and a pink childish face. He looked considerably less than his eighteen years and wished that he could grow a moustache like Whyton. But he didn't even shave more than once a month. Texas, only six months older, shaved every day and sometimes twice when Sergeant Hope decided that the first attempt had been unsuccessful. Poor Texas, he was everything that Hope disapproved of and got dreadfully bullied. William was fond of him in the way that he would have been fond of a large stupid dog, but a rudimentary education followed by a laborer's job in a gasworks hardly made Texas an interesting companion. William was no snob, but, himself the son of a scholarly dean with behind him a long peaceful childhood in a sleepy cathedral town, he found his comrades too alien in their ways and speech to make their undiluted company a continual pleasure. They were so unlike any of the people he had known before he joined the Army—except Hope. Hope was very much like a young curate who had been attached to the cathedral for some time and had left under a cloud after some peculiar hushed-up scandal that, as far as William could remember, had something to do with surplus vegetables at the Harvest Festival. Not that Hope was in the least likely to cause scandals; his entire life was sober and godly to an extraordinary degree.

Texas limped into the room and started to change into denim overalls. "You comin' down later, William?" he asked anxiously.

"Yes, in about half an hour."

"Shall I be gettin' on with the engine?"

"Yes—and for goodness sake bring back the tools. If Hope finds we've got them down there he'll put us on a charge."

William took his messages and went around to the old shed where Hope's truck, Texas' Norton, and the section bicycle were kept. The shed was covered by a mass of trailing morning glory creeper, but now in the later afternoon the flowers hung withered and apparently lifeless from the vines. By tomorrow's dawn every one of them would have sprung to exuberant life and for a few short hours the shed would be a glowing hill of peacock blue. The creeper was a source of continual surprise and delight to William.

William had never learned to ride a motorcycle, and so instead of the ferocious figure of Texas, helmeted, goggled and booted, with pistol at hip, bestriding his roaring machine through the town, the citizens of San Pietro saw a serious pink-faced youth in khaki shirt and shorts and a large topee pedaling slowly along the sun-scorched dusty roadways on an angular dun-colored bicycle. Arrived at the Palazzo Firenze he delivered his telegram to one of the native messengers and rode back to the dock area. He always enjoyed visiting the docks with their variety of small shipping berthed along the white stone quays, and it was his habit, having delivered his messages, to linger for as long as he dared among the crowds of grinning brown-skinned sailors, aloof native constables, and sweating, shouting stevedores. He would wander entranced along the commercial quay, staring down into the few feet of bright sun-shot green water in between the dark hulls and the stone wall where, unworried by their mighty neighbors, tiny brilliant fish picked and pulled at pieces of submerged refuse. Iron bollards stingingly hot to the touch, creaking ropes and groaning matted fenders, sacks of dates, bales of stinking hides, and, even more disgusting, *bêche-de-mer*, the tang of wood cooking fires from the high poops of the big painted dhows, and always the glittering, dancing water, vivid green and enticing.

This evening as he rode through the high gateway he noticed with amused surprise that the two Guardie di Finanza on duty were actually standing up; their old striped canvas deck chairs had gone. He had never seen them in an erect position before; it was commonly and jeeringly said that they had lost the use of their legs. Small, elderly, and sullen, in shabby drill uniforms with green and yellow epaulets, they took no notice of him, and he rode slowly through the variegated throng to the customs office. It was not a large office and it was crowded with people, the majority of whom were extremely angry. Despite the clattering ceiling fan the heat was intense. Against one wall leaned a row of six handcuffed natives guarded by two immobile port policemen.

One of the prisoners had evidently been recalcitrant, for his nose slowly dripped thick scarlet blood down his grimy blue shirt. From time to time he raised his manacled hands to wipe it, but for the most part he leaned, relaxed and impassive, against the peeling yellow distemper of the wall.

A disheveled Somali woman was being searched by two black customs guards in a corner. Her shrill recriminations and yelps of despair continually interrupted a running commentary of abuse leveled at her by a slim gray-haired Cypriot, whose dark aquiline face twitched and writhed with exasperation as, one after another, small bars of gold were pulled from her clothing. The center of the stage was held by two senior N.C.O.s of the Guardie di Finanza, their faces scarlet masks of fury. They were having a quarrel and conducting it in the invariable manner of their corps, as publicly and as vigorously as possible. Small elderly men, shabby and ugly like their colleagues at the gates, they were shivering and sweating with rage while they denounced each other in shrilling, strident voices and language which William, fortunately for his cathedral-bred ears, was unable to understand.

In another corner Captain Zvengetzov interrogated a surly Italian skipper and emphasized his questions by banging the table before him with the butt of his ever-present revolver.

In the middle of all this and seemingly perfectly indifferent to it sat a swarthy, stocky British officer, writing calmly at an ugly mahogany desk. On one side of him sat a young Greek, handsome and immaculate in white, and on the other a plump Egyptian with an upturned black moustache and a pink-striped shirt open to the waist. All three were in high good humor and busily engaged in examining and annotating a multitude of files and other documents with which the long desk was strewn.

William forced his way through a group of altercating Levantine ship chandlers and sketched a salute between the gesticulating arms of the Guardie di Finanza.

"Ah, thanks. We've been waiting for this." Lieutenant Baines grinned and ripped open the thin orange envelope. He glanced at the message and tossed it to the Greek. "Enter that up, Nick, and file it. Would you like some beer, Summerson?" Without waiting for an answer, he reached down into a bucket of ice below the desk and pulled up a dripping bottle. Jerking off the crown cork, he filled one of the many glasses that stood about among the tossed papers of the desk. "I don't *think* that's the one Zvengetzov's drunk out of—I hope not, anyway."

"Thank you, sir." The beer was cold and infinitely refreshing. There was always beer in the customs office; Baines seemed to live on it. Even now he was fishing out further bottles and refilling his glass and those of his two companions. A lot of what he drank, thought William glancing at him, must exude almost at once through his pores. The Lieutenant wore—perhaps in imitation of the Governor—full uniform. Not for him the light shirts and shorts of the Signals section, but tunic, trousers, tie, Sam Browne and cap. There was even a leather cane on the desk before him. But the heat of the docks and the crowded customs sheds invariably played havoc with all this finery, and Baines' clothes were dark and limp with sweat shortly after he had first put them on. He had been Chief Customs Officer on the island for three months now, and all the while the heat had been steadily increasing; soon, surely, he would give some sartorial sign of resignation to the climate. William had a bet with Whyton that Baines would abandon his Sam Browne before the end of August.

The Lieutenant had been set the formidable task of clearing up the dark tangle of graft and corruption and gross inefficiency that had for so long covered the Customs Department with the tenuous but elastic hold of a tough spider web, and he was slowly and with resolute toil getting it into some state of order. It was of the greatest importance to Major Lemonfield that the Customs and Excise Departments should work properly; they were responsible for a large percentage of government revenue, and by a great stroke of luck he had been sent the right man for the job. A Huddersfield police detective twenty-four years old, with considerable experience of financial fraud, Baines had also an inexhaustible patience and a sense of sardonic humor which baffled and infuriated the Guardie di Finanza and their polyglot associates. All the customs shed staff hated Baines with a bitter hatred; everyone connected with the services or administration of the port loathed the sight of the dumpy, jaunty, grinning figure in the crumpled uniform and the rakish cap. He had been nearly killed a month ago when set upon one night by a gang of black stevedores hired by a marine contractor whom he had accused of large-scale smuggling. But the leather cane that lay on

63

his desk contained a long, thin steel dagger, and the police for once had been near at hand. Lemonfield's rage at this attempted murder of his newest recruit had been great. The unsuccessful assassins had been savagely flogged in Fort Brocca until—and for some time after—they had disclosed the name of their employer, who had subsequently received a prison sentence of thirty years, a fine of ten thousand pounds, and the confiscation of his business and most of his other property. As Captain Naughton-Muirhead remarked afterward, the only thing the Governor had omitted was the cutting off of the miserable man's ears. It had been a salutary lesson to the dock area in general and proof of the Governor's determined attitude toward crime aimed at his Administration. Nonetheless Baines now carried two pistols and his assistants, Nicolides and Kanos, were both armed.

William sipped his beer, sitting on a small hard seat beside the long desk and watching Nicolides covertly taking shorthand notes of some of the wilder remarks of the two Guardie di Finanza, who under the stress of their anger were incriminating each other and sometimes themselves with the most complete abandon.

"By the way," asked Baines, looking up from his work, "is it true that they're sending us an officer for the police?"

"I don't know, sir," replied William guardedly. Hope would be furious if he discussed official signals outside the radio office.

"I've heard the Major wants one."

"Oh yes, he wants one all right. He's properly browned off with Mrs. Tamminetto."

"I don't think a woman is very suitable for the job of Chief of Police, I must say."

"That depends. Some might be all right. I once knew the matron of a hospital— However, I don't envy the man who gets the job."

William smiled. "I don't suppose he'll envy you, sir."

"Oh, we'll get straight in no time now," said Baines cheerfully. "Won't we, Franzoni?" He repeated the remark in Italian and, turning, William saw that the chief of the Guardie di Finanza, a villainous little creature with a scarred face and a short leg, had limped up to the desk. Sergeant Franzoni glowered, lowered his shifty eyes, and muttered something William could not catch through writhing lips. The thought of being straight in no time seemed to have no appeal at all for him.

Cycling to the narrow creek on the west shore of Ras Godron where they kept the boat, William forgot the customs office with its highly charged atmosphere of deceit, fear, and trickery in the pleasing thought that the rest of the evening was his own. There were still two hours to go before sunset and they would be contentedly spent caulking the gaping seams of the old motorboat, together with Texas and Silvana Angellini, the daughter of the senior Carabinieri N.C.O. and Mrs. Tamminetto's long-suffering secretary. The air was cooling as he bumped and rattled down the stony lane to the foreshore, and the tide, far out, exposed a long even slope of mud and grass-green weed. The old boat lay careened on its side, held by blocks of sea-stained timber just above high-water mark, and from its interior the metallic blows of a hammer echoed resoundingly in the still evening air. Texas was busy on the engine bedplates.

William clattered his bicycle down on a pile of pale shingles and ran toward the boat as Silvana, a pot of smoking tar in one hand, came around the curve of the high blunt bows.

"William!" she called. "You're late. You promised to be here half an hour ago."

"I know, I stopped with Baines for some beer."

"Idle bastard!" commented Texas without rancor from below.

"You get on with your work!" said Silvana, laughing. "Come on, William, this is hot now, but soon it will cool—it's very sticky tar, too thick, really."

William picked up the bag of shredded rope—they had shredded it yesterday, sitting cross-legged on the shingles like convicts picking oakum—and clambered beside her up the rough barnacled hull.

Silvana and William had been friends since the day they first met, nearly nine months ago, when William had taken the truck for the first time to the police office for gasoline. Silvana, who spoke a rudimentary schoolgirl English, had been sent down with him to the garage to interpret his desires to Sergeant Batinelli. Later they had returned to the office where Silvana had been soundly rated for tardiness. William had been sorry for her. They both had overbearing, unsympathetic employers—it had been their first link, their common tie. They had seen more and more of each other as the months passed, and the sight of them walking soberly together through the streets—the black-haired leggy girl, already showing much of the golden dark Southern beauty that she would so soon possess in full, and the serious fair-haired boy—had doubtless touched the hearts of the more sentimental citizens of San Pietro who had chanced to notice them.

William, who in some respects was young for his age, looked upon Silvana only as a companion—a delightful change from the company of Texas—with whom he could explore the rock pools along the heavily indented coast and collect specimens of sea urchins and curious crustaceans in jam jars and palm-leaf baskets. They taught each other their respective languages in those long sunlit evenings, splashing through the bright pools floored with coral sand, picking up twisted shells, laughing, exclaiming wonderingly over tiny iridescent fish. "William, William! How do you say in English this . . . ? And those?"

It was Silvana who was the better learner—she had the Latin's natural aptitude for tongues—and it was mostly in English that they spoke now. If she thought of William in any other way than as a friend she never showed it. Only sometimes, when he bent breathlessly triumphant over some marine specimen that had made more than usually strenuous efforts to evade capture, she would look at him, as he knelt with a frown of concentration on his flushed face and his fair hair falling over his eyes, with an expression of tenderness that, had he noticed it, would have embarrassed him greatly.

Their superiors both disapproved of this friendship almost as much as they disliked each other. Sergeant Hope rightly presumed it to be innocent, but was uncertain whether it would remain so long. Silvana Angellini was Italian and consequently oversexed. Sooner or later she would seduce young Summerson and then any scandal there might be would reflect on his section. It was a friendship that should be discouraged as much as possible at its present stage. Mrs. Tamminetto wrongly presumed it to be anything but innocent. There was, in her opinion, only one thing that an English soldier could want with an Italian girl. Scandal didn't worry Mrs. Tamminetto—there had been plenty of it in her own life and she had enjoyed it all—but she was fast deciding that she did not like the English nation. The English were neither easygoing nor gallant where women were concerned. The sharp, terse notes full of rebukes and reprimands that she

66

received from the Governor could never have been penned by an Italian officer, and the sarcastic and cynical remarks that Captain Naughton-Muirhead made on his visits to the police office were not of the sort she was accustomed to hearing from the lips of Southern gentlemen. Silvana had much better conduct her affairs with members of her own race.

But still they met in the evenings on the unfrequented shore, and sometimes William brought Texas, but mostly not, and they wandered far along the rocky coast exploring new bays and inlets, coves and grottos where fishermen seldom came and only the thin, delicate spider crabs danced weirdly over the glowing sand into the twilight sea.

7

THE monsoon rolled the huge clouds out of the sea and torrential rains masked Baressa in a silver-gray sheet of falling water. Streams turned to torrents, gutters turned to streams, the rain hissed and bounced over the slaty surface of the harbor and drummed on the iron decks of the grubby little freighters that tied up against the washed stone quays. In the Piazza President Wilson the battered oleanders shed their pink petals under the downpour and an occasional angry gust of wind blew them to stick like damp confetti over the statue of old General Cadorna, who stood wetly arrogant among a cluster of potted geraniums below the traffic lights. Some of the smaller mud huts on the outskirts of Daldacara melted like chocolate into the ground and a slight avalanche on the escarpment temporarily blocked the coastal road to Agamo.

Then the rains were over and the sky appeared a newly washed cobalt blue. The earth steamed and dried; everything was green once more; the summer was finished. Autumn came, sticky and humid. The Port Pilot developed prickly heat around his stomach and went about with his shirt outside his trousers.

It was during this time when no one exerted himself more than necessary and everyone felt slightly ill that Mr. Morle had his second dispute with the Administration. Ever since the day a year ago, when he had been turned out of Major Lemonfield's office in the Palace, the missionary had lain smarting under a sense of injustice and frustration. This was in part due to the loss of the hope he had nourished during the early days of the war and during his imprisonment in Fort Brocca—the hope that a British occupation would immeasurably increase his position and standing on the island. In his mind's eye he had seen a British Military Governor, an impeccable middle-aged family man preferably, driving to the mission church of All Saints in Daldacara every Sunday for Divine Service. He had seen himself in the role of padre to the English military on the island and, in more roseate moments, as unofficial adviser to the Governor himself. After all, he had been on the island for four years before the occupation—long enough, one would have thought, to be useful to a newly arrived soldier taking up the duties of Administrator in San Pietro.

He had sometimes spoken of these prospects to his wife and she, he knew, had entertained hopes of parties in the Villa and long, confidential chats to a religious, matronly Governor's wife —chats in which they would talk of England and English things, for, unlike her husband, Mrs. Morle did not feel called to the mission field and regretted with deep though hidden sorrow the small living in Somersetshire that they had once possessed. A bleak, large brick house with an eastern aspect, a small formal garden, green spiked railings.

But things had not turned out that way. Major Lemonfield was both unmarried and quite unlike the middle-aged, sound and religious, if rather stolid, soldier whom Mr. Morle had hoped for. The Major was not a soldier at all, to start with, but a sort of lawyer turned politician in uniform, and he appeared to be quite uninterested in the outward forms of the Anglican religion. Not only did he fail in his own religious duties, but he encouraged the other Englishmen to do likewise. Or, if he did not encourage them actually to stay away from All Saints—and Mr. Morle was convinced that he did—he certainly exerted no influence in a reverse direction. It was all very disappointing, quite unlike the way he had hoped things would turn out. But what really galled more than anything was the way Major Lemonfield ignored the missionary's existence on the island. By neither word nor deed did he give any indication that Mr. Morle meant more to him than the meanest of his new subjects. The attitude of the British Administration toward the Anglican mission was one of perfect indifference.

Mr. Morle had felt this indifference more and more keenly as the months passed, for he was a person who was quite unable to tolerate being ignored. Even downright hostility was better than that; at least it lent a zest to life. As British rule on Baressa entered its second blistering September Mr. Morle became convinced that it was his duty, if not as a religious minister then as a British citizen—a status he invariably invoked to cover any activity not expressly sanctioned by his cloth—to inform the Chaplain General's department of the low state of the morals and the torpid religious condition of the English soldiers on Baressa.

The more he thought about it through these days of humid heat the more important it became to urge the authorities to take action to put matters on a healthier footing. At last, one sultry evening late in the month, he walked firmly to his study after dinner and sat down at his plain wooden desk—so starkly, satisfyingly at variance with that vast ornate piece of furniture behind which the godless little Major sat daily in his great Palace. And, once at his desk, Mr. Morle's long suppressed resentment took control and his pen skimmed across sheet after sheet of foolscap. It was nearly midnight when, with a tight-lipped smile of satisfaction, he sealed and addressed the letter and next morning it was in the post.

Walking through the dirty, narrow, sunset streets of Daldacara that evening on his way to All Saints, Mr. Morle was grimly jubilant and yet a little perturbed. Had he said too much? Been, perhaps, a little too strong in his condemnation? But no, he told himself, it was his duty to condemn immorality and to use all the means in his power to prevent loose living wherever he could. Then there was such a thing as British prestige to be upheld. As a British citizen . . . He noted from the corner of his eye that a fellow British citizen, standing knee-deep in the middle of a small untidy garden full of wild marigolds that shone a violent orange in the setting sun, was at that moment removing a battered hat and bowing toward him. But Mr. Morle walked crossly on and glanced neither to right nor to left. Only the deep preoccupation of his thoughts could have led him to pass by Mr. Lillywhite's ramshackle hut in the native quarter, for usually he made a detour to avoid the embarrassing reminder of his compatriot's regrettable lapse from grace.

Arrived at All Saints, he went into the hot iron vestry to find his six half-caste choir boys chattering and laughing in a corner while they gambled mildly for centesimi, annas, and half-piaster pieces with a set of chipped wooden dice. Enraged by this behavior on a Sunday and in such a place, Mr. Morle cuffed them all with vigor until some began to cry and the others hurriedly to garb themselves in threadbare surplices over their dirty ragged shirts and shorts.

In his anger Mr. Morle failed to hear a knock at the door behind him and, having attired himself in his own ecclesiastical garments, he picked up a Bible and swept into the body of the church at the same time as Brigadiere da Vannia and three Carabinieri entered the vestry.

It was thus not until after the evening service that Mr. Morle was arrested. He was taken at once in a police car to the back entrance of the Palace and led up the stairs to the great office where a frigidly furious Major Lemonfield sat behind a desk on which were neatly arranged a dozen sheets of unpleasantly familiar foolscap. Mr. Morle had forgotten the censorship.

The ensuing interview was bitter but one-sided. It lasted for fifteen minutes, during which Mr. Morle was forced to listen to a stream of closely reasoned abuse and at the end of which he found it necessary to withdraw his letter—which he was requested to destroy there and then—and to make an abject apology under the threat of a trial for criminal libel.

When the missionary had been dismissed, white-faced and trembling with mortification, Major Lemonfield sat for a few moments in the shaded glow of his carved alabaster desk lamp, frowning and pinching his lower lip. He was pondering on the proper procedure for requesting the Missionary Society to which Mr. Morle belonged to recall their servant and he had almost completed framing the necessary letter in his mind when with a cursory knock Brinsmead opened the door and said, "Sergeant Hope to see you, sir."

Euan sighed. "Oh, very well. Send him in." Why was Brinsmead grinning in that silly and unusual manner? Hope entered also with a look of suspended jubilation on his ugly, pimply face and, saluting, proffered an orange signal envelope.

Irritated, Euan ripped it open sharply, to read with surprise and pleasure that he was now a lieutenant colonel.

"Congratulations, sir!" said Hope warmly. "And the same from everyone in the section."

"And from myself, too, of course," added Brinsmead from the doorway.

Euan looked up smiling. "Thank you, thank you both." He was oddly touched at the evident pleasure in his promotion evinced by these two rather somber N.C.O.s. Their opinion, their praise, he knew would be based on nothing but a sincere regard for true worth and hard ungrudging successful work. In a glow of pleasure he dismissed the matter of Mr. Morle from his mind. Let the fellow stay—he was bigoted, intolerant, narrow-minded and spiteful, but he had been twice severely frightened; he could do no real harm.

"Thank you," he repeated, smiling at the sergeants. "I hope you'll both have the same luck in the near future. And now will you tell Fortu to get my car, Brinsmead? I'm going home."

8

"WHEREAS the Island of Baressa is occupied by the Armed Forces of His Britannic Majesty King George VI.

"AND WHEREAS I, Euan Oliver Lemonfield, Lieutenant Colonel . . ."

For nearly two years now he had been doing this, he reflected. It seemed far less. The days had passed more quickly than he would have believed possible. It was, supposed Euan, because the work suited him; he enjoyed it all immensely. Mildly surprised, he realized that for him, at any rate, it had been a very happy time. Alone on his island, organizing and planning, patiently putting into effect reforms and improvements, working out his budget, spending thriftily, saving and economizing on govern-

71

ment expenditure, cutting out waste, fighting corruption. It was intensely absorbing. Looking back to that time twenty-two months ago when he and Brinsmead had struggled to take over from the voluble, sulky, slippery Giordano, he could not but compare the state of government as it had been then with what it was now. Under Giordano the administration of the island had been muddled along, chaotically in debt, inefficient, unenlightened, sleepy. Now the budget balanced with considerable surpluses and the government departments, in particular the judicial and fiscal ones, over which he exercised the greatest direct control, functioned smoothly, economically, and efficiently.

Even to outward appearances there was an improvement, visible and satisfactory, in the state of the island. The roads were in better condition, the harbor was regularly dredged, the city of San Pietro cleaner and neater and more orderly—everything showed that a firm and prosperous Administration had taken the place of its lax, poverty-stricken predecessor. Much more could have been done in this direction if only the Colonel had possessed the power to spend the government revenues as he pleased; that he did not possess this power was a source of continual nagging irritation. He might arbitrarily rule the lives of Baressa's entire population, might order curfews, communal fines, and confiscations, might requisition and seize property at his whim, imprison without trial and even sign death warrants in reams if he felt so inclined, but he must not spend a penny of public money without accounting for it to London. The powers of a military governor were almost entirely repressive; they were never intended to be progressive or beneficial; and while the Colonel was undoubtedly a despot he wished to be a benevolent one.

The only thing they had allowed him to do, he thought with bitterness, had been to build an isolation wing on the hospital, and it had taken many weeks and much correspondence to procure permission even for that. Nobody but himself and Dr. Valdonetti had particularly wanted an isolation wing—a fact that had made the reactions of San Pietro's citizens all the more extraordinary. He remembered with amusement and pleasure the day, less than a fortnight ago, when he had officially opened the new building at the request of the Mayor. The response of the townspeople had been as delightful as it was unlooked for—had almost overwhelmed him. It was not, as James had said, that they either desired or really needed a new wing to their already adequate hospital; no, it was, it could only have been, seized by them as a chance to show their appreciation of his rule—perhaps of himself personally.

For a few moments he sat motionless at his desk, staring unseeingly across the long room full of the soft gold light of late afternoon, pen poised over the half-finished proclamation. He saw once more the crowded streets, the waving flags—homemade Union Jacks mixed fantastically with black Fascist emblems and Italian tricolors, anything that came to hand—heard the cheering crowds, the Mayor's panegyric half inaudible above the noise. They had mobbed his car going home, clinging to the running boards, trying to shake his hands and patting with their own black, brown, or yellow ones any part of him they could reach. Streamers, flowers, Fortu forced to stop at last, turning in his seat, laughing delightedly. They had made it into a great public gala by sunset, a bacchanalia of tipsy black satyrs and hopelessly polyglot half-caste fauns. He had appeared four times on the balcony outside these very office windows, twice with James and the Mayor and twice alone. The crowd had roared its approval, singing, shouting, stamping, swaying under the strings and loops of fairy lights that the Mayor—prompted by Brinsmead, who exhibited a hitherto unguessed-at penchant for public festivities—had had festooned among the palm trees and lamp standards in the great square. And though a great deal of drink must have been consumed no violence or damage was done. Mrs. Tamminetto had alerted the police—insofar, at any rate, as their rather sluggish nature would permit—and had herself toured the town with Commino in a small police car, khaki jodhpurs, and a pistol. But this display of force and daring had been unnecessary; the crowds had only wished to serenade Colonel Lemonfield, and a heavy storm of rain had dispersed them before midnight.

Of course, the islanders had every reason to be grateful to him, considered Euan, for he was undoubtedly the best Governor they had ever had—not, admittedly, that that was saying much in view of the character of his predecessors. But if they had suffered maladministration and even a certain amount of repression under their former rulers, how much more of these might they have expected from the harshly indifferent autocracy of military conquerors? Instead of which they had found themselves financially better off almost from the start, for had he not immediately rescinded several semicompulsory levies to Fascist party funds and slowly reduced taxation and duties where, in his opinion, they were excessive? They had every reason to like his rule, and it followed that if good rulers were loved then they should love him. It seemed probable that they did so, and this had taken him completely by surprise, for he had never gone out of his way to win their affection. What he had done he had done because it needed doing and because of a natural desire to do his job well. He had, he told himself, theories on how to rule a country—most intelligent people must have them—and he was in the fortunate position of being able to put some of them into practice for a few years and see how they worked. And they seemed to work very well—or at least his subjects thought so.

He could not quite get over that demonstration twelve days ago. It continually recurred to his mind and left him with an extraordinary feeling—a feeling of elation and power, of intense possession. Surely there was nothing quite like the sincere adulation of crowds. He had often in the past smiled ironically over the reception of statesmen, royalty, film stars, and visiting potentates, and wondered coldly how they could bring themselves to grin and gesture and make emotional, flamboyant speeches. Now he felt he understood. Not, of course, that he would dream of making emotional speeches himself; it would be ridiculous and undignified. Still, he was sure that Giordano never had and never would have such a spontaneous ovation as he himself had so recently received. He wondered what the population's reaction would be if Britain and her allies lost the war and Giordano came back. Hardly contented, to say the least—but he pulled himself up abruptly here. Crowds were notoriously fickle; they would probably cheer themselves hoarse and erect triumphal arches.

In his small stuffy office Sergeant Brinsmead sat slumped behind his desk, feeling ill and listening impatiently to a complicated and nebulous complaint about Lieutenant Baines from the Port Pilot, who had taken severe umbrage at some fancied slight.

"So you will haf speakings to the Colonel about this things please, yes?" Captain Zvengetzov fondled his battered cap with its flamboyant but tarnished badge of the Vera Cruz Port Authority and spat out his words as if they tasted unpleasant while his mad blue eyes gleamed through the haze of his invariable black cheroot.

"Yes, yes! I've said so once already," replied Brinsmead testily. There was surely enough work to do without having to interview half-baked Hungarian noblemen who felt they'd been insulted. He pulled a file toward him—a trick he'd learned from Lemonfield—and the tall heavy Pilot grinned, a mirthless parting of his red-bearded lips, and rose to go.

"Good-bye, Sergeant Brinsmit!"

"Good evening, Captain."

Zvengetzov slammed his rakish cap onto his flaming head—he must have been nearly sixty but he hadn't a single gray hair; it was one of his many peculiarities which bordered on the freakish —and left the room.

"Damn!" swore Sergeant Brinsmead discontentedly. "Damn that Hungarian! And damn Baines, too! No bloody peace, that's the trouble! Can't I"—he addressed a picture of Marshal Chiang Kai-shek pinned to the door, an Army handout—"have a bloody moment to do my bloody work?" The Chinese leader gazed back at him aloof, almond-eyed, slightly contemptuous. "Huh!" grunted Brinsmead sulkily and turned back to the file before him. It was to do with the reconstitution of the Banda Governatoriale, Giordano's picturesque native corps of personal Palace bodyguards who had been demobilized at the beginning of the British occupation and had since eked out an unhappy existence on the dole. It was for this reason, and also to lend further dignity to the Headquarters of his Administration, that the Colonel had decided to reemploy them in their former capacity. Brinsmead did not really approve—he felt it was a waste of public money, for they would have to be completely reequipped—but if the Colonel had decided to have them there was nothing more to be said.

In two years the relationship between Brinsmead and Lemonfield had changed little. Perhaps they had grown closer together, but only in their work. Each admired and respected the other, though in Lemonfield's case admiration was mitigated by Brinsmead's continual carping jeremiad concerning the slackness, inefficiency, and mistakes of all the other members of the Administration from Captain Naughton-Muirhead downward. But nonetheless Brinsmead remained invaluable: he never forgot anything and he lived entirely for his work. He did not appear to want any reward for this devotion to duty and his thanks when Lemonfield had him promoted to staff sergeant had been purely formal. What short time he spent away from the office was passed in a small flat in the suburbs where he was looked after devoutly by a thin, pockmarked, ladylike Italian housekeeper.

The door opened and Captain Naughton-Muirhead strolled in waving his scarlet fly whisk in the smoke-laden air.

"A very good evening indeed to you, Staff Sergeant Brinsmead!" he remarked with the sardonic exaggerated courtesy he kept especially for the Chief Clerk. He wrinkled his nose and sniffed. "Have you been having a bonfire of secret correspondence?"

"No!" retorted Brismead sulkily. "I've been visited by the Port Pilot if you *must* know, sir. Now, what do you want?"

"I want you to cast your mind back, Brinsmead," replied the Captain, not in the least put out by the other's hostility. "Far, far back—let me see, over a year ago, about fourteen months, I should think. Can you cast your mind back fourteen months, Brinsmead?"

Brinsmead said nothing, but wearily replaced his pen in its tray with a gesture of bored resignation.

"About fourteen months ago," continued James, "an impecunious compatriot of ours was, I think, given a job in the docks?"

"Oh, Mr. Lillywhite, you mean? Yes, that's right."

"What sort of a job?"

"Junior clerk in the customs."

"Salary being?"

"Fifteen pounds a month."

"Hm. Does he earn it in your opinion?"

Brinsmead shrugged. "You'd better ask Lieutenant Baines that, sir."

"Yes, I'm going to."

"I might add," continued Brinsmead unwillingly, "that the Colonel and I put him there to keep an eye on the Guardia di Finanza."

"Setting a thief to catch a thief?"

"Oh, I don't think Lillywhite's a thief—not particularly. Merely a fool. What's all this about, sir, anyway?"

76

"Oh, nothing really. I'm just checking up on this and that."

"Well, now you're here I may as well tell you that the Colonel doesn't think much of your designs for the uniforms of the Banda. Too ornate." Brinsmead pulled out a file, opened it, and fingered his large moustache thoughtfully. "I can't help agreeing with the Colonel, either. Gold epaulets are all very well, but they cost money. The same goes for these silk cord affairs—anyway, we can't get them. None of the shops in the town have anything like them."

Naughton-Muirhead hitched up his pale biscuit-colored trousers and sat gingerly on the seat recently vacated by the Port Pilot.

"As a matter of fact, Brinsmead, I have found—or rather Fortu found for me—a little tailor who has a lot of all those trappings," he announced comfortably, "and he will sell them to us at a not unreasonable price."

"They'll look like a lot of cheap cinema commissionaires."

"Perhaps, but that is really what they are, in a manner of speaking. They were Giordano's Palace Guards, weren't they?"

"Yes," agreed Brinsmead grudgingly.

"And their main duties were to open doors and bow that dreary little man into his motorcar, were they not?"

Brinsmead grunted assent.

"Well, there you are! Except for asking if there are any more for the one-and-ninepennies, cinema commissionaires to the life."

"They'll look like the chorus in a comic opera," intoned Brinsmead morosely. "I don't see why we need go out of our way to look sillier than we are."

"Don't you, Brinsmead? And you may well be right. But the fact remains that this is a comic opera island. Some of us are the actors and the Colonel is the producer. He plays the leading part as well. The Banda and Captain Kellermann's men are the chorus; you're—let me see—yes, Brinsmead, you're the stage manager, an onerous job, more kicks than halfpence, I've always understood, and"—he was warming to his theme now—"the police are the low comedians, the clowns, with Mrs. Tamminetto as the chief clown, when she's not being the male impersonator. And, of course, the population is the audience. We must all keep them satisfied and give them their money's worth—hence gold epaulets for the Banda."

Twilight had descended outside as the Captain climbed silently on rubber-soled shoes the broad marble stairs to the Governor's office. The Palace messengers on the bench outside the tall white-and-gold double doors left off a whispered conversation as he appeared and jumped to their feet. He opened one of the doors and passed quietly within.

At the end of the long room the Colonel was writing rapidly by the light of his tall desk lamp. He sat very upright in his high-backed chair and the pool of golden light shining serenely on the vast glass of the desk was reflected back to glitter on his buttons and the gilded rank badges on his shoulders. It illuminated the pale, rather stern face, the broad brow, narrow nose, and firm thin-lipped mouth.

"I shall have to paint you like that, Euan," remarked James with a certain ironic benevolence. " 'Portrait of a Military Governor'—no, I think I'd just call it 'The Proclamation.' "

"In that case you'd be wrong"—the Colonel did not look up, but motioned with his pen to a seat in front of the desk—"for at the moment I'm dealing with the more mundane details of a report from Baines."

"But nonetheless"—James lounged forward to the chair—"it's an excellent title. For the sake of the title I'll paint you, Euan. You know you've always wanted me to."

"Nonsense!" The Colonel smiled, but went on writing. "But I am prepared to say that your picture of Fortu surprises me. You always said you were a landscape artist. Have you shown it to the Commendatore?"

"I have." James sighed. "He was violently complimentary, of course—what else could one expect from him? It may not mean much."

"Hm." Lemonfield wrote on rapidly. "I think he knows what he's talking about. Anyway, I consider it an excellent picture—unless you think my opinion doesn't mean much either. Are you going to do any more?"

James combed his fingers idly through his fly whisk. "Oh yes, I think so. I thought of painting the Commendatore next; he's got an interesting face—and besides, he'd be so flattered."

"That's right," said Euan absently. "You should get into the habit of painting flattering portraits of rich people. It must be comparatively simple to paint a straightforward picture of Fortu, but the real test is surely to take a subject like the Tamminetto hag and turn her into a Beauty Queen or a *grande dame* or something equally consoling. That's where the money lies." His pen continued to hover over the paper, making little darts here and there, swinging from right to left.

James said, "Somebody's given Mr. Lillywhite thousands of pounds—perhaps I'd better paint his portrait."

"What!" Euan laid down his pen and looked up at last. His face registered amused bewilderment and a certain weary apprehension. "What's all this, James?"

"One of Baines' customs contacts—a half-caste Greek named, I think, Miranos Allamara—reports that last night at 3 a.m. he saw Lillywhite go on board a small freighter, the *Anna Gabriella*, looking more than usually furtive. Not seeing a light in the deckhouse, this fellow got into the water—showing an extraordinary lack of interest in sharks, I must say—and paddled around to the stern where he saw a light from a porthole. He was able to look in and he saw Lillywhite counting quantities of notes at a table with another man."

"Did he recognize him?"

"He did. A captain Umberto Rossi, who owns a horrible, stinking little hulk called the *Bina* and goes fishing for *bêche-de-mer* in it."

"Ah! One of those."

"As you say—one of those."

"What else?"

"Well, I assume Miranos felt the sharks nudging his ribs by that time, so he came out onto the docks, looking like a drowned rat, I've no doubt, and was promptly arrested on suspicion by some dumb Port policeman. Baines got him out this morning."

"I see." The Colonel tapped a pencil reflectively on the desk top. Outside the dusk had deepened to night and, with a deferential tap on the door, the chief Palace footman entered with two assistants and began to swing the heavy purple-and-gold velvet curtains across the tall windows.

"This Miranos had no idea, of course, as to how much money was changing hands?"

"Not really, I'm afraid—except that it was a great deal. But heaven knows what he thinks *is* a great deal—probably he imagines fifty pounds to be immense riches. He says he saw a lot of

East African notes, mostly pounds, and some others that he thought were Egyptian. There's so much assorted currency in use here, that's the trouble."

The Colonel examined his fingernails, frowning. "Lillywhite has been in the customs for fourteen months. He came to me here soon after I got back from my tour early last year and said that he wanted a job. As you know, I'd seen him at the Balla concession and I asked him what had happened to the job he had there."

"He'd lost it, I suppose?"

"Yes. He was overcome with dismay and distress when I told him I knew he'd been working for Balla. I suspected at once that Balla had turned him out for dishonesty, and in ordinary circumstances I'd have checked up on it. But I knew I'd got to do something for him, whatever he'd done, so I gave him a junior clerkship in the customs. His actual job has been translating certain lists into English, which has had a rather baffling effect on the Guardie di Finanza and, I think, has stopped a certain amount of sharp practice. I knew, of course, that they'd find their way around it sooner or later, but it was only a temporary measure in any case. Since Baines has been here Lillywhite has lost any value he may have had from our point of view. I just kept him on because we can't have an English beggar in the streets."

"So you think he's in with the Guardie di Finanza?"

Euan nodded. "They probably employ him in a minor capacity as a go-between. I shouldn't think he's anything more—he hasn't got the nerve or ability for anything except crime on the smallest scale. In any case he couldn't do anything remotely criminal in that department without their active connivance—nobody can." He stared thoughtfully down the long room. "Well, this finishes *them*, James. I'll send for Baines tomorrow, and just as soon as it can be arranged we'll arrest all the Guardie di Finanza—at least all the white ones—and dismiss all the customhouse clerks and start again from scratch. The G.D.F. I intend to put away for good. Baines has been trying to catch them out for over twelve months and hasn't succeeded. He curtailed their activities considerably, but this Lillywhite business shows they've got some new ideas and are starting again. Heaven knows for how many years they've been using their official positions to make money by defrauding the Government! It's a habit they obviously can't be broken of. So into Fort Brocca they go for the rest of the war."

"What will you charge them with?"

"Fascists," answered Euan laconically. "Political animosity. It's easier that way and evades any legal quibbles later."

"Baines is going to be completely denuded of staff."

"He'll have to recruit some more, then."

"What about Lillywhite?"

"We'll keep an eye on him. But I think he'll stop whatever he's doing immediately the G.D.F. are arrested. I wish we had this new police officer they are always saying they'll send me. It's a nuisance having to arrange all this sort of thing myself."

"Then they *are* sending someone at last?"

"They *say* so—but God knows they've been saying so for a year now! I suppose he'll arrive one day."

"Mrs. Tamminetto won't be pleased."

"That woman," said Euan, coldly vicious, "is a jealous, crafty bitch if ever there was one! What I can't understand is how she manages to combine such amazing inefficiency with such an extraordinary capacity for low cunning. We're going to spring this one on her as a surprise and give her no time to lose the files and cook the accounts and generally cover up her shortcomings. God grant the new man—when at last he comes—is another Baines."

"Amen!" said James and rose to go.

9

IT was still very hot when Christopher drove along the dusty track that led to the small jetty far down the harbor where the police kept their two launches and where his own boat *Princessa*, a recent gift from the Colonel, lay sluggishly on the warm, oily green surface.

Two days before William and Texas had beached their old motorboat on the low sandy hump of Pelican Island, five miles down the coast, and, having been unable to start her again, had been forced to leave her and return to San Pietro in a native fishing canoe. Hearing of this, Christopher had volunteered to take them out on an attempted salvage expedition and now, as he drew up near the jetty, he saw that Silvana and Fortu had apparently been included in the party. William, dressed in faded blue canvas trousers as old, but not as filthy and ragged as those of Texas, explained apologetically that the two young Italians were the only competent engineers in the party, and anyway Sergeant Batinelli, the chief of the police transport section, had given Silvana the new spark plugs for their boat *Columbia*. But Christopher, for once in a comparatively carefree mood, would have been content to welcome even the Guardie di Finanza if William had somehow extricated them from Fort Brocca for the afternoon.

They cast off and chugged over the hot, calm water of the harbor with Pepino, the old native who looked after the boats, at the helm, while Fortu bent diligently over the engine and the three Englishmen and Silvana lounged on the hot white deck of the bows. The wharves and shabby shipping of the commercial docks slid past; the afternoon sun glared blindingly from the iron customs roofs, and as they passed the white stone pier of the Dhow Control Point the sluggish calm of the harbor gave place to the slow swell of the open sea and a breath of air, clean with the tang of brine and blowing gently from the west, dispersed the oily, spicy harbor smell.

"I hear you're going to stay on here after the war," said Christopher, looking with interest at Texas, who lay basking his naked mahogany torso in the heavy heat while his impossible trousers contaminated the *Princessa*'s white scrubbed planking.

Texas turned lazily and grinned assent—a flash of white teeth in his brown face. Just like any Italian sailor he looked, thought Christopher wonderingly. Only two years on Baressa and he could have passed unnoticed among the rough, burly *bêche-de-mer* fishers who lounged outside the Bar del Porto on the commercial docks.

"I think it'll suit you."

"I reckon so, sir." Texas grinned again as he told once more how he had been offered the job by Rossi, skipper of the *Bina*, one day in his deckhouse, where they had sat with some others drinking smuggled brandy out of teacups from noon to sunset. "So I'm here for good, sir," he continued, heaving himself into a sitting position and running a spadelike hand through his thick black hair. "They may take me home to demob me, of course, but I'll try to get them to let me go here, otherwise I'll have to work my passage back like."

"But the war may last for years yet."

"May do, sir." Texas grinned. "It can do for all I care. I don't care if the bloody thing lasts forever. I'm here now and I'm stayin'."

Christopher was half appalled and half amused at this, to him, fantastically impudent conviction. If he, an officer with the assistance and protection of the military Governor, never dared to be certain of his continuous employment on Baressa, how much less should this illiterate private, lacking any sort of influence, challenge Providence by such an assertion! But it was William who gave utterance to these thoughts.

"It's nonsense saying that, Texas. We might get posted any day. Any of us—to anywhere. Even you, sir"—he sought Christopher's corroboration—"you might get posted—or the Colonel, even. It's just up to the Army; you can't tell what they're going to do next."

Texas laughed and searched in his hip pocket for a squashed packet of native cigarettes. "They won't post the Colonel in a hurry. Who'd run the island then? An' I got a feeling they won't shift me neither. Me'n the Colonel, we'll be here in ten years' time —be old pals by then, I reckon."

They laughed. The *Princessa* chugged over the slow heaving swell and a small bow wave gurgled and splashed beneath her outwater.

Silvana said, "If Texas and the Colonel stay you must stay, William—and you, too, Capitano. We will all stay. No more English, no more Italian, we will be *indigeni*—natives of Baressa."

"What do you say, Capitano?" asked Fortu grinning as he adroitly cast a baited line over the stern. "Shall we all be islanders forever?"

Christopher, inwardly delighted to have been included in this sweeping program for the lives of the assembled company, smiled assent.

The rest of the afternoon was like that. Arrived at Pelican Island—low and sandy with no vegetation save a thick tattered fringe of mangroves swarming with huge black crabs—they

83

bathed and lay half in and half out of the shallow warm water at the sea's edge, talking and dozing, more than half drunk with the effects of sun, salt water, and a bottle of confiscated contraband brandy presented to Silvana along with the spark plugs by Sergeant Batinelli. Later Pepino and Fortu got to work on the *Columbia* and the others went to catch crabs among the mangroves.

It was a wild and risky sport. When a crab had been located and cornered it had to be held down with a stick while the hunter groped and fumbled for a hold behind its wildly snapping claws. Silvana and William were adept in this art—in fact, they had invented it—but Texas confined himself to pointing out crabs and holding the sack open to receive them.

Pushing ahead through the gray, whippy mangroves, he suddenly called excitedly to Christopher, a few yards behind, "Come here, sir, look at this!"

Christopher, splashing toward him through the shallow muddy water, saw a long torpedolike silver thing wallowing among the gray stems.

"It's a boat. It's Fortu's seaplane float!" he exclaimed. "It's upside down. It must have broken loose and been washed out of the harbor."

"It isn't, sir." Texas bent down and tried to heave over the long, narrow metal canoe, but it was too heavy for him. "Fortu's boat is in the harbor. I seen it as we come out."

"Well, let's get it right side up, anyway," suggested Christopher, and together they heaved it over with a crash that brought William and Silvana splashing through the mangroves to their side.

All four looked down at the open cockpit of the float. A snapped-off paddle with a flat aluminum blade floated in a pool of water and a tin bailer lay wedged under the combing.

"It's Fortu's boat," said William at once.

"It ain't," said Texas. "His is in the harbor—I seen it."

"There isn't another boat like Fortu's anywhere on the island," said Silvana. "It must be Fortu's."

"It can't be!" Texas replied in exasperation. "I tell you I *seen* Fortu's boat when we was coming out of the harbor. Now you ain't"—he put his hands on his hips and confronted Silvana with a pitying smile—"you ain't going to tell me that on a flat calm day that there float gets adrift and beats us to this island!"

"There is another," remarked Christopher suddenly. "I saw it

84

last year when the Colonel and I were on the road from Dinghité. We saw it right out to sea. I remember because I thought it must be Fortu's, but there was someone else in it. There was a storm coming up, and I remember the Colonel saying he wondered what it was doing out there."

"Well, it's not Fortu's, then." Texas sounded complacent. "And as I found it I reckon it's mine—that's right, ain't it, sir?"

"Well, so long as the owner doesn't turn up I suppose it is."

William had been rummaging in the half-submerged cockpit and he suddenly stood up with a small square tin in his hands.

"Look at this!" He shook it and it rattled. "Got a knife, anyone?"

Texas had, and they prized open the rusted lid. Inside, dry and quite intact, were several large fishhooks, a plain white handkerchief, and a wristwatch of good Swiss make. The same thought entered all their minds at once.

"Good Lord, a white man!" exclaimed William. "And he must have been drowned!"

They pondered excitedly over this new piece of evidence.

"Did you see who was in the float that time you were with the Colonel, sir?"

"It *looked* like a white man—yes, I remember I said so to the Colonel."

"But there aren't any Europeans at Dinghité—except when Brigadiere Veniero visits the place," remarked Silvana in a puzzled tone, "and he's far too fat and lazy to go out in a canoe like this. Anyway, he'd sink it."

"Then it must have been a native."

"Natives don't have handkerchiefs or wristwatches."

"There might be some who do."

"It's most unlikely."

Christopher cut short the discussion. "Well, anyway, we aren't certain that anybody's been drowned in it. It could have been washed away during the night, or the man might have swum ashore when it capsized."

"Not likely, sir, with all them sharks about." Texas, who wanted the float, was not prepared to concede that it might still possess a living owner.

In the end they bailed it out and pulled it through the mangroves to the bay where the *Princessa* and the *Columbia* now

85

rode at anchor. There it was attached by a length of rope to the stern of the latter and the two motorboats set out over the calm evening sea for San Pietro.

William and Texas were on their own boat with Fortu to watch the engine, but Silvana stayed on the *Princessa* with Christopher and, sitting together in the stern, they reeled out fishing lines as the low outline of Pelican Island faded into the glowing west.

It was quiet now without the others, and they lounged in comfortable tiredness on the canvas cushions behind the stolid back of Pepino at the helm. Christopher studied the girl beside him with growing interest and admiration. She sat idly paying out her line while the sinking sun shone on her slender coppery bronzed arms beneath the short sleeves of her red striped shirt. She was only a few inches shorter than he, though her small waist and too narrow hips accentuated her height and gave her, dressed as she was in shirt and shorts, a boyish air of which Christopher, who liked women to be short and feminine, would normally have disapproved. But there was about her thin, simply clothed figure, her small square shoulders and long legs, such a glow of youth and health, of sea and perpetual sun, that the defects of her form —the lack of that eighteenth-century classical plumpness so much in evidence among the statuary in the Casa dei Fiori and to Christopher the correct and desirable female shape—went unregarded and unmourned. He was fascinated by her small pointed face, in which the warm brown eyes seemed unnaturally large beneath the arched brows, the high delicate cheekbones, the wide, rather childish mouth, and the mane of heavy blue-black hair insufficiently brushed or combed.

She was fifteen, and there was something a little pathetic in the thinness and sunburn of this child of the police office and the foreshore. Christopher noticed with a curious mixture of amusement and pleasure and pity that she wore the same atrociously vivid nail varnish as Mrs. Tamminetto. He correctly surmised that the Police Chief had given it, with a quantity of patronizing but entirely erroneous advice on makeup and dress in general. He was glad to see that the sand and salt water were rapidly removing the gory paint from the girl's almond-shaped nails, though in the process of flaking and peeling the thin brown hands looked a sorry mess. There was a small triangular scar below her left eye, hardly discernible now with the passage of years.

"Silvana," he asked idly, "how did you get that mark on your face?"

The girl laughed and looped her line around a brass cleet. "This? Fortu threw a spanner at me. It was a long time ago—four, no, five years. We were in the police garage and arguing over the tools. Fortu had a fearful temper when he was a child."

"One wouldn't think it now."

"Oh, no! Not now—not since he's grown up. We all change when we grow up I suppose."

"Yes. Italians grow up quicker than English. Look at your friend William—half the time you'd think he was still fourteen!"

"William!" Silvana laughed. "I don't think he will ever change, do you? But he's nearly as old as you. I suppose it's because you've been a soldier longer."

"What is?"

"That you're more—more serious."

Christopher burst out laughing. "It couldn't be that. Captain —that is, Major—Naughton-Muirhead says that the longer one is a soldier the more trivial and frivolous one becomes. When one rises to be a General one takes one's frivolity seriously."

"I usen't to like the Major," remarked Silvana meditatively, "but I do now. He's the only man I know who continually stands up to Mrs. Tamminetto—and he's beginning to wear her down. My God, how she hates him!"

"You hate her, don't you?"

"Yes, most of the time. You've no idea what it's like working with her, Capitano." She looked into his eyes with an expression of amused distress.

"No, thank God!" Christopher leaned toward her. "Silvana," he said with a sudden urgency, "why don't you come and work for me?"

"For you?" The girl's huge eyes glowed with surprise and pleasure.

"You can come and type my letters. That's what you do for the police, isn't it?"

Silvana looked apprehensive. "Mrs. Tamminetto won't allow it. She'll make my father make me stay. I do quite a lot of other work as well as type the letters. She'd hate me to go."

87

"Mrs. Tamminetto's not going to run the police much longer. An English officer's being sent here to take over. You mustn't tell her that, though," added Christopher hurriedly. "It's supposed to be a secret at the moment."

Silvana's face lightened again. "And you really want me to come?"

Christopher smiled happily, his slant eyes glinting green in the colored evening light that shone on his dark blond head and illuminated each tiny fair hair on his bare bronzed arms. He knew he was beautiful and he knew Silvana knew it.

"Of course I do. I'll tell the Colonel tomorrow—or this evening, perhaps."

"Do you think he'll agree?"

"He's never said no to anything I've asked for yet."

When eventually they approached San Pietro the last red rim of the sun was sinking into the western sea and the multicolored sky of sunset glowed over the island, tinting the white buildings of the town to a bright orange and pink and gold and turning the vegetation on the high-rising escarpment behind the town to a vividly unnatural green. As the two boats turned the Dhow Control Point and entered the long stretch of the harbor, those on board saw a man sitting fishing on a rusty red iron bollard at the end of the short pier. Outlined against the shining sky, the shabby trousers, the bent, permanently dejected attitude, the old hat tilted over the long spectacled face, left no doubt of his identity. Mr. Lillywhite was making a lackadaisical attempt to supplement the diet of himself, his wife, and their eight regrettable children.

Lost to the world, sunk in some dim daydream of faraway happier times, he seemed unaware of the two boats until, when they were only a few yards off, William called out, "What luck, Isaak Walton?"

Mr. Lillywhite looked up with a start, looked down into the faces turned laughingly up at him. "Luck? Very little indeed. I have caught one squid and a red thing with spikes—my word, it looks villainous! I wonder, Summerson, if you know what . . ."

He was about to bend down and pick it up from beside him when his eye fell on the silver float tossing in the *Columbia*'s wake. For a moment he gasped at it in astonishment; then he hurriedly looked across the harbor to the Daldacara shore where, half a mile away, its silver body glittering unmistakably in the after-glow, lay Fortu's float. His mouth opened and shut twice, but no words came; then, his face white and his hands trembling violently, he jerked in his line and, collecting his two repellent catches, he set off down the stone pier at a shambling trot.

"No," said Colonel Lemonfield, selecting a thin yellow cigar from the big silver box at his side. "No, I'm afraid I really can't sanction that." He tried, without complete success, to keep from smiling as he looked from behind his great desk at Christopher, who stood, still dressed in his light sailing clothes, with an expression of surprised disappointment on his scarred sunbrowned face.

"You must realize," he continued, "that this is the first time I've refused you anything at all and I wouldn't refuse this if it were reasonable."

"But, sir——"

"One minute, please. You tell me that you want this girl to come and work in the barracks as a sort of secretary for you. Now, firstly, you are not entitled to a secretary, and certainly not a civilian one, and least of all to a female. Your position is purely military and there is no place for a civilian in the barracks. Secondly you don't need a secretary. I know all you have to do and I know how it's done. Your native officers and orderly room staff are perfectly adequate and competent to do it. Thirdly, a young girl like Silvana Angellini would be placed in a most undesirable position in an orderly room staffed entirely by men and, except for yourself, all of them black. It would be prejudicing her in the eyes of her compatriots and be most unfair for her father, the Maresciallo, and her uncle, Dr. Valdonetti—supposing they allowed it, which I am quite convinced they would not. Fourthly, it would naturally be assumed that I had concurred in the matter and would thus prejudice the Administration. In other words, I should be accused of playing the pander and assisting you in your immoral designs."

"I haven't——"

"And fifthly, there is, as you know, an officer coming to take over the police—a certain Captain Pirie. Now Mrs. Tamminetto is not going to like this, as you can understand, and she is not, I suspect, going to cooperate gladly with this officer. Silvana Angellini knows all the ropes of the police administration nearly as well as Mrs. Tamminetto—for, poor girl, I well know that she has had to do the most of the routine work involved. So she will, I trust, be of considerable assistance to Captain Pirie when he starts his duties, and it would be unkind to him and detrimental to the future of the police if I let Silvana leave at present." The Colonel relaxed in his chair and exhaled a cloud of cigar smoke with evident satisfaction; it swirled blue and heavy in the darkening air.

Christopher looked glumly at the floor and shifted his feet in their white sandals.

"But my designs *aren't* immoral," he said at last, sulkily. "She hates working for Mrs. Tamminetto. She'd much rather work for me."

"I'm sure she would," commented the Colonel dryly. "And, as to your intentions—a less sinister word than 'designs,' perhaps —they may not be immoral at the moment, but from what I know of you and your way of life they are more than likely to rapidly become so."

Christopher looked shaken; he rubbed the palms of his hands on his hips and took a deep breath. But before he could speak the Colonel continued, this time in a tone of amused kindliness.

"Look, Christopher, to put the matter quite bluntly, I don't mind you having one woman, but I'm not standing for a harem. You've got your half-caste dressmaker, you must be content with her." He smiled. "Polygamous practices shall not be indulged by English officers on this island. What's more, Silvana is, from that I know of her, a pleasant and respectable girl and she's perfectly happy with young Summerson as a playmate—and if he has any intentions at all I'm sure they're quite honorable. Silvana has probably taken a fancy to you because you're better looking than Summerson and far higher in rank. But I don't want you to encourage her anymore, because it will only make her most unhappy in the end, reduce the efficiency of the police, and almost certainly cause a scandal. And a scandal of that sort would seriously displease me, so——"

There was a slight knock on the door, which opened at once to disclose the tall, thin figure of Major Naughton-Muirhead. He looked with slightly raised eyebrows from Christopher to the Colonel.

"Good evening, Euan—and likewise to you, Christopher. Am I in the way?"

"No, no, James. We've just been having a talk. Come in."

"Idle gossip in the cool of the evening?" The Major wandered over to a shell-backed sofa of old-gold brocade that stood between two of the long windows and collapsed into a corner, seeming all long arms and legs.

"Christopher, I saw you out in the harbor with the *jeunesse dorée* this evening."

"Not an apt description of Signalman Dawson," retorted the Captain with a smile.

"No, perhaps not. What was that you were towing? Fortu's boat?"

"No, it wasn't. It's a funny thing. . . ." Christopher, glad to change the conversation to a new subject before the Major had a chance to mention Silvana, told at some length of the finding of the silver float, his belief of having seen it off the northwest coast during the Colonel's first tour, and the odd effect the sight of it had had on Mr. Lillywhite.

The Major almost purred with satisfaction. "You see, Euan," he said, "I was right. Mr. Lillywhite is obviously a criminal of the deepest dye. That float must be the means by which he lands his contraband up the coast. And, of course, it was he whom Christopher saw that time you were on tour. I understand it all now—don't you?"

"No," said Lemonfield irritably, "I don't. We haven't got any proof that Lillywhite is doing any smuggling himself. He may have been in league with the Guardie di Finanza, but——"

"We have a lot of circumstantial evidence," persisted the Major.

"I don't call it a lot."

"What exactly makes you think Lillywhite is smuggling? And what is he smuggling, in any case?" asked Christopher interestedly.

"We don't know what it is yet, but the man's been seen at dead of night accepting or delivering vast sums of money in the most suspicious surroundings. Now your discovery of this float confirms me in my assumption that the misguided fellow is a member of the smuggling profession. And this is, in my opinion, how he does it. He keeps that float somewhere around the coast—hidden, doubtless in some hole in the rocks

91

—and he paddles out on calm nights to a rendezvous with one of the *bêche-de-mer* boats—the *Bina,* presumably. Then he takes on board whatever it is he's handling and paddles back to a hiding place on the coast. He gets rid of the stuff and delivers the cash to the skippers involved and doubtless gets a very good commission himself. He must have been operating somewhere in the northwest when you first saw him, and now that he's an employee of the customs he feels sufficiently safe to practice nearer home."

The Colonel sighed irritably. "That man is a damned nuisance. Now I'll have to try to catch him—if possible *in flagrante delicto*—and then try him and imprison him. Well, there's one thing at any rate—it won't harm the Administration now as it would have two years ago. At that time everyone would have made unpleasant comparisons and said that we were all English and probably just as bad as each other—or perhaps that we were putting Lillywhite inside in order to take over his racket ourselves. Fortunately, they know me—and all of us—better than that now."

Naughton-Muirhead stood up and, sauntering to one of the tall windows, looked out across the interspersed lamp standards and palm trees of the square below to the dusky sea where the colored lights of the harbor buoys laid paths of red, green, and yellow over the still water.

"I believe they've got so used to us that they think of us more or less as islanders like themselves, now," he remarked musingly. "It is difficult to know whether to consider it a compliment or not."

Christopher said, "It's odd you should say that. This afternoon in my boat Fortu and Silvana were trying to make Summerson and me stay on here after the war, as Dawson says he will. Silvana said, 'No more English and no more Italian. We will all be *indigeni*—natives of Baressa.' " He suddenly remembered that Silvana was a name it might be unwise to bring up in the present company: the Lillywhite story had made him momentarily forget the Colonel's earlier remarks. "She was only joking, of course," he added hurriedly, blushing scarlet in the dusky gloom.

In the pause that followed the Major repeated dreamily, "*Indigeni*—natives of Baressa. A delightful idea, delightfully put."

"Nonsense!" Lemonfield's voice cut in harshly, angrily. "What on earth would you do here? You'd have no jobs and no positions. It's quite probable that Giordano will return here after the war's over—I doubt if he'd make any of us particularly welcome as residents. You forget that this isn't our island and that our occupation is presumed to be temporary. As for Dawson, he's rather different, I admit. He's nothing now and he'll be nothing after the war. If he wants to stay on here and be a beachcomber"—the Colonel's mouth turned down in distaste and his shoulders lifted slightly—"I suppose he might as well do that as anything else." He looked up and saw that both James and Christopher were eyeing him in amazement. His manner changed abruptly. He smiled and rose from his chair laughing. "You must forgive me. It's this Lillywhite business. It's infuriating! When I think what I've done for that man—yes, turn on the lights, please, James———"

There came a clatter of booted feet on the stairs outside and an urgent knock on the door.

"Come in!"

Texas entered, flushed and dirty, with an orange envelope clutched in his gauntleted left hand. He strode over to the Colonel's desk, clicked his heels, saluted, and proffered the message.

"There's a general comin' here to inspect us, sir, next week!" Texas could never deliver a telegram without informing the recipient of its contents before it could be opened. "Not from the Civil Affairs Branch, neither, sir," he continued, pushing back his helmet and wiping his hot face with the back of one heavy glove. "He's from Command, I reckon—why, I shouldn't be surprised if———"

"Quiet, Dawson! Quiet!" The Colonel lifted a hand in protest, smiling despite himself. He had grown fond of this big, clumsy, uncouth boy who for nearly two years had burst noisily into his office three, four, sometimes even six or seven, times a day. At first Dawson had been told to be quieter, to stand properly at attention, to hold his tongue. Brinsmead, outside in the anteroom, had delivered his most scathing rebukes—but to no effect; Dawson was incorrigible. In the process of time he had worn down all resistance and now he had the license of a sort of maladroit family pet, a heavy lurcher unfit for the house but smilingly tolerated by custom.

The Colonel looked up. "All right, Dawson, you can go. Tell Staff Sergeant Brinsmead I'll want him in ten minutes." He turned to the others. "Anyone heard of a Major General Glasscraft? No? Nor have I. He's a K.B.E.—Sir Herbert Glasscraft. He's from Command—worse luck. I wish they'd send us somebody from the C.A. branch instead."

"When is he arriving?"

"On the next *Napoleon*—that gives us plenty of time to prepare things. Let me see—she docks on Monday week, I think, doesn't she?"

"Yes, sir," supplied Christopher readily. "I know because there are supposed to be two of my men coming back from courses."

James said, "I suppose this new police officer will be on the same boat—if he's coming at all." He sighed and yawned. "I'm going home now. Don't be late for dinner, Euan, remember Saccomani and Da Ponte are coming. Christopher, would you like a lift back to your preposterous house?"

10

AT ten o'clock the following morning Staff Sergeant Brinsmead was giving the Colonel has assistance in the matter of the arrangements for Major General Glasscraft's impending visit. He stood beside the Colonel's great desk, holding a scribbling pad in one hand and tapping a pencil gently on the glass desk top with the other. His pale myopic eyes stared unseeingly through the thick lenses of his glasses and his forehead was deeply creased in a thoughtful frown.

"As you say, sir, he's not from our own branch, which makes it difficult to know what to do. In fact, we really don't know what he's coming here for at all. They'd hardly send a general from Command merely to inspect the garrison company, would they?"

"Hardly, Brinsmead, I should think. Anyway, I'll see that Captain Kellermann has everything as it ought to be—and perhaps

94

you'd better take a quick look at the company's files and books to see that they're right up to date."

"Very good, sir. You'll speak to the Captain about that?"

"Yes, yes, of course."

"M'm—well, otherwise all I can suggest, sir, is that we give him the full works and keep him busy—too busy to be a nuisance."

"Oh, he'll be a nuisance all right, whatever happens, and unfortunately a nuisance without any compensation. If he were from our own department we might at least get a little help from him on some subjects."

Brinsmead smiled. "You're thinking of the financial side, I imagine, sir?"

Euan threw himself back in his tall chair petulantly. "Of course I am! The whole thing is ridiculous at present. When I took this island over the Administration was only just paying its way—they somehow cooked the budget. A short examination over the first few weeks convinced me that there should be a sizable surplus not merely in hand but continually accumulating. We all know why there was not—the place was a mass of corruption from Giordano downward. Well, I have stamped that out and, as I had foreseen, there is an accumulating surplus. But when I suggest to H.Q. that I should spend some of it on a new school or better police barracks or widening the coast road—what happens? They say that all I must do is to keep the place exactly as Giordano left it and let the surplus cash amass. What infuriates me is that if we eventually hand the island back—as I assume we may—we'll be handing Giordano a vast sum as well, a free gift. He'll doubtless manage to embezzle a good deal and with the rest he'll put up some huge public building to celebrate his return and the departure of the detestable Colonel Lemonfield!"

"And the equally odious Staff Sergeant Brinsmead!" Brinsmead chuckled.

"Probably." Euan smiled reluctantly. "Now if only this fellow Glasscraft was in O.E.T.A. I could have a long talk to him here about all this. We'd go into the figures and I'd explain the entire situation and I'd probably get a working agreement out of him before he left. As it is, we've got to entertain some red-faced

95

gin-swilling old idiot who doesn't know the difference between a budget and a budgerigar!"

Brinsmead laughed heartily and, still chuckling, took off his spectacles and wiped them on a dark silk handkerchief. Though a man without much humor, he made a point of laughing when the Colonel let himself go on personal criticisms. This was not primarily to flatter the Colonel, but because he felt flattered himself. He knew that, with the exception of Major Naughton-Muirhead, the Colonel would make such remarks to no one else, and it pleased him intensely to think that he, Arthur Brinsmead, a mere N.C.O. in the eyes of the world, was the chief receptacle of most of the Governor's confidences and his often scathing opinions of other less fortunate mortals.

"Well, Brinsmead"—the Colonel, gratified and calmed by this small outburst of annoyance, pulled a writing block toward him and unscrewed a gold fountain pen, a gift from the Mayor and Council on the occasion of his last birthday—"the man's coming, so we must just make the best of it. Captain Pirie, our new recruit, knows of him. He speaks quite well of him on the whole and says he possesses a reputation for being efficient and thorough and a good soldier. Not that that's much use to us, for I flatter myself that I am efficient and thorough—though with no pretensions to being a soldier—and I don't think there's going to be much a general can tell me about running this island. However, that's by the by. The main thing appears to be that he's passionately fond of fishing and shooting—one of that sort."

"Ah!" said Brinsmead, in a tone which made it plain that he understood all about "that sort" and did not approve of them.

"So we'll give him plenty of recreation," continued the Colonel. "We must get up a shoot over the Commendatore's land—Major Naughton-Muirhead is a friend of his so he can arrange that—and somebody must take him fishing. Let me see—young Summerson would be best at that really, but we obviously can't send a general out in charge of a corporal. H'm—the Major? No good, of course—doesn't know anything about it. No more do I. I doubt if it would be satisfactory to send Captain Kellermann—in fact, I'm quite sure it wouldn't. We'll just have to send Captain Pirie, I think. He's keen on fishing. Now as to the other things. We will just show him this part of the island in as much detail as possible. Take this down, please, Brinsmead—ready?"

"Yes, sir."

"Right. *Emperor Napoleon* docks seven a.m. Monday. Reception on docks. Guard of honor—arrange with Captain Kellermann. Police motorcycle escort to Villa—arrange with Captain Pirie. Better wait till tomorrow, Brinsmead, he's taking over today."

"Yes, sir."

"Nine thirty, tour of Administration offices in Palace. Eleven thirty, visit Police H.Q. and barracks. That'll do for the morning. Then four thirty p.m.—visit docks, Port Office, Health Office, Customs—see Lieutenant Baines—Immigration Office and Passport Control. Eight thirty, dinner party at Villa. All British officers in attendance, also Mayor and Mayoress, Dr. and Mrs. Valdonetti, Commendatore Saccomani, and—let me see——"

"Mrs. Tamminetto?"

"No—oh, well, I suppose so."

"Captain Zvengetzov?"

"Definitely not!"

"Very good, sir."

"I may think of some more guests later. Now Tuesday—nine a.m., inspect garrison company—arrange with Captain Kellermann. That'll do for the morning; he'll enjoy that, I expect. Afternoon, fishing. Dinner with just myself and the Major; if he has anything confidential to say he can say it then. Wednesday, nine thirty a.m., visit Municipio and Chamber of Commerce and Sharia Court. Eleven thirty, Fort Brocca Prison. Five thirty, School of Domestic Science, Mrs. Morle in attendance. Inform her, Brinsmead, and if her husband's there, too, we can't do anything about it, but I'm damned if I'll introduce him to the General. Where was I? Oh, yes—six p.m., visit Catholic cathedral, and six thirty, visit Greek Orthodox Church."

"What about tea, sir?"

"Tea?"

"He'll want his tea."

"Oh—yes. Well, then, tea with the Archdeacon of the Greek church. Send him over half a pound of tea, Brinsmead, with instructions how to make it."

"Very good, sir. Do you think the General will like that?"

"I don't care what he likes. I'm showing him around and it will make a good impression if he visits the two biggest churches and meets the clergy. In the evening old Sheikh Mohammed Gedain can throw a Moslem dinner for him with all the trimmings. He hasn't got any money, so we'll have to pay for it—see to that, Brinsmead."

"Yes, sir."

"Then—Thursday, visit the High School in the morning and then lunch at Saccomani's. Get the Commendatore to invite everyone of any importance. Then fishing again in afternoon. Dinner at the Municipio as guests of the Mayor. Then—Saturday, thank God, he goes! The *Emperor Napoleon* sails at seven a.m., so lay on another guard of honor with the Captain and a motorcycle escort from the Villa with Captain Pirie—and that's that!"

At the same time as these plans were being laid in the Palazzo Firenze Major Naughton-Muirhead and the new Police Chief, Captain Pirie, were finishing a quick inspection of a small, rather shabby bungalow behind one of the slipways on the Daldacara shore. Captain Pirie had arrived most unexpectedly—he had taken a passage on a small Greek freighter instead of coming by the *Napoleon* in the usual manner—and most inconveniently. He had entered, suddenly and unannounced, the dining room of the Villa halfway through dinner the previous evening. A tall, burly man with a high color, small, angry gray eyes, and a clipped red moustache, he had been promoted only fairly recently from the ranks and he had still not entirely accustomed himself to his new status when a drunken French soldier, roaring berserk out of a brothel in Alexandria, had shot him in the leg with a .45 revolver. The heavy-caliber bullet had mushroomed out and removed most of one knee, thus disabling Pirie from any further active duties and resulting in his present appointment. It was not one that he would have sought himself, as he had been at rather unnecessary pains to indicate to his new employers.

"I fear our Sergeant Brinsmead has not made a very happy choice," commented James apologetically as they walked from one small, ill-furnished room to the next. "He's always been in charge of requisitioning accommodation here, but I really think in future I shall have to supervise his efforts."

"Oh, this is all right! I've lived in a hell of a lot of worse places than this in the last year or two! God Almighty, this is luxury, real luxury, compared to anything we had in the camps in Egypt

—let alone the Front, of course! After all, I don't suppose *this* place is full of rats and fleas and bedbugs."

"I sincerely trust not!"

"The place'll do me fine, sir." Pirie laughed. "You'll excuse me saying so, but if you or the Colonel had lived in some of the places I've lived in you'd look on this house as a veritable palace! Running water, proper sanitation, electric light—and furniture!"

James smiled. "Well, as long as you are satisfied that's all that matters."

"Well, I am, I can tell you! Up till I set out for this island I was living in a tent with four other bods. So you can realize it's good to have a bit of privacy. I'll make arrangmenets to get my kit dumped here."

"I've already told Brinsmead to have your luggage collected and brought along."

"You think of everything, sir!" There was the tiniest hint of derision in Pirie's jovial voice that a less sensitive ear than his companion's might have missed and that a less acute mind might have left untranslated. But to James it confirmed what he had already more than half guessed from the other's talk—Pirie both resented and disapproved of the standard of living upheld by the Colonel and himself. Probably he held some view based on an emotional and jingoistic patriotism that no one had the right to lead a life of comfort and ease during this war. There were, James understood, people who thought like that. His half-repressed dislike of the newcomer hardened to cold hostility. That a man of his sort—burly, uncouth, loud-voiced, and exhibiting, every time he opened his mouth, more than a hint of his plebeian breeding—should hold him in contempt was infuriating. He —James Naughton-Muirhead, the cultured, the civilized, the highly promising artist. It was laughable really, if it wasn't so exasperating.

James smiled—a rather hard smile—and said, "Well, then, I think we may betake ourselves to the scene of your new duties —the Police Headquarters."

At Police Headquarters they were doing the crime return. It was the busiest day of the month and one of the pleasantest, too. Everybody, and in particular Mrs. Tamminetto, was in a good humor on the day of the monthly crime return, for today the

99

somewhat spasmodic and slipshod efforts of the police to keep law and order and to detect and apprehend malefactors during the past four weeks were totaled up, neatly parceled into sections, and inscribed in a long, elaborate report glowing with self-admiration. This was then taken to the Palazzo Firenze and laid at the feet—or more correctly on the desk—of the too often skeptical Colonel Lemonfield.

As the work of compiling the return necessitated the presence of all the European police in San Pietro, it had long been the custom to serve light refreshments during the proceedings. During the course of years these light refreshments had grown progressively heavier until the Maresciallo had been heard to remark with satisfaction that they were really a meal in themselves.

The proceedings were held in the main charge room, where Mrs. Tamminetto sat enthroned behind a big desk covered with files and dossiers, plates of sandwiches and cups of coffee. She wore a girlish dress of white and scarlet linen, all her jewels—a varied collection of semiprecious stones—and a large rose pinned to her bosom with a little locket miniature of her late husband. Around her on chairs, desks, and tables were ranged all the members of the Carabinieri Reali, from fat, beaming Maresciallo Angellini, whose gray hair and air of benign avuncular authority marked him out as second only to the Police Chief herself, to lanky, sly, smiling Aldo Commino, that lady's personal assistant and at twenty-four the most junior member of the force.

Silvana, bright-eyed and laughing, sat near her mistress at a smaller desk and took down details as they were given to her. In her cheap cotton frock, with the small string of island pearls around her neck and her heavy black hair carefully brushed smooth for the occasion, she looked very young and very pretty. The Carabinieri, to whom she had been from babyhood a beloved pet, kept sidling up to her with plates of dainties and gallant little compliments and a weather eye on the jealous and vindictive Mrs. Tamminetto nearby. But while Silvana joked and laughed with all the Carabinieri, for every one of whom—even ugly, caustic Brigadiere Rondotto—she had a strong affection, it was her old friend Aldo who sat on a corner of her desk and shared with her a tin of sardines. They ate one each, turn and turn about, using an ivory paper knife instead of a fork; it was a messy and undignified business and quite in keeping with the rest of the proceedings.

Mrs. Tamminetto laid down with difficulty a particularly sticky éclair and banged a ruler sharply on her desk.

"Arson!" she called loudly, as one denouncing that crime in the dead of night. "Has anybody got any arson?"

Carabiniere Lucca, a small, spectacled, mouselike man who held the unenviable position of clerk to the Maresciallo, rustled timorously amongst his files. "One!" he called out in a husky, bun-muffled voice amidst a shower of crumbs. "I have one smallish arson on the night of the twenty-second."

"One," echoed Mrs. Tamminetto loudly. "One. Has nobody got any more? No? Very well, then. One, Silvana."

"One, *signora*." Silvana obediently made a note.

"Blasphemy and Outrage against the Dead!" announced Mrs. Tamminetto, unhurriedly turning over a page. "Has anyone got any Blasphemy? Outrage against the Dead?" Heads shook in every direction; jaws worked stolidly. Mrs. Tamminetto frowned slightly. "Commino, you're meant to visit the cemeteries once a week. Have you been doing that?"

"What's that? Oh, yes, *signora*. Yes, I have. Nothing to report."

"Very well. No Blasphemy or Outrage against the Dead this month, Silvana. I think we can mention in the report that we have at last managed to stamp out all crimes of sacrilege and desecration. We will make a special paragraph, 'Police Put an End to Religious Intolerance,' and send a copy to the Cathedral. Note that, Silvana."

"Yes, *signora*."

"And, gentlemen"—Mrs. Tamminetto raised her voice— "please don't let me hear of any more. If I say we've stamped it out then it mustn't appear in the report again. So if any of you *do* happen to find any sepulchers knocked down or graves dug up just see that they're put right again quietly without any fuss."

"Yes, *signora*," they all chorused dutifully.

"Now, let me see, what's next? Negligent Homicide. Has any-one——"

"Three fatal traffic accidents, *signora*." The Maresciallo was on his feet, a piece of cake in one hand and a cherubic smile on his round red face. But Mrs. Tamminetto was dubious.

"Does that come within the meaning of the act, I wonder?" She frowned hesitantly and tapped a pencil against her chin.

"They were particularly negligent," supplied the Maresciallo hopefully.

"Very well, then. Three Negligent Homicides, Silvana. Now —h'm"— Mrs. Tamminetto did not use the word "rape," but the Italian idiom she much preferred—"Defloration—how many persons have been deflowered this month? Brigadiere?" She turned inquiringly to Rondotto, the specialist in Carnal Violence.

"Come on, Carlo, here's your chance!" cried jovial, heavy-moustached Brigadiere da Vannia and was at once reduced to blushing silence by a glance of cold rebuke from the *signora*. Rondotto, dark and thin with a gleaming gold-filled smile, rose and said, "Six deflowerings, please, *signora*."

"Six!" Mrs. Tamminetto was delighted, but tried to appear shocked.

"I'm afraid so, *signora*—six."

"Six?"

"Six."

"Six, Silvana."

"Six, *signora*."

A pause. Mrs. Tamminetto drank some coffee and Lucca leaped up and offered her a plate of cheese straws. Not to be outdone, Aldo sidled around the desk and with his shy, almost pleading smile held out a little dish of anchovies on toast. Mrs. Tamminetto hesitated prettily and then chose an anchovy.

Back to work.

"Trade in Writings, Drawings, and Other Articles Contrary to Public Decency. I don't suppose anyone——"

"I'm afraid so, *signora*." It was the Maresciallo again, and though he attempted to force his features into a look of stern disapproval it was obvious that he was nearly bursting with merriment.

"Yes, Franco?" Mrs. Tamminetto's voice was a dulcet coo.

"I have two cases, *signora*—both concerning indecent postcards. One is a native, a hardened offender whom we will deal with in the prescribed way. The other is Mr. Lillywhite—he was selling them on the docks."

There was a gale of laughter and shouts of, "Who was buying them? Tell us, Maresciallo—who?"

The Maresciallo, chuckling benevolently, shook his head. "It would be unethical for me to tell you that, I'm afraid. Mr. Lillywhite said they were all pure art. He was arrested and let out on bail, but he seems to have disappeared. I——"

The Maresciallo got no farther, the laughter died away to a titter and jaws stopped munching. Carabinieri of all ranks slipped off desks and tables and rose from chairs. In the doorway stood Major Naughton-Muirhead and a strange British officer.

James advanced to the center of the room and smiled bleakly at the assembled company. "Ladies and gentlemen," he began, "for the last two years the work of supervising the Police Department has been mine. I have, however, other calls on my time and have not, therefore, been able to give you the full attention that your duties and position merit. The British Civil Affairs Authority has at last seen fit to send here an officer to take complete charge of the police. He will work in these offices and will take over absolute control of your department as from this morning. This then, ladies and gentlemen, is Captain Pirie, who arrived on the island yesterday. He does not as yet speak your language and therefore I must ask for your special coop——"

"Signor Maggiore!" Mrs. Tamminetto was on her feet, her eyes blazing with fury, her face white beneath its coating of paint. "Do you mean to say that I—that I am no longer Chief of Police?"

"Not chief, *signora*—no. Captain Pirie is now chief. You will, I am sure, understand——"

"I understand nothing! But nothing! No, no, no—it is not so! I am the Chief of Police. I cannot believe—no, no! This officer —he speaks no Italian. How can he do the work? It is impossible! I—for years now I—" Her voice rose to a hysterical pitch and she trembled with fury. James cast a quick glance at Pirie and saw to his satisfaction that that officer appeared both appalled and acutely embarrassed at this unexpected scene. "Oh, it is monstrous! It is intolerable! I cannot believe it!" Mrs. Tamminetto clapped a hand to her forehead and swayed dramatically. "Franco! Aldo!" she screamed and burst into tears.

Immediately all was pandemonium. The Maresciallo knocked over his chair in his eagerness to assist his ex-chief and Aldo leaped zealously around the desk to prevent a possible swoon. Mrs. Tamminetto chose the Maresciallo as being more suited to the occasion and, flinging herself into his arms, sobbed loudly and brokenly, protesting meanwhile at the gross ingratitude of the English in general and Colonel Lemonfield in particular.

The effect on the Carabinieri was all she could have hoped for. They must, felt James, have surely had a thousand good reasons to dislike her extremely, but either this was not the case or else they forgave her on the spot, for now all of them from the Maresciallo down to Commino—yes, and even Silvana— were throwing glances of genuine indignation and reproof at both himself and Pirie. Not only glances, either, but oblique remarks expressive of the strongest resentment and disapproval.

"Ah, but it is a shame! The poor *signora!*"

"After so many years!"

"Such service——"

"The poor unhappy lady!"

"Oh, what a base act!"

James held up a hand and called for silence; he got it eventually, barring Mrs. Tamminetto's loud sobs.

"Please, ladies and gentlemen!" He spoke with an exaggerated weariness and exasperation. "All this is both unnecessary and ridiculous and completely out of keeping with the tradition of the Carabinieri Reali. Had I been permitted to continue, I was about to explain to Mrs. Tamminetto that whilst Captain Pirie is going to take over the duties of Chief of Police—and I may say, in passing, that the Occupying Power has every right to appoint one of its military officers to that position—Mrs. Tamminetto is requested to remain as chief of the clerical side and the Criminal Records office and to——"

"Never! never! never!" Mrs. Tamminetto tore herself from the Maresciallo's arms and crashed her fist on the top of an adjacent desk. "If I have no longer my position here, I go! I go—I finish!" and, sobbing bitterly, she ran across the room and out of the doorway.

"Go after her, Commino," ordered James brusquely. "Drive her home and then return here. Silvana!"

"Yes, *signore?*"

"Come here." Silvana walked rather uncertainly out of the crowd of sullen police and approached the two officers. "Silvana"—James spoke in English—"I want you to explain—not now but later—to these people that Captain Pirie has been sent here by the British Army and not by Colonel Lemonfield.

Secondly, you will have to take over a lot of Mrs. Tamminetto's work on the clerical side, for she is not coming back. You know all about it, so it should not be difficult. Thirdly, you must give Captain Pirie all the help he needs and be his interpreter until he speaks the language."

"If he ever does," commented Pirie, smiling down at Silvana.

"I hope that you will try to learn it," said James seriously. "You will find it a great handicap if you don't." This was obviously intended as a rebuke and the smile left Pirie's face to be succeeded by a dull flush.

"Well, sir," he said abruptly, "if this young lady will act as my interpreter I'm ready to take over now."

"You are? Very well, then, I'll leave you to it. I shouldn't try to change too much too quickly."

"I think I know how to deal with these people. I'll give them a bit of a pep talk now—quite friendly—just to let them know what I want and how I expect things to be done and then I'll have a look at the office stuff."

"You'll find them quite a nice lot—a bit sloppy by Army standards, perhaps, but I shouldn't worry too much about that if I were you. I——"

"Look, sir, don't think me impertinent"—Pirie gave a slight chuckle—"but if I can have a free hand that's all I want."

James laughed. "Oh, very well then, I'll get along. Ring up the Palace if you want anything more in the way of office equipment; we've got plenty to spare. Brinsmead's in charge."

"Yes, sir." Pirie saluted stiffly and James turned away. As he went down the steps he heard Pirie saying, "Now I want you to tell these men that I'm a soldier and I like things done in a soldierly fashion. Now we'll get along well together if . . ."

I I

SEVEN o'clock was not an hour at which the English officers—with the exception of Lieutenant Baines—generally visited the docks, but on this still, hot Monday, with the sun rising swiftly over the bleak outline of the Daldacara Orphanage on the eastern side of the harbor, they were all there. A square had been roped off on No. 1 berth to protect them from the milling crowd who waited with pleasurable curiosity to see the English General arrive.

The officers were in their best clothes and feeling hot and uncomfortable in consequence, for the morning breeze did not rise until after nine o'clock. Even Captain Pirie, in ostentatious charge of the police arrangements, had put on a tie, though to the Colonel's annoyance, he had explained that he had lost his last drill tunic some months ago. They weren't worn much any longer except by people at Base, he had explained. "We wear them here," had replied the Colonel with cold finality, "therefore you must get some more."

A dozen yards behind Euan, who stood close to the edge of the quay, a guard of honor from the garrison company was drawn up under a black lieutenant—a glittering array of starched white, rows of brass buttons, vivid green epaulets, ostrich plumes, and flashing silver bayonets. Behind the guard of honor waited the Colonel's big blue car surrounded by six Carabinieri on gleaming motorcycles. Everything was ready and only the *Emperor Napoleon*—stubbornly, stolidly stuck with engine trouble out in the roadstead beyond the harbor mouth—delayed the consummation of this imposing spectacle. But at last the small, squat hull that had steamed punctually over the horizon at half past six and had hung inexplicably about outside the harbor entrance for twenty minutes was seen to move again. The hot and fretful officers on the quay straightened their ties, the commander of the guard of honor brusquely called his men to attention, and as the little ship passed the Dhow Control Point and turned her blunt bows toward No. 1 berth an air of intense expectation filled the crowd.

Colonel Lemonfield, shifting irritably from one small, immaculately shod foot to the other, was far from happy. The more he thought about this visit the less he had liked the prospect. It was all very well to map out a large agenda in the office with Brinsmead, but what a bore the whole thing was going to be in practice! What an interruption of his normal routine—to no purpose, he felt sure. Added to this feeling of irritation was one of resentment. All these junketings and inspections were in honor of a visitor—of high rank, certainly, but of no importance in the island. What had this General Glasscraft done for Baressa that he should be entertained and feted by the Municipality and taken shooting over some of the best country on the plateau? Euan looked forward with no pleasure whatsoever to watching the Mayor and Corporation, Commendatore Saccomani, and the rich concession owners fawning around someone other than himself. The thought of having to play second string to anybody at all on his own island was a bitter, nagging pain which nothing could dull.

With a hideous scream from its siren—which made everybody jump and the Colonel determine to give Captain Zvengetzov a piece of his mind later—the stocky, grubby eight-hundredton mail boat came alongside the berth. On the bridge the Hungarian pilot was giving rapid raucous orders through a megaphone while the skipper—blond, fat Captain Rekelhof, a native of Holland—leaned placidly on the rail and acknowledged aquaintances among the crowd with a condescending lift of the steel hook which served him in place of a left hand. On the small boat deck a group of British officers surrounded a tall thin figure whose red-banded hat and scarlet collar tabs proclaimed him to be the General.

A bump, the creaking groan of rope fenders, the churn and thud of the screws dying away to the sharp tinkle of the telegraph, and a dozen burly brown stevedores were running the white gangway up to the deck. A sharp command from the officer of the guard, followed by the stamping, clicking, crashing rattle of the soldiers presenting arms, and General Glasscraft was on the quay and shaking hands with the Colonel.

"So you're Lemonfield, eh? I've heard a lot about you."

Euan looked up into a bony red face, a high-arched intimidating nose above a clipped gray moustache, cold gray eyes. So unmistakably like everyone's idea of an English general was this face that Euan almost smiled, but to his distress and annoyance the resemblance ended there. Instead of the smart, precise, soldierly figure in spotless pale gabardine whom he had expected to greet, the General looked almost like a tramp—a military one, perhaps, but nonetheless a tramp. His gaunt figure was draped in a faded drill bush shirt that fitted nowhere, baggy creased shorts that were far too long, and wrinkled stockings above shoes that were more suited to the golf links than the parade ground.

107

A web equipment belt with unpolished brasses that sagged beneath the weight of a revolver completed this unsoldierly outfit. It was particularly mortifying for Euan that the crowd, which he rightly guessed to be looking for a general of the glittering Italian pattern, should be shown this military scarecrow instead. However, he must put the best face possible on the matter and he performed the necessary introductions quickly. James first.

"This is Major Naughton-Muirhead, sir, my Civil Affairs Officer—Captain Kellermann, commanding the garrison company—Captain Pirie, our police officer—Lieutenant Baines, who is in charge of the Customs Department."

The General acknowledged them all with quick handshakes and a bleak smile. He was in a bad temper, for the breakdown of the mail boat had been infuriating, and not only that, but during the delay he had been accosted in a familiar manner by a voluble foreign naval officer who had puffed smoke from a filthy black cigar into his face while he expatiated interminably on— as far as one was able to understand the fellow's vile English— the nobility of his own pedigree and the glories of a family estate near Kluj. Now the General wanted his breakfast and the sooner he got it the better he would feel. But first the guard of honor. He passed down the glittering, rigidly motionless ranks of giant Nubians, and it was obvious to everyone that he was impressed.

"A very good guard," he remarked to Christopher, who walked, sweating with apprehension, beside him. "A very good guard indeed—and a very smart turnout. It does you credit. I know these fellows—damn good at drill, but not too strong up above, eh?"

"No-no sir."

"How d'you find 'em on field craft? Do you have any difficulty training them to the new two-pounders?"

"Two-pounders, sir?" Christopher was startled. He had never heard of two-pounders; he had no idea what the General was talking about.

"Yes, two-pounder antitank guns, man. Haven't you got yours yet?"

"No, sir."

"Good God!" He turned to a thin, spectacled major behind him. "Pole! Make a note to get those ordnance fellows to damn well hurry up and get the new G1098 out here at once—and up to scale, too!" He turned back to Christopher with a short grunt. "I suppose you'll tell me your Carriers haven't arrived either?"

"No, sir. I—we—that is, nothing's arrived. We haven't got anything except what we came with—just our rifles."

"What—no Brens?" The General seemed genuinely startled.

"No, sir."

"But, good Heavens, man—this is absolutely monstrous! No Brens! My goodness, I'll make those ordnance fellows sit up when I get back!" He paused, frowning. His staff and the Administration officers stood silently around; Major Pole scribbled furiously; the guard stood like ebony statues.

"You've been here all the time, Kellermann?"

"Yes, sir." Christopher gazed unhappily at the others and received a glance of amused condolence from James.

"H'm!" The General suddenly turned to the industrious Pole. "This boy had better go back to the mainland for a course. It's no good getting their new G1098 up to scale if there's nobody to instruct them in it when it comes. Yes, fix up a course for him, Pole—or, let me see. Two years——" he surveyed Christopher thoughtfully. "You've certainly served your term of exile. Would you like to go back to your own regiment?"

"No, sir—thank you." Christopher controlled his voice with difficulty. "I—that is——" He looked wildly around at the Colonel, and Euan slid up to the General's elbow and came gently to the rescue.

"As a matter of fact, sir, if I may take the liberty of saying so, I should be extremely sorry to see Captain Kellermann leave the island. He has cooperated with me to the very best of his ability, and as you are aware the Civil Affairs branch and the Army don't always see eye to eye." He laughed deprecatingly and smiled blandly up at the General, who gave him a cool, shrewd glance by way of return.

"Well, if that's the case I suppose he had better stay—though I'm not altogether sure. . . . However, he'll have to leave you for a few weeks, Lemonfield—if you can bear to be parted from him."

Euan smiled, but his face paled slightly—a sign of fury, frustrated in this case and, as James correctly guessed, billowing inside him like a blast furnace. The General, however, noticed nothing, and if he had would not have cared. Privately he thought this Colonel Lemonfield a rather nasty little man—pushing and smooth, too smooth. They thought a lot of him at O.E.T.A. Headquarters, but then O.E.T.A. were a queer lot with queer opinions—a good many foreigners amongst them, too. It was derisively said that the initials of the organization stood for Our Enemy's Timorous Admirers—though why this should be when so many of them appeared to be Jews the General could not understand.

"Very well then, Kellermann," the General said abruptly, "you can come back here after you've done a course in the new weapons. The question is, who's to do your job while you're away? I suppose we'd better try and find a relief. See what you can do about that, Pole."

Major Pole shook his head lugubriously. "Very well, sir, but it won't be easy to spare anyone at present."

"I know, I know. But we can't take a company commander away from his men and not re——"

"Sir, excuse me." The General turned with a slight frown and beheld Captain Pirie beside him. "I could take over Captain Kellermann's job while he's away if that would help. I've only just come from the mainland and I know all the new weapons. In fact, I was instructing in them only a month ago and——" He looked toward the Colonel for assent and received instead such a glare of cold fury that he stopped abruptly.

Before the General could reply Euan said, "Captain Pirie has only just taken over the police here and is by no means sufficiently conversant with his own duties to be able to undertake those of another officer as well." This savage snub caused the unfortunate Police Chief to flush to the roots of his hair and the General, who had no intention of becoming involved in the intricacies of a dispute between O.E.T.A. personnel, made a noncommittal noise at the back of his throat and finished the inspection of the guard.

The breakfast provided in the wide loggia of the Villa was sumptuous. Every island delicacy suitable to the meal was present and the General, in a rapidly mellowing frame of mind, swore that never had he eaten such fine avocado pears and, delighted to hear that they actually grew in the grounds of the Villa, he graciously accepted Lemonfield's offer to send a couple of crates of them aboard the *Napoleon* at the expiration of his visit.

The talk during the meal was mostly concerned with fishing, a sport in which, as Pirie had foretold, the General took a lively interest. Neither Euan nor James was able to contribute much to a conversation which rapidly turned into a duologue between the General and Major Pole, who seemed if anything a still more knowledgeable enthusiast—probably, thought James cynically, he had been chosen for his present position on purely piscatorial grounds.

At last the meal was over and, rising, Euan suggested the first item on his agenda—a visit to the Palazzo Firenze. But the General demurred.

"No, no. No reason to go down to the town again just yet. Isn't there somewhere here where I can have a few words with you, Lemonfield?"

"Certainly, sir. If you'll come to my study. . . ." Euan, wondering what the few words were going to be about and distinctly dubious concerning the satisfaction he might receive from them, led the way to his study. This was a small room by the standard of the Villa, in which no room could really be termed small, semicircular in shape, paneled in soft green and silver with many long narrow windows that commanded a dull view over the vegetable garden. The General sank into an armchair, accepted a cigar, and motioned Euan to be seated as well—a gesture that particularly annoyed the Colonel, who felt that, general or no general, he could do as he liked in his own study.

"Now, Lemonfield, I expect you've been wondering what I have come here for, eh? Well, I'm afraid it's not merely to inspect everything and to look around generally, so if you've laid on a schedule for me—which I fear you probably have—I'll have to disappoint you by scrapping it. Now I don't suppose there's any need for me to outline the general situation in Africa at the moment." This was not strictly true, for the General, who held a firm belief that O.E.T.A. personnel were interested in nothing but lining their pockets at the expense of their temporary subjects, did not really suppose that Colonel Lemonfield had any more notion of the military situation than one of the garrison's black soldiers. But one had to observe a certain form when dealing with field officers, even noncombatant ones. "So I'll merely say that from the point of view of the C.-in-C.'s staff things are not only just as bad as they appear on the surface, but considerably worse."

"I'm sorry to hear that."

"So are we all," remarked the General dryly. "Well, what it all amounts to is that we don't know whether the front will hold. If it breaks—then things will look pretty black and where we'll manage to hold the enemy next I don't know. It's very possible that he'll be right across the continent and nearing the east coast in a month or so's time. If that happens you will realize that there'll be just a few hundred miles of sea between you and the German Army. Now this island is not, we know, an ideal base, but in the circumstances it is at least a base of a sort between Africa and India and for that reason will be very important to us—and to the enemy."

He paused, and through Euan's racing mind flashed a series of equally unpleasant possibilities. Were they going to send more troops to the island? That would almost certainly mean friction with their commanders over a host of problems. Were they going to mine the waters? That would put an end to the island's trade and disrupt his entire economy. Was General Glasscraft himself going to make his headquarters here as a sort of G.O.C. in exile? If that was so he would probably demand the Villa—mainly on account of the avocado pears. Was—but the General continued.

"Now, what I'm here to do is—putting the matter in a nutshell —to get this island on a war footing. I'm going to examine it from the point of view of security and, of course, defense. If the worst comes to the worst the C.-in-C. is determined to hold this island, and as the enemy may well be equally determined to take it we've got to make it as impregnable as possible."

"You mean more troops are to be sent, sir? I really don't——"

The General shook his head impatiently. "No. No more troops are to be sent—yet. Good God, we haven't got a man to spare in any case, and we are naturally trusting that we won't have to fight on this island or anywhere remotely near. What I'm going to do is to look for defensive positions and get some idea as to how this place can best be held against airborne and seaborne attack. I'll want to use Kellermann's men—it's a damned nuisance they haven't got their two-pounders, but that can't be helped now—and the police and everyone I can lay my hands on for tests in this respect. There will be far too few, of course, but nonetheless the whole thing must be regarded as a practical exercise by everybody. I'm only here for a few days, so we must start as soon as possible. I've got maps of the island, so I won't have to trouble you for yours. We'll plan the maneuvers—if one may call them that—at your office today, and tomorrow I'll tour the island with my staff; then I hope we'll be able to start the day after. That will give you time to instruct the civil authorities in their part and to take the necessary administrative measures."

Euan looked as doubtful as he dared. "Well, sir, naturally, if the C.-in-C. has really determined to hold this island at all costs——"

"He has, I can assure you."

"In that case I suppose it is useless to tell you that the Italians handed it over without a fight because they knew it to be indefensible."

The General flushed slightly. "What d'you mean?"

Euan spoke carefully, persuasively. "I have read the reports of their Military, Naval, and Air Force authorities drawn up at the beginning of the war. They unanimously say that Baressa is indefensible from attack by sea or air. Its long coastline is completely exposed and in most places the beaches are ideal for landing craft. The nature of its terrain makes it particularly difficult to defend for a variety of most cogent reasons, and there is no possibility of constructing any sort of airfield without——"

"Lemonfield, are you trying to instruct me in defensive strategy?"

"No, sir!" Euan spoke urgently. "I'm only telling you what the Italian Government——"

"Damn the Italian Government!" The General was becoming really angry now. Arguments and obstructions, just what one might have expected from an O.E.T.A. colonel. Of course he didn't want the place defended—upset his blasted Administration and disturb his beauty sleep. And this pallid little creature with the manicured hands of a woman and the unctuous voice of a priest was going to explain exactly why his precious island should be handed over to the Italians again, was he? "What the Italian Government thought, said or did is of no relevance at all! Kindly remember that, Lemonfield. Do you suppose that because the Italians—the Italians, of all people!—say that a place can't be defended that we should necessarily agree with them?"

He snorted. "You appear to have a remarkably high opinion of the Italians. If you'd seen them at rather closer quarters as soldiers instead of reading their reports you might change your mind!"

"Oh, I make no pretensions to being a military strategist," disclaimed Euan hurriedly. "It only seemed to me—however, if the decision is to defend the island there is no more to be said. I will give you what cooperation lies within my power."

"Thank you," said the General shortly and rose. "We'd better be getting on. We'll go down to your office and call a conference of everybody."

Turmoil. That afternoon sleepy Baressa started to wake up to the fact of the General's presence. The staff officers—there were four of them as well as the invaluable Major Pole—harried the Administration officials in the Palace to the point of frenzy and then scattered outward over San Pietro, bent on causing the maximum of alarm and despondency. Official cars, hurriedly requisitioned, shot through the streets of the city on urgent errands and Texas, seized as a permanent hostage by the General, was given a sharp rebuke for not standing still while receiving orders and sent off sweating and swearing on a dusty round of messages. William, too, was told to stand by and with a "II" set to accompany the General on his tour of Baressa the next day. He spent the evening in company with Fortu trying to install his machine in Colonel Lemonfield's big blue car, in which the General had decided to travel.

Major Pole visited the barracks and found the soldiers practicing guard drill. He looked on sourly for a few minutes and then sought Christopher in his office.

"I'd advise you to get your men ready for the General's exercise. They'll have plenty of time to practice ceremonial drill when the war's over." He looked bleakly around the office. "Also, you don't appear to have read the orders that came out early last year concerning full dress. These white uniforms ought to have been withdrawn months ago."

"Oh, but they've only got one set of khaki each and that's not in very good shape. They normally only wear it for fatigues, you see."

"Do you mean to tell me they wear full dress all the time?"

Major Pole looked incredulous. "These white uniforms were damned expensive even before the war; they're only supposed to be worn on very special occasions. Have you been drawing replacements from Base? I wonder why the hell they let you have them without saying anything."

"Oh, no!" Christopher hurried to correct this error on the part of Major Pole, an error that he felt might lead to trouble. "Colonel Lemonfield's had them made here. You see, he likes the palace guard to be full dress and—well, he thinks they look best in white, really, so when I told him the uniforms were wearing out and I couldn't replace them from Base stores he arranged to have them made here."

"Who paid?"

"The Administration, I suppose—I didn't."

"Good God!"

The officer sent by Major Pole to Police Headquarters met with a more enthusiastic welcome than any of his fellows. Captain Pirie ushered him into the office and sent Commino out for two bottles of beer, then he offered him a cigarette from a cardboard pack and slumped down behind his desk.

"Well, old boy, and what can I do for you?"

"It's a question of what you've got, really. Can you tell me how many men you can possibly spare from duty for the next three days?"

"H'm—you mean natives? You don't want my precious little Wops, do you? Frankly, old man, you can have 'em with the compliments of the season and half a pound of tea if you want them—but I don't advise it."

The Staff Captain laughed. "No, I don't think we'll have them —the old man's not keen on Eye-ties. Anyway, I don't think they'd be much use."

"I'm bloody certain they wouldn't! Stinking lot of bastards —pardon my French—just like that lad I sent out for drinks— you know, slimy. Frankly, old boy, I wish to hell I was out of this racket, and if you could help to get me back you'd be a pal for life. I never wanted to come to O.E.T.A. in the first place, and it's a bloody sight worse than I thought it would be."

The Staff Captain looked sympathetic. "The island seems okay to me. A bit remote and out of touch, but——"

"Oh, the island's okay!" Pirie spoke with unconcealed bitterness. "Just the job, in fact. A nice comfy little place to spend the war in. Haven't you noticed how popular it is among my compatriots in exile?"

"You mean——?"

"I mean, among others, my young colleague with the scarred face." Pirie grinned without humor. "He was scared stiff this morning when it looked as if he'd get posted back to somewhere more warlike."

"But surely not! Why, he got the——"

"Oh yes, he's got a couple of bloody good gongs—and I often wonder how the hell he got them. All I know is he spends his time here fawning around the Colonel, saying, 'Yes, sir!' 'No, sir!' 'Very good, sir!' and having his picture painted by Number Two, who treats him like a tart—if you'll excuse my rudery. It's, 'Christopher, be an angel and find the cigarettes,' and, 'Christopher, need you wear *quite* such green shirts—the color clashes with your eyes!' "

"No!"

"I've bloody well heard it, old boy!"

They roared with laughter and Commino, returning with the beer, was pleased to find his new and invariably taciturn master in such a good humor.

Major Naughton-Muirhead's private apartments were a suite of first-floor rooms in the right wing of the Villa and the largest, his sitting room, opened on a small balcony from which could be observed a magnificent view down the escarpment and far out over the sea.

At a quarter to twelve on the evening of the day of the General's arrival he was sitting before the open French windows of the balcony, calming a troubled mind with the high-souled meditations of Marcus Aurelius in preparation for retirement to rest. Outside in the soft warm darkness of the garden, frogs croaked from the ornamental pools and tropical night birds whistled intermittently among the fruit trees. A great bat hovered for a second in the open window and then flitted away with a dry rustle of its furry leather wings.

It had been an exhausting day and James was tired and worried. He had seen little of Euan, who, after emerging in company with the General from his study, had driven at once to San Pietro and only returned in the early evening—apparently he had lunched with the General and his staff in the Palazzo Firenze. James himself had spent much of the day making arrangements for the accommodation of the General's staff and canceling the orders for the visits and inspections that had been issued during the past week. It had not been until the afternoon that Brinsmead, pale with indignation, had explained the reason for the General's visit. James sighed and put down his book; as he did so there came a light knock on his door.

"Come in."

Euan entered, holding a small, flat leather case in one hand. "I'm not disturbing you, James? I saw your light shining out on the garden so I knew you weren't asleep. I've brought you a little present." His voice was weary, but there was a glint of humor in his dark eyes.

"Oh—how kind! What is it?"

"One of Giordano's pistols." Euan laid the weapon in its leather holster on an inlaid octagonal table and sank into a nearby chair.

"Oh!" James eyed the black shining butt with mock distress. "Is this a delicate indication that the General desires me to do away with myself?"

"Not at present." Euan smiled wanly. "It is, however, an indication that he expects you, in common with all of us, to participate in these ridiculous maneuvers of his."

"But, even so, does one have to appear in public armed to the teeth? Why?"

"To foster an illusion of reality, I suppose. You don't seem delighted with my little gift, James. There were three in the safe in my study. One for you—received without enthusiasm, I note. One for me—which I fear may be loaded, though I dare not ascertain that by letting it off. And one for Fortu, who was overjoyed."

"Bless him!"

"But thrilled. He started to take it to bits at once, so I sent him away hurriedly. I only hope he understands it."

"Perhaps he'll accidentally shoot the General," suggested James hopefully. "Then we can spend the next few days acquitting him of manslaughter instead of playing soldiers. I'm afraid you've had a horrible time, haven't you?" He looked with sympathy at Euan, slumped whitely in the big chair.

"Simply frightful! You've no idea what things were like at the Palace today. I gave him the big room next to the Financial Clerk's office, and he spent the entire morning calling for information about roads and woods and bays and so forth. He seemed to labor under the delusion that I and Brinsmead were cartographers and general surveyors. We were continually being questioned rather as if we were field commanders just back from a prolonged reconnaissance." He smiled. "The only thing that kept me from losing my temper was the speed and splendor with which Brinsmead lost his."

"I'm sure he did."

"You must excuse me if I seem a little light-headed, James"—the Colonel laughed shakily—"but today's been a distinct strain. Not only have all my plans for this visit been upset, but everything's being turned upside down—all for the sake of this utterly fantastic exercise. It obviously won't be of any value, because we know the island's indefensible. However, the General won't listen to me, so there we are!" He shrugged resignedly. "We'll just have to put up with it, I suppose, and thank God that he'll be gone by this time next week. But it's all so highhanded! That's what annoys me. I mean, the man isn't even from our own branch, yet he orders me about and takes my servants and requisitions my car just as if I were a damned infantry subaltern instead of a military governor—monstrous!"

James saw he was working himself up into a rage as he thought of his ruffled dignity—the dignity that for two years of absolute rule no one had dared to affront. "I——" he began, in an effort to avert the coming storm, but Euan went on in a tone of growing fury.

"Here am I with the entire responsibility of this island on my hands and what help do I get? What help do I get after two years during which I've worked nearly twenty-four hours a day putting this place on its feet? An ignorant, conceited old fool who's got less brains in his head than one of our own domestic fowls—a witless, pompous, red-faced ass—in fact, my dear James, a typical goatlike British General comes here, looking like something that's rolled off the municipal garbage tip. Surrounded by a bevy of clumsy clowns hiding their cretinous faces behind vast dingy moustaches, he starts throwing his weight around in order to bolster up his own overweening ego by going home, filled to bursting with our food, and laboriously writing a misspelled and ungrammatical report on grubby foolscap to the effect that General Sir Herbert Glasscraft has actually found that Baressa *is* indefensible after all and recommends the C.-in-C. to think of somewhere else!"

When the breathless flow of invective came at last to a stop, leaving Euan panting and smiling wryly, James said, "Baines seems to have discovered that this man Glasscraft made nonsense of some operation in the desert a few months back, and for that he's been sent right away from the front—discreetly sacked really. If that's true it explains his present fire-eating attitude. The ridiculous old creature's all burned up inside, as the Americans say. He knows he won't get another chance of the limelight unless the war comes here and he's just praying that it will. I'm convinced that all this chatter about the front not holding is nothing but wishful thinking on his part."

Euan got tiredly to his feet. "I shouldn't count too much on that, James," he said with weary viciousness. "If this fellow has had a hand in things, as Baines says, then I can't see the front holding in the desert or anywhere else. Why, he must have been absolutely God's gift to General Rommel! Try to imagine a very large house with a very large room in which sit about a dozen or so replicas of Sir Herbert all shouting and contradicting each other and piling up masses of irrelevant information. Occasionally they gang up to eject one of their number and replace him with something equally dreadful from elsewhere—that, surely, is a picture of a typical British General Staff. England will lose the war. Giordano will have the last laugh yet. I am now going to take some of Dr. Valdonetti's bromide and go to bed."

12

"SIR, will *you* sign these?"

"But really, Brinsmead, I hardly think I should. You say the Colonel hasn't seen them——"

"Well, somebody's got to. We can't hold up the process of running this island because Colonel Lemonfield's been forced to go and play soldiers!"

It was two days since the General's arrival, and Major Naughton-Muirhead sat at the Colonel's desk in the Colonel's office, unwillingly signing orders and instructions which that officer, by reason of his absence from his capital, was unable to confirm with his neat, backward-sloping, "E. O. Lemonfield, Lt. Col. & S.C.A.O."

In theory the authority of the Colonel was temporarily vested in his deputy, but that, as James knew, would not prevent angry remarks if documents which the Colonel would not approve were given official assent. So he hedged and procrastinated and read through all sorts of unimportant letters, to Brinsmead's evident impatience.

"Why not wait until the Colonel gets back, Brinsmead? A day or two can't——"

"Yes, it *can!* It will make a *lot* of difference! I always get these done on Wednesdays and I'm not going to have my entire office routine upset just because——"

"Oh, all right, all right!" grumbled James, unscrewing his fountain pen. He would just have to rely on Brinsmead, and if things were signed that should not have been it would really be the Chief Clerk's fault.

Having won his point, Brinsmead relaxed slightly. "I say, sir, how long is all this nonsense going on? Is the Colonel going to be away until Friday?"

James shrugged. "I rather think so. The main idea seems to be that he's the Military Administration in exile as it were. According to this preposterous exercise, San Pietro is being so heavily bombed that the Administration has had to leave. So the Colonel's gone to Saccomani's place. I'd be there and so would you, only the Colonel pointed out that there must be somebody in San Pietro in case of emergencies and that you and I must be left out of the present folly at least until tomorrow. As a matter of fact, Colonel Lemonfield should be at Addi Jesus —that's where the General wanted him to go. But he said he was damned if he would, for there's nowhere to live there except the church. He said——"

There was a knock on the double doors, guardless now since all the Banda had been taken off for the exercise, and they opened to reveal Captain Kellermann, looking hot and sullen and exhausted and dressed in a sweat-stained khaki shirt and dusty trousers. From behind the great desk James eyed him with amusement.

"Good morning, Christopher. We have got our blinds half drawn, but as you see we are not quite closed. What can we do for you today?"

"They want you, James." Christopher lounged across to the desk and sank down in an armchair, taking a cigarette case from his hip pocket. Now that the awe-inspiring presence of the Colonel was temporarily removed the impressive surroundings had lost much of their portentous atmosphere; the virtue was gone out of them.

"Well, they can't have me. I've got a lot of things to sign— haven't I, Brinsmead?"

"You have, sir."

"The Colonel says you'd better come, James." Christopher examined his dirty, scratched hands with displeasure. "That dreadful old man's been making us chase through fruit plantations all the morning."

"Not the Colonel, too, sir, surely!" Brinsmead sounded shocked.

"No, of course not. Me and that—that new person, Pirie. He likes it."

"He would!"

"Anyway, he won't be able to do it anymore," continued Christopher with gloomy triumph. "The Colonel came and caught him cutting down some of Saccomani's tangerine trees to clear a field of fire or something."

"Good Lord!"

"You can imagine what the Colonel said, so I needn't repeat it. While it was going on this Glasscraft man turned up and said a field of fire was necessary and that it would be a good idea to cut down most of the trees on the concessions—or at any rate to cut great avenues through them to guard against parachutists. So the Colonel said, with great politeness, that he agreed entirely that the only satisfactory way to make the plateau safe from guerrilla war was to do as the General suggested. In fact, if the General would issue the orders he would see to it at once. He must, he said, point out that the present small amount of trees that Pirie had cut down would mean compensation claims on the Army for about two thousand pounds, and if the General's idea was put into practice the sum might well be over a million, perhaps two. However, if the General would like to take the responsibility. . . ." Brinsmead and James laughed delightedly and Christopher grinned and continued, "Well, anyway, Glasscraft was furious, but he couldn't do a thing. He went redder than ever in the face—bright scarlet, just like an angry turkey—and swore that no cooperation was being given him and so on. Absolutely childish, of course, because the Colonel had offered to cut the trees down if the old fool would order it—only he didn't dare. So the Colonel followed up his first remarks by saying that unless the maneuvers were kept off cultivated land entirely he feared the inevitable damage would cause compensation demands of considerable magnitude from the concession owners. His very own words, James! So there we are. The Colonel has almost managed to ruin the exercise—he's as pleased as hell. When Glasscraft had shot off in an absolute fury he said to me, 'Christopher, you have just seen a small exhibition of the military mind and how it may be politely baffled by the use of a modicum of intelligence. Let your very natural pleasure in the spectacle be modified by fitting apprehension for the prospects of the Armed Forces of the Crown.' I think that's one of the nicest things I've ever heard the Colonel say."

Brinsmead rubbed his hands. "Ah, no one ever gets the wrong side of Colonel Lemonfield without ruing the day!" he exclaimed with relish. "I bet he'll encourage the Commendatore to send in a huge bill and we'll forward it to H.Q. with comments. Then we'll keep the pot boiling with continual reminders and this General will be followed all over the place with correspondence about it for months and months. It will give him something better to do than upset other people's office work with stupid pranks like this. But why has the Major got to go, sir?"

"Purely out of spite, Brinsmead, I think. You'll be next, probably. Now the Colonel's wrecked the exercise the General's going to try and hamstring the Administration by way of return. San Pietro is now supposed to be obliterated and the entire Government has got to get up to the plateau. You've been forgotten for the moment, but he'll probably remember you later."

"I'm damned if I'm going till I've had lunch!" remarked James firmly. "You stay and have lunch with me, Christopher, then we'll go up together."

Christopher relapsed into gloom. "I daren't. I'm only down here to arrange about having Diaz's old field guns towed up. I'm not O.E.T.A. You know what he can do to me. He's already been half threatening to get me posted again. I have to pretend to be extremely keen on this bloody exercise. And by the way, Brinsmead, how can I get off going on a course? He's threatening to send me to some dismal place on the mainland for two months."

"We'll fix that sir, don't you worry," replied Brinsmead with vigor. "We'll let them fix it all up and at the last minute we'll say you're ill. Valdonetti will sign any certificate required, of course. I doubt if they'll worry about finding you another vacancy, but if they do I'll lose the letter and we'll get at what the Colonel terms 'clerical cross-purposes' until they get fed up."

Christopher gave him a grateful smile. "You know all the answers, Brinsmead, don't you?"

"Yes, sir. It's my job."

In the end James' curiosity about the goings-on in the interior forced him up the escarpment before lunch. He had two suitcases packed, put them, together with his valet and a case of Giordano's old cognac, into the back of his white Bugatti, and drove off at a leisurely pace through the blazing midday heat. A couple of miles beyond the Villa he found the narrow road effectually blocked by four heavy diesel trucks grinding slowly upward at a snail's pace while behind them four old-fashioned field guns lumbered through the clouds of white dust and blue oil fumes. It was therefore in a state of some exasperation that James drove half an hour later along the winding avenue of huge shady banyan trees that led to Commendatore Saccomani's *azienda*.

Leaving the valet, Mahmud, to attend to his baggage, the Major ran up the long flight of shallow steps under the wide portico and almost into the arms of the Commendatore himself. The gaunt old man was delighted to see him. "Ah, my friend!" He beamed, screwing his eyeglass into his yellow face. "This is a true pleasure! I am already honored with His Excellency's presence and now you come!" He laid a hand on James' shoulder and guided him toward the dining room. "We were just about to sit down to lunch, so you will join us and my people will meanwhile see to rooms for you. Excellent!" He lowered his tone and became somewhat graver. "Major, I can ask you—for I know you better than your excellent colonel, whom I should otherwise of course ask— is there any real danger?"

"Danger, Commendatore?" James was mystified. "Danger of what?"

The Commendatore halted beneath a huge shining trophy of ancient Arab swords, scimitars, and spears that glinted fearsomely in the diffused light of a great stained glass window. He looked, thought James, a trifle embarrassed.

"Danger of occupation—I should perhaps say reoccupation— by the Germans or my—ah—fellow countrymen."

"Dear me, no—I don't think so. Oh, I see! You feel that these military goings-on presage an invasion? No, I'm sure they don't. If the worst happens in Africa—from our point of view, Commendatore, of course—I believe this island would be evacuated by the British."

"Oh, I see—yes, yes—evacuated." Instead of looking relieved, the Commendatore's parchment face took on a still more distressed expression; he hesitated, and when he spoke again it was with an embarrassed unwillingness. "I have been, as you know, friendly—helpful—to the British where it has been in my power, for as you must have realized I do not like the regime." He gesticulated vaguely. "Perhaps I am too old—too old for trumpets and flags and speeches—that sort of thing. But you can understand that a return of Colonel Giordano would——"

James said at once, "I think, Commendatore, that it would be best if we discussed this matter later when this General has gone. Doubtless we can find ways and means of assuring your safety. I am sure that the Colonel would never dream of abandoning any of his friends."

They passed into the dining room to find Euan standing near the long table, a damask napkin in one hand and a slip of paper in the other. In front of him at rigid attention stood a dusty Negro soldier.

"Ah, James, you've come—only just in time, too! This"— he crumpled the paper viciously in his hand—"is a message from the Great Panjandrum himself to the effect that this house has been destroyed by enemy air action and that the Administration is to move to Calgarini's *azienda*. So don't unpack. Commendatore, I fear we must cease to be your guests from this afternoon."

The old man registered polite and doubtless sincere concern at the news and the meal was resumed. James regretted the forthcoming departure with equal sincerity. Saccomani's house was by far the biggest and most comfortable on the plateau and his cuisine was the envy of all on the island. Euan, as James saw at once, was in just the state of bitter, frustrated, irresponsible resentment that he had feared. All through the long and excellent meal he calumniated not only General Glasscraft but the entire British General Staff in a flow of sarcastic vituperation that left the unhappy Commendatore more than ever convinced of the inevitable and catastrophic defeat of Allied arms. Euan, James realized, might be capable of considerable creative endeavor when he chose, but there was no doubt that his razor-edged legal mind was equally happy when engaged on destruction. Having verbally torn the command and organization of the British Army to shreds, he tossed the ragged remnants aside and started with equal gusto to repeat the performance with the Home Government. He was just concluding—to the Commendatore's excusable surprise—a concise and closely reasoned lecture on the overwhelming disadvantages of parliamentary democracy when Fortu, dirty, sullen, and with his new white uniform stained with sweat and oil, was shown into the room.

James stared at him in surprise. For two years now this Italian boy had been part of his daily life. From his original position as Euan's driver Fortu had gradually risen to be a sort of factotum and unofficial A.D.C. to both Administration officers, and his devotion to his employers' interests had earned him their complete approval. Curiously aloof in his dealings with them, generally unsmiling, scrupulously neat, clean, and respectful, there was about him an air of remote, somber dignity unyouthful, almost Spanish in its cool hauteur, which pleased the Colonel by its contrast with the average Italian's gay garrulity and fascinated the impressionable James. "Fortu unbent quite a lot today," he was wont to say on returning from some painting expedition. "When he unbends he makes a charming companion." "He unbends all right when he's out boating with Christopher and the Signals," Euan had remarked. "His official presence is reserved solely for our benefit, I think. Very suitable, too," and James, with a slight sigh for his own youth now past, had agreed. But in the grimy disheveled figure that now approached it was almost impossible to see the youthful, dignified, confidential servant of the past two years. James was shocked.

"Good Heavens, Fortu! What *have* you been doing?" The note of displeasure in his voice and the frown of annoyance on the Colonel's face—though this in fact was not due to Fortu's appearance, but to his interruption of the exposure of the British Constitution—were, it seemed, the last straws. Fortu's eyes blazed, his face flushed a dark fiery red and he went all Latin.

"Signor Colonnello! Signor Maggiore!" he stormed furiously, and suddenly for the first time in anyone's experience burst out into broken English. "This no bloody good! I not go on! I finish! Is no good this bloody General and work for him! All day is say, 'Fortu, go there! Fortu, go here, quick! Go to Captain! Go to Colonel!' All over bloody country—and all last night. Now is say you come to him please for attack, but I finish, *signori*—I not go on any bloody more!" He relapsed into silence on the point of tears.

Euan put his napkin down on the table; he spoke in a carefully controlled voice, though his hands were trembling with rage. "Commendatore, I'm very sorry about this regrettable exhibition." He turned to his unhappy driver. "Fortu, if you can't control yourself in public there won't be any question of *you* giving *me* notice. If this sort of thing ever occurs again you'll be dismissed at once! You need not imagine that this present business is any pleasanter for myself or the Major than it is for you, but we do not make disgraceful scenes about it and we shall not permit you to do so. Now go back to the General and tell him that we shall be at the Calgarini concession in an hour's time."

Fortu went without a word and the Commendatore, who had noted with distress the Colonel's meager appetite, hastened to break the ensuing uncomfortable silence by pressing food upon his guests. "Colonel, you are not eating. Will you not try some of this pork? You have often been so kind as to compliment me upon my pigs."

"I'm not very hungry, thank you, Commendatore." Euan forced a smile.

"But you must keep up your strength, Excellency—you may be working half the night."

"I always do work half the night."

"Of course, of course." The old man shot a sidelong glance at James. Now that both the officers were about to go he felt more than ever impelled to procure confirmation or denial of his fears. "I trust"—he laughed deprecatingly—"that these maneuvers do not anticipate any real danger of attack from the Germans?"

"There's not the slightest chance of such an occurrence in my estimation," replied Euan sharply. "Completely out of the question." It was, he told himself bitterly, typical of this blundering imbecile of a general to carry out his accursed exercise in such a way as to stir up fear and apprehension among the population.

As if to confirm this Saccomani said doubtfully, "But your general——"

"Oh, he is only exercising the troops. He has, you see, recently been relieved of a more important position which he was quite unfit to hold by reason of his lack of intelligence. But he has to be employed somewhere, so——" Euan shrugged his shoulders contemptuously and smiled.

"I hope that you are right." The Commendatore still sounded a little doubtful.

"I am. Even," continued the Colonel firmly, "if this General *does* think an attack likely, I myself say it is not so. You can take your choice of those two opinions, but you will find mine to be the correct one."

The old landowner bowed and smiled and looked considerably relieved. In two years he had never heard of this formidable little man making a mistake in anything he said or did; his infallibility had become almost a byword. If Colonel Lemonfield said that the Germans would not attack the island then one could be quite sure that they would not.

As they drove through the wide fields and fruit plantations on the way to their new headquarters James tactfully but persistently attempted to draw his superior's attention to the inadvisability of quarreling with General Glasscraft and his staff. "I can't help feeling that however right we are and however disgracefully he behaves we will only be the losers by allowing him to return to the mainland full of hostility toward us. I know he's nothing to do with our branch—which doubtless takes very much the same view of him as we do—but even so a persistent reiteration in all the bars and messes of Africa of slanders concerning us might have unpleasant consequences."

"Such as?" inquired Euan sarcastically.

"Oh, God knows!" James saw with half-amused irritation that his attempt to urge restraint was failing. "Perhaps what we would most desire to avoid."

"You're not, surely, suggesting that O.E.T.A. would dream of removing *me* purely because a man like Glasscraft complained about me!" Euan gave a short, incredulous laugh.

"No, no—of course not. However, if we can avoid entirely alienating——"

"Alienating! Good God! Why, the moment the man set foot on the docks I could see exactly what was going to happen!" Euan flung himself back in his seat. "Listen. There is a certain large class of regular soldiers, many of them high-ranking and most of them elderly, to whom O.E.T.A. is anathema. They cannot bear that there should be within the framework of the Services a temporary organization whose members wield a more comprehensive power than they. And when those members are selected for knowledge and intelligence which ordinary soldiers are expected neither to possess nor acquire it is an addition of insult to injury. Worst of all, they are powerless to deal with us. They can and do collect millions of boys like Kellermann and Summerson and stamp them as hard as they can into the military mold—with indifferent success, if the two examples I have quoted are in any way typical. But us they may not touch, for we are administrators and, whether they like it or not, administrators there must be— hence O.E.T.A."

James had listened to this harangue with admiration but impatience; at this juncture he put in, "Since we have got onto generalities I must remark, at the risk of being taken to disagree with you, that I have always understood that one of O.E.T.A.'s main roles is to assist the military in the execution of their duties."

But the expected outburst never came. Instead Euan laughed easily, happily. "*Et tu, Brute!* Rank heresy—such an assertion is deserving of the stake!" He picked his briefcase from the floor beside him and began searching in it briskly with hands which, James' quick eyes noticed, shook slightly. Second only to an affront to his dignity, Euan hated to be caught out.

In a moment he continued in a quiet, pleasant, almost persuasive voice, "Of course, Sir Herbert can't abide me. I'm the archetype of all O.E.T.A. stands for in his narrow and highly biased mind. I don't suppose he thinks any better of you, James, either—but it's me he has to deal with. Of course, he doesn't like dealing with me—he'd much prefer to spend the time bullying Christopher. He's furious that I've ruined his exercise, but he can't do anything about it."

It was James' turn to laugh; he saw clearly that to pursue the matter would be fruitless. Euan and the General were the antithesis of each other in every way possible and the hostility between them was as inevitable as it had been spontaneous. But it might, he felt, so easily have been damped down and concealed beneath a surface of amiable acquiescence if Euan had used more intelligence and been less absorbed with the glittering sacrosanct structure of his official dignity, less obsessed with the fact that he was the ruler of Baressa, less——

James was jerked suddenly forward as the native driver stamped on the brakes and the car screeched and slithered to a halt. Less than five yards from the radiator and obscured until a moment before by a sharp bend in the road lay one of Captain Diaz's old field guns, slewed sideways at an ungainly angle across the red earth while one detached wheel leaned against a tree at the roadside.

"What in God's name——" began the Colonel furiously, but a gang of natives who had leaped into the tangled hedges at the car's approach now emerged thornily from their retreat and a stocky, red-faced young man with a shock of bleached towlike hair and a wide gold-toothed grin came up to the window.

"Signor Colonnello? Excellency"—he bowed—"I am very sorry—we didn't hear you coming. I was trying to get this cannon off the road before you appeared. I hope no harm is done?"

"No, no. We're all right, Pietro." Euan smiled wryly. Inwardly the shock had put such pressure on his long bottled-up exasperation that he felt he might explode at any moment. His hands itched to slap Pietro Calgarini's happy, ugly face. "Your father is expecting us?"

"He is, Excellency. It is a great honor."

"Is the British General here?"

"Excellency"—Pietro's troubled glance sought his dusty riding boots—"he lives at present in a tent near the river. We—my father and I—have both begged him to honor our house, but he will not."

"Ah. Doubtless he finds such a position more satisfactory for supervising the maneuvers," said Euan dryly. Not content, he thought bitterly, with causing all this unnecessary disturbance, the old fool had to make himself a laughingstock and bring contempt upon his entire nation. Couldn't he understand that Spartan ideas among the High Command which might appeal to Nordic races were totally out of keeping with the traditions of Latins and Moslems? The Italians would consider him a fool; the natives would believe him mad. Both would laugh—was there not even now a glint of sardonic amusement in young Calgarini's pale eyes?—and say to each other that this, then, was the sort of man who held high rank in the British Army. This was the sort of man who was their Governor's superior officer.

"Well, Pietro," he said tightly, "are you going to get that gun cleared away?"

"Oh yes, Excellency—at once!"

"How did it happen?"

The young man grinned. "It was slung wrongly to the truck. It's amazing it got as far as this in the circumstances—and it's done it no good. I'm afraid it won't be much use until the trail has been rewelded."

"You seem to know a lot about artillery."

"Well, Excellency, when—that is, before the occupation I was in the Avanguardisti"—he stated this fact with an apologetic grin—"and Captain Diaz used to instruct us on the guns. He was interested in cannons, though he was not an artilleryman himself. He used to say I'd make a good gunner and if I'd had to join the Army I'd have——"

"Yes, yes, Pietro. I'm sure you'd have been another Napoleon. Now demonstrate your skill and shift the wretched thing out of the road."

The young man grinned hugely, clicked his heels, and started shouting directions to his gang of laborers.

James lit a cigarette and offered his case to Euan. "That boy always reminds me of Dickens' Kit—an uncouth youth, but worthy."

"I wish their house were a little more comfortable," remarked the Colonel gloomily. "The father's been widowed twelve years and the place is an absolute barracks. Vile cooking and beds hard as iron and nothing to drink but cheap spirits of the most indigestible sort. The old man is kindness itself, but I'm afraid we shall live little better than Sir Herbert Hermit in his tent."

13

A NIGHT spent under the hospitable but bleak roof of the Calgarini *azienda* convinced James of the justice of Euan's disparaging remarks. After a bad dinner they retired to bed—to the distress of the two Calgarinis, whose idea of correct hospitality was a drinking orgy into the small hours—and passed restless dream-filled hours on ancient lumpy beds. Next morning Euan was in such a state of nervous irritability that James thought with growing apprehension of the coming meeting between him and the General. It was to his great relief that word was brought late in the morning that Sir Herbert was heading northeastward toward the lonely trackless foothills that sloped down to the coastal plain near Cascio.

After lunch, as the Colonel was getting ready to visit a new bacon-curing plant at some distance from the *azienda*, Fortu arrived. Tired and scratched, for he had been following the General through miles of bush country on the plain, he was still too chastened to dare to look sullen, but as a mute reproach to his masters he had dressed himself in dirty, ragged dungarees, fastened around his waist with a piece of rope. "He needn't think it worries me if he adopts the sartorial habits of his temporary master," Euan remarked later. "I think it quite suitable that Glasscraft should be followed around by something looking like a sewage worker from a Naples slum."

Fortu brought a message to say that the Calgarini concession had now been occupied by enemy parachutists and that the Administration Headquarters must leave at once for the north and take up residence at Signor Balla's estate. The order was received with exasperated fury by the Colonel and some wearily cutting remarks from James; there was nothing to be done, however, but comply.

"I'm certainly not leaving at once," said Euan as he shredded the message between his fingers. "I don't come out here often and I'm going to see Calgarini's new equipment before I go. You'd better take your car and go ahead and warn Balla. You can warn him also in a discreet way that if I'm not made extremely comfortable and provided with the best of everything he will find difficulty in renewing his export licenses next year. I don't like that man and I don't wish to see him. I merely want rooms, food, and servants put at my disposal."

Driving through the long bright afternoon with Mahmud silent and wooden-faced behind him, James thought, not for the first time, that it would be pleasant to have a little farm up here on the green undulating plateau. Five thousand feet above sea level and still climbing slightly, the rolling verdant farmland stretched out on both sides of the road, a patchwork of fields and woods, little hamlets, and silver shining streams and irrigation ditches under the cerulean sky.

The air was fresh and cool and smelled of crops—the sweetness of billowing fields of white-flowering beans, the warm drifts of scent from the acres of oranges and tangerines out of which the plantation owners did so well. But as James drove north the vegetation became visibly poorer and the farms smaller and more scattered. By four o'clock he had arrived at the beginning of the Balla plantation and was wondering, as he passed thicket on thicket of unpruned fruit trees clogged with rioting undergrowth, why Balla did not retire and sell the plantation to someone more capable, when he came upon a roadblock. A loose coil of barbed wire stretching from tree to tree across the road was guarded by a brightly uniformed member of the Banda. James drew up with an exclamation of annoyance, and the soldier approached, saluted, and proffered a much thumbed piece of paper. Turning it the right way up, James read:

> This road is heavily mined. Not to be used on any account until termination of exercise.
>
> J. D. POLE, MAJ.

"Signor Maggiore, do you wish me to open the road?" The guard grinned.

"Yes," said James, and then thought better of it. After all, the General or Pole or one of the staff might suddenly appear like a jack-in-the-box, and tiresome recriminations would be less tolerable than making a detour to the *azienda*. Euan would probably insist on using the road when he came by later, but for himself he felt too weary for a verbal contest with the General's staff.

"No—wait. Is there another road to Signor Balla's house?"

"Yes, *signore*—that one." The man pointed to a half-hidden leafy track that disappeared into an orange plantation on the left of the road. It looked just wide enough for the car.

"Very well." James reversed and, acknowledging the guard's salute with a nod, plunged into the green gloom of the winding lane. For about a mile the Bugatti bumped and lurched over the uneven surface, disturbing parrots and monkeys and a small herd of half-wild pigs. The pressing branches of the overhanging trees rattled against the car's sides; there was no breeze and it was very hot. Suddenly James came upon another roadblock; a great banyan gashed and seared by lightning lay across the track. Each end of the giant tree was firmly bedded far in the undergrowth and the way was effectually barred.

"So here we are, Mahmud," he remarked with weary resignation as he braked to a halt with the car's chromium bumpers gently swaying a few inches from the rugged gray trunk.

"*Signore?*"

"We can't be far from the *azienda*. I'm going to walk there and arrange to have men sent to clear this tree away. You stay where you are."

"Yes, *signore*."

133

James got out of the car and, clambering over the fallen banyan, strolled off down the track. As he walked he turned over in his mind the speech he would make to Balla. Of all the concession owners Balla was the one Euan liked the least, and though James had only met him once, he concurred in this dislike. Balla was not exactly rude, but he lacked respect. On an island where one was entitled to, and invariably received, a flatteringly large amount of respect one perhaps became unduly sensitive to anything that hinted at civility rather than servility—not that Balla was even particularly civil, by all accounts. This visit would not be welcomed, for unlike most of the other farmers, to whom the prospect of visitors was a genuine pleasure, a bright break in the dull if profitable round of agriculture, Balla seemed to wish only to be left alone—a taciturn, misanthropic old man of reputed Fascist sympathies. Well, he would be left alone, for Euan certainly did not desire his company. He must nonetheless—James stopped short in the track, jerked suddenly from his thoughts by a choking shout that seemed to come from somewhere in the woods on the left. In a moment it came again, a short gurgling cry, not loud but penetrating clearly the other conglomerate noises of the woods, the whistle of parrots, the melancholy cries of hoopoes, and the interminable high-pitched conversation of the small gray monkeys. James listened motionless and once more the rough, muted yell—agonized, inarticulate, but certainly human —reached out from the woods. He looked quickly around and, rubbing the damp palms of his hands on his hips, touched the unaccustomed leather pistol case. The knowledge of being armed steadied his nerves; carefully he slipped open the holster flap and took out the shining black automatic. With its compact, complex mechanism he was totally unfamiliar and, standing there in the sun-shot leafy lane with the neat shining thing in his hand, he wished acutely that he held instead the Port Pilot's simple rusty .45 revolver.

Once more the harsh, painful cry broke from the woods to his left and, summoning such resolution as he possessed, James pressed cautiously into the undergrowth at the side of the track and moved as quietly as possible through the tangled trees of the plantation. He heard the cry twice again before, parting a natural screen of thick bushes, he came upon a low brick building, old and almost obliterated by masses of creepers and vines which made it appear a sprawling hillock of greenery. From within he heard a low, continuous muttering and once again, but more loudly this time, the choking yelp of agony. His curiosity, insatiable where human beings were concerned, forced him forward. He must find out who was making those noises and why and under what conditions. Yet such a discovery might be highly dangerous. Visions of a homicidal maniac, a snorting, red-eyed apparition on the pattern of Mr. Rochester's wife, brought the perspiration coldly out on his forehead as he edged his way carefully around the creeper-clad tumbledown building, a place sufficiently sinister and remote for the concealment of the most appalling inmate.

Aware now of a peculiar mephitic odor—perhaps he had trodden on some rank fungus in the spongy undergrowth—he turned a corner and came upon a small unglazed window and, approaching this with extreme stealth, he parted a tangle of creeper and peered over the rotting, ant-eaten wooden frame. The inside of the low building was filled with a gloomy green filtered light that percolated through gaps in the broken roof and two further windows as derelict and obscured with vegetation as the one through which he now looked. A sagging timber door a few yards from his present position let in one shaft of bright sunlight, and in the very heart of this, narrowing his eyes against it and holding up a glass as if to measure its contents, stood Mr. Lillywhite.

Disheveled, unshaven, haggard, his old gray flannel trousers bagging shapelessly around his gaunt legs, an incongruously gay sports shirt clinging to his emaciated chest so that every rib stood out, Mr. Lillywhite presented an even sorrier spectacle than usual. There was something else in the room with him, something from which the fetid stench seemed to emanate, something that shifted and moaned and muttered incessantly on a low bed in the shadows, something for which the liquid Mr. Lillywhite held was intended, for now the lanky figure turned and with soothing, nervous sounds approached the bedside. Whatever it was it could not, James felt, be particularly malign if the shady but timorous beachcomber was prepared to remain alone with it in this remote hut in the depths of a tropical wood. He rose to his full height and sauntered gently through the door, still holding his pistol.

"Good afternoon, Lillywhite."

There was a crash of breaking glass and the ex-customs official turned, gaping unbelievingly, from the bedside. His mouth hung open ridiculously and what color he had drained from his face, leaving it a grimy gray under the reddish stubble. Still half crouching by the bed, shabby, trapped, anemic, he gazed with horrified eyes at the intruder. From the bed a waft of nauseating stench stretched out miasmalike to fill the room.

"Stand up!" ordered James abruptly and Mr. Lillywhite, a look of fascinated horror glassily reflected in his pale eyes, lurched unsteadily to his feet. James, gripping hard the pistol which his inability to use failed to rob of its powerful reassurance, approached the bed, and at the sight of what lay there his stomach heaved. He retreated, holding his breath, toward the door. "Who is it?"

Mr. Lillywhite gasped and stuttered and then, to James' disgust, was noisily sick on the stone floor. Turning from him, James steeled himself to walk once more up to the low bed. He looked down at a panting, sweating, half-naked skeletal figure—the chest a skin-covered cage of ribs gashed in places to the bone with half-healed wounds, the belly so hollow that it seemed to press against the spine, and below a pair of filthy blood-stained shorts a left leg swollen to nearly twice its correct size and horribly discolored. James stared with fascinated repulsion. From knee to ankle it was a distended mass of corruption, the skin a deep purplish blue spotted here and there with velvety patches of decay. Most of the left foot was missing and the stump was bandaged in tattered cloths stained yellow with unavailing antiseptics. Then, tearing his eyes away from this spectacle of living putrescence, he gazed down at the skull-like face from which fever had sucked all the flesh till the high flat cheekbones seemed about to burst through the taut skin. Mr. Lillywhite must have administered the greater part of a strong sedative before dropping the glass, for his patient was unconscious and, except for his heavy, rasping breathing, unmoving; his eyes were bright narrow slits beneath the nearly closed lids.

Curiosity had impelled James into the low ruinous building, and though that curiosity was still unsatisfied it was lost in a wave of shocked disgust. He had never seen anything remotely like this before; he had profoundly hoped never to see anything of the sort in his life. He was suddenly angry with the anger of a child who wordlessly but intensely rebels against the limp squalor of the dead dog that yesterday sprang briskly barking in the sunshine. He felt personally soiled by this abrupt exhibition of human degradation by the obscene, stinking, dying creature on the filthy truckle bed. Some dim, age-old instinct urged him to kill it at once and hustle it out of sight, burn it, bury it, cover it up.

Recovering himself with an effort, he turned back to Mr. Lillywhite, only to find him sprawled facedown in his own vomit in a dead faint. A great earthenware crock of water stood by the door and, ladling this out with a small enamel saucepan he found beside it, James emptied several quarts over the unconscious man without avail.

Curiosity rose again, mastering his repulsion of the dying ruin of a man on the bed, and he was afire with the desire to learn who he was and why he was being kept in this remote and utterly inadequate shed in the depths of Balla's plantation with Lillywhite, of all people, as a nurse or warder or both. He glanced rapidly around the room for further clues; it was as bare inside as without; beyond the truckle bed and the crock of water there was no single stick of furniture. But under the bed his sharp eyes detected something squat and bulky. Holding his breath against the sickening smell of corruption, he knelt down and pulled out a cheap tin trunk of the sort commonly sold in the native markets. He carried it to the open door and, lifting the lid, saw that it was half filled with a small supply of cleanly laundered clothes. He took out a couple of shirts of the common checked cotton material worn by the poorer farmers and a pair of blue denim trousers before he came on the plain greenish khaki drill tunic bearing on the right breast the eagle emblem of the Third Reich.

James stared from the stylized swastika-clutching eagle to the unconscious man on the bed with a mixture of astonishment and fear. Was General Glasscraft right, after all? Were the Germans actually contemplating the seizure of Baressa in the near future? But no, it was nonsense; they were still thousands of miles away at some sort of stalemate with the Eighth Army. He turned back to the tunic in his hand and examined it more carefully. The collar bore rectangular tabs of strange insignia in colors of black and salmon pink; otherwise the drab-colored garment was austerely plain. It told him nothing. He turned back to the trunk for further clues and soon found them. A cap of khaki drill of the sort issued to German troops in Africa, bearing the small *totenkopf*

137

badge of the S.S., and a broad belt with great metal clasp emblazoned with eagle and swastika and the motto, *"Meine Ehr hiest treue."* At the bottom of the box, under a couple of khaki shirts, he came across a small leather case containing an identity card. With a muttered exclamation of satisfaction James opened it and was confronted with the photograph of the head and shoulders of a burly, youngish man with a wide Slavonic face, high cheekbones, small light eyes, and thick lips. It was just possible to recognize the ghoulish lineaments of the man on the bed. S.S. Hauptsturmführer Konrad Joseph Stralowski.

"So *that's* who you are," muttered James, rising to his feet. He prodded the sprawling Mr. Lillywhite, but without eliciting any response, and stood momentarily hesitating what to do. But there was little point in remaining longer in this malodorous hut with a dying man in a coma and one who stubbornly remained unconscious. Putting the S.S. man's identity card in his pocket, James emerged with relief into the clean bright sunshine outside. As he had expected, a thin but clearly visible track wound away between the trees and, following this, he came in ten minutes to the outbuilding of the *azienda.*

Two days later James sat beside Major Pole in one of the Palace cars as they drove behind Euan and the General to the docks. The early morning streets of San Pietro were hot and crowded, for it was market day. The breeze had not yet risen and clouds of pungent white dust hung heavy in the air behind the hooves of laden donkeys and the feet of plodding, swaying camels.

"Well, Major, I trust you've enjoyed your visit?"

Pole turned his myopic gray eyes on his host and blinked behind his spectacles. His face was expressionless.

"We didn't come here for enjoyment"—the words were a prim rebuke—"but if you were to ask if it had been a satisfactory visit I would say yes."

"Ah, I'm glad of that."

"Yes," confirmed Pole with an air of serious smug complacency. "We have done what we came to do and, despite one or two unforeseen difficulties, everything has turned out very much as the General expected. We work as a team, you know. The General selected all of us from different units at different times and welded us into a team. When we go to work we each have our allotted jobs and we know exactly what is expected of us. The General—he likes to refer to himself as the team skipper—coordinates our efforts. We generally succeed in our work and I think that's the reason—team spirit."

"It sounds delightful."

"It's efficient," said Pole, shooting a suspicious look at his companion, "if that's what you mean."

Why, James wondered, should he think I meant "efficient" if I said "delightful"? Anyway, I meant "bloody."

In the leading car the General, full of breakfast and content in the knowledge that quantities of island delicacies were at that moment being stored away in the *Emperor Napoleon*, felt more forgiving toward his host. During the last part of the exercise Lemonfield had been much more cooperative, though he had seemed strangely absentminded and quiet. Probably, thought the General, he had been impressed with the vigor and keenness displayed by himself and his staff. These O.E.T.A. people might pretend to be little tin gods, but they all knew inwardly that they couldn't compare to the regular Army when it came to drive and grit and determination. With more than a touch of self-satisfied benevolence he turned to the Colonel.

"Well, Lemonfield, I'm afraid we've disorganized you a bit this last week."

"Not at all, sir," Euan answered mechanically.

"I'm afraid we have though. Still, a bit of a shake-up doesn't do anyone any harm—and, as I said last night, things have turned out very well." He shook his head and gave a short barking laugh. "I still can't get over what you told me when I arrived. This place indefensible! Why, I'm dead certain from what I've seen that it could be made absolutely impregnable! The trouble with the Wops is that they don't *want* to defend things; they're hopeless in defense and they know it. So of course they pretend everything's indefensible in order to save themselves from foredoomed failure in the attempt. Now when those strongpoints I've marked on the map are built and the gun emplacements constructed and equipped this place will be capable of holding out against anything the enemy likes to send against it. Given a few battalions I'd guarantee to hold it indefinitely against the pick of the German Army. However, as I said before, we can't spare any more troops at present—and it's not yet necessary. If the worst comes to the worst of course they'll be sent, but for the moment—except for a company of Engineers to build the strongpoints—I shan't recommend any immediate reinforcement."

"Oh, I see." Euan sighed inwardly with relief.

"I'm going to send land mines as well for mining the roads. The Engineers will give you instructions as to how and where they should be laid in an emergency. And I'll see about getting some sea mines off to you, too. I know, Lemonfield, that they are not really within the Army's province, but in an emergency it's far better to have them handy—much of my plan of defense depends on minefields close inshore. There are plenty of little ships in your harbor that could lay them. I don't suppose you've got anyone who knows about that sort of thing though, have you?"

"Well—there's the Port Pilot——" began Euan dubiously.

"That foreign fellow, you mean?"

"Yes."

"Oh, you'd better not let *him* touch them, Lemonfield. No, you'd better not do *that*."

"I quite agree, sir." It was, thought Euan with mild surprise, the first and only time that he and the General had reached genuine unanimity.

On the docks the Negro guard of honor was drawn up once more, but now in shabby khaki and bulging webbing equipment they lacked the magnificent appearance of a week ago. The inspection was quick, and within a very few minutes General Glasscraft was shaking hands with Pirie, Christopher, the Major, and lastly Colonel Lemonfield, and speaking a few brief words of thanks for the hospitality extended to him. Then he was on board, standing with his staff on the boat deck as the gangway was rumbling back onto the quay. The bridge telegraph clanged and was answered immediately by a remote tinkle from the engine room, and then the churn and thud of the ship's screws thrashed the water to mottled foam while a line of sparkling green widened between the *Napoleon*'s dingy hull and the quayside.

For minute after minute the Colonel stood silent and still on the white stone quay with his officers behind him and behind them the rigid ranks of the guard of honor. The *Napoleon* was past the Dhow Control Point now and out on the glittering morning sea. Small, black, and ugly, she was silhouetted against the vast blazing glory of the eastern sky and all the figures on her

140

bridge and deck were lost to view. Still the Colonel stood motionless, staring with unseeing eyes across the great expanse of gleaming water to the dark hull with its long trickle of greasy smoke stretching up and back until it disappeared into the clear serene blue of the sky.

14

FOR a few days after the departure of General Glasscraft the Colonel remained in the Villa, suffering from the results of the fatigue and nervous strain incurred during the visit. But he was not idle, and from his study he issued orders that both relieved his feelings and encouraged the citizens of San Pietro to discountenance the wild rumors of Allied defeats, impending invasion, evacuation, and bombing that the General's behavior had caused to be put about. The *Napoleon* was hardly hull down over the horizon before the khaki-clad guard outside the Palace was ceremoniously changed by reliefs in all the old glory of glittering white, brass buttons, and ostrich plumes, while in his office Sergeant Brinsmead set to work with a blue pencil on the General's carefully worked out training schedules.

The official cars which had suffered the indignity of camouflage in brown and green blotches were sent to the Administration garages for repainting, and even the spiked heads of the Palace railings were defiantly given a fresh coat of gilt. Barbed wire was cleared from the streets, trenches were filled in, half-constructed air-raid shelters demolished, sandbags emptied, and San Pietro was restored to its normal appearance of sleepy tropical prosperity.

As if to confirm the Colonel's faith in Baressa's security, the news of the great German defeat at El Alamein broke on the island. It was received with general acclamation by the native islanders, upon whom two years of quiet but skillful propaganda had impressed the iniquity of Fascist rule as conducted by Colonel Giordano and the progressive probity of the British Administration under Colonel Lemonfield. The Italian population viewed the defeat of their armies with mixed feelings. It was nationally humiliating, perhaps, but—one did not really want the war to come any closer to Baressa, because it was so bad for trade. A victory the other way might have meant the return of Colonel Giordano and the reimposition of the Fascist levies and party taxes and goodness knows what imposts besides to help pay for this ridiculous war. Things were far better as they were.

Owing to some obscure claim to royal blood the Count Giulio Brocca was believed to have possessed, the island had always had vague monarchist sympathies and the slow contented tenor of its life had proved an infertile breeding ground for Fascism. So much so that the upper strata of colonial society, the people who really mattered, had been quite open in their lazily tolerant amusement at the regime and its trappings and its leader. Baressa was their island and what happened in faraway Italy was no concern of theirs. If their sons liked to play about in the Avanguardia—well, boys would be boys, and so long as they did not hold their weekly romps over growing crops or damage the fruit plantations with campfires it was doubtless a healthy enough way of passing the time. They paid the Fascist levies grumblingly, but without real rancor. One naturally had to keep in with whatever government was in power, and all governments continually demanded money for one thing or another; besides, though one did not admit it, one was rich and one could easily pay. Some enthusiast once started a fund for a statue of Il Duce, but so little money was forthcoming that Signor da Ponte was able, by personally contributing fifty percent, to get the committee to agree to a statue of his uncle, the second Governor, instead. Even at the time of the Ethiopian war the islanders had only with difficulty been shamed into the grudging gift of a small motor ambulance, and Mussolini's curtly sarcastic letter of thanks had not been forgotten.

Thus, when Colonel Lemonfield ordered a public holiday to celebrate the Allies' first great victory of the war, Signor Belotta, the Mayor, did not feel it improper to hold the municipal banquet—so unreasonably and impolitely declined by the visiting British General—on the eve of the proclaimed fiesta. Colonel Lemonfield himself should be the guest of honor, and after the banquet there should be a ball in the big assembly room of the

142

Town Hall. The Municipality had not given a ball since the war started and it was high time they gave another; if it could be taken to celebrate anything it could be that the war had withdrawn still farther from remote Baressa. That, surely, was worth a ball.

The invitations were sent out to everyone of any note within reach of San Pietro. Businessmen, shippers, and public officials from the town, burly bronzed farmers from the uplands in tight-fitting evening clothes, their wives, sons, and daughters, all flocked to the Town Hall, proudly bearing the Municipality's card of invitation. Italian, Greek, Armenian, Turkish, Dutch—Captain Rekelhof, back with the *Napoleon,* beaming and flashing his steel hook in cheerful greeting—all the variegated nationalities that made up the white population of Baressa were represented. All the English soldiers, both officers and other ranks, had been in-vited and so, too, though not without misgivings, had the Port Pilot. It was common knowledge that Captain Zvengetzov's at-titude toward the war had undergone a sudden and embarrassing change. Exactly why this was no one knew but it had something to do with some Russian remarks about Transylvania, a renegade cousin, the estates near Kluj and a silver mine. It was all very complicated apparently, but after receiving a bulky letter cov-ered in exotic stamps and seemingly written in runes Captain Zvengetzov had overnight become violently pro-German. When sober he kept these opinions to himself—but his sobriety was never guaranteed. It would be awkward if he offended the Gov-ernor in the Municipality's own building, but he was an official of undoubted position and Colonel Lemonfield, a stickler for eti-quette, might be equally offended if it were neglected to invite him.

When at last the long dinner was over and the speakers had said all they could think of in praise of Colonel Lemonfield, the ball began. The Colonel himself did not dance, but stood con-versing with the wealthy and more elderly members of the Cor-poration at one end of the great flower-decked hall. One by one personages of importance—the chief of the Armenian commu-nity, the Senior Engineer of the power station, the head of the Greek Orthodox Church—duly presented themselves to bow, to flatter, to receive a few words from the little man in the pale sand-colored uniform and to retire, smiling obsequiously, knowing themselves still in favor. The Chief Rabbi, spectacles gleaming —Captain Rekelhof, hook flashing—Signor da Ponte, pulling at his black beard a shade nervously.

When the dancing was in full swing the Mayor, seeking among the crowd for his own daughter, came upon Silvana. She was standing alone by a pillar in a gay new dress of broad green and white stripes with a glowing scarlet hibiscus flower in her hair. Signor Belotta smiled with upraised eyebrows.

"My dear, the prettiest girl at the ball—and not dancing?"

Silvana laughed. "Mrs. Tamminetto asked me to get her bag from the cloakroom, and when I came back everyone had started. Now there aren't any partners."

"There are plenty of servants to wait on the guests," remarked the Mayor smilingly, looking around the crowded floor. "I would ask you to dance with me, only I'm sure you'd prefer someone younger—ah, come along!" He took the girl's hand and led her through the couples who sat out and gossiped among the pillars till they reached the group about the Colonel. Silvana saw with a tightening of her heart that Christopher stood with the other officers behind the Governor and Commendatore Saccomani.

"Excellency"—the Mayor beamed—"here is one of the senior police officers without a partner. May I borrow one of your staff for her? Perhaps Captain Kellermann——?"

The Colonel, who had broken off his conversation with the Commendatore to smile at Silvana as she approached with the Mayor, gave a quick frown at these words, but he could hardly oppose them. He turned to Christopher, who was hesitating at his elbow. "Go along then, Christopher. Signor Belotta, the Commendatore tells me that he is prepared to help finance. . . ."

The rest of the words were lost to Silvana as, blushing angrily, she was swung away by Christopher into the whirl of waltzing couples. For a few moments they danced in silence, then Silvana said, "Didn't you want to dance with me?"

"Of course I did!"

"You didn't seem to! I thought you were going to say you wouldn't—and I haven't had a chance to speak to you for days!"

"Nonsense! I've been waiting to get away from the Colonel to find you."

"You've been dancing before," accused Silvana. "I've seen you with three other partners."

"The Mayoress, Mrs. Valdonetti, and Mrs. Tamminetto!" retorted Christopher contemptuously. "The Colonel made me dance with the Mayoress, and the Mayor made me dance with Mrs. Valdonetti——"

"And who made you dance with Mrs. Tamminetto? You must have enjoyed that!"

"She did, of course—who else? Silvana, you're cross with me, but it's the Colonel you should be cross with. He doesn't want me to have anything to do with you. That's why I've had to be careful."

Silvana was startled; she looked up into his smiling face. "But why? What have I done? I don't understand——"

"*You* haven't done anything. It's *me* he's worried about. He thinks I'll make you unhappy or something. He wouldn't hear of your coming to work at the barracks."

"But he's never objected to William being friends with me." She was hurt and puzzled. "I don't think you asked him, Christopher. You changed your mind. You don't really want——"

"Oh, all right, all right, have it your own way! The Colonel's madly in love with you himself and is keeping you in reserve for his private use—after which you'll be handed over to the Major, which will embarrass him considerably, I've no doubt. It's a question of *jus primae noctis*—only not being educated like me you don't know what that means."

Silvana was not amused. "No, but seriously, did the Colonel really say we mustn't see each other?"

"I keep telling you he did!"

"Then—aren't we going to?"

Christopher looked down at her anxious, flushed face and grinned. "Yes, we are, of course. But we are going to be very careful. You don't want to get me sent away from Baressa, do you?"

"Ah, he wouldn't do that!" Silvana was shocked.

"He almost said he would," replied Christopher with a certain complacency.

"Then—should we be dancing?" She tried to loosen her hand from his and her dark worried eyes sought the far end of the room where the Colonel was still talking to the Mayor and the Commendatore. But Christopher had already steered her through the swinging dancers until they were nearly at the tall entrance doors and as far from the Colonel as it was possible to be.

145

"He can't complain—he told me to. Silvana, I like your dress. It is very flamboyant, but it suits you."

"Mrs. Tamminetto doesn't like it. She says it is garish and unbecoming a young girl—but I know she was jealous."

"Mrs. Tamminetto is an evil old whore."

"Christopher! Really!"

"You must never let her choose your clothes again. She has horrible taste. I'll choose them in future."

"Will you?" She laughed, and he guided her suddenly out of the throng of dancers, between two rotund marble pillars and out onto a small balcony half hidden behind them from the main room. Flushed and excited, his green eyes glittering, he looked down at Silvana and she seemed more than ever desirable in the rustling finery of her bright dress.

"Now I am going to disobey the Colonel completely!" He took her in his arms and kissed her long and passionately and many times.

William leaned against the bar, drinking beer and angrily repulsing the attempts of the Mayor to find him a partner. He was furious with the old man for the way he had seized Silvana and handed her over to Captain Kellermann without reference to her rightful owner. They had disappeared somewhere into the maze of dancers ten minutes ago and, try as he would, he could see no sign of them. He answered distractedly the occasional questions of Captain Pirie, who, unable to dance by reason of his stiff leg, had sought him out at the bar and was disparaging the proceedings in a grumbling monologue.

". . . Isn't very nice in the present circumstances, I must say. When you consider that England and Italy are supposed to be at war, all this fraternization is absolutely wrong, to my mind. Surely you see that, Summerson, don't you?"

"What's that, sir? Oh, I don't know. I mean, the war isn't very important *here,* if you see what I mean."

"I bloody well don't! Of course it's as important here as anywhere else. These people are our enemies, can't you understand that? But I don't suppose you can. You're just like the rest. You think that because the war's a long way off you can forget about it." He stared glumly into his glass and William, standing on the

146

brass footrail of the bar, scanned the whirling dancers for some glimpse of Silvana.

"Of course," Pirie continued sourly, "you've no excuse for not being an officer, Summerson, you know. You're the officer type. Everyone who's the officer type ought to make the effort."

"What—? Well, no one's suggested making me one, actually."

"Have you even applied?"

"No."

"Well, there you are! You should apply to the Colonel."

"I'd have to leave the island, though—and I don't want to do that."

"You might just as well," said Pirie unkindly, "for Kellermann's pinched your girl and you won't get her back from that little sweetheart in a hurry, I shouldn't think." But William wasn't listening, for far down at the end of the long room Silvana and Christopher had emerged suddenly from behind two pillars near the door. They immediately moved away in opposite directions, but not before William's straining eyes had caught the quick, flushed, smiling glance that passed between them. A cold hand seemed to press his heart.

"What's that, sir?" he asked dully, turning back to Pirie. "I didn't——"

"Oh, forget it!" The Captain swirled the brandy around his glass and, emptying it at a gulp, motioned the black barman to fill it again.

Behind the distrait William Captain Zvengetzov and Mrs. Tamminetto were drinking Cointreau that had been smuggled into the island by Captain Rossi and sold to the Mayor at a specially low price. The Hungarian, his tarnished epaulets glinting in the bright light and his face pale with emotion, held one of the ex-Police Chief's crimson-nailed hands in a clammy grasp. "Gina, I tell you this, you may have lovings with many other men, but not one will love you like I—for I will love you until you scream for mercy!"

Pirie looked at them with disgust. "Oh, for God's sake—this bloody island!"

A hand rested for a moment lightly on William's shoulder and a voice, half mocking, half sympathetic, said, "Poor Summerson! *La donna è mobile.* I feel for you." He looked up into the long

147

smiling face of Major Naughton-Muirhead and, not knowing what to answer, smiled slightly and shrugged his shoulders. "After such constancy on your part. Really, it's too bad!" He was piloted gently away from the bar and toward the group around the Colonel. But on the way they were stopped by Pietro Calgarini, who stood, mopping his hot, damp face, beside a plump, pale girl equally hot and damp in a dress of heavy purple silk.

"Signor Maggiore—one moment."

James halted, smiling. "Good evening, Pietro. How are you?"

"Hot, *signore*." Pietro grinned and all his gold teeth flashed. "I have danced every dance!" he announced proudly, and then, "This is Giacinta da Ponte—we are engaged."

"Indeed? Congratulations to you both!" James glanced from the ugly youth to his equally paling fiancée. So two of the richest families on the island had made an alliance. "I'm sure your parents are very pleased."

"Yes, they are. We've known each other all our lives, haven't we, Gia?" He glanced at her with a mixture of pride and shyness. The Da Ponte girl smiled, showing, James noted with satisfaction, several gold teeth of her own.

"Well, you had better come along and receive the Colonel's blessing. I'm sure he'll be delighted to hear about this, considering how well he knows your respective parents."

They all approached the Colonel and James was beginning, "Euan, our young friend here——" when from the direction of the bar there suddenly came confused shouts and the tinklings of broken glass. At once there was a general movement toward the scene of the commotion where, surrounded by a gaping group of guests, Captain Zvengetzov was discovered lying flat on his back with his unconscious head pillowed in the lap of a weeping Mrs. Tamminetto. Above him, red-faced, angry, and embarrassed, towered Captain Pirie.

"And what," asked the Colonel in a frigid voice as he eyed first his Port Pilot and then his Police Chief, "is supposed to be going on here?"

"This bloody bastard drank 'to the success of the glorious German Army'!" declared Pirie furiously. "So I told him to bloody well shut up. A lot of my pals have been killed by the bloody Jerries and I'm not going to stand for——"

"Are you trying," cut in the Colonel in an awful voice, "to tell

148

me that you actually struck the Port Pilot? That you so far forgot yourself as to knock him down?"

Before the icy sternness of that gaze and the cutting clarity of that voice—a combination brought to dread perfection by constant practice on many a recalcitrant witness—Pirie wilted. The hot words of self-justification withered on his lips.

"Well—he asked for it," he mumbled at last.

"Whatever the Port Pilot may or may not have said you had no excuse whatsoever to strike him. A flagrant breach of conduct most unbecoming in an officer of the Administration! I suggest you go home at once!"

"I very much fear," remarked the Colonel later in the evening and apropos of nothing in particular, "that the new Police Chief won't do—won't do at all."

15

NEXT day it was noticed that the Colonel, taking the salute from a flag-bedecked dais as the troops and the Banda and the police and fire brigade went swinging past, looked in a thoroughly bad temper, quite out of keeping with the general gaiety of the occasion. In his office half an hour before he had had a short but annoying interview with Dr. Valdonetti.

The doctor, tired and dirty, was back from one of the continual trips to the far end of the plateau which had already caused some surprise among the hospital staff.

"So you really think he will live?" Euan had rattled a pencil irritably on the glass desk top before him.

"I think so, Excellency." There was a hint of pride in the doctor's weary voice. "The man has an incredibly strong constitution. When I operated seventeen days ago I was certain that it was a waste of time. In that state, with that leg—well, you saw him yourself."

"I did." Euan's face twitched at the memory. "I suppose you removed the entire leg?"

"At the hip, yes. Even so, it seems to me like a miracle that he still breathes."

"Is he conscious?"

"He regained consciousness for the first time last night. He was unconscious again when I arrived an hour later. But I think— though it is still too early to be certain—that slowly, very slowly, he will recover. Gangrene invariably sets in quickly after shark bite unless the wound is properly treated at once. A shark's multiple teeth are so full of decaying organic matter that even when the victim is not sufficiently mangled to die from shock or loss of blood——"

"How long will it be before this man can be brought to San Pietro?"

The doctor shrugged. "Two months at the least, I should say, before it would be really safe to move him."

"I see. Well, in the meantime I don't want the matter discussed by anyone. Your assistant at the Balla estate must be informed of that if you have him relieved. I don't want anything about this man to become known until he is well enough for me to talk to him."

At breakfast next morning in the Villa the Colonel appeared preoccupied and irritable. He had spent most of the preceding night in Fort Brocca questioning—in company with Baines—Mr. Lillywhite and Signor Balla alternately. Pouring out a third cup of coffee, he suddenly broke a long silence to remark, "Now that Valdonetti says this damned man's going to live the whole affair takes on a much more unpleasant complexion."

"For us, I assume you mean?" commented James absently from behind the *Baressa Courier,* where he was pleasurably engaged in reading an article on modern art contributed by himself.

"For us, of course!" said Euan crossly. "For *me,* really, that is. I can't report him now, can I, after having failed to do so for weeks? Besides, it's the very last thing I *want* to do. It would create all sorts of inquiries and complications."

"Well, I suppose the Army would want to know what he was doing here." James folded the paper and handed it to a hovering footman. "But then, we'd like to know that ourselves. Did you get anywhere last night?"

"No, nowhere at all, really. Lillywhite knows nothing of any importance except that he was used as a go-between to try and arrange this man's getaway with Rossi, but for different shifty reasons on Rossi's part and general inefficiency on Lillywhite's it hadn't come off."

James looked skeptical. "But why on earth should this German still be here more than two years after the occupation? Don't you think Lillywhite may know more than he says?"

Euan poured himself some more coffee. "I doubt it. He's in the most appalling state of fright at present. Baines has only to look at him and he screams out everything he knows. My only fear in that respect is that he'll start inventing things soon and implicating perfectly innocent people in order to ingratiate himself with us."

"What's Balla got to say for himself?"

"Very little," replied Euan grimly. "He's in a stronger position and he knows it. His main line is, firstly, that he's a patriotic Fascist; secondly, that he's no idea why Stralowski came to this island, but that as he failed to get off before we arrived he had to hide, and Balla hid him as in duty bound to an ally of his country. Thirdly, he says that what he's done is no crime and that he has committed no contravention of the Laws and Usages, and that I'd better let him go or he'll complain to Geneva."

James burst out laughing. "Really, the man's got a nerve! Is he right—I mean, about the Laws and Usages?"

"Well, that depends how one interprets them. As the British interpretation holds good here he is more or less right, I suppose."

"You can't do anything, you mean?"

"I could intern him, I suppose, but I hardly think it's worthwhile in the circumstances. I'd have to explain to everybody why I'd shut up a concession owner—as you know there's a fairly strong fellow feeling among them all—and that would mean telling everyone about Stralowski, which is the last thing I want to do. I'll keep him in prison until we've got this indestructible German in San Pietro and then let him go back—with considerable safeguards and a lot of bail. You see, we've got so little to go on at present. Baines has made a thorough search of the concession, but found nothing. No papers or maps or incriminating letters or secret codes or anything dramatic like that. Just the old fool's out-of-date laboratory full of bits of gold-bearing rock—mostly dated 1910."

"Nothing serious there, you think? He's not inventing a death ray or building a spaceship?"

Euan frowned; he did not care for jokes at breakfast. "It's well known that he's been looking for gold ever since he came here. He's sometimes found a few bits, but nothing to make him rich. That's why his estate's always in such a mess—he takes no interest in it. Oh, but we did find out he's a virulent Fascist. All the literature was there—the whole works—and a little plaque of Mussolini looking more than ever like an inebriated old pugilist."

"Well, everyone's always said he was a Fascist, anyway."

"Exactly."

On New Year's Eve Mrs. Tamminetto gave a small party in her handsome bungalow at the end of the Corso Vittorio Veneto next to the slaughterhouse. The late Captain Tamminetto had bought it cheaply from a bankrupt Armenian merchant in the thirties before the municipal abattoir was built. As Police Chief he had done everything he could to prevent the erection of that dismal building beside his residence, and owing to his official position he would normally have been entirely successful in preventing it. Unfortunately, the site happened to have been acquired by Colonel Giordano, and as he was bent on selling it to the Municipality the Captain of Carabinieri came off second best. He and his wife found it best to entertain only in the winter months when the seasonal wind was blowing away from the abattoir.

Mrs. Tamminetto's sitting room was large, but it was considerably reduced in size by the collection of Oriental bric-à-brac and the multitude of fat, vivid satin cushions with which she chose to furnish it. The walls were covered with photographs of herself and her husband and various friends, mostly snapshots enlarged and emanating an atmosphere of the *passé* gaiety of the twenties. Silvana, who attended the party by command, spent much time pondering on the extraordinary clothes with which her late mistress had bedecked herself in her youth. And who could possibly have wanted to marry Captain Tamminetto? Small, prim, with a little waxed moustache, pince-nez and wiglike hair, the photographs made him look still more unattractive than the balding, snappish, prematurely aged little man she recollected occasionally seeing in her early childhood. For the first time Silvana, comparing the late Captain of Police with Christopher, looked at Mrs. Tamminetto with half-pitying contempt. But beyond occasionally saying, "Hand these around, dear," "Give the Maresciallo some more coffee." Mrs. Tamminetto was far too busy with her otherwise all male party to spare much time for her erstwhile secretary.

All the Carabinieri were present and Captain Zvengetzov and Texas. Texas was Mrs. Tamminetto's new favorite and on his half-pleased, half-embarrassed face she lavished all the caresses she had been wont to bestow on Aldo Commino. She treated him like a household pet, and now he sat on a frilled cushion at her feet, taking no part in the conversation, while from time to time she ran a hand through his thick black hair or pinched his ear affectionately between scarlet fingertips. Texas enjoyed it. Nobody had made a fuss of him before in his short life, and it was a pleasant change to be petted and coaxed with food and drink.

To the ill-concealed disgust of the Port Pilot the party was almost a temperance one, for beyond a small bottle of mandarino, the tangerine liqueur of which their hostess was particularly fond, the guests drank nothing but coffee and lemonade. The Carabinieri, not a bibulous set, were content to munch colored cakes and sip from little porcelain cups, but Captain Zvengetzov was not pleased and, after a halfhearted attempt to make improper advances to Silvana—which she easily repulsed—and an unsuccessful effort to interest Texas in the lost glories of the estate near Kluj, he picked up his battered cap and drove home to his large squalid flat near the docks in disappointed dudgeon.

Nonetheless Mrs. Tamminetto's party was, from her point of view, a complete success, and this success was demonstrated the following morning when the Police Force went on strike.

Colonel Lemonfield did not discover this until late in the morning, owing to the depressing behavior of Sergeant Brinsmead. For, on arriving at his office at 9 a.m., the Colonel found on his blotting pad a short, neatly typed request for a posting to the mainland and with incredulous dismay saw that it was signed by his Chief Clerk. When Sergeant Brinsmead was summoned to give his reasons for this shocking demand he stated coldly and firmly that he was no longer prepared to go on working against obstruction and inefficiency and at the same time to be subjected to insults and abuse. It was not what he was used to or for what he joined the Army. He would put up with it no longer. Euan lay back in his chair and stared at him in amazement.

"Just what and who are you complaining about, Brinsmead?"

"I'm not complaining about anything or anybody, sir. I'm just requesting a posting—as I have a right to do, I believe."

"And I have a right to ask you why—and to refuse such a request if I consider your reasons unsatisfactory," retorted Euan with a touch of grimness. "Now let's have no more prevarication, Brinsmead—surely after all this time we know each other well enough to speak and hear the truth. What *is* all this about?"

"Well, sir, since you *insist* on knowing, it's Captain Pirie."

"Ah! Yes?"

"Ever since he took over the police I have had no cooperation at all from him in the matter of returns. Under the—the last person who ran the police I always got my returns."

"My good Brinsmead, *no one* could have complained more bitterly or more often of——"

"Be that as it may, sir," interrupted Brinsmead doggedly, "I *did* get them. They were often inaccurate, but they came. Captain Pirie will *not* send in his returns. At first I let the matter go on for some time, as I understood he was new to the job, but after I had sent several respectful reminders, with no effect, I rang him up."

"Yes?"

"All he said was something about 'bloody red tape.' "

"Ah? And then?"

"I eventually got some of the returns—weeks overdue and utterly useless, for they were all wrong. I sent them back and asked him to do them properly and resubmit them as expeditiously as possible. And yesterday he rang me up and was"—Brinsmead's fiery moustache twitched with fury—"excessively rude and abusive."

"What did he say?"

"He said—among a lot of other things—that I was being 'bloody insolent' and"—Brinsmead swallowed with difficulty—"that he would do his job as he pleased despite all the—all the miserable, officious little clerks in O.E.T.A.!"

"He said that, did he?"

"He did!"

"I see." Euan kept a straight face with extreme difficulty. Not only straight, but he managed to assume a look of stern vexation. While he was, in fact, exceedingly annoyed by the conduct of Captain Pirie, he had grudgingly to admire his nerve. In Pirie's position he would never have dared to use such language to a senior N.C.O. like the aggressive and formidable Brinsmead. However, the pressing necessity at the moment was to make Brinsmead see reason. He tried hard. He used all the arts of persuasion and tact with which he was endowed. He hinted at promotion and he offered to have the work on police returns removed to another quarter. He said he would "speak" to Captain Pirie. It was all to no avail, for the little man's touchy and arrogant nature had been so insulted that nothing would pacify him. He would leave the island and never set foot on it again. Euan tried appealing to the past, to the two and a half years of hard but satisfyingly successful work that they had shared and to the personal friendliness that had grown up between them. It was no use. Frustrated and furious, his hands shaking with suppressed emotion, he at last told Brinsmead to go; he would sign the request.

As Brinsmead left the office Lieutenant Baines, agitated and sweating still more profusely than usual, passed him in the doorway and entered the Colonel's office with the news of the police mutiny.

He found the Governor in such a state of anger that he wished he had not come. And his news, when broken, threw the little man into such a dreadful rage that Baines, standing unhappily before the great desk, really thought that his master was about to start smashing the furniture. However, after striding rapidly up and down the long room for a few minutes, the Colonel was restored sufficiently for the necessary drastic action to be taken. Orders were rapidly given by telephone for the garrison troops to take over police duties and to surround the native police barracks and confine its inmates indefinitely. The Carabinieri were ordered to report in a body to the Palace, and lastly Captain Pirie was brusquely summoned to attend at once. Then at last the Colonel put down the receiver. For a moment he stood lost in thought and biting his lip.

"How old are you, Baines?" he shot out suddenly.

"Me? Twenty-five, sir," answered the surprised lieutenant.

"You joined as a private, didn't you?"

"Yes sir."

"Have you been in action?"

"No."

"Thank God for that!" exclaimed the Colonel devoutly. "One way or another it seems to have had a thoroughly bad effect on those of my officers who have been."

Baines felt that no reply was expected to this statement and the Colonel continued, "Why don't you like Captain Kellermann?"

"I—I do like him. I mean, he's all right. That is, I've got nothing against him," stammered Baines confusedly.

"Oh—I thought somehow you two didn't get on very well. I'm glad to hear such is not the case, for it is vitally necessary that the civil and military authorities should cooperate trustfully with one another. Now, Baines, after this little effort of today Captain Pirie's got to go. I'm going to make you Chief of Police as well as of Customs, and also I intend to allot a certain sum for the expansion of the plainclothes agents you seem to possess into a—a security force. I'll see you're made a captain as soon as possible, and further promotion will depend on your success, of course." He gazed into the lieutenant's face with a friendly yet searching smile. "I think you'll do this job very well, Baines—very well indeed. I only wish I had some more officers like you."

Embarrassed, Baines flushed redder than ever and stammered his thanks. Then he was dismissed and Pirie was shown in.

The Colonel's interview with Captain Pirie, as described by him at lunch that day, was short and to the point. "I told him that this mutiny—one can hardly call it a strike—was an altogether disgraceful affair, and asked him why he thought it had happened. He started a long and irrelevant denunciation of the Carabinieri in general and the Maresciallo in particular. Well, as you know, James, we've dealt with old Angellini for ages without the slightest difficulty. He's not particularly bright and he's idle, but otherwise he's not a bad old thing at all and he knows his job from A to Z. The rest are equally satisfactory within their limitations. I told Pirie that, but of course he wouldn't see it. The fact is he loathes Italians and thinks it unpatriotic even to be civil to them. So I told him I had little doubt that the police were behaving in this way because they were dissatisfied with him as their chief, and in the circumstances—though I should, of course, go carefully into the whole matter—I had decided to relieve him of his duties."

"Ah?"

"He was furious, of course. Said it wasn't his fault and that he'd only been trying to get things straight and instill a little British discipline into his men."

James laughed. "That's obviously been the cause of the trouble."

"Of course. So I read him a little lecture on the principles behind O.E.T.A. and told him that in my opinion he was quite unfitted for a position in the organization. He agreed in an insolent sort of way, so I told him that he could either write out his resignation there and then or else I should send in a thoroughly bad report, which would have a worse effect on his future. That shook him, and he went off to an empty office and wrote out a request for a posting at once and brought it back to me for endorsement. He can't spell. I had to get one of the clerks to rewrite it and type it. Now it goes off and he follows on the next *Napoleon*."

"Good riddance to him, I say."

The news of Captain Pirie's dismissal, discreetly broken by James late in the afternoon, had such a soothing effect on Sergeant Brinsmead that he went at once to the Colonel and withdrew his application for posting. It was thus with a comparatively light heart that as dusk was falling Euan gave the order to admit the Carabinieri to his office. Summoned to the Palace in the morning, they had been kept waiting in a set of disused offices for eight hours without any refreshment and were now in a suitably chastened mood of fear and penitence. They wished on the whole that they had not gone to Mrs. Tamminetto's party. They wished it still more devoutly for the next quarter of an hour, during which they were treated to a vivid display of verbal pyrotechnics which left them dazed and stunned but humbly thankful to have escaped with no more than superficial singeing. They trooped off sheepishly in search of sackcloth and ashes and the Colonel wiped his forehead with his silk bandana and went home to dinner.

Captain Pirie had only met Mr. Morle on two occasions since he had come to Baressa, but in the interval between his dismissal from the police and the arrival of the *Napoleon* the missionary was the only man on the island with whom he felt inclined to speak at all. He sought him out in his house on the day after the abortive mutiny and found him sitting at a deal desk in his bleak study, correcting some pious essays by the senior class of the Mission School. He looked up as the Captain came in with a half-suspicious smile on his hard, thin-lipped mouth.

"Good morning."

"Good morning to you, Padre. May I sit down?"

"Certainly."

Pirie lowered himself carefully into a creaking cane chair and put his cap on his knees. Mr. Morle, waiting to discover what this visit might portend, carefully stacked the tattered marbled exercise books on top of each other as if their perfect alignment were of the greatest importance. On the dusty windowpane the flies buzzed noisily.

"I've come to say good-bye," announced Pirie morosely. "I'm off on the next *Napoleon*."

"Indeed!" Mr. Morle looked surprised. "You've made a very short stay on Baressa. Hardly three months, surely?"

"Too bl—too darned long, if you ask me!"

"Oh? You're pleased to be going?"

"I am. And if I wasn't it wouldn't matter—I'd still go. Tell me, Padre, you've had trouble with Colonel Lemonfield yourself, haven't you?"

Mr. Morle's mouth tightened. "Trouble? Hardly. It wouldn't be suitable for a missionary to have 'trouble' with the military. I and the Colonel don't see eye to eye on many matters, I'm afraid. I must admit that I don't think he's made things very easy for me since he's been here. But am I to understand that you've had—h'm—difficulty with him?" The missionary looked with sharp interest at his visitor.

"I've been sacked, Padre, if you want to know," replied Pirie with an attempt at bland indifference, "for not being nice enough to the dear Italians."

"Oh, I see. I'm sorry."

"Well, I'm not!" returned Pirie truculently. "I'm damned glad—excuse me—to get out. I never wanted to come to O.E.T.A. in the first place and what I've seen since I've been here has sickened me completely. They're all a useless lot of shirkers."

This happened to be exactly the opinion held by Mr. Morle,

158

but he was not prepared to corroborate it unreservedly. For one thing Christian charity forbade him to condemn quite so generally, and for another—well, it was his experience that walls on Baressa had more ears than anywhere else. So he replied with a thin smile, "Ah well, I wouldn't like to say that myself, you know."

"I would!"

"After all, someone's got to do these jobs and we can't spare our best men for them in time of war. No, no, one must have a little sense of proportion—no, thank you, I don't smoke. But I must say that I think that on this island there's a distinct leaning too far toward—what shall I say?—a rather sycophantic paternal autocracy that I can't say I care for."

"Meaning what, exactly?" This last was slightly beyond Pirie. "That the Colonel's too bloo—too big for his boots?"

Mr. Morle laughed. "I didn't really mean that, you know. You certainly call a spade a spade. Would you like a cup of tea? I'm going to have one." He picked up a small brass bell and rang it. Soon a black mission boy in grubby white shirt and shorts knocked at the door and was dispatched to the kitchen. "Strictly between ourselves"—Mr. Morle lowered his voice—"I think the real trouble is that Colonel Lemonfield is much too interested in his own position. He's presumably here to administer—during hostilities only—a captured enemy island. Instead of which it seems to me he considers himself—well, more or less as a permanently placed indigenous ruler."

"A darn dictator, you mean?"

Mr. Morle smiled primly. "I rather think from what I have seen and heard of the Colonel that he would term himself a benevolent despot. His is the sort of mind that believes in benevolent despotism. It is a political theory which has, like so many theories, a certain amount to recommend it. The ancients considered—however, that's not germane. As I was saying, I believe that Colonel Lemonfield thinks of himself almost as an independent ruler here. He behaves rather as if he does, I must say."

"You mean he's absolutely pro-Wop?" suggested Pirie scornfully.

Mr. Morle put the tips of his fingers together and studied them thoughtfully. "He certainly seems to conciliate them as far as possible," he said guardedly, "and doubtless he has his reasons. I

159

can't myself, however hard I try, like the Italian nation. None-theless, as a clergyman I must of course prefer to see them—to see anyone—ruled by kindness rather than by force and coercion. However, even so, I can't approve of Colonel Lemonfield's obvious attitude that because he is a highly intelligent person and an able administrator he is entitled to blatantly cast aside all pretenses of patriotism—which is more or less what he does."

"I'll say he does——" began Pirie furiously, but was compelled to halt while Mr. Morle's morning tea was brought in and laid before him. When the servant had retired and closed the door Pirie continued, "They're all as bad as him in that respect—the whole lot from Naughton-Muirhead down to young Dawson the D.R.!"

"H'm!" Mr. Morle sipped his tea. "Yes, perhaps. Some of them are good enough in their own way doubtless, but—well, of course, they're all under the Colonel's influence." He paused. "I once wrote to my Bishop—a long letter—and pointed out what I considered to be the situation here. After all, I've had far more experience of this island than the Colonel and his staff, and I thought the Bishop might be sufficiently interested to pass the matter on to some authority who might look into things. Though I am only a missionary clergyman and a noncombatant, I feel I have a duty to my country."

"I should say so! What happened?"

"Well, I regret to say that the Colonel intercepted the letter—one might almost say he stole it—and, of course, it caused—friction." Mr. Morle put down his cup slowly. "But as you're going back—a word or two in the right quarter—eh?"

"I doubt it." Pirie shook his head and stared gloomily out of the window across the hot morning street. "I'd like to see them all kicked out as much as you."

"I never said——"

"But no one will take any notice of me. I haven't been in O.E.T.A. long enough to know the high-ups—and, anyway, I expect they'd all back Lemonfield up to the hilt."

Wandering impatiently about the picturesque smaller quays of the inner harbor on the following afternoon—the *Emperor Napoleon* had docked and was to sail next day—Pirie caught sight

160

of Christopher, William, Fortu and Silvana. They were sitting at the end of a low wooden jetty in a palm-edged backwater that was separated from the main harbor by a curved sandy spit. Beyond the jetty and moored to a leaning barnacle-encrusted old pile the *Princessa* and the *Columbia* and a couple of police dinghies lay motionless on the flat, oily green water. For a few moments Pirie stood in the shade of a faded blue boathouse, watching them with sour resentment. In light sailing clothes they sat on the flat iron bollards or sprawled on the jetty's edge, talking and lazily fishing, while Pepino squatted farther away, baiting hooks and coiling lines. They were speaking Italian, and to Pirie the accents and inflections of the Englishmen were indistinguishable from those of their companions. Gone completely native, he thought disgustedly. There's no difference between any of them; they even think the same way.

After a moment's irresolution he walked toward them, his stiff leg thumping on the hollow boards of the jetty. He was not greeted with pleasure, he noted, or even with any pretense of it. They knew he was going and he knew they were glad of it. Kellermann merely looked up and then bent with feigned concentration over his line while Summerson, who should at least have gotten to his feet in the presence of an officer, took no notice at all, presumably thinking that in the company of Kellermann such a formality was unnecessary. The Colonel's driver alone greeted him with an amused, cynical glance and a *"Buon' sera, Capitano."*

"Fishing, eh? Caught anything?"

"Not much."

There was a pause, and Pirie felt his resentment ebb abruptly while in its place stole inexplicably a calm, tolerant approval. He looked with sudden surprised appreciation at the scene around him—the sun-warped little jetty, Pepino's vivid orange shirt, Summerson's deft brown fingers unhooking a silver-blue fish, the girl's dark, intent face peering down into the still green depths, the shaggy palm-heads reared high against the blue sky. And beyond, the long view of the hot, peaceful harbor with the swooping white lateen sail of a dhow cutting across the sparkling translucent green as she made for the open sea. The long golden afternoon and this scene fixed in it, fired and glazed as on some great porcelain bowl. For the first and last time the island

161

laid its spell upon him, too. Enviously, the war—his war—forgotten, he thought, if I had been younger . . . if things had been different. . . .

He said mildly, "Well, I'm off tomorrow."

For a moment there was silence and he realized with a return of his former mood the barriers—intangible, but utterly uncrossable—that separated him from these people. It was not only the difference in age and upbringing and ideas, but the fact that they were islanders and he was not; they were the painted figures behind the glaze on the porcelain bowl and he stood outside.

Then Kellermann said with stilted formality, "I hope you will have a comfortable trip."

Pirie grunted. "I suppose *you're* here for good, eh?"

"For good?" He was on the defensive at once.

"For the duration, at any rate?"

"I certainly hope so. It suits *me* well enough."

"So I can see."

Kellermann flushed angrily. "For those who do their work properly," he said with prim venom, "and give satisfaction to their superiors Baressa is a pleasant enough place."

Pirie gave a shout of genuine laughter and slapped his thigh. "That's the spirit, old boy!" he declared. "You do your duty by Colonel Lemonfield and he'll look after you—God help you! I'll leave you to it, for this is the best place for you. Good-bye—and I do hope you come safely through the war. Good-bye, Summerson." He turned and stumped off across the jetty—at least he had thrown a stone into the still calmness of their afternoon.

"What an absolutely foul man!" exclaimed Christopher furiously and loudly enough, he hoped, for the retreating Pirie to hear. "Common as hell and just typical of what they make officers out of these days! The Colonel should have sent him back the moment he arrived! I knew he was a swine the moment I set eyes on him!"

16

IT was not until mid May, when the heat of Baressa's early summer was rising rapidly to its intolerable peak, that Colonel
Lemonfield interviewed his German prisoner. The reason for
this tardiness, though he would not admit it, was his indecision
concerning the man's future disposal. Every week from January
onward Dr. Valdonetti had reported a slow but certain improvement in the condition of the man who lay carefully secluded in
an empty wing of the old isolation hospital at Daldacara. Sooner
or later he would be completely recovered and then, presumably,
something would have to be done about him. It was all very
awkward. The Colonel had not reported his capture in the first
place, because to do so would have corroborated General Glasscraft's belief in a German attack and led to severe strictures on
the Administration's security measures—also, Euan was convinced that the man must die. Later, of course, a report on the
matter was almost out of the question. It would have meant a
most embarrassing explanation, probably before a Court of In-
quiry, and might well have cost the Colonel his position. Now
it was far too late. Short of murdering the man—not a course
compatible with Euan's idea of benevolent despotism—there
seemed no alternative but to keep him indefinitely. As Major
Naughton-Muirhead had remarked, if the war continued for long
enough he would die of old age.

By mid May Dr. Valdonetti stated that the German had made
as complete a recovery as was possible. Owing to the high amputa-
tion of his leg, an artificial limb was out of the question, but the
man had learned to move on two crutches and was now able to
be interviewed at the pleasure of the Governor.

Euan had not seen the prisoner since that afternoon many
months before when with James, Christopher, and Balla—the
latter escorted by two guards of the Banda—he had pushed his
way into that ruinous, malodorous hut. It was due both to the re-
pulsive state of the German on that occasion and the nagging

nuisance of his undesired presence since then that Euan had taken
no opportunity of visiting him in the old hospital where he lay.
It was therefore with a sudden quickening of interest that on
this early summer morning he received Brinsmead's information
that Baines had brought the man to the Palace as instructed.

"All right, Brinsmead, show them in."

"Very good, sir."

Euan leaned forward slightly as the doors were opened and
Baines entered and saluted, followed by Dr. Valdonetti in his
white coat, assisting with one arm a broad, limping man of me-
dium height who tapped uncertainly across the parquet on two
crutches.

The approach of these three across the long, shining yellow
floor of the office was slow enough for Euan to study the German
carefully. In this heavy, youngish man—his age might have been
somewhere in the late twenties or early thirties—it was only
by stretching his imagination to the limit that he could recognize
any resemblance to that dying scarecrow of eight months before. Dressed in curious olive-brown drill shirt and trousers and
a belt with a heavy embossed clasp instead of a buckle, he really
seemed to have made a complete and miraculous recovery. His
missing leg gave him an oddly lopsided appearance, but his
battered face had a healthy color beneath a deep tan—he had
been allowed out in the walled hospital grounds for the last
month—and his coarse dark hair was neatly cut and combed.

There was something ineffably foreign about that face, thought
Euan. It was far more Oriental—more Slav—than Aryan German. Somehow that big head with the high, flat cheekbones, the
thick Negroid lips, the small, wide-set, almost colorless eyes, was
oddly akin to the harsh Slavonic skull of Captain Zvengetzov. Presumably the man was a German, but he looked much more Euan's
idea of an eastern Pole.

When the little group had at last reached his desk Euan briefly
indicated the chair before it and the German, panting slightly,
was lowered into it by Baines and Dr. Valdonetti, who then took
up their places at each side and a little behind him. At close quarters the Colonel decided that there was something quite horrible
about the man, and because of it an indefinable feeling of unease
pervaded him for the whole of the ensuing interview. The Ger-

man sat there, four feet away across the great desk, bent a little forward, breathing heavily and eyeing the Colonel with a sort of ghastly conciliatory grin—a half-crushed snake at the mercy of its opponent, but still possessing a hopeless deadly will to strike. If he smelled of anything it must have been only the clean smell of hospital soap and freshly ironed clothes, but to Euan's imagination there seemed to hang about him that charnel miasma of corruption and decay that had nauseated him that afternoon months before. His stomach heaved slightly.

Then, with a slight shake of his head, as if to free himself of these ridiculous, imaginative sensations, he drew a pad of thick bright-blue Palace notepaper toward him and picked up a pencil.

"You appear to have made a very satisfactory recovery." He spoke in Italian and the German answered in the same language, speaking in a low, pleasant voice with the same careful fluency and grammatical correctitude as the Colonel himself.

"I have. Thanks to the skill and patience of Dr. Valdonetti." The soft voice, denoting in its every tone a high degree of intelligence and civilization, was so wildly at variance with that uncouth low-browed face, marked for life with the livid scars and gashes of the sharp coral rocks, that Euan blinked with surprise.

"H'm—I'm glad to hear it," he lied. "You are extraordinarily lucky to be alive in the circumstances."

"I am, indeed." The German's blubber lips writhed into a smile and he waited.

"Yes. Well, now—ah—Captain Stralowski"—Euan refused to use the politico-military title of Hauptsturmführer—"I am going to ask you a few questions. You have already been questioned by Captain Baines and I have a copy of your answers here. I intend to go over some of them again."

"Very well."

Euan looked at the man again—a sharp, intent glance. "Now," he said briskly, "you came to the island on 28th May, 1940."

"I did."

"And reported to Colonel Giordano on that day?"

"On that night."

"What were your instructions from your superiors?"

"To report on the island and to suggest whether or not it

165

could be—or was likely to be—defended in time of attack. I was also to report on the Governor, the Administration in general, and the garrison."

"Is that all?"

"At the time that was all. Later, after the British occupation, I was ordered to remain on the island and report when possible on everything that went on. Your Administration, Colonel Lemonfield—and yourself, too. Should it interest you to know it I reported very favorably on both—from the British point of view of course."

"Don't be impertinent!" snapped Euan, assuming his coldest, sternest frown, before which many an unfortunate had trembled. The German smiled slightly, quite unabashed.

"Was I being impertinent? I did not think so. If, however, I have unintentionally offended you, I am sorry."

Euan glared at him in amazement. From a captured German officer he had expected either formal military respect—after all, the man was a junior officer, only a captain—or arrogant, half-veiled insolence, which he would have well known how to deal with. He had not been prepared for this air of almost friendly equality, the weary, kindly air of condescension with which this battered man answered his questions. He tried once more.

"You had no other motives for remaining here?"

"None."

"It seems a rather odd task for an officer of the Waffen S.S."

"We are a rather odd corps, you know."

"You were able to communicate with the mainland, yet we have found no trace of a radio of any sort. Had you one?"

"No. After the British occupation of the island I was, of course, unable to use the radio station."

"Of course," assented Euan impatiently. "Then how did you communicate?"

"I can't tell you that, I'm afraid," said the German, as if he were denying some adult knowledge to a child still too young to be enlightened.

"I insist on an answer!"

The German smiled amusedly and eased his remaining leg before answering. "Colonel, you are certainly aware of the Geneva Convention regarding interrogation of prisoners of war. I have given the Captain my name, rank and number. I will repeat them

166

to you if you wish. Beyond that information, as you very well know, I am not bound to answer any questions."

The Colonel raised his eyebrows. "The Geneva Convention quoted by the German S.S.—this is indeed finding Saul amongst the prophets!" The German gave a short chuckle of genuine appreciation. "But in any case," continued the Colonel, "you have already answered several questions, according to the Captain's report, which I have here."

"Yes, I have. I feel that my unhappy situation when I was captured and the gratitude—the very real gratitude, I assure you, Colonel Lemonfield—that I feel toward you for being instrumental in saving my life makes it pardonable for me to explain my reasons for being on this island."

"H'm." Euan was not impressed with this line of argument. "You were little better than a spy, then? In fact, you were a spy— you have admitted it, have you not?"

"Oh come, Colonel!" The German almost grinned, displaying a set of large yellow teeth. "I was a soldier cut off from my base by fortune of war. I admit I was not in uniform when captured, but that was because I was very ill and in bed. My uniform was with me—in fact, I'm wearing as much of it as the climate permits at present. No, you can't seriously believe me to be a spy. You could not prove it."

"On the contrary, I believe I could prove it quite sufficiently to have the necessary action taken!" countered Euan sharply.

"The Geneva Conventions——"

"Please don't quote the Geneva Conventions to me! I happen to have read them."

"Oh, well, one can have anybody shot for anything in this war," said the German, losing interest. He glanced boredly out of the window.

Euan, for once completely at a loss, started to make unmeaning notes on his writing pad. His mind worked rapidly but unavailingly in an attempt to discover a way of wrenching at least some acknowledgment of his position from this peculiar prisoner. But he was hampered by the extraordinary sensations which Stralowski evoked within him and which were so strong that they seemed to clog his usually swift brain in a clammy fog. Surprise, irritation, amusement and even a grudging admiration—they were all there. But the strongest sensation was one of repulsion and—yes, almost fear. There was something deeply sinister about this mutilated man. Before he had even opened his mouth, while Euan was yet expecting, if not obsequiousness, at least the formal respect of a junior to a senior officer, he had felt something of this repellent power. And as soon as the man had spoken he had realized that for the first time for many years he was confronted with someone as clever, as intelligent, and as strong-willed as himself. He had procured no fresh information from the German and he had been openly thwarted in front of Baines and Valdonetti. Two things were clear at any rate. The man was not going to answer any further questions, and he was both formidable and dangerous. Formidable and dangerous? A hopeless cripple, unarmed and thousands of miles from his own countrymen? It seemed ridiculous. And yet . . . and yet. . . .

Euan looked up. Though inwardly extremely annoyed, he spoke with a guarded friendliness, a condescending waiving of the differences in their ranks and present positions.

"Well, Stralowski, I don't think there's any point in prolonging this interview any further in the circumstances. You are technically right in your assertion that you are not compelled to answer questions—though you should consider yourself lucky that I don't believe in resorting to painful methods of coercion in the notorious manner of the corps to which you belong. I will tell you candidly that I am not completely satisfied with your explanation of your presence on Baressa, but in the circumstances I suppose I shall have to accept it. Now, as to your future. It is not at present convenient to send you back to the mainland, and you will therefore remain under guard in the hospital, unless that accommodation is required for other purposes. If you behave yourself we shall do our best to make things as comfortable for you as we can." Euan eyed him narrowly. "You seem to me, Stralowski, a young man of considerable force and ability. I warn you that if you are detected in conversing with civilians or attempting to communicate with any unauthorized person, or making any sort of attempt to arrange to leave the island, the consequences will be unpleasant for you. Do you understand?"

"Oh, yes, perfectly."

"Good—then don't let that happen. You had better continue to wear that uniform, but without badges of any sort. We are a long way from hostilities and I don't particularly wish to advertise your presence here. Is there anything further you wish to say?"

The German unhurriedly picked up his crutches. "No, I don't think so—except to thank you once more for saving my life. I am sorry if I have been unhelpful in the matter of answering your questions, but of course you realize that I am still technically under the command of my own service and must not infringe standing orders."

"Yes, yes, I understand that. Very well then, you may go. Good morning."

"Good morning, Colonel."

"Valdonetti, take him out. Baines, you stay here. I want a word with you."

Euan remained silent until Stralowski had shuffled out on the steadying arm of the doctor. Then he threw his pencil into the ormulu tray and leaned back in his chair.

"A particularly odious person, Baines!"

"A 'hugly brute,' sir, as Mr. Jorrocks says"—Baines grinned—"but he's nice enough to talk to."

"He is not! I thoroughly object to being addressed in a tone that one can only describe as 'maty' by a junior officer of the German S.S. I suppose he *is* a German? He doesn't look it."

"Nor he is, sir—at least only by naturalization. He's half Pole, half Latvian by birth."

"A horrible mixture! But I thought that fellow was a Slav the moment I set eyes on him." Euan drew Baines' notes of the earlier interrogation across the desk. They told little. "He says he knows nothing of Captain Rossi of the *Bina*?"

"Yes, sir."

"And that he only lived at the Balla estate because it was remote from here and Balla was a good Fascist?"

"Yes, sir."

"H'm, we know that already. There's nothing we don't know here. However, I'm still not really satisfied. You must keep him secluded from civilians and if you see as much of him as possible you may find out something more."

"Yes, sir—that's what I thought."

Euan frowned. "He's dangerous, Baines, I'm sure. He must be kept under just as close guard as would be the case if he were not crippled."

"Very good, sir."

169

"You will be entirely responsible for him." He paused. "In the circumstances, I think we can now release Balla. He's to go straight back to his farm and not to leave it except to report to Police Headquarters once a fortnight. All right, that's all. Tell Sergeant Brinsmead I want him."

"Yes sir." Baines saluted and left.

Taking some files out of his tray, Euan began to examine the letters and minutes clipped to their fronts for his attention. Brinsmead came in, bearing more files, and the routine of the morning was recommenced. Papers were signed, visitors shown in and out on official business, the two telephones rang from time to time as departments requested instructions or clarifications, orders were drafted, court proceedings perused, returns checked. Yet through all this the face of Stralowski still hung and hovered at the back of Euan's mind—ugly and scarred, the small pale eyes coldly expressionless, the wide thick mouth twisted into a mirthless smile.

An uncanny feeling that he had been hoodwinked, a vague foreboding for the future lay over him like a thin, intangible cobweb of doubt. His personal clerks and secretaries declared that the Governor was working up for a storm. The branches eagerly discussed the question of whose fault it was and which of the departments was likely to bear the brunt when it eventually broke. The more timorous wished gloomily that the Municipality would soothe their master's mood with another laudatory banquet.

17

A MONTH later in the Headquarters of the O.E.T.A. two high-ranking officers were discussing a reallocation of personnel. The remains of the Afrika Corps had surrendered at Cape Bon and the whole of Italian North Africa was in the hands of the British. Soon, it was assumed, Sicily and perhaps much of the Italian mainland would share the same fate.

"I'm not really very keen," one of the two red-tabbed officers remarked as he flicked through a heavy file. "No, I can't think in the circumstances——"

"Isn't it rather a question of seniority?" asked the other, who, with his back to the room, was gazing out of the window.

"Oh, there *is* that, of course. But——"

"I thought he was earmarked for something like this."

"He was—yes, he was, but that's a long time ago. I agree the man's good at his job—very. He's supposed to be brilliant. The trouble is, he doesn't get on with the Army, so I understand. That's a failing I've seen many of our people acquire if left on their own too long. They begin to associate themselves too closely with the territories they rule and resent the military as inconvenient intruders. Well, you know all about that, of course."

"Yes, but I still think we should give him a chance. He's done spectacularly well where he is."

"Perhaps. But I can't agree. He'd be far closer to the vital theaters of action and if he really *is* the prickly customer I understand him to be he'd be jumping up and down on the Army's toes like a damned trip hammer every hour of the day. We'd have nothing but complaints and possibly courts-martial and recriminations all around. No, thank you! I've got two other fellows' names here and they're both much more in the picture—much more the Army's cup of tea—than your friend on his little island."

The officer at the window turned with a chuckle. "Good Lord, he's not my friend! I don't know the man from Adam. I've seen his reports, and they're all they should be and written in beautiful English—a sort of sham-Augustan style, but perfect in its way. He can't have gone completely native."

"Good. Well, he'd better stay where he is and continue to report in beautiful English. I know it's a bit hard on the poor man, but we've got to think of the efficiency of the Organization. Anyway, he probably doesn't want to leave his blessed island—he's never hinted at a desire for something bigger. We'll promote him and see if we can't get him some small recognition of his exquisite prose—a medal of some sort, perhaps."

So, one hot, damp, steamy day of July when the seasonal rains were at their peak and the great rumbling blue clouds lowered over the plateau, Lieutenant Colonel Lemonfield became a full colonel and received the O.B.E. Everyone congratulated him profusely, and the Mayor sent a huge bouquet of tuberoses to the Palace with a card of felicitations from the Municipality. A dinner party was given at the Villa to which all the Colonel's friends were invited, and after a magnificent meal of thirteen courses he sat, surrounded by the wealthy estate owners and businessmen whom he had carefully wooed ever since he came to the island, basking in an atmosphere redolent of luxury and success and listening to their suave compliments.

Next day, as the rain cataracted down on the sodden city, hissing and bouncing on the murky water of the harbor, Euan sat liverishly in his office and listened to Baines' reasons for requesting Mrs. Tamminetto's reemployment in the Police Headquarters.

"She's the only one who really understands the paperwork and at the same time can get proper cooperation out of the Carabinieri, sir. They like her—heaven knows why, but they do. They've been suggesting we should reemploy her ever since I took over."

"Have they indeed?"

"Yes sir. And there's another thing. I just haven't got time to do the police returns and reports myself—what with the customs to run as well. Sergeant Brinsmead's been complaining."

"Good God, Baines! Surely you know by now that Brinsmead *always* complains. It's a matter of principle with him. He'll be complaining on the Day of Judgment for inaccuracies in the entries of the Recording Angel or that he hasn't done them in triplicate or something. If he's only been complaining to *you* there's nothing to worry about."

"Still, I'd like to have her back, sir," repeated Baines stubbornly, "if it's all the same to you."

A knock on the door was followed by the leisurely entry of Major Naughton-Muirhead. "May I come in, Euan? I've received a most extraordinary telegram. Good morning, Baines."

"Good morning, sir."

"Baines wants the Tamminetto woman back in the police office," announced Euan, "if it's all the same to us."

"Are you feeling quite well, Baines?" The Major looked him up and down in feigned bewilderment. "Do you know what it is you ask?"

172

But irony was lost on the Police Chief. "It'd only be for the paperwork, sir."

"The Police Gasoline Account—I know." James shuddered.

"I'd see she didn't try to pull any fast ones."

"The whole reason," Euan declared wearily, "why the Administration went through the trouble of getting that fellow Pirie and the disappointment of employing him and the embarrassment of dismissing him was solely in order to get rid of this woman. Now if I agree——"

"For goodness sake don't do anything of the sort!" interrupted James hurriedly. "You know what——"

"Yes, yes, James, but Baines is in charge now. If he wants her—if he really is sure——"

"I am, sir."

"All right. But I personally am not going to sack her again. If she comes back, she comes back for good. She'll hang around your neck like the Old Man of the Sea and stay there. On your own head be it."

"I'll manage her, sir. Thank you, sir." Baines grinned broadly at James, who was looking extremely put out, saluted, and left.

"I think that very ill-advised Euan, I must say. I——"

"Nonsense, nonsense!" soothed the Colonel. "Baines will manage her—he's no fool. If he wants her back he's got a very good reason for it, I'm sure. He'll keep her under his thumb. Now, James, what's your extraordinary news?"

The Major took a cigar from the big silver box on the desk, clipped it, and lit it before replying. "Do you recall the parting remarks of that amiable old General who visited us last October? Remarks about building fortifications and strongpoints?"

"I do. Yes?"

"Well, a company of Central African Engineer troops is on its way here to build them. It's due to arrive next week."

"But good God, James, this is fantastic! There must be a mistake. They couldn't want to build fortifications *now*. The entire mainland's free of enemy!"

"Here's the telegram." James laid the flimsy orange paper on the desk before the Colonel.

"Yes, by God, I believe they must be coming! How utterly ridiculous—and typically Army! So this is the way they waste the taxpayers' money, is it?"

173

"Not our taxpayers'."

"Well, really, it's too absurd. However, if they come they come. Tell Brinsmead to find them somewhere to live, will you? I'll just have to see they don't do any damage. I can't very well send them straight back again, I suppose?"

"Not very well."

"No."

"Huh!" grunted Brinsmead morosely. "Live? Why should I find them somewhere to live? Do you think I'm a house agent, sir, or what? Anyway, there isn't anywhere for them to live." He sat under the glare of a bare electric light—even in fine weather his office was dark and during the rains he had the light permanently on—behind his high-stacked multiple wire trays and stared through them at James like a bad-tempered ginger cat in a cage.

"Well, Brinsmead, they can't just sit out in the rain, can they?"

"They can for all I care, sir. It's immaterial to me what they do."

"I'm sure it is. But the Colonel wants you to find them accommodation."

"It's impossible—there isn't any," growled Brinsmead, and then in the same breath, "They'd better go into the old Cinema, I suppose—there's nowhere else. The roof leaks, but they're engineers, so I suppose they can mend it."

Christopher sat in his small office in the barracks, staring blankly out at the empty, rain-soaked parade ground. A few of his soldiers sat huddled unhappily under dirty blankets in the arched doorways of their long, low barrack rooms, messily eating dark maize porridge, their staple diet, out of smoke-blackened tins with their fingers. A splendid sight on parade, they were extraordinarily slovenly, uncouth, and sullen at all other times. Christopher disliked them impartially, but with indifference.

After a further half hour of routine office work his duties for the day were completed—at any rate to his own satisfaction. Christopher decided to go home and, having done so, wished he had not. There was nothing to do, and he mooned about the oddly shaped, overdecorated dusky rooms, peering out of arched and pillared windows at the great walls of dripping tangled greenery that surrounded his strange dwelling. The ceaseless hiss

174

and rustle of rain pervaded the Casa dei Fiori; wherever one went one could not escape it, drumming on the many cupolas of the roof, rattling on the stained-glass skylights, gushing through gargoyle-mouthed gutters, bouncing on the marble flags of the circular courtyard—everywhere the sound of water.

Zeki pattered in and laid lunch in the dining room. He had run in from the backyard and the wet imprints of his bare feet glistened across the mosaic floor. Christopher ate without appetite and wondered wearily when the rains would cease and he would be able to meet Silvana again. They had been meeting regularly at agreed places, generally somewhere along the shore, for several months, but now, with the entire island covered with its gray pall of vertically falling water, all that had had to come to a stop.

Of course, he could have made a pretext to visit the Police Headquarters—but then there was Baines, and Christopher distrusted him. Baines was too much of a policeman, too quick to notice things—and probably too much in the confidence of the Colonel. He resolved to get to know Baines better; there was no reason why they should not be friends. It was, he realized, probably his own fault that they were not, but in the days when Baines arrived every stranger in uniform had been a potential enemy. But they had found common ground for the first time in their dislike of Pirie, that devout worshiper at the military shrine. Their motives for this had probably differed, but he had felt a genuine warmth for the genial, grinning secretive Yorkshireman on the day that he had replaced Pirie in the police office.

He sighed, and, pushing his chair away, wandered out onto the long veranda. Outside the thick man-made jungle rustled and dripped, pressing hungrily ever closer toward the house. The Colonel had suggested only recently the desirability of setting a squad of black soldiers armed with machetes to clear at least a broad entrance drive of the crowding tangled stems and vines and cut the pressing vegetation back from the Casa itself. Christopher remembered how, looking at the dense mass distastefully, he had said, "I don't know how you can bear to live in the center of such a wilderness. It's—it's almost disgusting." But Christopher had done nothing in the end. He liked the feeling of being surrounded by that impenetrable flower forest. In his first days on the island it had seemed a friendly, darkly screening guard against the world. Its very inmates—the bright parrots, noisy mongoose, and slithering snakes—had seemed sentinels posted to warn off intruders. Now that three long island years had interposed their silent sunlit hours between him and the dark past he no longer really needed these outward symbols of refuge, but he had been obscurely loath to have even one tree felled, to disturb even a single bird, and so he had evaded the Colonel's suggestion and his private jungle remained.

At half past two Toki dived out of the overgrown path and up the marble steps between the wet statuary. She wore a gleaming scarlet mackintosh and carried a small leather suitcase and a long parcel wrapped in sacking. Christopher sighed inwardly, but disguised his feelings with a surprisingly convincing show of pleasure. He helped her off with her mackintosh and kissed her with every appearance of ardent passion.

"I've brought you some more shirts, *carissimo*," Toki announced breathlessly as soon as Christopher had released her from his embrace, "all like this." She indicated the gaily flowered cotton two-piece she was wearing, her almond eyes glinting up at him with admiring pleasure in the greenish gloom.

"I can't wear shirts made of that!"

"Ah, but you can, my own! You will look very, very beautiful."

"The Colonel won't think so."

"Ah, no? And it is for the Colonel that you dress? You want to make him fall in love with you, yes?" The Colonel was the only subject upon which ever Toki displayed anger or irritation. So much had been vetoed or postponed because the Colonel might not like it. She could only come covertly to the Casa because, while all the island knew of their relationship, Christopher thought that the Colonel would prefer them to maintain at least a semblance of discretion. She must never be seen in Christopher's company outside the house. She must never speak about him to her friends. The money he gave her she must not flaunt as she would have liked for fear of causing a scandal that would embarrass the Colonel's Administration. And Christopher even viewed the clothes she made him with an eye to their effect on Colonel Lemonfield!

"It is only," she announced indignantly, "because he himself is so small and thin and—and"—she put a wealth of scorn into her voice—"so *pallido*, that he is envious of you, Christopher, my beautiful one!"

"Nonsense!" Christopher grinned and pressed his thumb gently on her nose, squashing it flat to her face. It was a gesture he always employed when they disagreed, and it never failed to restore his quaint little mistress to gay good humor. "What's that?" He pointed to the long thin parcel that Toki had left lying on top of the broad balustrade.

"This—ah! Yes, I nearly forget. For you, too, Christopher. There—you open it." Picking it up, she placed it triumphantly in his hands.

Unwrapping a yard or two of canvas, Christopher found he was holding a long two-handed Japanese sword in a lacquered scabbard. He looked with amused surprise from the heavy shining weapon with its thick silk-corded handle to the smiling expectant face of his mistress.

"But—what's this for?"

"For you, Christopher, my dear one. It is a proper samurai sword. It belonged to my uncle—oh, a long time ago! He was not a noble, you understand, so he could not wear it, but he always kept it. Look—yes, pull it out—you see how sharp? And look, here is the *tsuba*—the little piece to guard the hands. It is of *shakudo*—copper and gold—yes—and here these little flowers, chrysanthemums, you know, the Japanese emblem. You like it —yes? My uncle could not wear it, for he was not a noble, but you——"

"I'm not noble either," denied Christopher hurriedly.

"But an English officer—you can wear it. It is nicer than your own, isn't it, my lovely one?"

"It is very nice, Toki." He bent to kiss her, laughing into her adoring black eyes. "It's a beautiful sword—but I can't wear it. I really can't."

"Because of—Colonel Lemonfield?"

"No—well, yes, that's one reason of course. He'd have a fit if he saw me on parade with this. But, anyway, I couldn't possibly wear it—don't you see, it's quite the wrong *sort* of sword. Look —we'll hang it up here, that will look nice, won't it?"

"Well—" said Toki disappointedly, but Christopher kissed her again and, taking her hand, led the way into his bedroom.

177

18

CONTRARY to expectation, the Central African Engineers—when they eventually arrived, a fortnight late—were totally unlike any of the previous military visitors to Baressa. From the first they endeared themselves to their younger island compatriots by their almost spectacular inefficiency and lack of any sort of military *esprit* or discipline. The state of confusion on the rain-swept docks as they disembarked was indescribable. They had lost their advance party on the way to the coast and with it most of their N.C.O.s. They had also sailed without their officers' baggage and they even managed to drop a considerable amount of their technical equipment into the harbor as they landed. No one, least of all their Commanding Officer, knew how many of them there were supposed to be, and for two hours they milled raucously about the commercial quays and eventually set fire to the customs sheds in a vain attempt to make some tea. To make matters worse, an irate Captain Zvengetzov informed Baines with a sort of sneering nonchalance that the after hold of the transport was full of naval mines sent on board by General Glasscraft's instructions for the defense of the harbor. Baines at once ordered the ship out into the roadstead, and it departed with two or three dozen African Engineers who had reembarked in despair.

Christopher, impelled by a morbid fascination to view the arriving troops—whose officers, he felt sure, would be further editions of Captain Pirie—walked briskly down to the docks through the thin rain. He was wearing a smart pale mackintosh over his uniform, carrying a cane, and had his hat at a haughty angle. He had a feeling that attack, in the form of an aggressive display of military bearing, would be the best sort of defense for the future. He watched, from the shelter of the Bar Regina Elena, the erratic disembarkation of the Africans with an expression of the sternest disapproval.

"I say, are you in charge here?"

Christopher looked around to see a man at his elbow. A tall, slender, unshaven young man, wearing a grubby pink shirt lacking several buttons and gaping open almost to the waist to reveal a bony chest, and faded khaki slacks that appeared to have come in recent contact with a good deal of wet green paint. He gazed doubtfully at Christopher through horn-rimmed glasses and with one hand pushed the lank, rain-wet black hair from his narrow forehead.

"Good Lord, no! Certainly not!" disclaimed Christopher hurriedly. "Captain Baines is."

"That's the little Yorkshireman, I suppose? Not that quaint foreign sailor type?"

"No, no. That would be our Port Pilot—and he's in one of his bad moods today, I think."

"Well, your Captain Baines doesn't like us much either, I'm afraid. Some of the men set fire to the customs houses and he seemed to take umbrage."

"Yes, he would—he's the Chief Customs Officer."

The young man shivered dismally and thrust his hands into his pockets. "Oh, that accounts for it then. God, isn't it a bloody day? Is it always like this?"

"No—only for another week or so."

"I suppose we might be just about sorted out by then," grunted the Engineer officer morosely.

"It *is* a bit of a shambles, isn't it?" suggested Christopher mildly as he glanced toward the yelling docks where a free fight appeared to be underway and the Port Pilot, attempting to dock the *Anna Gabriella*, was spitting Balkan curses at Baines through a megaphone.

"Not for us it isn't! God, you should have seen the embarkation the other end! God!" The Engineer spat with a gloomy pride on to the wet roadway. "There's a —ing little Army booklet called *Embarkations and Disembarkations*—ever seen it? No? You're bloody lucky. Some diseased sod of a staff officer from Area sent me the thing a couple of months ago—to prepare for this." He jerked his head toward the milling men, stumbling and shouting over the haphazard piles of equipment. "I actually read the —ing thing, too!" he said aggrievedly. "You can see what a lot of —ing good it is! After this bloody war's over I'll take it to the War Office and I'll find the current C.I.G.S. and I'll * * * *."

Christopher recoiled slightly at the obscenity of the following

179

remarks, but he concurred broadly with the sentiment expressed.

"Come and have a drink," he suggested.

In a few moments they were leaning against the zinc-covered bar near the tall, gleaming chromium coffee machine while Mario, the burly proprietor, served them with rum and pineapple juice.

Christopher introduced himself. "I'm supposed to be commanding the garrison here. I've got a company of blacks up at the barracks."

"Blacks? Like ours?"

"No," replied Christopher firmly, "not like yours. Mario! Two more."

"My name's Paige," announced the Engineer sternly. "I'm a lord."

"What?"

"I'm Lord Paige. I tell you now because the others would tell you later in any case, and then it looks as if I were trying to hide it out of shame or pride or modesty or something. Our second-in-command—a man called Collis—once introduced me to some stray old staff colonel he found in a club and then quoted Belloc. You know—'I do not think you want to hear about this unimportant Peer.' The old fool turned out to be a friend of my father's—God rot him—and was most upset. So I tell most people myself now. I hate being misconstrued." He surveyed Christopher with a grave, horn-rimmed gaze. "I always try to make myself plain on all occasions."

"So it would appear." Christopher eyed the newcomer with amusement. "Who's your C.O.?"

"Major Sherwood. He's a dear old thing—quite clueless and always drunk as an owl. He's an old poppet, really. Who's yours?"

"Well, I haven't got one actually. The boss here is the Senior Civil Affairs Officer—a Colonel Lemonfield."

"Is *he* a poppet?"

"No—no. I shouldn't call him that. He's certainly not at all clueless—quite the reverse—and nobody's ever seen him drunk."

Paige looked sympathetic. "A bit of a bastard, eh?"

"Oh, no," replied Christopher quickly, rather resentfully. "He can be extraordinarily nice when he wants to. He's always been very good to me."

The Engineer ordered two more double rums—he seemed,

180

thought Christopher, to be following faithfully in the footsteps of his major—and turned his dark, absurdly serious gaze back to his new acquaintance. "Is this colonel of yours a military type? He shouldn't be. O.E.T.A. aren't generally."

"No, he's not at all military. His opinion of the Army is abysmally low."

"I think the —ing Army's * * * * myself."

"So do I," agreed Christopher wholeheartedly, and their friendship was sealed.

At the inevitable dinner party at the Villa that night Colonel Lemonfield and his officers made formal acquaintance with their visitors. Formal, perhaps, was hardly the word, for the appearance and behavior of the Engineer officers was informal to a degree hitherto unexperienced within the dignified walls of the Villa. None of them had changed their damp, dirty clothes since the morning, and they explained unworriedly that what little personal luggage had survived the mishaps of the journey was on the ship which still lay, full of mines, in the roads.

Their commander, Major Sherwood, was a fat, vacuous little man with a floppy white moustache, watery blue eyes, and a severe natural impediment in his speech, which was rendered all the more unintelligible by being very fast and seldom having any direct bearing on the subject under discussion. His addiction to the bottle was so obvious that even in his presence it was a matter of jocular comment among his subordinates. The second-in-command was a big plump Irishman, Captain Lycett-Collis, whose round red face, crowned by an unruly mass of auburn curls, was continually creased into a simpering grin. He invariably took it upon himself to answer all questions addressed to his superior, which he did in such a gay, good-humored way that it might have been taken for the most natural thing in the world. Of the two juniors Lord Paige was the elder by a year or two, while his colleague, Lieutenant Ventham—equally thin, shabby, and ironic—possessed a sudden screeching laugh with which, being a taciturn young man, he frequently startled large numbers of persons.

On Christopher's arrival he found the four newcomers sitting with the Colonel, the Major, and Captain Baines in the blue reception room where Giordano had made his last speech as Governor three years before. Lord Paige greeted him as a long-lost friend and, forestalling the Colonel, to that officer's evident annoyance, introduced him to the others.

"God, Kellermann, what a bloody day we've had! You've no idea! It took all the afternoon to get the men into their billets. They're in a —ing Cinema, you know."

"Yes, I understood that's where they were going."

"I expect they'll burn the bloody place down—but I don't suppose it matters."

"On the contrary!" interjected the Colonel, who had listened to these last remarks. "It will matter a great deal! I trust they don't do anything of the sort. Are they in the habit of burning down their own quarters?"

"Yes, they are, sir, actually. They don't do it on purpose, of course, but it's making their continual tea. You see——"

"Baines!"

"Sir?"

"Get on to the telephone and tell Brinsmead to send some extra fire extinguishers to the Cinema at once."

"Yes sir."

"I'm hungry," announced Lieutenant Ventham suddenly in the awkward pause that followed. "I haven't had any breakfast or lunch."

"I had lunch in a quaint little restaurant with a couple of young signalmen," remarked Captain Lycett-Collis. "William and Texas, they called each other. I borrowed a quid from William—otherwise I haven't a bean."

"I hoped *you* would invite me to lunch"—Paige glanced reproachfully at Christopher—"but you didn't, and I had only enough money to buy a bag of peanuts from a boy on the quay. Not digestible or filling."

"Sherry had a glass of gin for lunch—didn't you, you old dear?" Ventham smiled at his major, who nodded mildly and muttered something behind his moustache.

"What's that?"

"He says," interpreted Captain Lycett-Collis, "that he *did* have a glass of gin for lunch."

"I think," said the Colonel with unnatural calm, "that you would all probably like your dinner now. Let us go in."

Conversation at dinner was reduced to a minimum by the

necessity of gratifying the Engineers' ravenous appetites. The two lieutenants in particular ate as if they were never going to stop.

Euan once attempted to address Major Sherwood, but the result was not encouraging. "Will your visit be a long one, Major, do you suppose?"

The old man drained his glass for the eighth time and looked around expectantly at Zubier, who at once filled it again.

"Long time? Long time?" he was understood to mutter. "Yesh, I expectsh we will be a long time, Colonel. Yesh. You shee, we've losht a lot of shtuff, one way and other—lotsh. We'll have to shend for more. That'll take time. Yesh. And then there'sh the Advansh Party—we losht them, too, you know. They musht be shent here—or perhapsh they's better go back to Bashe—eh, Fred? I shaid perhapsh the Advansh Party should go back to Bashe?"

"Yes, Sherry, I heard the first time." Captain Lycett-Collis lifted a piled fork to his mouth. "I think they'd better." He turned to the Colonel. "Well, sir, as the Major says, we'll be here a long time, I expect, what with one thing and another."

"How long do you think?"

"Can't say, sir, really."

"Six months?"

"Oh, longer than that."

"Nine, perhaps?"

"Oh, I don't know—longer than that, I expect. A year or two, perhaps."

"That's the idea, Colley!" chimed in Lord Paige. "We'll stay here for a few years—anyway, till the bloody war's over. I think I'm going to like it here. Christopher—that *is* your name, isn't it? I hate calling people by their surnames—please pass the salt."

Major Sherwood suddenly leaned toward the Colonel and said something with great speed and indistinctness. Then he sat back in his chair and gazed up at the ceiling.

"I beg your pardon?"

"He's asking you if you'll lend him five pounds," explained Captain Lycett-Collis, "for a day or two only, you know."

Euan was taken aback, but replied, "Certainly—yes, of course."

Major Sherwood nodded vigorously and said something in which the words "very kind" and "bed for the night" were just distinguishable. On a sudden surmise Euan turned to the Captain.

"You *are* fixed up all right in your quarters, aren't you? My Sergeant Brinsmead arranged for two houses to be put at your disposal in the Via della Costa. They're rather small, but we thought they would do for the present, until you know where your work is going to take you. One of them was used by an officer who was commanding the police here for a few months last year."

The Captain shook his auburn head firmly. "No, sir. Know nothing about it. Nobody told me anything."

"But——"

"Wait a minute!" interjected Paige, with his mouth full. "There was a young chap—Italian, I think—who spoke a bit of English—why, good Lord! That's him over there in that picture!"

"That's my driver," remarked the Colonel coldly. "Well, we're getting somewhere at last. What did he say or do?"

"Well, he had a big green boxcar and he said something about houses and our baggage. I didn't follow him quite at the time— some of the men were having a fight with pick helves and I was trying to stop them—but I sort of understood he had a place for our equipment. Anyway, I saw Peter stuffing it into the boxcar. What did you do with it, Pete?"

"Took it to those two houses. I went with him. Nasty little places they were, too."

"I beg your——" began the Colonel angrily.

"You *are* a bloody fool, Pete," interrupted Captain Lycett-Collis genially. "Do you mean to say you've put all the technical stuff in the houses we were meant to sleep in?"

"It had better be got out at once," said the Colonel hurriedly, foreseeing an unpleasant possibility. "I'll give orders for it to be——"

"I shouldn't sir—not in the dark."

"Why not?"

Ventham let out a sudden high-pitched, harsh laugh. "A lot of it's dynamite," he said, and relapsed into blushing silence.

"Oh, I see. Well, that's very awkward. I think perhaps you'd all better spend the night here," suggested the Colonel in a voice from which cordiality was noticeably lacking.

"Paige and Ventham could come and stay with me, sir," offered Christopher suddenly, "if you agree."

Euan shot him a grateful glance. "Yes, I think that's an excellent idea."

"I *should* have liked to have stayed here," remarked Paige regretfully. "I think it's a lovely house."

"You go where you're told, you precocious peer," retorted Lycett-Collis. "The Colonel doesn't want you here and I don't blame him. I——"

"There's one thing I think we should get cleared up," said James decisively from the foot of the table. "At present there is a ship standing hove to just outside the harbor with its stern crammed full of mines—at least, the Port Pilot says that's the case. No one knew about it until it had been four hours in the docks, and I assume that if an accident had happened—doubtless in a unit of your sort accidents are very well guarded against, but nonetheless they might occur—if, as I say, an accident had happened and the mines had gone off, considerable damage would have been done to the docks."

"To the docks?" Ventham laughed caustically. "Crikey, the whole bloody town would have been flattened!"

"The town!" It was Paige's turn. "Why, the whole island would have rocked! Just like an earthquake!"

"You've no idea," remarked Captain Lycett-Collis complacently, "how powerful those things are."

"Baines!"

"Sir?"

"How far out is this ship?"

"I think about two miles, or perhaps one and a half. I'm not quite sure, sir."

"Then you should be. Telephone Zvengetzov and have it taken right out to sea—right out."

"Yes sir."

"As I was saying," continued James equably, "accidents might occur. We have only just discovered that there is a house—two houses—in the Via della Costa which contain dynamite—enough dynamite we shall doubtless be informed, to disintegrate Baressa completely. In the circumstances I suggest that these gentlemen declare any further stocks of these things they may have in their possession—before it is too late."

185

"Yes, certainly. I quite agree." The Colonel spoke firmly. "How much more have you got?"

For nearly a quarter of an hour the Engineer officers argued hotly with one another about the quantities and types of explosives they had brought with them. Several totals were put forward, all varying to a wide degree. Only Major Sherwood failed to contribute to the argument and it was belatedly noticed that he was fast asleep.

"Poor old thing!" said Ventham compassionately. He habitually, James noticed, referred to his commanding officer as if he were an aged house dog whom it would soon be a kindness to have painlessly destroyed. "He's absolutely exhausted; he's had a dreadfully tiring day. Can't he go to bed?"

"He's got no pajamas," said Paige.

"Never mind—he's too tired to worry about that." Ventham got up and came around the table to his dormant superior. "Come along now, Sherry. Ups-a-daisy! That's a dear old thing! Where does he go, sir?"

"I'll show you." James rose hurriedly and, preceded by the skinny, grubby boy supporting the unsteady, fat old man, left the room.

"We often have to put Sherry to bed," explained Captain Lycett-Collis, refilling his glass with port.

"Practically every night," supplemented Lord Paige.

"I see," said the Colonel.

19

IT SOON became apparent that the Engineers had no intention of getting on with the work they had ostensibly arrived to perform at anything save the slowest speed. It took them a fortnight to sort out their men and equipment and a further month to await the forwarding of the countless things they had left behind. Then their Advance Party appeared—it had not, after all, been sent back to Base—and a further two weeks were wasted in settling them in. Even then the Engineers would doubtless have procrastinated still further had they been allowed, for their officers, placed for the first time in two and a half years in a civilized community, were enjoying themselves to the full in their different ways. They had emerged from a remote malarial swamp in Central Africa after a prolonged and completely fruitless effort to drain a small portion of it for the construction of an airfield. They found Baressa delightful and it was their undisguised intention to remain there as long as possible.

Major Sherwood spent his time drinking himself into a stupor and sleeping it off—only to wake and drink again. He seemed to have no intention of leaving the Villa, and though he gave his hosts no trouble they found his continued presence increasingly irksome. At first they attempted to control his alcoholism by keeping the cellars locked and the decanters empty, but he merely sent his batman down to San Pietro and started to run up a heavy debt at an Indian wine merchant's. After a fortnight Euan got him into a car and sent him off with Fortu to examine the sites of the intended fortifications. He returned early, complimented Euan on the island scenery, and said that the fortifications were well planned. Fortu reported that he had slept soundly throughout the trip.

Captain Lycett-Collis was so attracted by the island that within a few days he had openly announced his intention of settling there after the war and actually started negotiating for the purchase of a small fruit plantation on the plateau. For some reason this behavior particularly incensed the Colonel, and very shortly Lycett-Collis was coldly informed that no land might be bought or sold during wartime without the consent of the Administration. He immediately applied and the permission was at once refused. Thereafter he was kept sulkily busy answering notes of protest from Brinsmead and Baines concerning the behavior of his troops.

The two lieutenants looked upon their new posting as a prolonged seaside holiday. They were forever out in the harbor fishing, or making voyages along the coast in the company of Christopher or William or Texas. They never put on a uniform and they were never very clean, but their thin, fever-racked bodies filled out and darkened to the copper-brown color of their new friends. Nobody ever saw them at the Cinema where their men were billeted, and their idea of reporting for duty was to stroll up to the Villa from time to time to inquire affectionately whether "Sherry was all right."

The end of this halcyon period came about after two months when Colonel Lemonfield visited the Cinema unannounced. What he found going on there so shocked him that he drove straight back to the Villa and had a stormy interview with Major Sherwood, from which the old man emerged quite sober and trembling violently. In the evening Captain Lycett-Collis and the lieutenants were summoned to the Colonel's office and, to their dismay and chagrin, were given explicit orders to get on with their work or leave Baressa.

Next day on the Governor's orders a fleet of trucks conveyed the Central Africans to the inhospitable site of the first strong-points on the coastal plain beyond Cascio. Their officers were brusquely informed that they must be there every day by 10 a.m. and remain until five in the afternoon. Failure in this respect would be followed by a request to the mainland for their removal.

"Not a bastard?" remarked Lord Paige angrily to Lieutenant Ventham. "Why, the man's a bastard of the very first water!"

During the autumn of that year Captain Stralowski first began to be seen outside the hospital grounds. Since he had been brought to the Palace in May the news of his capture had slowly become known. Owing to an official directive to soft-pedal the matter, the information that a German prisoner was in the hospital had not caused much of a sensation, particularly since he appeared to have been there for a considerable time.

William and Texas, looking at him over the wall of the hospital garden, saw an ugly scarred man wearing dark glasses and sitting in a deck chair, reading the daily paper. Christopher, introduced by Baines, found the crippled officer civil enough in a dry, matter-of-fact way. But the memory of that afternoon a year ago on the Balla estate haunted him, and he found the company of this cold-eyed, gentle-voiced, man, brought miraculously back from the lip of the grave, both embarrassing and obscurely frightening, and the fact that he was a German associated him too closely with the war. He did not repeat his visit.

Major Naughton-Muirhead, whose duty it was to inspect the hospital once a month, always visited Stralowski on these occasions. He did not like the man and when speaking with him he felt the same undercurrent of critical hostility that he had known with Pirie. But whereas Pirie's hostility had reached upward from below, an envious resentful anger at someone wealthier and more intelligent and more indolently assured than himself, Stralowski seemed to be looking down. There was a weary, cynical malice about the man, a slyly humorous condescension about his venom, that was far more perturbing than Pirie's self-righteous animosity. James would leave his room upset and irritated and continue his inspection in a snappish manner, crossly finding fault with the smallest things, while Stralowski, watching the door close, would display his large yellow teeth in a grin of genuine amusement and return to the book or paper he was reading.

Only Baines saw much of the German. At first his intention had been to lure Stralowski into some damaging remarks concerning Captain Rossi's activities, for, though Rossi himself had been refused admittance to Baressa, since the previous October, it was known that he still touched at points on the coast and presumably, therefore, he had associates in San Pietro. The German was as uncommunicative to the Police Chief as he was to everyone else, but Baines was a man of infinite patience—sooner or later Stralowski would let some useful hint drop. So, evening after evening, he visited the hospital and sat drinking iced beer with the prisoner for hours on end. They both became slightly drunk by about nine o'clock, but it made no difference to either of them; Baines was just as alert for a slip of the tongue on the part of the German and Stralowski himself remained as secretive and discreet. After a few months of this Baines' hopes of acquiring information began to flag, but the habit of spending almost every evening in the German's quarters remained. They talked little and drank more, sitting in silence looking at each other for long periods of time, but they had become so used to each other's presence that if the German had any friendly feelings for any of his captors they were for this short, heavy, swarthy man who resembled him physically and perhaps mentally more closely than anyone on the island.

His manner toward Baines displayed neither the slightly derisive politeness with which he had treated the Colonel at their one and only interview or the sardonic dislike that annoyed James on his monthly visits, but a sort of friendliness—tinged undoubtedly with mockery, but genuine enough for all that. He taught the Police Chief to play chess and his highly developed powers of concentration shortly made him an excellent player, though never in the same class as his master. Baines would ponder over the board until the sweat dripped down his face and then, moving his piece, would see the German's great teeth bared in a wolfish smile and hear the gentle voice say, "No—no, I think not. Look, I go here and—checkmate again, Baines, I'm afraid."

But they did not play chess every evening, and it was not long before the stringent orders that Lemonfield had made for the German began to be tacitly relaxed. At first Stralowski did little more than limp along the outside wall of the hospital, two hundred yards and back again. He did this in the evenings, and after a few days Baines walked with him. It was not long before they visited one or two of the bars in the nearby Via della Costa before returning to the hospital.

20

THE capitulation of Italy and her reentry into the war on the Allied side were greeted with considerable relief by the easygoing European population of Baressa. It was felt that no recriminations or wrathful charges of collaboration could now be leveled against them in the unlikely event of a return of the Giordano administration.

Large bouquets of flowers were sent to the Palace and Colonel Lemonfield, who personally considered floral tributes effeminate and theatrical, wrote short notes of thanks to the senders and asked the Mayor and Corporation to dinner at the Villa. The walls of the dining room were hung with Union Jacks, Italian tricolors, and the flags of the Allied nations. On a last-minute inspection before the guests arrived James added the black double eagle of Imperial Austria which he had found amongst a bundle of old flags in the Palace. Captain Zvengetzov was so overcome by this delicate compliment to his feelings that he remained sober throughout the evening with his gaze fixed unmovingly upon the old emblem under which he had fought many bloody battles long ago. Before he left James gave him the flag and the poor old savage wept with emotion. It was, so those who witnessed it were understood to say, an affecting sight.

The native population, to whom the international event meant little, decided to celebrate it nonetheless, and on the next evening the city was in gala dress and the crowds roared and sang and shouted for the Governor in the great square outside the Palace. Euan, working late in his office in secret expectation of this, appeared suddenly on the balcony above the main entrance —a tiny figure on that vast floodlit façade. He was greeted by roar after roar of thundering applause. The crowd in the square went wild with delight and surged shouting up to the glittering sentries on the marble steps. High up above his tempestuously loyal subjects the little Governor smiled, lifted a hand in farewell, and disappeared within. Nor, though the packed square bellowed again and again, would he reemerge. Sergeant Hope, Sergeant Whyton, and William, who witnessed it, considered this, too, to be an affecting sight.

Visiting the prison of Fort Brocca just before Christmas, James encountered Mr. Lillywhite in the main courtyard. He was disconsolately haranguing a gang of sullen prisoners on the subject of a wilted geranium in a small flowerpot which he held in one hand. Since his imprisonment fifteen months before Mr. Lillywhite had been restored gradually to a certain amount of freedom. After six months of solitary confinement in a dungeon he had been promoted to a small room in an upper story and given the job of superintending the female prisoners' work. After a further six months he had been released—but only on condition that he work in the Prison Service. He was now overseer of the gangs of prisoners which the thrifty Administration rented to the Municipality to undertake the upkeep of the flower beds, trees, and lawns in the city squares. This kept Mr. Lillywhite in conspicuous places throughout the day where his absence would at once be missed. At night he returned to his black wife and mud-colored family in Daldacara.

As James' white Bugatti swept into the yard Mr. Lillywhite called his gang to a shambling attention and raised his old brown hat. His present attitude to the Administration was one of the utmost servility, for though they had frightened him almost to

191

death with threats of the prison firing squad they had, in the end, treated him with leniency and actually provided him with a sine-cure at seven pounds a week. This was double the salary he had been getting in the Customs Service and, had he known it, was only due to Colonel Lemonfield's inveterate habit of driving hard bargains with the Municipality.

Lined up to receive James on the prison steps were the senior warders under Maresciallo Riccomini, a portly, dignified, bald man whose gray beard and regal air lent him a striking resemblance to King Edward VII. He was a cousin—several times removed, as he repeatedly explained—of Colonel Giordano.

"Good morning, Maresciallo."

"Ha—good morning, Major—good morning!" Riccomini smiled, bowed slightly, and rubbed his hands. "A nice morning, sir—a little cool, perhaps, but that's all to the good—all to the good! We have enough heat at other times, do we not? And Christmas next week, Major! How the years do fly past! To an old man like me it seems as if it were only yesterday——" Still talking affably, he led the way into his neat office, pushed a chair up to the desk for James, and, after proffering a box of cheroots, sat down himself.

"Well, Major, here are the books for you to see." He opened several large ledgers. "I think you'll find they're all up to date and in order. Yes, I think you'll find that." James flicked through them boredly and scribbled his signature here and there in red ink. The Maresciallo lit a cheroot and sat back in his padded chair with the tips of his fingers together and a look of satisfied complacency on his majestic features. Outside in the yard Mr. Lillywhite's voice could be heard rising to a shrill, angry falsetto as he badgered and worried his morose blacks into the back of a truck.

James snapped the last ledger shut and looked up. "Yes, Maresciallo, all in order, thank you."

"Thank *you*, Major," returned the Prison Chief with a courtly inclination of his head.

"Is the staff all right? Working well?"

"Ha—h'm." The Maresciallo affected to consider this question with a thoughtful care; he gazed at the ceiling and meditated. "Yes—yes, I really think I can say they are. Sergeant Zanoni is due for a short holiday. He's getting old—getting old, yes. But

192

he's a good man and knows his work. I'll give him a week off if you agree, Major."

"That's not very much, is it?" ventured James. "How about letting him have a month?"

Riccomini slowly shook his head. "No—no, Major. I think a week is ample. If I may say so I think a week is quite sufficient."

"Very well." James was not prepared to be drawn into an interminable discussion of the faults and foibles of Sergeant Zanoni and the rest of the prison officials. He knew from bitter experience that a long, cozy, repetitive monologue on the shortcomings of his staff—with reiterated assertions that they were all getting old—was what the Maresciallo enjoyed above all things. So he said quickly, "There's one thing I must tell you, Maresciallo. The Colonel, as you know, is very keen on the engagement of prisoners in profitable work. He argues—rightly, I'm sure you'll agree—that criminals should work hard and the benefits of their industry be reaped by the Administration. He is not content for a prisoner to make only enough money to offset the cost of his personal imprisonment, but considers that there should be a profit as well. As he says, an industrious workman usefully employed cannot only support himself and perhaps a family but can generally put by a little money every week as well. How much more, therefore, should a prisoner, unhindered with any family responsibility and living in an extremely simple material manner, be able to show a profit on his work." James drew a long breath and continued. "Before the Colonel came to this island the prisoners worked at the most unrepaying pastimes. They rolled the prison paths all day or repaired damaged rope fenders for the Port Department. We have put an end to that, but the Colonel still thinks that the prisoners are not making enough money at their occupations. They must work very long hours and very hard and at remunerative labor."

The Maresciallo's august brow had darkened into a frown as James concluded this speech and his well-manicured fingers drummed irritably on the leather top of his desk.

"Of course, if the Colonel is not satisfied——" he began huffily, but James cut him short.

"You mustn't misunderstand me, Maresciallo," he soothed. "These are the Colonel's ideas. They are still new and have to be explained—you can't be expected to understand them by telepathy. The Colonel is perfectly satisfied with progress up to date; he merely wants to see the prisoners making still more money."

"Ah—well, so long as the Colonel is satisfied at present," Riccomini remarked, all smiles once more, "we'll see what we can do to make the prisoners' occupations still more remunerative in the future. Yes—we'll see what can be done in that direction. And now, Major"—he rose—"perhaps you'd like to inspect the interior?"

Together they threaded their way through long stone corridors, across courtyards and into bastions. Here were row upon row of cells, then kitchens smelling of native bread, latrines smelling of disinfectant, an infirmary smelling of carbolic soap, a dispensary smelling of ether. The stone floors echoed their tread and the old fort seemed filled with the noises of grating locks, the slamming of heavy doors, and the click and clash of warders' rifles as they came to attention at the sight of James and their imposing Chief. From high barred windows shafts of sunlight fell like aimless, probing spotlights, illuminating places of no importance, falling on blank white walls or scrubbed stone flags.

They passed through the female prisoners' wing, where a few sullen Negresses made fishing nets and palm leaf hats under the eye of a massive half-caste wardress. Then, traversing a long, narrow paved yard, the outer wall of which was pierced with old gun embrasures looking out across the sparkling blue sea, they came to a heavy iron-studded door.

The Maresciallo knocked loudly with his baton of office and they were admitted by an elderly, obese Italian warder—Sergeant Zanoni, who was about to receive a week's holiday. James walked down two stone steps and found himself in a large, low workroom, where the six Guardie di Finanza arrested eighteen months before were busily engaged as tinkers, mending pots, pans, oil drums, and other small metal articles. They did not look up as James entered, but bent sullenly over their tasks. The tap of hammers and the whine of a hand forge echoed in the low room.

"Any complaints?" James asked.

Silence. The hammers tapped. Ex-Brigadiere Franzoni picked up a blowlamp and with an expressionless face applied its roaring blue flame to the back of a frying pan.

"They have no complaints, *signore*," said Zanoni, coming to a slovenly attention.

Despite their unpleasant personal appearances, accentuated now by the drab prison clothes, and their heinous past, James felt a spasm of pity for the degenerate criminals at the benches.

"Are they all right, Maresciallo? Quite happy?"

"They are quite all right, Major, quite all right. They do not come to prison to be happy, though." There was a hint of respectful reproof in Riccomini's voice.

James picked up an old kettle from the workbench. "Do you really consider this the most repaying occupation for them? Couldn't they make more money at something a little more technical?"

Riccomini smiled. "They could, Major, certainly. For instance, if we hired them out as auditors, as cashiers, or even—ha, ha!—even as customs officials! They understand all about figures and bookkeeping. Ha, ha, ha!" He rubbed his hands together, pleased with his joke. Then he reverted to gravity. "No no, Major. Their occupation is most repaying, I assure you. They are the only tinkers in the city and, what with the extreme shortage of hardware and household utensils due to the war, everyone makes use of them. I assure you they are making quite a lot of money."

"Ah, well," James remarked as he turned to climb the steps, "I expect you're right."

The Maresciallo followed him out and the door clanged after him. As he did so the Guardie di Finanza all stopped work and stood waiting silently until the footsteps had died away across the yard.

"Very well!" said Zanoni sharply. "Get the stuff out and get on with it. We've been hindered enough for one morning."

Immediately the Guardie di Finanza started to open drawers in the benches and to shift an iron screen from a small furnace in a corner. Zanoni walked up and down, examining a mold or two here, a pot of molten metal there.

"Let's have a look at that last batch, Franzoni," he grunted. The onetime Brigadiere opened a mold and displayed six well-cast East African shillings, opened another and showed the guard four big Egyptian 20-piaster pieces.

"A bit rough—the lettering."

"Not when Morosoni has done it with the acid."

"The Maresciallo," remarked Zanoni severely, "said last night that Gonzaga did not finish those rupees properly. He was most annoyed about it. If a thing's worth doing, he says, it's worth doing well. Unless more care is taken in future he will reduce your shares by ten percent."

"The rupees are difficult, Zanoni," muttered the hunchback Gonzaga discontentedly. "If the Maresciallo would only get us better lead——"

"He gets you the best he can. You must remember there's a war on," retorted Zanoni virtuously. "Besides, you do the Ethiopian dollars perfectly well with it. Now Dumini, what *are* you doing with that block tin? You *know* how expensive——"

The Guardie di Finanza were—as Maresciallo Riccomini had assured James—making quite a lot of money.

21

"COME here," said William, catching Silvana by the wrist and dragging her up to the top of the old seawall. "I want to discuss your love life."

"Why?"

"It interests me. I have a personal interest in it."

"That means you are going to suggest again that I should marry you, I suppose."

"I wasn't actually. Why? Have you suddenly decided that it would be a good thing, after all?"

"To marry you? No. I don't think so really. I'm not sure, but I don't think I will, somehow."

"That's an improvement on last week. Last week you said it was only a remote possibility."

"Did I? Yes, I did. I had remote possibilities on the brain, I suppose. A letter came to the office from Sergeant Brinsmead inquiring whether there was a remote possibility of us submitting a correct gasoline account for the month. Mrs. Tamminetto was furious; she hates sarcasm."

"I believe," said William, ignoring this digression, "that you would have been very pleased to marry me once."

"When?"

"Three years ago, when we'd been on the island about nine months and you and I used to go for walks along the shore in the evenings."

"But do you think the Colonel would have approved? I was only fourteen, after all. He might have issued a proclamation banning child marriage."

William took a coin from his pocket. "I'll toss up for it. Heads you marry me—tails you marry Christopher."

"That's a ridiculous way to choose a husband."

"No, it's not. Marriage is a lottery."

The coin spun in the air, fell on the white sun-baked stone, and rolled edgewise into a crevice.

"Well, whom do I marry now? Or does that mean I'm to stay an old maid?"

William kicked moodily at the flaking stone. "I think you'd enjoy being married to me. There would be a lot of advantages to it. And I'd make an excellent husband. Much better than Christopher."

Silvana said, "I wish you wouldn't go on about it so. If you go on like this I'll have to marry someone just to get some peace."

"Christopher, I suppose?"

"He hasn't asked me, so I can't—can I?"

"He won't either," said William. "I believe he'll marry his Japanese in the end. After all, they've been married to all intents and purposes for three years."

"Nonsense!" Silvana flushed.

"It's not nonsense. They're as good as man and wife in the sight of everyone except perhaps God. Once they settle down properly and have a lot of little hissing, slit-eyed yellow babies——"

"Don't be so disgusting, William!"

"I'm not being disgusting—it's all perfectly natural. I can't understand why they don't regularize themselves and——"

"All right then, I'm going!" Silvana slipped off the wall and walked away.

"So you'd only be destroying his domestic happiness if you *did* marry him!" called William loudly. "You'd be a home wrecker!"

Then he, too, slipped off the wall and wandered gloomily toward the docks to look for Texas.

Spring came in with its usual burden of growing heat and discomfort. Once more the Port Pilot was seen with his shirt outside his trousers, once more the Government offices started to close an hour earlier and to release their streams of tired, hot clerks and accountants and messengers into the dusty, sweltering afternoon streets. Soon the monsoon would sweep the rain clouds out of the west and cataracting torrents would once more envelop the island. The days would be hot and steamy, the nights humid and damp; it would not be comfortable, but it would be better than the present vicious, iron heat that shivered the air into distorting waves. Island tempers frayed under the strain of the brick-kiln days and the tossing sleepless nights on beds that felt like oven grills.

Christopher was alone again in the Casa dei Fiori—alone except for Toki. Lieutenants Paige and Ventham had been forced to leave for Dinghité to superintend the construction of concrete redoubts at the island's inhospitable northern extremity. They had not wanted to go and had left in a spirit of angry despair, taking with them in an old diesel truck their few shabby belongings, a quantity of cheap spirits, and two scrofulous young Negresses whom they had picked up in the docks and had, despite Christopher's protests, been keeping in an outhouse near the kitchen.

Apparently they found Dinghité a most unsatisfactory substitute for San Pietro, for after they had been there a week Christopher received a letter informing him that they considered their present location rather worse than the Central African swamp they had abandoned a year before. It was devastatingly hot, there was no ice, Captain Lycett-Collis was ill with what he believed were measles, and the Negresses were unsatisfied financially and were demanding money with threats. Sherry had run up a wine bill he was unable to meet at the only shop, and the Indian storekeeper had cut off supplies and was also demanding money with threats. The men had got savagely drunk on palm toddy and had wrecked the mission church. That very morning the black priest had appeared and was still in Sherry's tent. They could

198

hear his voice from their own and it seemed that he, too, was demanding. . . .

Christopher thrust the letter, half finished, into his pocket and drove down to Police Headquarters ostensibly to regale Baines with the gossip it contained, but actually to try and see Silvana.

At Police Headquarters Baines was correcting the gasoline account, a document that, having been recently exposed to the fury of Sergeant Brinsmead, was thick with blue-pencil underlinings and acid remarks in red ink. Mrs. Tamminetto sat beside him, finishing her elevenses and wiping her fingers on his handkerchief, which she had borrowed. She had transferred her affections from Texas, who soon palled, to her new chief and amity in Police Headquarters was complete. Baines put up with playful smacks, kisses, hair-rufflings, and little gifts of buns and creampuffs with weary, grinning good humor. He even pinched Mrs. Tamminetto's behind from time to time, eliciting shrieks of mirth and furious mimic pummelings. It was all a nuisance and not the way he would have liked to run his department, but it served its end. Mrs. Tamminetto did her job—with the exception of the gasoline account, which she was congenitally incapable of rendering correctly—with zeal and efficiency. She told him everything and showed him her files on the smallest invitation. The Carabinieri were happy and worked fairly hard. It was, thought Baines, well worth the slap-and-tickle interludes which it necessitated.

"I wish I understood how you ever got these totals, Gina. Brinsmead says they are all deliberate falsifications, and I'm pretty sure he's right."

"Ah, Brinsmit! That man—he has no heart! Ah, how he hates me! And for nothing—nothing at all. Wait one moment and I will get my copy and show you how I get these figures. First let me explain about the oil." Mrs. Tamminetto gobbled up the jam tart she was finishing and leaned over her chief, breathing heavily. "Now what is it that he complains of in this?"

Commino knocked and put his head around the door. "Captain Kellermann to see you, *signore.*"

"Oh—all right. Tell him to wait a minute. I'll be ready to see him when I've finished this."

"*Si, Signor Capitano.*"

In the small, dusty anteroom outside Baines' office Christopher found Captain Stralowski. The German sat patiently on a wooden kitchen chair with his crutches propped against the wall beside him. When Christopher entered he turned his pale eyes on him with a look of annoyance, as if he had been interrupted in doing something far more important than merely gazing expressionlessly out of the grimy window.

"Good morning, Captain," he said with an air of weary boredom. And then, as if to forestall an inevitable query, "I am waiting for Captain Baines."

"Oh, I see. How are you getting along with your crutches?"

"Progressing." Stralowski sighed. "I make progress. I can walk farther now—but it is tiring."

"Didn't I see you near the police jetty yesterday afternoon?"

"I expect so. I was watching the radiomen coming in from a fishing trip. They had caught an octopus. They brought the creature ashore and now it lives in a glass tank outside their house. That is why I am here. Captain Baines was anxious to see it and suggested I should come, too. Why are they decorating the town?"

Christopher laughed. "Oh, some nonsense of the Mayor's. It's the Colonel's birthday tomorrow."

"Ah, so?" Stralowski raised his eyebrows. "And it is the custom to rejoice publicly on the anniversaries of Colonel Lemonfield?"

"Good Lord, no! He doesn't know about it yet—he'll be furious when he does."

Baines came in. "Hullo, Kellermann, what can I do for you? Have you heard about the octopus?"

"Yes."

"We're just going to have a look at it. Why don't you come, too?"

"No—I've got other things to do." Christopher blushed.

"Oh, very well."

"By the way, what's the Colonel going to say about all these birthday decorations in the streets? I saw Lillywhite hanging them on the trees as I drove here and he told me it's to be a surprise. But I don't really think the Colonel likes surprises—hadn't you better tell him?"

Baines frowned and bit his lower lip in pained concentration. "H'm—it's awkward for me," he muttered. "If I ring the Colonel and tell him about it the Mayor will say I've spoiled his surprise. He'll probably think I complained on purpose to get one up on the Municipality—don't want that. Then if I don't do anything the Colonel'll say the police are slack and unobservant—I dunno. . . ."

"Well, then I shouldn't say anything if I were you. Somebody's bound to tell him soon. You can always explain that you thought it was for some Italian fiesta."

"We're supposed to know about them beforehand," grumbled Baines. "However, I won't say anything until this evening. Surely by then he'll have been told by somebody."

Major Naughton-Muirhead was telling him at that moment. ". . . and I believe Lillywhite's engaged in hanging colored lights on all the trees in the squares! You mustn't be too cross with poor old Belotta; I'm sure he really thinks he's being terribly complimentary. Perhaps it would be better if I rang him up myself and explained that while we considered it a charming gesture——"

Euan was sitting back in his chair, laughing in high good humor. "I think it's quite delightful! What will old Belotta think of next, I wonder? No, James. Neither of us will ring him up. We'll pretend we've noticed nothing."

"You mean—let him go on?"

"Yes, I think so. Why not? It won't do any harm and will amuse the townspeople. *Panem et circenses,* you know."

James looked doubtfully at the Governor. "I hope it won't make us look rather ridiculous. They're putting big wooden shields with 'E.L.' painted on them on the lampposts."

"In what colors?" asked Euan sharply.

"White on a blue ground, I think it was."

"Good. I'm glad they've got that right. I've always chosen blue and white as the Administration colors."

James was at once delighted and intrigued at this new facet of his friend's character. "So you really *are* going to let them go on?"

Euan's brow creased into a small frown. He said stiffly, "I've already told you so, haven't I? I don't see why you should want to stop people celebrating my birthday. I'm the Governor, and it's perfectly suitable that my birthday should be celebrated as a public holiday. After all, there are a great many rulers whose birthdays are marked in that way—you'll admit that, I suppose?"

"Oh yes, I'm sure there are."

"And you'll admit I rule this island?"

"Yes, but there is a——"

"Then, really, James, I think your objections—whatever they are—must be quite illogical." He smiled suddenly. "Come, this isn't like you at all! Let's see what we can do to make the festivities still gayer. I'm going to give a garden party at the Villa. I think we should invite at least three hundred people."

"Rather costly, I should think?"

"I and Brinsmead have managed to set aside a little money from the revenue for such eventualities. We do it very discreetly, and it comes under all sorts of headings—'Building Repairs,' 'Wear and Tear on Office Furniture,' 'Electric Fittings'—we've collected a few hundred in one way and another."

James was thunderstruck. "Euan—do you mean that you and Brinsmead have been embezzling the——"

"Good God, no! Really, you don't make the slightest effort to comprehend me! We have had to do an increasing amount of entertainment—largely by way of return to the Municipality —since relations with the Italians altered by their change of front last autumn. I can't possibly pay for it on a colonel's salary, and I know that H.Q. would make the most mountainous difficulties if I asked for a reasonable entertainment allowance—so we do it this way. We're not embezzling anything. It's our own revenue, isn't it? And a large amount of it is solely due to my early work here, so if anybody has a right to decide how it should be spent I should have thought I am that person! People don't seem to realize that a certain display is expected from the rulers of Oriental territories. . . ."

Mr. Morle sat in his study writing his monthly letter for the Mission magazine. Most of it was an account of the difficulties he was finding in inducing the Administration to pay for the rebuilding of the Church of King Charles the Martyr at Dinghité. On the next page would be published Manoah's piously turn-the-other-cheek account of the sufferings of his churchless flock. Mr. Morle hoped both articles would have an embarrassing effect on Colonel Lemonfield.

Behind Mr. Morle and at a table in the center of the room sat his wife, a depressed, gray-haired woman in the middle forties, peering shortsightedly at some tattered prayer books laid out for repair. On the floor between them sat their five-year-old daughter Vera—the same "infant daughter" whom an exasperated Colonel Giordano had incarcerated in Fort Brocca with her parents nearly four years before. She was a fat, pallid child who turned the glossy leaves of a book of mildly illustrated Bible stories with an irreligious lack of enthusiasm. The quiet, broken only by the ticking of a peculiarly ugly clock enshrined in a miniature Egyptian temple of black marble—a present to the Morles from a Missionary Society in England—was suddenly shattered by the approaching roar of a motorcycle on the road outside. Mr. Morle looked up.

"It's that Dawson boy, I suppose," he remarked angrily. "Up and down! Up and down! All day and every day! Why can't he take his messages by another road occasionally? It's a—he's coming here!"

"Here, dear?"

"Yes. At least, he's pulled up by the gate. Yes, here he comes." The front door opened and Texas could be heard stamping about in the hall questioningly. "In here!" called Mr. Morle.

"Mornin'," greeted Texas unenthusiastically as he came into the study. He drew off a gauntlet, fished in the slanted pocket of his breeches, and pulled out an envelope. It was not the usual red one, but broader and pale gray with the new Palace crest, a large crown, embossed in gold on the back. Even though it was crumpled and bent from its journey in Texas' pocket, it retained its expensive, aristocratic look.

Mr. Morle, swiveling around in his office chair, took it and turned it over suspiciously. "We shall no doubt see His Majesty's *complete* Arms on the Colonel's letters soon," he remarked sarcastically.

"I wonder what he wants with us?" sighed Mrs. Morle in such a martyred tone that it might have been assumed that Colonel Lemonfield was in the habit of making pressing and unreasonable demands upon them every day of the week.

"I will tell you when I have opened it," replied her husband with a hint of reproof in his voice.

"I c'n tell you now," announced Texas boredly. "It's a invite."

"A what?"

"A invite. To his birthday party." Texas took off his crash helmet and rubbed a hand through his hair. "*Caramba!* Ain't it stiflin'? Yes, the Colonel's givin' a garden party on his birthday. That's tomorrow and you're invited—you lucky people!"

Mr. Morle, shooting him a look of dislike, ripped the letter open and took out a heavy pasteboard card stamped with another gilt crown. He looked at it, his lips compressed.

"Yes, Eva, what this boy says is true. Colonel Lemonfield 'desires our presence.' Does he, indeed? A very high-handed sort of invitation, I must say! And what's more, I notice that it's signed by his driver—extraordinary!"

"Fortu's his private seketry now," remarked Texas. "He was twenty the other day so the Colonel made him his seketry—promoted him like."

"I see—and how many secretaries has the Colonel got now? And who is going to drive his car?"

"They got a nigger, I think. He's got four seketries now, what with Fortu. There's Miss da Mosta an' Miss Falcino, what always has toothache, an'——"

"Yes, yes; never mind. We all know our Governor has become quite a personage. Quite the amateur Viceroy." He smiled wryly. "Sit down, Dawson. Would you like a glass of lemonade?"

"No, thank you very much," replied Texas, suddenly polite, but he sat down opposite Mrs. Morle and stared fascinatedly at the battered prayer books.

"This party will cost a lot, won't it, Dawson?"

"I expec' so. There's to be three hundred guests. I know," said Texas gloomily, " 'cos I've got to deliver most of the invites."

"Well, if the Colonel's as rich as all that I wonder why he doesn't help the Church instead of hindering us. It's absolutely disgraceful the way the Administration is procrastinating about compensation for that shocking business at Dinghité. They say it's nothing to do with them, but of course that's mere shilly-shallying. The Engineer troops are here to work for them, I suppose?"

Texas was not interested in this subject. "We got 'n octopus in a glass tank," he volunteered by way of diversion. "*Caramba!* You should see it eat fish!"

"Why do you keep on saying '*Caramba*'?" questioned Mr. Morle crossly. "I don't suppose you even know what it means!"

"I do, then! It's Spanish for 'Crumbs!' "

"Nonsense!"

"Well, anyway, Captain Rossi tol' me it was." Texas sounded defiant.

"Are you still going to work for that man after the war, Dawson? I must say I don't approve of the idea at all, myself."

"Well, the Colonel don't neither, s'matter of fack," grumbled Texas. "He don't like Rossi, that's what it is. He stopped him coming to the island. I ain't seen him for nearly a year now."

"Why is that?"

"I dunno. Cor—coo! It gives me the sick, I tell you straight! There I was, all fixed up nice, an' now I dunno where I am. I dunno whether I'll have a job here after the war or whether I'll have to go home."

"This island's no place for a young man like you," said Mr. Morle sententiously. "I've been here a longish time now and I can tell you that most people—Italians or English, but particularly English—who come here go to the dogs sooner or later. Look at that wretched fellow Lillywhite! But I agree that the Colonel's done you a bad turn."

22

CAPTAIN BAINES lived in a second-floor flat in the center of San Pietro's main shopping thoroughfare, the Corso Thaon de Reval. It was the second flat he had occupied since he had been on the island, and it had been specially requisitioned for him by the Governor when he had assumed the duties of Police Chief. Before his tenancy it had belonged to the General Manager of the Arabian Sea Shell Company and it was large, modern, and sumptuously furnished. The Administration had not only paid the General Manager heavy compensation for the eviction, but had purchased all his furniture and fittings at something very near his own figure. It had cost over nine thousand pounds to set Baines up in this way, but it was typical of Colonel Lemonfield to spare no expense when rewarding a useful subordinate.

It was money wasted though, for Baines, living only for his job, would have been perfectly content to have remained in the small, dingy apartment in the Via della Costa that he had occupied as Customs Chief. He only came to the flat to eat and sleep and never entertained there, the most he was prepared to do in that respect being to give his plainclothes agents cognac if they had to report to him late at night.

One evening, when the seasonal rains were at their height, he decided to break this rule and ask Stralowski to dinner. It was nearly six o'clock in the evening when he thought of this, and outside dusk was falling in the almost deserted, rain-swept street. He had left the office early and, having bathed and changed into white drill shirt and trousers, he intended to spend the evening in his study examining some files of customs accounts which he had collected from Kanos earlier in the day. His anger when he found that the files were not the ones he had supposed was considerable, but by habit suppressed. The habitual half-grin on his swarthy face widened and tightened as he prowled restlessly in his rubber-soled canvas shoes up and down the softly lit study, composing a stinging rebuke to be delivered to Kanos first thing in the morning. It was too late to do anything now. The customs offices were locked, Kanos was in his suburban home, and Mrs. Tamminetto, who could have supplied him with other equally interesting documents, was, he knew, out playing bridge with Captain Zvengetzov at the Mayor's. And, anyway, it was pouring with rain.

Baines padded into the big white kitchen where Dora, his half-caste cook and the sister of one of his agents, sat reading the *Baressa Courier* at the kitchen table. She looked up with a start as her master appeared silently in the doorway.

"Dora, I want to have someone to dinner tonight. Can you manage?"

The cook rose respectfully. "Yes, *Capitano,* I think so. If you don't mind having crayfish again for the fish?"

"No, that will do nicely."

"Very well, *Capitano.* At what time will you want dinner?"

"Eight," replied Baines and padded out. Dinner at the Villa and the Mayor's and up at the Commendatore's and at all the other important private houses on the island was invariably at ten, but Baines liked to work between nine and the small hours.

He went into the hall and rang the hospital. "Put me through to the old isolation wing."

"*Si, signore.*"

The telephone buzzed and the Police Chief waited. He could hear it ringing emptily at the end of the hospital passage and pictured Stralowski reaching for his crutches and heaving himself from his chair in his small green-painted room and tapping slowly down the long tiled corridor.

After a couple of minutes the phone was answered by a native, speaking in guttural Italian. "*Si?*"

"This is the Police Chief speaking. Is that the guard?"

"*Si, Signor Capitano.*"

"I want to speak to the Tedesco Captain."

"Is he not with you, sir? He said he was going to see you."

"Did he? When?"

"An hour ago. He said you had told him to take one of the cars as it was raining. He took the small green Fiat."

Baines' almost permanent grin vanished abruptly. "Did you see which way he went?" he asked quickly.

"No, *signore.*" The guard's voice sounded puzzled. "I didn't watch."

"If he comes back lock him in his room and ring me at once—see?" He put down the telephone and stood motionless, a short, stocky white figure in the calm, soft glow of the concealed lighting in the hall. What was Stralowski up to? Was he making an attempt to escape or was he just visiting—who? Or had he really been coming to the flat, but had broken down in some deserted part of the town and, rather than limp slowly about in the downpour, was waiting to be rescued? Yet he had never even mentioned the car that day and had never driven it or any of the others before. Also, he had always informed Baines beforehand of any excursion he proposed to take outside the grounds of the hospital.

It looked bad. Baines was silently furious with himself for abating in any way the Colonel's orders concerning Stralowski. The German was never supposed to have been let out of the hospital at all, yet bit by bit he had edged farther out as the weeks and months went by, and somehow nothing had been said. He had at last come and gone more or less where he pleased and no one had stopped him. Baines had been content with the German's invariable request for permission and the knowledge that Miranos, the best of the plainclothes agents, had been set to keep an eye on him and report his movements should he venture near the docks or enter a private house or do anything else that might give rise to the smallest suspicion. Then, after Italy's *volte-face,* it had seemed that Stralowski, now without any allies on the island or within thousands of miles, could not seriously consider escape to be a practical possibility. And, after all, he had only one leg.

But excuses, Baines told himself bitterly, would be useless, for in direct contravention of the Colonel's orders he had time and time again permitted Stralowski to leave the hospital. If the German somehow got off the island and was recaptured by Allied forces elsewhere there would be hell to pay. The Colonel would probably lose his job and perhaps his commission—Baines would undoubtedly lose his. Everything depended on finding Stralowski as soon as possible.

This meditation had taken Baines less than ten seconds—a series of unpleasant pictures whisked across the magic-lantern screen of his mind's eye—and he had alerted the police and ordered his agents out into the streets and docks within another three minutes. Then there was nothing to do but wait. And, after all, Stralowski might at that moment be sitting in his car in the dark in some deserted street waiting for assistance. Or he might be visiting some unsuspected contact with the mainland. Or—but in his heart Baines doubted these possibilities. In his heart he believed that Stralowski was off on what he presumably hoped was the first stage of a journey back to the Reich.

Half an hour later, as Baines paced noiselessly up and down the hall, waiting with gnawing impatience for the telephone to ring, there came a knocking on the door. He flung it open and found Miranos. The emaciated, pockmarked little half-caste stood on the mat, trying to furl a wet umbrella while rain dripped slowly off his old glinting rubber mackintosh. He was coughing and his thin face looked ill and drawn. The most efficient and devoted of Baines' agents, Miranos at twenty-two suffered from tuberculosis and chronic anemia to such a degree that the slightest extra physical effort left him coughing, pale, and shaking. He was a morbid little creature, glumly convinced that he was dying, and with a habit of explaining in depressing detail exactly how and why to anyone who would listen. He possessed a quick intelligence, a good memory, and a clever knack of piecing seemingly irrelevant odds and ends of gossip and hearsay into significant information. Embittered by ill health and—until entering Baines' service—poverty, he lived entirely for his work. For the results of it, in Baines' hands, generally got someone into severe trouble, and Miranos disliked the human race individually as well as collectively.

Now he said, smothering his cough with difficulty and leaning wearily against the doorpost, "He's on the plateau."

"Ah!"

"A truck driver passed the car nearly an hour ago at the top of the escarpment. He told Spiros. Where's he going, Capitano? Balla's place?"

"Yes. Stay here a minute!" Baines dashed down the corridor and returned a few seconds later with a heavy Service pistol and a long electric torch. "Okay, you'd better come with me, Miranos. We'll get the car." Together they ran down the stairs and into the street.

Baines kept his car, a small, fast Alfa Romeo, in a side-street garage. It was the work of a moment to unlock and roll back the well-oiled aluminum doors and toss the gun and torch into the back of the car, and then they were off, roaring down the Corso Thaon de Reval at a speed far in excess of the legal limit. The rain seemed to be lessening, but the humidity was such that Miranos continually had to wipe the inside of the windshield with a duster to prevent it fogging up.

At the top of the escarpment the night was clearer and the rain had abated. Through the frayed clouds a few small wet stars blinked fitfully. On the way up, as he wrenched the car perilously around the hairpin bends of the twisting road, Baines had been too preoccupied with his own skillful driving to give a thought to the probable intentions of Stralowski, but once on the long flat road that looped and turned through the estates of the concessionaires he was able to give at least half his mind to the problem of the German's goal. It seemed certain that he would make for the north of the island, for not only were the rich anti-Fascist farmers of the southern uplands all strong supporters of Colonel Lemonfield's Administration, but with the docks of San Pietro guarded there was no possibility of escape in that quarter.

To the north, where the plateau sloped brokenly to the long bleak plain, there were a thousand hiding places for a fugitive and it would take weeks, or even months, before they could be combed. The coast, too, was fretted and worn into countless small deepwater creeks and inlets—lonely, desolate places which, owing to the intricate coral reefs and jagged rocks of their treacherous waters, remained unvisited for years at a time by even the native fishermen. Stralowski must make for the north to avoid recapture, and if he intended to conceal himself in some cave on that inhospitable coast he would need supplies of food, and Balla's *azienda* was the only place where he might get them. Even if Balla was unwilling, now, to connive at the German's escape Stralowski might still possess hidden supplies somewhere on the estate. That he knew of some means of leaving the island was also certain, for he could not hope to live the life of a hunted fugitive indefinitely. Somewhere along the tangled northern coast there was an accomplice with a boat, and perhaps farther out to sea a little smuggling ship—Rossi's *Bina* probably, but there were others—that would take him to the mainland.

Tearing through the dark, his headlights shooting long white beams up the glistening road, Baines blamed himself with sullen fury for his failure to prevent this escape. He had not even the slight consolation of feeling that he had been deceived into underestimating the German. Like the Colonel he had been quite aware that Stralowski was clever, formidable, and dangerous, a man of fanatical, wicked strength both of the mind and the body, for had he not struggled back to life from a comparatively advanced state of decomposition? Nor could he defend himself by pleading the extreme unlikelihood of a friendless one-legged cripple escaping from a garrisoned island across more than six hundred miles of shark-infested sea. It must, Baines told himself bitterly, have been obvious to anyone who had known him that Stralowski would have attempted, probably successfully, to escape from a far worse position with no legs at all.

The man had fascinated him. In a careful, snakelike way those pale eyes had half hypnotized him and weakened him and inveigled him into a lazy feeling of false security. He had known that Stralowski was dangerous, yet he had tacitly consented to granting him more and more liberty. Baines groaned audibly as he thought of the morrow when he would have to report his fearful blunder to the Colonel. He had a stronger respect and admiration for Lemonfield than anyone—even Brinsmead—on the island. Lemonfield had promoted him and praised him and given him the work he liked above all things and showered gifts upon him. Now this business would probably cost Lemonfield his position—might well lead to his conviction before a court-martial. As he pressed the accelerator down to the floorboards, Baines' eyes narrowed and his mouth hardened to a grim line. If, against all probability, he caught Stralowski he would kill him, either at the moment of recapture or at some conveniently isolated spot on the way back. Miranos would neither object nor talk afterward. They would bring the body back and have it buried quietly in the hospital grounds—or, better still, take it out by night in the customs launch and drop it weighted into the sea. He would explain matters to the Colonel in a private interview, and he judged shrewdly that Lemonfield's relief at this final disposal of the prisoner would induce him to take a lenient view of his erring subordinate.

The rain came on again as they swept past the hill-crowned village of Addi Jesus, outlined dimly by a veiled moon against the swinging blackness of storm clouds. Then the road ran between the long empty fields of Da Ponte's estate and they were in the northern half of Baressa. For another forty minutes they drove through the rain along a road that, no longer straight, made wide zigzag detours, first toward one small untidy *azienda* and then toward its fellow a few miles on. The vegetation perceptibly thinned and worsened, the road dipped slightly, and once when they topped a rise they could see, far to the east, the moonlight glinting bleakly through shattered clouds on the dark night sea. Then they turned off the road at a tall kilometer post and roared downhill into the Balla estate.

It was as he squelched to a halt in the muddy yard that Baines noticed with a leap of his heart that something unusual was taking place in the *azienda*. Servants were running hither and thither with flaming, hissing oil lamps and buckets of water. Even as he and Miranos jumped from the hardly halted car a billow of orange flame puffed up from one end of the big house. Together they ran up the steps and onto the wide porch. There, by the hot white light of several oil lamps, four house servants were grouped, chattering shrilly, around Balla, who lay panting in an old deck chair with blood from a wide head wound trickling down his face. Behind him, through the open doors, the police officers could see flames spurting in the depths of the house.

"*Silenzio!*" snapped Baines at the strident servants. "Where's he gone, Balla?"

The old concessionaire stared up through dazed, pain-filled eyes. "He's gone," he groaned, "gone. He's away. He tried to kill me—he shot me." For the first time Baines noticed blood seeping through the old man's shirt high on the shoulder.

"It was a damned bad shot, then," he muttered, as he quickly examined Balla's wounds. If the old farmer was going to die there were some questions he wanted to ask him first. But though the head wound was deep and gory it had been too far to the side to do much damage and the gunshot in the shoulder was unimportant.

"You're all right, so stop moaning!" said Baines hardly, and as the shocked old man still continued to groan and swing his head restlessly he leaned forward and slapped him smartly across the face. Balla grunted and spat but remained still.

"Now, quickly! Where's he gone?" Baines' intense urgency seemed to communicate itself to the farmer through the haze of shock and pain.

"To the creek five miles along the road. Yes—that's where he must have gone, for they said he drove down that track to the right."

"What did he want here?"

"I think—he—came to—kill me."

"When did he leave?"

"About ten minutes ago. The servants heard him. They ran when he fired and he dropped his pistol. I think—" But Baines waited to hear no more. He dashed through the crowd of panting natives carrying water buckets into the flaming house, leaped into his car, and rocketed out of the yard with Miranos still struggling into his seat.

The track to the right. It showed up almost immediately in the glare of the headlamps—a dripping rough earthen lane overhung by low trees and masses of trailing creepers. The Alfa Romeo lurched and bounced down it at breakneck speed. Ten minutes. They were hot on his heels. Baines was grinning again now, and he chattered nonsense to Miranos as they crashed and jumped over the uneven surface. Stralowski wasn't lost. He wouldn't get away. All would yet be well.

Even the unemotional Miranos was affected by his patron's mercurial rise in spirits and grinned sardonically at the effrontery of a one-legged cripple trying to escape the Captain.

"We're going to fix him this time, Miro! We'll be taking home a corpse in the back. Just like the time we found old Pagila stabbed down on the road to Agamo."

"This corpse has got to be killed first, Capitano," reminded Miranos cautiously, "and while it still lives it is dangerous. It may have another pistol. You will be careful—please."

They suddenly emerged from the embowering tunnel of the track and shot down a steep incline to a sandy beach. There before them, gleaming wetly through the rain in the beam of the headlights, was the hospital car—the green Fiat. With a shout of pure relief Baines seized his revolver and leaped out.

"Stralowski!" he called loudly.

"Baines?" The German's voice, surprised, almost admiring, seemed to come from the shore, and as the Police Chief, followed by Miranos, ran down the shelving beach of soft sand the moon, appearing through the torn rain clouds, flooded the desolate scene with cold white light. Nearly in the middle of a long, thin reef of rock that projected out into the sea stood the German, propped on his crutches. Twenty yards farther out at the reef's end was a rowing boat with a dark figure on the thwarts. A quarter of a mile away on the flat, rain-pocked moonlit sea lay the small black hull—unmistakable to Baines—of the *Bina*.

For the first twenty yards the reef was narrow and edged, only a few inches wide. Stralowski must have crawled slowly along it on his hands and single knee, and even so it must have taxed his strength. Baines, attempting to run along it, stumbled and slipped on the slimy green weed, falling painfully to his hands and knees every few feet and nearly losing his pistol. The German, who had gained the wider, smoother part, made what speed he could toward the waiting dinghy, and at one moment, when his ankle twisted agonizingly on a loose stone, the Police Chief thought his quarry might yet evade him. But Stralowski, too, was in difficulties; his rubber-tipped crutches, skidding on the wet rock, doubled him up, and though he strove frantically to regain his balance he had hardly done so before his pursuer was upon him. They stood for a second face to face, panting and grinning, Baines with his pistol leveled at the German's chest, Stralowski with his crutch raised for a blow. At the end of the reef Rossi bent to his oars and drove the dinghy vigorously out to sea.

"So!" Baines grinned breathlessly into the German's face.

"So!" mocked Stralowski. He lowered his crutch and slipped it under his armpit. For a moment longer they stared at each other, half-laughing with a queer embarrassment at this too-dramatic meeting. Neither knew quite what to say. Everything somehow seemed inappropriate to the occasion.

Baines, filled with hysterical relief, noted, oddly without surprise, that Stralowski was shaking with suppressed laughter and in another moment he, too, would have done the same. But, hearing the receding splash of Rossi's oars, he yelled in a high, crowing, triumphant voice, "Okay, Rossi! We'll get you one day!"

There was no reply. Miranos, scrambling up behind him said, "All right, Capitano?"

"All right."

"Here?"

"No—later." Baines stuck the gun into the waistband of his white trousers, still gazing with rapture into the smiling face of his captive. All was well. He could still scarcely believe it, for at the bottom of his mind he had been convinced for the last three hours that Stralowski would make good his escape. By some miracle he had prevented it by a hairsbreadth. The disaster to Lemonfield—to himself—was averted and never should it be repeated. Soon this broad, ugly, smiling, sinister man would be dead—tomorrow's dawn would break on a Baressa freed of his malign presence. Face to face they stood in the drenching rain under the wan moonlight on the rocky sea-girt reef, and to Baines it was the greatest triumph in his young life—the most exhilarating success he had achieved in his twenty-six years.

Stralowski shrugged his broad shoulders, still laughing, and hooked a hand in his belt. His thumb moved to the heavy emblazoned clasp, pressed, and the front fell forward and downward, bringing with it two stubby barrels. As they reached the

214

horizontal they exploded with a crashing detonation that drove two heavy soft-lead bullets into Baines' stomach and threw him flat on his back at the feet of the astonished Miranos. Before the latter could understand what had happened Stralowski stooped, tore the pistol from the Police Chief's trousers, and fired rapidly three times into the half-caste's face. The little body in the black rubber mackintosh dropped silently to the rocks and lay still. Stralowski bent over Baines who, speechless and blue-lipped and staring with agony, was trying ineffectually to rise to a sitting posture. Blood leaked from his gasping mouth and welled, black in the moonlight, between fingers clutched across his torn stomach.

"All right, all right," muttered Stralowski, much as he might have soothed a sick child. He grinned suddenly. "It's checkmate once more for you, Baines, isn't it? Poor Baines!" Then he pushed the Police Chief gently back against the rocks, pressed the muzzle of his pistol into his right eye and fired. The back of the head flew open and brains and blood fell out in a long tangled coil. Then, as the moon was once more obscured by cloud, Stralowski turned and swung slowly away down the reef, calling to Rossi as he went.

Ten minutes later, as the splashing of oars grew fainter and ceased, there was a sudden vivid flash of lightning and the rain redoubled its force, falling almost solidly from the sky with a hissing roar that muffled the chug of the *Bina*'s engines as she made for the open sea on a northerly course.

For the rest of that night as the tide came in the storm crackled and growled over the coast and flash upon flash of lightning lit up the two motionless bodies sprawled on the disappearing reef.

23

Two days later, after the first fury of his rage had subsided, after he had visited the Balla concession and the secret cove at the end of the track, after he had done all that was possible to hush up the entire occurrence, Colonel Lemonfield sat in his office considering the position with his assistant.

"Of course, if he is recaptured and it is discovered where he has come from our position here will be extraordinarily unenviable. But I think he realizes that and I don't think he will give us away."

"Really?" James shook his head, smiling. "You place a lot of reliance on his so-called gratitude for our helping to save his life. I must say I don't consider he's exhibited very much gratitude in slaughtering Baines before escaping. As a farewell gesture it lacks good feeling."

"I don't expect any gratitude or anything else from that man," retorted the Colonel irritably. "But he has his own reasons for not wanting it to be known where he comes from. Firstly, he will not wish to be placed in the hands of trained and competent interrogators who will not be content until they have found out considerably more about his doings here than either I or Baines could. Secondly, he undoubtedly murdered Miranos and almost certainly poor Baines as well. Now Baines, being a soldier, might be considered fair game, but Miranos was a civilian, and killing him counts as murder. He could probably be shot for that—even if I were unable to prove him a spy, which I should certainly try to do if he were so foolish as to admit to his recent whereabouts. But, even so, the situation is still unpleasantly dangerous. For if he *did* get caught and *did* explain that he had been here for four years, eighteen months of which he had spent as a prisoner, and if he further admitted to shooting a British officer in order to escape—why, then, my good James, I should be—h'm—*persona non grata* to quite an unexampled degree as far as the Army was concerned." Euan examined his polished, almond-shaped fingernails critically. "I should be in a very, very difficult position."

He sat up briskly. "Well, that may never happen—I don't think it will, for somehow I don't think Stralowski is going to get caught. But as I have deceived the Base authorities up to the present I fear I must continue to do so. Will you therefore please render a report stating that Baines was drowned in the performance of his duties. As chief of the Customs and Excise it is perfectly possible that he might have been apprehending smugglers off Pelican Island and, being stunned by a blow on the head from an oar, fallen overboard in the darkness, and not been missed until too late. Anyway, you invent something along those lines—you've been a journalist, so it should be easy."

"Very well."

"And I fear you'll have to supervise the police once more"— Euan sounded apologetic—"at least until we can make some other arrangement. But whatever we do we'll never be able to replace Baines, I'm afraid."

"No, I suppose not." James gazed sadly out of the window. "He was a quaint young man—I never got to know him well."

"I did, I think. He was so wrapped up in his work he never thought of anything else. That is what made him seem quaint, I expect. A great loss—you might put that in the report, by the way."

Later that morning Fortu opened the door and said, "Corporal Summerson is here, Excellency. He says you sent for him."

"Tell him to come in."

William, entering the long room, thought that it never changed. For four years he had been sent or called from time to time to the Colonel's office. It was always exactly the same—no piece of furniture against the white paneled walls, no Persian rug on the shining yellow floor, had been moved an inch from its original position on the day that Colonel Giordano left the room for the last time. If the Italian Governor were to return tomorrow he would find no difference save for the twin-framed pictures of the King and Queen of England that hung on the wall behind the great desk. The Colonel himself had changed as little as his surroundings. He still sat, small and very upright in his ornate high-backed chair; he still failed to acquire a tropical tan; and his rather stern face with the thin nose, compressed lips, and large dark eyes retained its distinctive sallow pallor. Blandly ignoring dress regulations, he still wore expensive white linen shirts and semistarched collars—a touch that he must have known managed to remove any possible suggestion of the battlefield from his immaculate red-tabbed uniform and that subtly stamped him once and for all as an administrator, a man of the desk. Nor had the heavy atmosphere of authority and power always felt in his presence changed, unless perhaps it had increased slightly with the years. Entering that presence, one still felt a natural awe of

217

this little man, a feeling of relief if he seemed in a good humor, a coldness in the stomach if he did not.

Today William was unable to read any signs of good or bad humor on that pale, aquiline face. The Colonel looked tired and perhaps worried, but the furrow between the arched black brows that warned of impending storms was absent.

"Ah, Summerson, come in. Come in and sit down."

"Yes, sir." William looked at him with surprise; he had never been told to sit in the Governor's presence before. He drew a chair up to the other side of the desk and the Colonel looked at him closely for a moment.

"Have you heard about Baines?"

"No, sir. That is, nothing definite. People say—" He hesitated.

"Go on," prompted the Colonel.

"—that he's dead."

"How do they say he died?"

"No one seems to know."

"Well, you and the rest of the Signals must know now. Three nights ago the German prisoner escaped, and in trying to recapture him Baines appears to have been killed."

"Good Lord!"

"It's a shocking business altogether and, I'm sorry to say, the blame rests entirely on Baines' own shoulders. He had express orders from me to keep Stralowski closely under guard in the hospital and even, if he thought it necessary, to transfer him to Fort Brocca. Instead of obeying these orders, I now find he had been in the habit of letting the man out more or less when he chose, and often unaccompanied. I am quite at a loss to understand such crass disobedience—such incredible folly—from an officer who in every other respect was excellent." He paused, drumming on the glass desk top with the fingers of his left hand. "For certain very good reasons I don't want anyone to learn the truth except the British personnel here. You will therefore tell Sergeant Hope and the rest of the section what I have told you and inform them that I want it put about that Baines died attempting to intercept armed smugglers who killed him and one of his men and made good their escape. And I intend to let it be known that Stralowski is ill—shortly I shall give it out that he is dead. You understand?"

"Yes, sir."

"Good." The Colonel was silent for a minute and William, still shocked by what he had heard, sat musing over Baines' untimely end. Outside in the Piazza del Re the rain had temporarily ceased and a watery gleam of sunshine glistened across the wet roadways and made a great rainbow sash of iridescent color from a long streak of motor oil at the corner of the Via della Costa.

Then the Colonel said, with a brisker note in his voice, "I did not send for you merely to tell you what I have, Summerson. Naturally, the correct person to tell would have been Sergeant Hope, but I'm busy and as I have something else to discuss with you I thought I would kill the proverbial two birds. Now let me see, where is . . . ?" The Colonel let his sentence trail off unfinished as he searched rapidly through a drawer—he never permitted wire trays to cumber his desk's surface—and pulled out what appeared to be an architect's plan of a building. He studied it silently for a moment and then looked up.

"Now, Summerson, you're very fond of fish, I believe?"

"Fish, sir? Not particularly." William looked on this surprising question as an accusation of gluttony and rather resented it. It was not the Colonel's business what he ate, and in any case it was not true. It must be Texas he was thinking of—Texas adored fish.

"Oh." Lemonfield frowned. "Everybody told me you were. And you keep some unhappy octopus in a cage, don't you?"

"In a tank, sir. I don't think it's unhappy, and we're not intending to eat it, in any case."

The Colonel waved these matters aside. "What you keep it in or intend to do with it or what the state of its spirits may be are not subjects of speculation on my part, I assure you. The fact remains that you do that sort of thing, presumably, because you like fish."

"Oh, yes—I see what you mean. Yes, I do like those sort of fish, sir," replied William, drawing a firm distinction between fish as a study and as a meal.

The Colonel appeared satisfied. "Would you consider yourself to be—in an amateur manner, of course—a student of marine biology?"

"Well"—William hesitated modestly—"in a very amateur way, perhaps."

219

"Amateur or not, you appear to be the only one on the island. Are there any interesting or unusual fish in our waters?"

"Oh Lord, yes! There are an amazing amount of different sorts of fish around the coast," said William enthusiastically. "I've collected as many as eight different types of——"

The Colonel laughed. "I can see you're keen enough about fish, at any rate. Now I'll tell you what this is all about. The other day I and the Mayor and one or two others were talking about the future of this island after the war. I won't bother you with all we said, for it is not relevant to the matter in hand. The fact is that Baressa is a very unimportant little island from the international point of view, in any case. However, sooner or later we— that is you and I and the Major and Captain Kellermann and all the Englishmen here at present—will presumably be recalled." He paused.

"Yes—I suppose so," said William slowly. "It will be rather a —a wrench. I mean leaving, after all this time, won't it, sir?"

"Perhaps," said the Colonel shortly, shying away from a subject which he obviously found distasteful. "However, while we've been here I feel we have done some good. That feeling is shared by those of the inhabitants who are persons of standing and authority and they want us to leave behind some—some memorial of our stay. I happened to be discussing public amenities with the Mayor the other day when he remarked that it was a pity that San Pietro had no aquarium for he believed there was enough interesting marine life to justify one. The upshot was that I decided to set up an aquarium as a memorial of my—of our time on Baressa. It is not to be a very large one nor—as we have no professional man to stock it—will it presumably be of much scientific value. But it will be interesting for future visitors and an acquisition for the city. I want you to catch the fish for it, Summerson, if you think you can."

William's face lit up enthusiastically. "Yes, I can easily get plenty. I know most of the best places where the different sorts are to be found. It will take some time to get really good specimens, I expect. How many tanks are you thinking of having, sir?"

The Colonel examined the plan on his desk. "As it happens, there is an ideal building for the Aquarium—the old Casa del Fascio in the Piazza President Wilson—do you know it?"

"I've never been inside."

"A lobby and one large hall. It used to be used for meetings of the local Party organizations. You'd better visit it today—get the keys from the Mayor's secretary at the Municipio—and look around. I think we might manage forty tanks. Fifteen along each side wall and ten across the back. We'll have them built in, of course, with the necessary lighting and apparatus. You see, the building is confiscated property as it belonged to the Fascist Party, which is now outlawed and dissolved, so we pay nothing for that. Then the Engineers have kindly offered to build the tanks and install the necessary apparatus before they leave, so that will cost us very little either. Consequently we can use what little money Brinsmead and I can scrape up on the interior decoration and the external inscription and so forth."

William was enchanted. "I think it's an excellent idea, sir! I can't think of any other sort of memorial that would be nearly as good!"

"Exactly." The Colonel smiled. "The Municipality will be able to see to its upkeep for a very small outlay, in which, of course, it compares favorably with some sort of charitable institution like an orphanage or a home for the aged. Well, that's all then, Summerson. I'm giving orders for the building to be prepared right away. I'll let you know when you can start to collect the exhibits."

"We could put the octopus in as soon as a tank is ready."

"Yes, yes, by all means. Now please tell Sergeant Brinsmead I want him."

Colonel Lemonfield had one further interview that morning. It was with Captain Kellermann. He was ushered into the office on the stroke of noon and found the Colonel sitting at an empty desk, his hands clasped before him on the shining glass top.

"Good morning, Christopher."

"Good morning, sir. Did you want to see me about the promotion of those corporals? I've brought some reports on them and their——"

"No. Brinsmead will deal with that. I've got something else I want to say to you. Sit down."

Christopher did as he was told with an uneasy feeling that Silvana was going to be the subject of the ensuing talk. He was right. After a few moments of silence, during which the Colonel examined his fingernails and Christopher's unstable nervous system was subjected to an ever-increasing strain, the door opened and Fortu looked apologetically in.

"Are you busy, Excellency?"

"I am. What do you want, Fortu?"

"Only to bring this from Sergeant Brinsmead, *signore*." Fortu crossed to the desk with some note pinned to a blue file. The Colonel read it, scrawled a reply on the bottom, and sent his secretary out. Christopher, by now in a state of acute distress, licked his lips and tried to rub his damp palms unobtrusively on the sides of his chair.

The Colonel, having frowned at the desk and pondered for a few more agonizing moments, confirmed Christopher's worst fears by saying, "It's about Silvana Angellini. Exactly what *is* the present relationship between you and her?"

"N-nothing. There isn't any relationship. I mean, you said a long time ago——"

"I know, I know. But, regardless of what I said, you seem to see a great deal of her. Also, I am informed that she is in love with you."

Christopher flushed. "Who says so?" he asked sullenly.

"Never mind!" snapped the Colonel. "Is it true?"

"Well," said Christopher reasonably enough, "it might be. I wouldn't know. All I can say is I can't help it if she is."

The Colonel was silent for a moment. When he spoke again his voice had lost none of its sternness. "You knew perfectly well, after I spoke to you the first time about this, that I wanted you to leave that girl alone. I am not going to stand for a scandal concerning you and Silvana. It would upset a great many people and I will *not* allow it! If she believes she's in love with you I can only suspect you've had a hand in it. You've been seen about together with increasing frequency, and that lends considerable substance to my suspicion. Now, once and for all, Christopher, I tell you to leave that girl alone! If I hear that you've been seen about together once more I shall write to the mainland and ask for your removal." A sudden thought seemed to strike him. "You're not really in love with her yourself, are you?"

"How can I be," muttered Christopher bitterly, "if I'm not even allowed to talk to her?"

The Colonel pondered this deeply for a full minute, eyeing

Christopher musingly the while. At last he said wearily, "Let me try to clarify the situation. Silvana is alleged to love you. It seems to me that you are—or want to be—in love with her. Supposing such to be the case, there are two courses, either of which it might be considered natural for you to take. Either you could keep her as your mistress or you could marry her. The first I absolutely and utterly prohibit. The second would almost certainly be vetoed by the Army. If you attempt to follow the first course I shall have you sent away from here as quickly as possible. If you write to the Army and request permission to marry the girl it will probably be refused and you will be hurriedly put out of temptation by being transferred elsewhere. And even"—the Colonel's voice took on a kinder, more persuasive tone—"even if by some extraordinary chance the Army overcame its inherent dislike of its junior officers attempting to wed alien nationals in occupied territories and granted permission—even then, Christopher, I really think you would be unwise to avail yourself of the opportunity. Silvana has been born and brought up on this island. She might, perhaps, become eventually acclimatized to life in Italy, but in England—no. It would be too completely different. She would be unhappy and so would you. Then I doubt if your parents would particularly welcome the child of an Italian N.C.O. in the colonial Carabinieri as a daughter-in-law." He paused and eyed Christopher, who glowered darkly out of the window. "Anyway, as I have already said, you can be nearly certain that the Army would not allow it. If you really want to marry the girl and wish to apply for permission, you may do so, of course. I can't approve, but I won't hinder you. If you don't want to do that, then you are to let her alone. Now that's final, Christopher, so don't forget it!"

It was raining again when the Colonel left the Palace. The great Negro sentries stood disconsolately in the ornamental stone boxes, doubtless envying the guards of the Banda whose duties kept them within the vast building, and the square was deserted. There were none of the usual passersby to stop and gaze in respectful awe at the Governor coming down the steps, the sentries taking a pace forward and stamping to the "present arms" and the two uniformed footmen holding open the door of the long gray Packard sedan that had recently taken the place of Giordano's blue tourer. As he was driven rapidly through the rain toward the Villa Euan pondered, as was his custom, on the events of the morning. Through all the many official duties, through all the conversations, orders, suggestions, demands, that crowded back in this habitual brief review there was one short remark that stuck like a burr in his mind. "It will be rather a wrench. I mean, leaving, after all this time"—a casual remark of Summerson's. A wrench—that, thought Euan somberly, was an understatement. For if it would be a wrench for Summerson what would it not be for him? And yet, he mused, I have much to go back to. My career, my opportunities in a world far greater and more important than this little island—at least, to everyone except me. And I might go far—the King's Bench, or Parliament. Perhaps a peerage, or in due course of time Lord Chief Justice. Yes, he had much to return to. Professional success, future honors, almost certain wealth. Then why did he view the prospect with such queer distaste? Why did he seem to look on that prospect of success, honors, riches with a sort of indulgent, slightly contemptuous indifference, as if they were mere toys, the desire for which he had outgrown in the accustomed use of one more splendid thing? Because, thought Euan with a flash of insight all the more painful for being starkly true, I have almost absolute power here, and when I put *that* down, as I must, the highest place of professional eminence will be meaningless; no honors can indemnify nor can all the wealth in the world reimburse me for that loss.

24

BY the end of September the Engineers had completed the last of General Glasscraft's fortifications—in plenty of time, as Major Naughton-Muirhead remarked, for the next war, when they would doubtless prove invaluable to some enemy opposing a British landing—and had all returned to San Pietro.

A section under Lieutenant Paige had been in the city since July and were still engaged on work in the new Aquarium. It was a consolation to Colonel Lemonfield that the Engineers' prolonged visit had thus not been without some profit to his Administration. Major Sherwood's hopeful expectation of being once more invited to live in the Villa had come to nothing and he now resided in one of the two small houses originally put at the Engineers' disposal by Brinsmead. He shared it with Captain Lycett-Collis and they spent most of their time sitting in two shabby deck chairs on the creeper-smothered back veranda, drinking and dozing through the long hot autumn days.

The two lieutenants shared the second house and soon reverted to their dock-gamin habits. They were to be seen at most hours of the day drifting about the calm, oily surface of the harbor in a patched-up old dinghy with fishing lines trailing from the stern, or loitering, hands in pockets, along the crowded commercial quays where the dingy little tramps and long, gaily painted dhows jostled each other at the berths.

Their departure, with the rest of their unit, was due in late October, and it was some two weeks before this that Major Naughton-Muirhead, sitting idly beside the window in his comfortable office, was surprised by a visit from Lieutenant Paige. He was still more surprised to see that his visitor was dressed in a neat, freshly ironed khaki drill uniform complete with cap and Sam Browne belt.

"I want to talk to you about something, sir—if I may," said Paige with that invariable gravity of expression which, with his narrow head and large spectacles, lent him, when he pleased, the air of some prim, industrious student of divinity.

"Sit down, then." James proffered a box of cheroots. "Would you like one of these?"

"Are they what the Port Pilot smokes?"

"Good Heavens, no! Certainly not!"

"He's always offering me cigars. I had one once. I was disgustingly sick—on the floor of the *Silver Lizard*, I think it was."

"Most embarrassing for you," remarked James dryly.

"Oh no, sir. Not really. People are always doing that. They're used to it there—the floor's concrete, you see. But I haven't come to talk to you about that."

"I should hope not, indeed. It's entirely outside my province."

"Yes." Paige paused, looking, James thought, a trifle embarrassed. "Actually I've come about a job. I wondered whether it would be a good thing if I became Police Chief here."

"Did you? What makes you think it might be?"

"Well"—Paige frowned—"after all, Baines is dead and you need someone, I suppose, don't you? And I speak the language. And I know the island—every ——ing foot of it by now," he added with a touch of bitterness. "Also, I'm on the spot. I thought perhaps I'd ask you what you thought before I asked the Colonel."

James looked at him while surprised amusement gave way to speculation. "H'm—I wonder what the Colonel would say?"

"Well, I thought you'd have an idea. That's why I came to you first."

"Myself"—James shrugged—"I'm all for letting anybody have the job who wants it, for I've had to try and supervise the police since Baines'—ah—unfortunate demise, and, frankly, they bore me. But"—James looked critically at Paige—"tell me, why do you want it?"

The lieutenant hesitated a moment, then he said, "A lot of things, really. I like this island and I don't want to leave, and I really don't think there's much future in Sherry's unit, somehow."

"Very little indeed, I should imagine."

"Yes—and when we get back to the mainland somebody may find out that he's permanently pickled—in fact, I think it likely that they will. Then we'd get another boss and he'd probably be a bastard. We wouldn't like that—not after Sherry."

"No. I can understand that," commented James with becoming seriousness. "Nonetheless, these all seem rather negative reasons for wanting to become Baressa's Chief of Police."

"You don't think I ought to tell them to the Colonel, then?"

"No. I think he would be more impressed if you adopted a more positive attitude. I think you'd much better say that you have always had a great ambition to become a police officer and that you believe you could do the job and are very keen to try. Tell him you were a friend and admirer of the late Chief and that he often talked to you about the job and that you picked up a lot from him. Tell him that you possess a natural love and understanding where the Carabinieri are concerned. Tell him——"

"Well, Paige," said the Colonel an hour later, "this request of yours has surprised me. However, I am prepared to apply for your entry into O.E.T.A. and if it is granted—as I think it will be—to employ you here. But"—he looked sternly at the would-be Police Chief—"I shall expect you not only to work hard, but to behave in a fitting and dignified manner. You will find that working for me is a very different thing to working for Major Sherwood. I will tell you candidly that I am extremely unimpressed with your present unit. If you revert to type at a later date I shall not hesitate to dismiss you."

At lunch he said to James, "I'm not sure it's very wise, but I'm frightened of being sent another Pirie."

"Oh, he may be all right. He knows the island and speaks Italian. Did he tell you he was fond of the Carabinieri?"

"He did. An extraordinary admission, I thought it. Do you think he's all right? Has he taken some erotic fancy to Commino or Amerigo or one of the Brigadieri, do you suppose?"

"No," said James decidedly. "His tastes, if low, are quite orthodox."

"I hope so, I'm sure. A scandal of *that* sort, after all these years," remarked the Colonel gloomily, "would be *too* shaming!"

"Too shaming!" corroborated Mrs. Giordano's parrot in a falsetto shriek. "Too shaming! Too shaming!"

"Take that bird out," said the Colonel.

The weeks went by and the Engineers departed. Not all of them, for, as was to be expected, several were accidentally left behind. They went, as they had come, in a state of dismal confusion—the men fighting over their rations, the three officers quarreling tipsily about their cabins. Captain Lycett-Collis took away five crates of coconuts, which he had some scheme for shipping to England and selling at a great price. Lieutenant Ventham unknowingly took away his half-caste mistress and a drab dun-colored child—they smuggled themselves into a lifeboat on the transport and were not discovered until halfway through the voyage. Major Sherwood's batman took away a pair of Colonel Lemonfield's shoes which he had somehow managed to steal from the Villa. They left Lord Paige sitting in Police Headquarters dressed from top to toe in an exact replica, except for buttons and badges, of a Carabinieri officer's uniform.

When the police had discovered that their new chief was an English milord they were hugely impressed. They addressed him alternatively as Conte, Commendatore, Marchese, and even Altesso. Mrs. Tamminetto voiced their sentiments when she said, "We like very much indeed to have as our chief a noble. We feel it is both high and honorable and in the Carabinieri tradition to be commanded by an aristocrat. My husband, though he had no title, was descended on his mother's side from persons of very high social rank. His aunt, too, was the second wife of a Papal Count. I myself have always had admiration and pleasure in the nobility. Now I am very happy, for I am a friend of two, for you, Marchese, are noble in the same way as my dear friend Captain Zvengetzov—is it not so?"

"No," said Paige firmly, "it's not. English milords are quite different from Hungarian sailors. They are far more noble, for one thing."

"Captain Zvengetzov is a Knight of the Order of St. Stanislaus," informed Mrs. Tamminetto in a disappointed tone.

"And I shall be a Knight of the Order of the Boot unless we get a little work done this morning. To start with, will you be kind enough to explain to me why Brigadicre Rondotto considers it beneath his dignity to be employed on anything except the detection of carnal violence? I don't think we have enough N.C.O.s to allow one of them to specialize in rape."

"It was considered quite all right by Captain Baines," declared Mrs. Tamminetto provocatively. Brigadiere Rondotto was, after the Port Pilot and the Maresciallo, one of her greatest admirers.

"And it is in the tradition of the Carabinieri Reali, I suppose?"

"Oh yes, I think so."

"Well, then," said Paige gravely, "there is, of course, no more to be said. Brigadiere Rondotto shall continue to deal exclusively with sexual crime."

"Dear Marchese!" Mrs. Tamminetto smiled benignly and raised a hand to pat the thin, spectacled, boyish face. But she prevented herself just in time. There was something about the Marchese that hinted strongly that such frolicsome gestures would be out of place. He was not gay—no. He was serious and had much official dignity. But he was quite delightful, nonetheless. One had only to say that such a thing had been the practice of Captain Baines and that such another was in the Carabinieri tradition and he invariably agreed to continue them.

Despite his outward gravity, Lord Paige was enjoying himself ecstatically in his new position. Seeking ever the complete rock bottom in military values and ideals—the utter antithesis of the Grenadier Guards into which family tradition had tried unavailingly to force him—he had at last found his Eldorado. A corps which put even the Central African Engineers in the shade, a unit which made even Sherry's company look drab and serious by comparison. His continual parody of the Carabinieri, so blandly unperceived by its victims, was a source of excruciating inward delight that caused him, at the end of each delirious day at Police Headquarters, to fall helplessly on his bed, his meager frame racked by spasm after spasm of uncontrollable laughter.

As well as their clothes, he copied their dramatic gestures, their clumsy clicking and bowing, their ridiculous salute, their overpolite, ingratiating pomposity of manner—even their incurable habit of melodrama and histrionics in the most inappropriate places. As the weeks went by he rapidly acquired a lonely, perverted passion for this amusement, acting daily a continual delicious satire of which he was the sole admiring audience. Soon it became almost second nature to him, so that for much of the time he really was a Carabinieri officer, vain, futile and furious. Only at the very back of his mind the thin, wiry boy still stood shaking with sardonic laughter.

His peculiar virtuosity in this performance became weirdly brilliant. He managed to fly into the semblance of a towering rage while untidily eating an elaborately sticky cream bun at his desk. He delivered a passionate and rhetorical harangue on certain astonishing modes of behavior, which he asserted were Carabinieri traditions, while standing in the doorway of the native constables' lavatory, nor would he move aside when those desirous of entering humbly explained their need.

Nonetheless he was careful to do his work, if not with the intense methodical devotion of Baines, at least with a sort of slapdash efficiency which gave Brinsmead no chance to increase the even flow of his perennial complaints. He took, too, a leaf out of Christopher's book, and constantly visited the Governor for orders, punctiliously clicking his heavy jackboots and trying to remember to salute in the English manner. And though the Colonel eyed him a little oddly he said nothing, except afterward to his friend and assistant.

"James, I think young Paige must have been telling the truth

229

when he told me he was fond of the Carabinieri. Have you noticed his clothes?"

"I have. So has everybody else. The Signals refer to him as Brigadiere Paige, or 'Brig' for short. He told Brinsmead that he intends to apply for a transfer to the Carabinieri after the war."

"Indeed? I wonder," mused the Colonel, frowning, "whether Dr. Valdonetti knows anything of psychiatry?"

25

CHRISTMAS came and brought with it even gayer festivities than usual. The war was surely in its last stages, victory seemed assured, and by next Christmas the world would be at peace—exhausted, perhaps, but still at peace. On Baressa everyone whose social or financial position enabled him to do so gave a party. These ranged from the dignified feast, drawn out to interminable length by flowery pre- and postprandial speeches, which the Senior Sheikhs of the Sharia Court gave to Colonel Lemonfield and the heads of his Administration, to an impromptu and uninhibited alfresco supper on board the floating crane given by Texas to a small gathering of disreputable female friends. Between these two extremes there were four civic dinners, a pigeon shoot followed by a large lunch party on the Saccomani estate, a cocktail party given by the Port Pilot to celebrate the razing of the Kremlin by German fire bombs—an event which Captain Zvengetzov erroneously believed himself to have heard announced on the radio—and a tea party, followed by rather childish indoor games, given by Lord Paige to the Carabinieri.

Among the many events that took place at the Villa was a party given solely for the British military personnel. Colonel Lemonfield was at his most charming, and though the younger Englishmen felt at first as if they had been invited to dine with a formidable headmaster this sensation soon wore off under the influence of the Villa's excellent champagne, of which the Major had seen to it there was an abundance.

During the last week a quantity of booklets and prospectuses had arrived from the mainland, explaining the various ways and means by which, on demobilization, the Army authorities intended to assist their released personnel to resettle themselves in civilian life. Brinsmead and the Colonel had examined these with their usual thoroughness and Euan, who after four and a half years as their overlord felt a genuine paternal affection for the young men under his command, moved unostentatiously from one to another, endeavoring to ascertain their future plans. It was therefore with some surprise and a certain repressed annoyance that he found that, with one exception, they appeared to have given the future no serious thought at all. The exception was Texas, who, in default of Rossi, had induced Captain Vrontas of the *Anna Gabriella* to half promise him a job as second mate. At least, it was an advance on his colleagues.

"But surely," Euan inquired of Sergeant Hope, "you have something to go back to? What were you before the war?"

"Me, sir?" The lanky Sergeant took off his spectacles and rubbed them. "I was a clerk in a firm of tea importers—Stenthorpe, Blackwell, and Monckhouse—quite a large concern in the city."

"I suppose you'll go back to them?"

"Well, I can't actually, sir. You see, they used to keep up with the Service members of the staff—I used to get a circular once a quarter full of the firm's news. But they were bombed out in 1940 and last year I got a very nice letter from Mr. Blackwell himself saying that things were bad and they'd had to cut down their expenses and—well, he was very sorry and all that, but——"

"I see. But you're a trained clerk. I suppose you'll go to some other firm?"

Hope looked doubtful. "I suppose I might, sir. But, to tell you the truth, I don't know that I really fancy the life anymore —not after living out here all these years."

"Then what *will* you do?"

"Well, I *had* thought I'd try to avoid demobilization for as long as possible and hang on here while they keep the radio going."

Euan shook his head. "Not very wise, Hope, I consider. You'll be getting older and the jobs at home will be snapped up in your absence. I'll get Brinsmead to send you down a few pamphlets on one or two things you might like to try."

He fared worse, if anything, with the others. Sergeant Whyton wanted to leave the Regular Army and get a job in Colonial Posts and Telegraphs. But at thirty-six he thought he might be too old. The Colonel thought so, too, and pressed him to think well before he left the Service.

William believed that he might like to go in for marine biology—if he could get a job of that sort.

"It will mean a long time of study and a lot of exams, I expect," said the Colonel. "You will have to work hard to make up for the time you've lost."

William shied away from the prospect of prolonged and studious labors. "Perhaps I'll think of something else," he said.

Christopher agreed with disconcerting lack of enthusiasm that he would presumably enter his father's great cooked-meat business. "I'll probably have to, I suppose. But I don't want to."

"Why not?"

"It seems so dull."

"I thought you were keen to have a quiet, settled sort of life."

"Well—in a way, sir. But I'm sure I shan't like being an executive in a sausage factory."

"But what would you do if you didn't do that?"

"I don't know, really."

Euan was getting a little tired of this vague attitude. "You must realize," he said firmly, "that once the war's over you'll have to get down to a serious, sensible job of work. You'll have to take your place in the general scheme of things. You can't spend the rest of your life as a sort of Peter Pan, boating perpetually around the coast of a tropical island."

Christopher sighed. "I suppose not," he said.

Then Euan tried his new Police Chief. "You aren't seriously intending to join the Carabinieri after the war, are you, Paige?"

"I don't think it would be wise to join them seriously, sir. But I shall try to do so in a lighthearted manner. The Carabinieri tradition——"

"I suppose you realize that you would have to take Italian nationality?"

"Is that a very expensive thing to do?"

"I don't think so—but expense is hardly the point, is it?"

"Oh, yes, sir. Carabinieri pay is very low by comparison with—say, the London Metropolitan Police."

"Now there's a lot to be said for the Metropolitan Police. If you're really set on being a policeman why not——"

"No, sir. I couldn't do that even if I wanted to. My relations wouldn't allow it."

"If your social position forbids you to join the English police it seems odd that no objections have been raised against your joining the Carabinieri."

"There *have* been objections. My parents wrote and said it was a ridiculously frivolous idea."

"I'm inclined to agree with them. It certainly looks like frivolity to me."

"Frivolity, sir? Oh, I don't think so. The Carabinieri tradition——"

"What exactly *is* the Carabinieri tradition, may I ask?"

But Lord Paige was saved from answering this difficult question by a sudden mad scream of blistering foreign curses from Mrs. Giordano's parrot, which had seized and swallowed a burning cigar butt from a nearby ashtray. The poor bird had been fed by Texas on bits of biscuit soaked in gin and was fast losing control of itself.

"I don't think the Colonel's succeeded in finding out anyone's future plans," remarked the Major to Brinsmead as they sat drinking port at the end of the table after dinner. "I don't think anyone has any, as a matter of fact."

Brinsmead sipped his wine thoughtfully and then made much ado with his moustache and his napkin—it was a Victorian performance that pleased James immensely.

"In my opinion, sir, they don't want to think about their future. It's easy to understand why. We all came out here soon after the war really commenced—before England had really felt very much of it. And there's not been the slightest atmosphere of war here, of course. In fact, time stands still here, as the Commendatore is fond of saying, and consequently we're still prewar people. If England has changed as much as newspapers and letters lead us to believe, then we are in for a considerable shock on our return. And again"—he twirled the stem of his glass between his fingers gazing abstractedly at the ruby wine—"we have been out here—most of us, that is—long enough to have really settled down. We have had to adapt ourselves to the way of life on Baressa." At this James barely repressed a smile. For over four years Brinsmead had fought untiringly to make Baressa adapt itself to *his* way of life. "And now we shall have to readapt ourselves to England. And that"—Brinsmead clipped a cigar with careful attention—"may not be so easy."

"I daresay you're right. I understand, by the way, that the Colonel expects to be requested to stay on here until some decision on the future of the island is reached. That may be several years, of course, for it's so small and unimportant that it probably won't be considered for ages—not until all the other problems have been settled. Will you stay with him?"

"Yes, sir. I'm glad to say that he has asked me to and I've agreed to stay, subject, of course," he added grandly, "to safeguarding my business interests in England meanwhile. What about yourself?"

"I'm not sure." James smiled musingly. "I really don't know what my plans will be. I certainly don't intend to return to Europe for a few years. I might go to America. I have several friends there."

"So I've always understood, sir. You were once in the newspaper business over there, weren't you?"

"I was indeed. Odd as it must seem, Brinsmead, I was for a short space a columnist on the staff of the New York *Herald Tribune*. A most entertaining experience in many ways. More port?"

The conversation drifted off onto subjects of administrative concern—Court Fines, Native Welfare Clinics, and the Public Works Department's consuming desire to incorporate the Fire Service within the framework of its own organization. Brinsmead could never avoid talking shop.

The party ended at midnight and James, returning to the library, found the Colonel sitting in a deep armchair pensively surveying the litter of glasses and bottles.

"I've drunk too much, Euan, I'm afraid. Much more than I intended. I was led astray by Brinsmead." James chuckled. "Brinsmead surprised me—he drank more than anybody else and went away stone-cold sober. To all appearances, at any rate. Tell me, have you any idea what these mysterious 'business interests' of

234

his are? Apparently they need safeguarding or something—he's very pompous about it all. Is he a tycoon in the city?"

Euan laughed. "Don't you know? I thought you knew everything about everybody here. Brinsmead's got two pet shops in Kent. One at Broadstairs and one at Herne Bay. Quite small affairs, I believe, but they do well in the summer if the season's good."

"How most peculiar! But Euan, how very odd! How most un-Brinsmead-like! When *did* you discover this?"

"Oh, I've known it for ages—ever since he first came, I think."

"Extraordinary!" James seemed unable to assimilate this fascinating new information. "I suppose I had never inquired because I thought he *must* be some sort of clerk in peacetime. Does he *like* animals?"

"Loathes them, I understand. He is allergic to tortoises, which bring him out in a rash, and he's convinced all parrots carry psittacosis. He told me he thought it was highly unwise of us to keep the Giordanos' one in the dining room."

"I doubt if we shall be able to much longer. Hark at it! Dawson made the wretched thing drunk."

"Dawson was drunk himself. He and the parrot will be feeling very sorry for themselves tomorrow morning."

"Do you know, Euan, I believe that bird was given drink by the Giordanos? It's had four and a half years' total abstinence and tonight it's broken out at last." From the dining room the pot-valiant parrot could be heard whistling, screaming, and calling out the names of servants past and present, until the Colonel was forced to cover its cage with a cloth.

When Euan said that Texas was drunk he spoke the truth. Texas was quite frequently drunk, but tonight he was drunker than usual. Yet the wine of the Villa had a refining effect on his drunkenness, so that instead of being clumsy, inarticulate, and pugnacious, as he was invariably rendered by a stomachful of cheap spirits in the dock area, he was gay, garrulous, and amicable. He shook hands with an embarrassed native constable on his beat in the Piazza President Wilson and stayed with him so long that when at last he tore himself away his colleagues had disappeared.

235

It didn't matter. The night was fine and Texas had no intention of going to bed for some time. Finding himself in the vicinity of Mr. Morle's house, he made his unsteady way there, ran up the steps, and rang the bell loud and long. After a brief interval the door was opened by the missionary himself.

"Well? Oh, it's you, Dawson, is it? What do you want? It's late. I'm just going to bed."

"I come to say 'Merry Christmas,'" announced Texas, grinning disarmingly, "an' a very happy New Year. I bin to a party."

"So it appears." Mr. Morle eyed him coldly. "Whereabouts?"

"At the Governor's Villa—we all went."

"Oh, indeed." Mr. Morle's inveterate curiosity impelled him to add, "Who else was there?"

"Oh, everyone. Cap'n Kellermann an' L'tenant Paige the new police bloke—you know, the one that's dressed up like a Wop sergeant. Brigadiere, we calls him. Coo, he's a queer bloke, he is! Not s'good as Baines, I reckon. I liked ol' Baines. We was—you know, chummy like. If that bastard Jerry hadn't of killed him I reckon he'd'a been in the party tonight. Funny when you come to think——"

"What did you say?" snapped Mr. Morle suddenly.

"Me?" Texas looked blearily innocent. "I ain't said nothin'."

"About the German prisoner killing Captain Baines?"

A sudden look of consternation wiped the grin off Texas' face. "Did I say that? I didn't mean it, then. Forget it."

Mr. Morle studied him for a long moment in silence and Texas blushed to the roots of his hair. "I reckon I didn't know what I was sayin'," he mumbled foolishly.

"Well, anyway, come in!" The missionary's voice took on a sudden genial, hospitable note. "Come in, Dawson, and have a drink. I think there's a bottle of beer about somewhere. Come in, come in!"

26

B^Y mid March of the new year the Casa del Fascio in the Piazza President Wilson had undergone a complete metamorphosis and was ready to emerge as the Euan Lemonfield Aquarium. The Colonel had wished it to be called the English Aquarium, but the Mayor and his friends had persuaded him to allow his own name to be given to it. They had pointed out that while the other Englishmen on the island were regarded with both respect and affection by their many friends none could be said to have contributed toward Baressa's welfare to anything approaching the same degree as the Colonel. It was he who had reformed the government, brought integrity to the administrative departments, justice to the courts, trade and prosperity to the island. It was he who had swept away the old corrupt practices of the Fascist regime, the restrictive monopolies, the exorbitant taxes and imposts which, while crippling commerce and lowering the island's standards of living, had gone to line the pockets of Colonel Giordano and his associates. To him, and to him alone, Baressa owed a very real debt of gratitude and it was his memory in particular that they wished to venerate.

"A statue," the Mayor had said wistfully, "would have——"

"No, no. Out of the question, Belotta," Euan had interposed, almost equally wistfully. "It wouldn't do at all. But if the Civic Authorities wish the Aquarium to be named after me I must, of course, agree. I think, though, that the words 'and other members of the British Administration' should be added."

"Yes, Excellency, if you say so." Belotta pursed his lips. "In small letters," he added by way of an afterthought.

"Yes, yes. In small letters, naturally."

So the shabby weathered silver fasces had been removed from the façade and the timeworn legend, *"Credere! Obbedire! Combattere!"* above the portico had been overlaid with a facing of finest white marble, and under cover of canvas screens and scaffolding were carved the English words:

THE EUAN LEMONFIELD MEMORIAL AQUARIUM

This Aquarium was given
to the city of San Pietro
by and to commemorate the
government of
H.E. COLONEL E. O. LEMONFIELD, O.B.E.,
and other members of
the
British Administration.

Opened on   1945.

The date was left vacant for a few days and then a mason scrambled up the scaffolding and inserted the words "21st April."

The twenty-first of April was the Colonel's birthday. Exactly a week earlier William had landed the last marine specimen and now the forty big glass tanks were full of strange and beautiful monsters swimming in illuminated water between carefully laid out coral rocks and trailing colored seaweeds. Those members of the Administration who were allowed to attend a preview on the twentieth were astonished and delighted at what they saw.

The twenty-first dawned with the pale whitish sky and dry, still air that betokened great heat, but long before noon the populace was out in the flag-decked streets and by eleven o'clock the Piazza President Wilson, with the municipal band playing operatic music in the palm-shaded center, was packed to suffocation. Punctually at a quarter to twelve the black troops marched to the roped-off square outside the aquarium and formed up in the rigid lines of a guard of honor. As the hour boomed out from the Cathedral clock tower the big gray sedan of the Governor was seen turning into the narrow lane through the crowds that had been kept open with great difficulty by the guards of the Banda. Preceded and followed by a police motorcycle escort, the glossy car moved slowly across the square to the accompaniment of an ovation that drowned utterly the concerted roar of the twelve motorcycle engines.

For several minutes the rattle and clash of rifle butts, the braying of the band, and the tumultuous applause merged into a kaleidoscopic riot of sound that continued until the Colonel and his officers had mounted the steps of the Aquarium, to be greeted by the Mayor and Corporation and the heads of various societies and associations—in fact, by everyone who really mattered on Baressa.

Then came the speeches. The twin themes of the many speakers were the greatness and goodness of Colonel Lemonfield and what they were pleased to term the joint successes of the armed forces of England and Italy, now at last about to be consummated in final victory. No one had the bad taste to refer to the reason for Colonel Lemonfield's presence on the island, and a visitor from another planet must certainly have assumed that he had originally taken office at the request of an admiring and applauding Italian Government. Every recognizable mention, however obscurely pronounced, of the Colonel's name brought forth fresh applause and spurred the Mayor and his loquacious henchmen on to ever greater excesses.

By contrast the Governor's speech was short, and if it could not be termed modest neither was it particularly boastful. Tacitly agreeing that under his sway Baressa had, for the first time, been properly governed, he expressed his deep gratification that the islanders were sensible of the benefits he had conferred upon them. He had, he believed, proved that a firm hand, backed by integrity of purpose, resolute industry, and a sincere regard for the public weal must make for the increasing happiness and prosperity of a people so governed. His pride and contentment at what he had been able to achieve were considerable—but they were as nothing compared with the genuine affection he had come to feel for all the races and classes who made up the inhabitants of Baressa. He did not know how much longer he would remain amongst them as their Governor; it might be a matter of years or only of months. But whenever the time came for him to leave, and wherever he might afterward go, he would remember with deep pride and love the people whom. . . . The rest of his speech was lost in roar upon roar of cheering, and the bellowing, flag-waving crowds surged and jostled against the close-packed ranks of Banda and police that lined the Aquarium steps.

Euan tried a few more sentences, but, seeing that any attempt to make himself heard was useless, he turned laughingly to the

239

Mayor and, with a slight shrug of his shoulders, seized the cord that looped upward to the coverings of the façade and pulled. Two great flags, those of England and Italy, swung slowly apart and the carved and gilded inscription glittered out of the white marble: "THE EUAN LEMONFIELD MEMORIAL AQUARIUM."

The Colonel still had the cord in his hand and the roars of the populace in his ears when someone touched his shoulder and Christopher's voice shouted urgently, "Look! Who are those?"

"What?" Euan turned, smiling, and stared out over the seething square to where Christopher's pointing finger indicated the exit into the Corso Thaon de Reval. There, struggling hopelessly in the unregarding press, he saw figures in British uniforms. The pale khaki of the Army, the tropical white of the Navy.

27

NOON next day. The sunlight flickered across the bright surface of the harbor, glittering on the small waves that splashed gently at the foot of the Dhow Control Point. On the stone quay stood William, Texas, and Commino, staring out at the long gray hull of a cruiser and the clumsier forms of four troop transports that lay at anchor in the roads. To and fro along the warship's side dashed pinnaces and launches, towing glittering white wakes through the cobalt sea. Now and then they would detach themselves from their grim parent and, making quickly for the harbor entrance, round the Dhow Control Point in a flurry of spray and come to rest under the cranes of the commercial docks. Most of them contained two or three naval officers and a shore party of ratings packed side by side in rows of white and blue.

"She's a big ship," remarked Commino at last to break the silence which was growing oppressive.

"Too bloody big." Texas spat glumly into the water and an officer in a passing launch eyed him coldly. "All them others is full of troops. They'll be comin' ashore later."

"Only to stretch their legs," said William.

"Still, I don't like it. I don't want to see a lot of —ing soldiers hangin' around our docks, drinkin' in our bars. After all it *is* our island."

"Well, you're not the only one who feels that way," retorted William morosely. "Nobody likes it—and the Colonel least of all, I should imagine. We've just got to put up with it until they go."

"I still can't see why they got to come here," growled Texas dourly.

"Hopeless explained exactly why at breakfast. If you'd listened to him you'd have understood. They're a troop convoy returning from the Far East and they got hit by some freak storm—some sort of a hurricane, I suppose—and what with the transports being old and unseaworthy they had a rough time. They got scattered and the cruiser told them to make for this island to join up again."

"Why did they all arrive together, then, if they got scattered?"

"How do you know they have? There may be some more to come yet. I——"

The sudden blaring of a motor horn on the docks behind them cut him short. Sergeant Whyton was beckoning to them from the section truck.

"Wake yourselves up there!" he called angrily. "Hope wants you back at once. Come on—run!"

Leaving Commino to his lone vigil, the two signalmen walked slowly back to the docks. They never obeyed Whyton's orders promptly—somehow he never seemed to expect it.

"Well what's all the hurry, Whytey?" demanded William as he swung himself up into the back.

Whyton, swearing under his breath, reversed and turned the old oil-stained vehicle between two cranes before he answered. Then he said, "We're to be inspected in an hour, if you want to know."

"Inspected? Who by? The Colonel?"

"God, no!" Whyton laughed shortly. "He's got plenty on his plate at the moment without that. No. By some bloody twirp of a Signals Major from that sodding outfit." He jerked his head in the direction of the sparkling sea.

"Why?"

"Christ, boy! How in hell should I know? I suppose because the Corps wants to see what we're doing. We haven't seen a Sigs

241

officer since we came here. We can't complain." He pressed the accelerator down to the battered footplate and shot forward, narrowly missing a group of naval officers upon whom the beaming Port Pilot was pressing his black cheroots.

"I'll tell you one thing—the order for the inspection was brought to Hope by someone from one of the troopers—someone you know." He grinned sardonically, his thin mouth twisting under the narrow line of moustache.

"Who, Whytey?"

"No. You guess."

"There couldn't be anyone we know on the troopers," said William, puzzled. "How could there be? Go on, Whytey, who was it?"

The Sergeant's grin widened. "Ever heard of a lad called Pirie?"

"What?" William was aghast. "Not—not the man the Colonel sacked? You don't mean——"

"Don't I? I do then."

"Christ-all-bloody-mighty!"

"Naughty!" reproved Whyton, chuckling as he wriggled deftly through the traffic. "Nasty foul-mouthed little bastard you are, young William, for a padre's son. What would your poor old dad say? Take on something terrible, I bet. Give you a bleedin' good larrupin' more like an'——"

William cut these irrelevant hypotheses short. "But what's he doing on the transport? Has he been to the Far East?"

"I'll tell you what he's doing all right! He's on this sodding General's staff—that's what he's doing. And I'll tell you something else," added Whyton impressively. "I've seen a good many troublemakers one way and another in my time. The old Army's full of them. But if ever I see a lad really out to stir up just as much bloody daylight for everybody as he can—then that lad's our ol' pal Pirie."

"This is all very awkward—very awkward indeed." Colonel Lemonfield strode up and down his office floor, occasionally stopping at one of the long windows to peer angrily out at the distant prospect of the gray hulls lying in the roads. The Major and Sergeant Brinsmead sat together on a brocaded settee, the former smoking his habitual cigar, the latter ready with pad and pencil to take down the Colonel's spoken word. "We must do what we can for these people, I suppose, but it's still very awkward. They'll want their troops to come ashore, but I'm against it. We've built up a lot of goodwill since we've been here, and if the town is suddenly flooded with British troops—who are never well behaved when they disembark from troopships during voyages—we may lose it."

"They'll get drunk and disorderly," prophesied Brinsmead gloomily. "They'll probably wreck a bar or two and a few restaurants and play hell in the brothel quarter. I shouldn't be surprised if they still look on Italians as enemies and try to treat them as such. When one considers all we have—" He was almost taking the word's out of the Colonel's mouth.

"The *worst* thing, the *very worst* thing that could happen! And, of course, as Governor *I'll* be blamed! The islanders will say that I permitted it. They'll say that I am really only another English soldier and much more interested in pandering to the amusements of national troops than to their own welfare. But I'm *damned* if I'll agree to shore leave for this convoy!"

"You'll find it hard not to, I'm afraid," said James sympathetically. "It will naturally cause a lot of resentment."

The Colonel stopped his pacing by the window. "I don't mind being resented by a lot of people out there"—he pointed toward the sea—"but I thoroughly object to the same feeling being manifested by a few people here. That's the point."

"The sailors," remarked Brinsmead darkly, "will be worse than the soldiers. If *they* come ashore there will be hell to pay."

"We might try a system of strict bounds," pondered Euan grudgingly. "If we said they must remain on Ras Godron, for instance. That gives them the waterfront, but stops them getting into the town. They might be a nuisance in the dockside bars, but then those places should be used to that sort of thing."

"They might break into the customs sheds," argued Brinsmead. "I'd ban them from setting foot on the island at all, sir, if I was you."

"As a last concession—" began the Colonel, when Fortu knocked and entered.

"The British General and his staff, Excellency."

"Oh—oh, yes. Very well, show them in, Fortu. You two stay here."

Major General D'Aumont, a big, florid, burly man in the

243

early forties, entered the office accompanied by two staff officers. He strode up to the little Colonel and shook hands with a bluff good humor that was obviously intended to be friendly.

"Good morning, Lemonfield," he growled in a deep bass voice. "I'm afraid we arrived at an awkward time for you yesterday, and I expect you've been cursing us ever since. But we'd no more notion that you were doing the honors at a public occasion than you had that a sudden Armada was going to descend on you, hey? Never mind—everything sorts itself out in time. Now you don't know these two members of my staff, I think. Major Dilke and Captain Cassells." He turned to his officers. "This is our unfortunate host, Colonel Lemonfield."

The two staff officers smiled and shook hands deferentially, and Euan introduced James and mentioned Brinsmead.

"Please sit down, sir—and you, too, gentlemen." He indicated the chairs grouped around the window while James fetched the big silver cigar box from the desk.

"Brinsmead, ring for Fortu and tell him to have some coffee sent up."

The General held up a hand. "No, no! It's very kind, but I've got to get back on board just as soon as we've fixed up one or two things."

"Very well, sir." Euan drew up a chair and smiled, though his mind dwelt tensely on the inevitable question of the troops' shore leave. Sooner or later it would come up, but he was not going to give way if he could help it, even if it meant thoroughly offending this big, genial man with the darting brown eyes and the rubicund face of a youngish John Bull.

"Well"—D'Aumont puffed out a cloud of cigar smoke with evident pleasure—"the situation has only changed slightly since we had our short talk yesterday afternoon. Apparently the *Lewes Victory* and the *Empire Sunrise* are both on their way here, but owing to damage and cargo shifting they'll probably take another twenty-four hours to make it. When they *do* get here I understand from the cruiser captain that they'll need at least three days, probably four, to put things to rights. That means we'll be here approximately a week, so we'll take this opportunity to get some fresh fruit and vegetables on board. Can you help us in arrangements of that sort?"

244

"Certainly, sir. Brinsmead, make a note to contact some of the shipping contractors about that. Yes, that will be easy." He sounded relieved. "My Chief Clerk will advise your catering officer on the most suitable island products at present available. I'm happy to say there's a wide choice."

"Good!" exclaimed D'Aumont, rather as if the Colonel, against all expectations, had succeeded in performing some clever parlor trick. "Now the next thing"—his mouth twitched in a slight smile—"is the question of shore leave for the troops. I fear that will mean a little extra work for some of your staff, but naturally we don't want to have the troops cooped up on board for a week."

"Well, sir"—Euan drummed his fingertips lightly on one knee—"of course, I agree it would be an excellent thing to get your troops ashore, but, in the circumstances, I feel that I must—with great regret—say that I think it would be unwise. Please," he added quickly as the General's brow puckered in a slight surprised query, "don't misunderstand me, sir. I am most reluctant to be unable to agree and it is not through any lack of——"

"Exactly what do you mean by 'in the circumstances,' Colonel? What circumstances?"

Euan felt the atmosphere becoming chilly. He took a deep breath. "This island, as you know, was occupied without any resistance from the inhabitants as early as 1940. After the first two weeks there were not, nor have there been since, any signs of obvious military occupation beyond the presence of myself and my staff and a small garrison of native troops. The latter have never been resented, for they merely took the place of a similar company of Italian colonial troops. They occupied the same barracks, and performed the same duties. Also, their discipline has been rigidly maintained. Consequently we have had to overcome hardly any feeling of national resentment and have thus attained the cooperation of the Italian inhabitants, who make up the most important section of the community, to an exceptional—I might say a highly gratifying—degree."

"So I have been led to understand," agreed D'Aumont smoothly and slightly to Euan's surprise. "In fact, the general atmosphere of friendship and goodwill was very noticeable—yesterday."

Euan felt himself flush a little at this reminder of what, he had to admit, must have been to the visitors' eyes an extraordinary scene.

"Ah, yes. Yes, indeed. Now, as I was saying, we have achieved this cooperation largely through the fact that there have been no combatant units of British troops on the island to remind the Italians of their defeat and thus to arouse feelings of humiliation and resentment." He paused.

No one spoke, but he felt the atmosphere was becoming increasingly hostile. The General was frowning and slapping a small notebook softly on the palm of one hand; the two staff officers sat still and expressionless, as if any sudden movement on their part might derange some delicate balance and precipitate a crash. Euan continued with an air of calmly impressive rationality that he did not feel.

"This cooperation and goodwill have been of inestimable value to the Administration and, as you can understand, I am therefore very loath to allow the town to be flooded with British troops—particularly at this time when victory is just being achieved. It is not, I think, a suitable moment to remind the colonial inhabitants that their country was defeated." He stopped, and for a long moment there was silence.

"I see," remarked the General and there was something in his tone—a sort of tolerant weariness—that Euan did not like at all. "Your devotion to what you consider to be the best interests of your Administration does you credit, Colonel. I understand your point entirely—in fact, you've made it very clear. However, I, personally, don't think that the presence of British troops in the town will have any serious repercussions for O.E.T.A. They'll probably spend a certain amount of money—I suppose, by the way, rupees are accepted here? Yes? Good—and, of course, that will be good for the tradesmen. I think you overrate the unpopularity they'll bring you."

"I was thinking of the Administration, sir, not of myself," corrected Euan stiffly.

"Of course, of course. But the same thing applies. And, in any case, I naturally can't allow such a small consideration to stand in the way of the well-being of the troops."

"To me," said Euan, smiling but pale, "it is no small consideration, I assure you. I have already said how reluctant——"

"Your reluctance is beside the point," growled the General impatiently. "Let us get this quite clear. I want the troops to have a reasonable amount of shore leave while we are kept here. They've been bucketed about for a week in a severe storm and they need to get their feet on firm land once more. You can go into the matter of prohibited areas and bounds with our D.A.P.M.—but the troops must come ashore."

"Then my objections carry no weight, sir? You do not mind if considerable and enduring damage is done to the relationship— the very carefully built up relationship—between the Administration and the inhabitants of this city?" Euan spoke with a repressed fury that was apparent in every word. His hands shook with rage and his dark eyes gleamed.

D'Aumont rose with a slight sigh of vexation. "No. To be quite frank with you, Colonel Lemonfield, I don't care in the least—and in any case I think you overrate the situation fantastically. But you can write and complain to O.E.T.A. Headquarters if you want to, I suppose. I'll send the D.A.P.M. to arrange about bounds. Come along, gentlemen." Followed by his two officers, he left the room.

"Excuse me, I've come to see the British officer in charge of the police if he's available at the moment. I'm Major Defoe, the D.A.P.M. from the convoy."

"Well, I'm the Police Chief," said Paige, "and I'm English— at present."

Major Defoe, tall and spruce and grim, looked in astonishment at the thin, lanky young man in the flashy foreign uniform. "Oh —ah—I'm sorry. Your clothes seemed to me——"

"When I was a young officer," interrupted Lord Paige with a hint of reproof in his voice, "we were always told it was more democratic and sensible to dress like our men—and I have always done so."

"H'm. Well, I've come about fixing bounds for the troops. By the way, this is Captain Pirie from the General's staff." He stood aside and Pirie once again entered his old office.

"Pirie?" Paige's brow wrinkled in thought. "I've heard that name before somewhere, I know."

The ex-Police Chief grinned mirthlessly. "Yes, I'm sure

247

you must have, old boy. I had your job three years ago."

"Oh Lord, of course! Now I remember. Yes." They eyed each other narrowly and with renewed interest, standing on either side of the shabby leather-topped desk at which they had both worked. Neither liked in the least what he saw.

"I noticed a few of the old gang as I came in," remarked Pirie with a sort of malicious geniality. "Commino and young Silvana Angellini and Amerigo. It gave them a bit of a shock to see *me* again. Commino's getting fat. I told him he ought to take more exercise, but I don't think he understood. I never could speak the language. You do, I suppose?"

"Of course. Fluently."

"Good for you, old boy. But tell me, what's happened to young Baines? He took over from me."

Before answering, Paige fumbled in a drawer and offered his visitors a crumpled packet of the inferior native cigarettes that the Carabinieri smoked for want of anything better. They were refused.

"Baines? Oh, he met with an unfortunate accident. He was drowned while apprehending smugglers somewhere off the coast —near Pelican Island I think. He was Customs Chief as well, you know."

"Good God! Poor man!" Pirie looked sympathetic. "I always thought he was the best of the bunch."

Major Defoe said, "Well, now you two are acquainted, perhaps we can get down to business." He turned to Paige. "I understand that you are deputed by the Senior Civil Affairs Officer to arrange with me about the bounds for the troops."

"Yes, His Excellency has instructed me to that effect," said Paige gravely. Pirie grinned broadly and even Defoe's rat-trap mouth twitched.

"Well then, let's start. You've got a map of the town?"

For the next half hour Paige enjoyed himself thoroughly while he needlessly and irrevocably compromised the Administration in the eyes of the D.A.P.M. He had been given orders by the Colonel to keep the bounds clamped around the smallest area possible and only to enlarge them bit by bit under pressure. Though Defoe, abetted by Pirie, who of course knew the town, was intent on opening up as much as possible to the troops, tact and good humor might have done much to assist him in driving a hard bargain and at the same time saved him from falling out with the D.A.P.M. But Paige had by now come to identify himself too closely with his caricature of a Carabinieri officer to be able to lay aside the part without an effort of will, and this effort he regrettably saw no reason to make. For half an hour he was by turns pompous, niggling, evasive, choleric, and even tearful. He shilly-shallied, flattered, and wheedled. At one moment, in an ecstasy of despair, he flung his hat on the floor. He made long irrelevant digressions and dramatic, embarrassing appeals to such abstract virtues as Honor, Justice, *Amour-propre,* and Chastity—this last when discussing the brothel area. He continually spoke of the Colonel as His Excellency and was loud in his efforts to safeguard what he termed "the official dignity of the Administration." And in the end, in a fit of simulated cold rage, he said that the troops could go exactly where they liked for all he cared. He hurriedly withdrew this, but it was too late to agree to anything but the very widest bounds, and when the two convoy officers left the Headquarters they had every reason to congratulate themselves.

Major Defoe was too angry to do this, however. Despite the excellence of Paige's acting, he had a faint suspicion that he had been made the victim of a prolonged and ill-timed joke.

"I don't believe," he said stubbornly, "that whatever that fellow says he's English—not even at present."

"Whatever he may have meant by that," added Pirie.

The D.A.P.M. grunted something about "an utterly atrocious setup" and "going native," and they retraced their steps to the docks.

That evening Mr. Morle had a visitor. He had just returned from a trip to Dinghité where, as usual, heresy had been raising its stupid head. A large number of petty thefts had been attributed to the Holy Ghost, whom several witnesses swore they had seen slinking from hut to hut in the dark. The missionary was not in the best of tempers as he and his wife finished dinner that evening and Captain Pirie was announced. Nonetheless Mr. Morle greeted him enthusiastically and led him into the sitting room.

"My dear fellow! How nice to see you again!"

Pirie smiled pleasantly. "It's good to see you, Padre, and Mrs. Morle. You both look as if you had been keeping fit. How's your daughter?"

"Vera's very well, thank you—very well, considering the time of year. This heat's not really good for children. Do sit down."

"Thank you." Pirie sat and looked around him. The room had remained exactly the same since he left Baressa two and a half years ago. The same scrubbed floor of boards covered with the same old imitation Persian rugs. The same colored copy of Holman Hunt's "Light of the World" wrinkling in the heat behind its glass. A few shells—an unlooked-for gift from Captain Diaz—in a shallow wooden cabinet. The uncompromisingly stark colonial furniture.

"It doesn't seem any time since I left, Padre, you know."

"Doesn't it, indeed? And it's well over two years. I expect you've been to a lot of places since?" There was a certain envy in Mr. Morle's voice. He, too, would have liked to travel, but somehow the Society never offered him a change of station.

"Oh, I suppose I have—a bit. Mainly in India."

"Really? That must be very interesting. I've always wanted to go there. It would be far pleasanter to live and work in a British possession—though, of course"—Mr. Morle corrected himself dutifully—"I must subordinate my desires in that direction to my calling."

"You're da—that's to say, you're quite right, Padre—about India," confirmed Pirie with enthusiasm. "It's a place that's really British. It's got that atmosphere of—well, belonging, if you know what I mean. Everyone seems to have the right ideas there —except, perhaps, the Indians—and even some of *them,* particularly the Gurkhas, are first class! It's quite different from this place—absolutely different. It's on a higher level entirely. It's a gentleman's country—I think that's the best thing I can say about it. It's a place where a good soldier is still respected—a place with a military tradition, and proud of it! It's a 'fit' country, too, if you understand me. There's a feeling of strength and independence about the people one meets in the clubs and the messes. Of course, years of British rule have done that for it. It's a place where an Englishman is still respected for being English. And for that reason, I think, all the English there seem to be more English than anywhere else. They've got something to live up to and they live

250

up to it. It's a bl— an extremely fine place." He grinned, suddenly, embarrassed. "But, good Lord, I'm making a speech! Tell me, Padre, what's your news? What's been happening in this little beauty spot since I left? How's the dear Colonel?"

Mr. Morle smiled sardonically. "Colonel Lemonfield—or the Viceroy, as we're beginning to call him now—enjoys the best of health as far as I know. If he suffers from any complaint it's a hallucination that he's Hitler, King George, and the Pope all rolled into one!"

Pirie laughed loudly, but Mrs. Morle, till then sitting silently in her chair by the table, made a little tutting noise at this uncharitable remark of her husband's and said warningly, "Dear!"

Mr. Morle, who resented his conscience being prompted in this manner, gave her an irritated glance, but, his features stiffening, said, "Well, perhaps I shouldn't say that. No, I'm sure I shouldn't. But he remains as he was when you knew him."

"Which comes to the same thing," commented Pirie succinctly. Mr. Morle did not deny it. "And my handsome young friend with the scarred face and the pretty medals? How does he fare? Still sticking like a limpet?"

But Mr. Morle was not to be betrayed into further remarks unseemly for one of his calling. "They're all the same as when you left the island—with the exception of our new Police Chief, Lord Paige."

"*Lord* Paige?" queried Pirie, surprised. "Do you mean to say that fellow's a lord?"

"Certainly he is," confirmed Mr. Morle. "I mentioned his arrival to my Bishop, who wrote back to say that he knew the father, Lord Sandhill, quite well. In fact, he's apparently an important person in the diocese."

"Well, he's got a damned queer son then!" declared Pirie with fervor. Mrs. Morle gave a slight quiver, but remained silent.

"I believe he's going to join the Italian police after the war," remarked the missionary disapprovingly. "Unless he's joking, which I more than half believe."

"I say," said Pirie suddenly, "it was a bad show about Baines, wasn't it? What exactly happened?"

Mr. Morle's eyes lit up at the name of the dead Police Chief and he leaned more closely toward his guest.

"It's a very odd thing you should ask that. I can tell you one thing—the whole business is most mysterious. I've managed to sort out a little, however, owing to an indiscretion on the part of young Dawson of the Signals last Christmas. Now I don't think you know that a few months after you left it became generally known that Colonel Lemonfield was keeping a prisoner in the old hospital. A German officer. Now this man. . . ."

28

THE troops came ashore. They came singing and cheering and noisy, glad to be on land again and away from the dull, cramping discipline of shipboard life, glad to see another foreign town. The sailors came, too, and together the two Services wandered gaily through the city, caps on the backs of heads, hands in pockets, shirts open to the waist, cigarettes hanging from lips. "Hi, George!" they accosted the vendors of souvenirs. "How much? Garn! It ain't worth half! Where c'n we get a drink? *Drink!* You know—booze! Look, like this! See? An' girls? Where's the place? You know—women—girls! Garn, the bloke's daft! No, you silly idiot, *not* like that!"

There were, as Brinsmead had gloomily prophesied, incidents. Three privates got slightly drunk in the Bar Regina Elena and started throwing the phonograph records—to which, being all Italian, they took objection—into the sea. Mario complained and asked the Administration for compensation. Some naval ratings stole the Mayor's car, drove to the Aquarium, and tried to abduct the octopus. They were apprehended and spent the night in Fort Brocca.

A lance corporal and two sergeants, who should have known better, found their way into the brothel quarter and outraged the professional feelings of the prostitutes by frequenting a very sordid little place whose horrid threshold was only crossed by the lowest and most degenerate. They were surprised, on emerging, by Brigadiere Rondotto, who was slinking around his chosen field of operations with that hangdog lack of zeal which characterized his corps. In the interests of his clients—for the prostitutes paid him a small retainer fee for his dubious services—he admonished the soldiers, who thereupon seized him, pitched him into the noisome den from which they had just come, and, shutting the door, locked him there.

A very small stoker exchanged hats by rapid sleight of hand with Commino in broad daylight in the Piazza del Re. Before the astonished Carabiniere knew what was happening the stoker ran fast but proudly back to the docks and was last seen, flourishing his trophy, in a pinnace making for the cruiser.

All these unfortunate occurrences were reported in letters couched in varying degrees of mortification and distress to the Colonel, who saw his worst fears being realized. The troops were *not* liked. The townsfolk were *not* amused. He felt his popularity sinking rapidly like the mercury in a thermometer on a frosty day.

Frigid little notes of protest signed "E. O. Lemonfield, Col. & S.C.A.O." were forwarded daily to the D.A.P.M.'s office on the convoy and that officer learned to groan with weary vexation when news was brought that the big white government launch *Principe di Piemonte* was emerging from the harbor. But official notice of these protests had to be taken, and the convoy's daily orders were filled with long paragraphs under the heading, *"Discipline*—It has been brought to the notice of the Officer Commanding. . . ." The old Army custom of passing the buck came into its own. Badgered and harried by the Governor, the D.A.P.M. turned a flow of caustic complaint on the lieutenant colonels commanding battalions. They, in turn, worried their company commanders, who rounded on their N.C.O.s, who cursed and threatened the sulky rank and file.

Far from improving matters, this spate of general recrimination only served to make them worse. The war was practically over and the troops' discipline had slackened. Resentful and sullen and sick to death of the continual threats that "all shore leave will cease unless . . . ," that "severe disciplinary action will be taken if . . . ," that "any further conduct of this kind will be drastically dealt with," they went out of their way to make trouble. They knew quite well who was responsible for all the bickering and nagging, and the "incidents" began to change from the playfully mischievous to the deliberately malign. Whatever the state of Colonel Lemonfield's popularity in San Pietro, there was

253

no doubt about his lack of that asset on the convey. As the great gray car, accompanied by the invariable roaring escort of police motorcycles, sped through the city it was received with scowls, derisive shouts, and insolent gestures from the khaki- and white-clad servicemen in the streets.

It was not till three days after the arrival of the convoy that Euan learned of Captain Pirie's renewed presence on the island. He blamed Paige severely for his omission to report this and remarked bitterly that had Baines still been Police Chief Pirie's arrival would have been known in the Palace within three hours. Paige received an acid letter of rebuke commenting on his shortcomings and inquiring what had happened to the efficient intelligence system his predecessor had fashioned and for which the Administration was still paying out good money. But though the Police Chief was sufficiently shaken by the letter to snap Mrs. Tamminetto's head off when she mentioned the Carabinieri tradition, and to assemble his leisurely agents and administer a surprisingly English dose of plain speaking, he did no more. In this respect he showed a naïve disregard for police intelligence that would have aroused the derision of Baines. For the dead officer would have had Captain Pirie watched and followed whenever he set foot ashore and in so doing would have had a verbal report of his long interview with Texas on the fourth evening of the convoy's stay.

Pirie, on the lookout for the dispatch rider, found him outside the Silver Lizard bar near the customs sheds at six o'clock on a sultry evening. He greeted him genially.

"Hullo, Dawson! How's life been treating you since I saw you last?"

Texas grinned. "Okay, sir, thanks. It's a surprise to see *you* back again."

"I bet it is! Well, come and have a drink, anyway. It's just about time for one. By the way, this is Mr. Halkett of the Provost branch. Mick, this is Dawson—one of the signalmen here."

"Pleased to meet you, sir," said Texas amicably to the short, dark young officer thus introduced. Halkett smiled but said nothing.

They went into the Silver Lizard—a long, garish bar full of flyblown mirrors and archly naughty advertisements for different kinds of aperitifs. Despite its new paint and polished chromium it had an indefinable atmosphere of the twenties about its decor which pleased those of its customers whose youth had been spent in that period.

Sitting at a chromium-legged table with a black glass top near the wall, Pirie engaged Texas for some minutes in half-bantering gossip of a general nature.

"Are you still going to work for Captain Rossi after the war, Dawson?"

Texas' face clouded. "Not now, I reckon. I haven't seen him for ages. But I think I've more or less got fixed up with Cap'n Vrontas of the *Anna Gabriella*."

"What's happened to old Rossi? He always used to be around in the old days. I remember him coming to my office for licenses to buy diesel oil. Did he fall out with Lieutenant Baines, or something?"

"Dunno," repeated Texas gloomily. "I ain't seen him around for ages."

Pirie attempted a shot in the dark. "I expect he helped Stralowski to get away and doesn't dare show his face here now."

Texas jumped as if he had been stung. "What's that?"

Pirie assumed a look of amused surprise at Texas' reaction. "I said perhaps he helped Stralowski to escape—you know, after he killed Baines."

Texas' jaw dropped. "You *know* about that!"

"Of course I do. Why shouldn't I? *You* obviously do."

The dispatch rider's mouth closed with a snap, his brow darkened. "I don't know nothin'," he growled sulkily.

"Mick, he knows nothing! You hear?" Pirie grinned.

Halkett, speaking for the first time, said, "He certainly knows quite a lot for someone who knows nothing!"

"Three more cognacs!" Pirie hailed a passing waiter. Then he turned back to the wretched Texas, his face hard, his small gray eyes steely. "You'd better not lie to me, Dawson," he said evenly. "I've already heard enough to realize that you know exactly what happened. Mr. Halkett heard it, too. If you want to avoid serious trouble you'll answer my questions."

"You can't do nothin'—" began Texas, but it was easy to read the doubt and fear in his voice.

"I can do quite a lot," rejoined Pirie grimly. "I can, among other things, get my friend the Senior Signals Officer on board the convoy to arrange for your recall to the mainland for further training and discipline. And that will be the last you'll see of Baressa and of this idea of a job here after the war." For a moment the three sat in taut silence while Pirie glared with all the purpose and willpower he could muster at the dispatch rider.

Then Texas, lowering his eyes unhappily to his heavy boots muttered, "Well, if you *know* that Jerry killed Capt'n Baines, I don't see as there's much more I c'n tell you."

"Perhaps not. But there are one or two small points I'm anxious to clear up. Firstly. . . ."

Entering, rather later than usual, the staff officers' mess on board the convoy, Pirie found his colleagues were already seated at dinner. He noted, with a feeling of relief, that the General was absent—probably dining with the Captain of the cruiser, as was often his custom. Major General D'Aumont disliked unpunctuality at meals. With a muttered word of apology to the senior officer present, Pirie slid into his chair amidst a few genially insulting guesses as to his lateness, and ordered a whiskey and soda from a passing Indian steward.

"Have you been having a tête-à-tête with His Excellency?" chuckled a florid major opposite. "Making your kowtow at the steps of the throne?"

Pirie smiled slightly. "No, sir. I may, perhaps, have an interview with that exalted personage before we sail—or perhaps not—but this evening I've merely been having a drink in one of my old haunts."

"I don't believe you!" retorted a fiercely moustached captain with a black patch over one eye. "You're an old crony of the Great Panjandrum and you've been bending the knee at a gilded levee in his royal residence." He turned to the other diners. "Old Pirie pretends he's not an intimate friend of the Great Man, but I've discovered that when he was last here he was invested as Hereditary Lord of the Golden Ducal Chamber Pot. It's pure modesty that prevents him from mentioning it!"

A roar of laughter greeted this sally. Pirie grinned, but said nothing.

"Is it true," asked the major who had first spoken, "that when

256

the Old Man went ashore he found them all having a gala in a zoo? High jinks and feasting and fun—lovely!"

"Trust Applecroft to get it wrong!" remarked the one-eyed captain with feigned exasperation. "If you *want* to know, Bill, they found Colonel Tom Thumb opening an Aquarium to the greater glory of his own name and making a speech in his own praise to a huge crowd of wildly cheering townees. Pass the mustard up here, Denning, damn you! Why do you have to collect every condiment around your plate like a blasted palisade? Don't you want us to see what you're eating, or something? Really, the table manners of you junior officers leave much to be desired, if little to the imagination. When I was—" But he was shouted down, and a glum red-faced lieutenant colonel at the top of the table said, "It's all very well to make a joke of it, but it's a damn bad show. I've got nothing more than the next man against O.E.T.A.—some of them do a fairly good job, some don't. This Colonel wallah is typical of the worst sort. Puffed up with the fact that he's boss of a lot of conquered Wops, he's just out to lord it in luxury for as long as he damn well can. And, of course, he hates the sight of British uniforms because they remind him that he's supposed—God help us!—to be in the Army himself and not a bloody Little Tin God on wheels." He paused amidst approving silence. "I've been ashore twice and that was enough. The place is full of Wop police and parade-ground nigger troops and fantastic sorts of Palace Guards—looks like a bloody comic opera scene most of the time. And what the devil's wrong with our boys' landing, may I ask? They do no harm—no real harm, at any rate. My God, it makes me furious to think that here's a man who's sat on his backside in an office for five years and he can't even let his own country's soldiers have a bit of shore leave without making wretched prim little complaints about their behavior! The lads know about it all right. I bet they'd like to tell Mr. Lemonfield just what they think of him!"

The troops needed little encouragement to misbehave themselves and were becoming aware that their officers felt much the same hostility as themselves toward the ruler of Baressa. On the morning after Pirie's interview with Texas a short but luridly adjectival description of the Governor was found painted across the shining new double doors of the Aquarium. Lemonfield requested the D.A.P.M. to visit him and in a frigid interview demanded that all shore leave should be canceled forthwith. Major Defoe replied that as there was no proof that the outrage had been committed by British troops he saw no reason to punish them. Perhaps, he suggested blandly, some disaffected element in the town was responsible, some petty malefactor smarting under a court fine? Or even, perhaps, a practical joker among the English signalmen of the island radio office? At this suggestion the interview terminated abruptly at an Arctic temperature.

That evening when the Colonel drove, surrounded by his roaring escort, to the Palace, he found the Piazza del Re full of loitering groups of British troops. Dusk was falling and the tall ornate lamps around the dusty square and in the palm-treed central gardens threw their yellow glow over the pale khaki of the soldiers and the white of the naval ratings. Row upon row of lighted windows, the Palace towered up into the hot darkening sky, and he saw, with feelings of surprise and annoyance, that not only were the two Negro sentries patrolling the front of the long shallow steps but the steps themselves were lined by guards of the Banda. As the car drew to a stop, swaying gently on its soft springs, Fortu, his face worried and apprehensive, ran down the steps as the sergeant of the Banda flung open the car door. As the Colonel emerged he was aware of a rising chorus of shouts and hisses from the groups of soldiers in the great square.

"What's the matter, Fortu?"

"Excellency, the British troops have been shouting insults about you and the Administration in the Piazza for the last quarter of an hour. Some of their officers came down the Corso, but when they saw what was happening they went away again."

"Scandalous!" exclaimed the Colonel angrily. Mounting the steps with his young secretary at his side, he cast a furious look over his shoulder at the loitering groups who now seemed to be converging around the bottom of the steps. As he climbed higher and came more plainly into view from below the jeers and catcalls increased in volume and obscenity and a couple of oranges bounced on the marble steps at Fortu's feet. Trembling with rage and mortification, the Colonel reached the doors of the Palace, flung open by bowing servants, and crossed the threshold into the calm and quiet of the great hall.

He stormed upstairs and past the two great sentries of the

Banda who swung their curved sabers to the salute before his office door. Alone in the privacy of his long room he paced rapidly to and fro. He had been insulted and hooted on the steps of his Palace! The impossible had happened. He, Colonel Lemonfield, the highly esteemed and universally popular Governor of Baressa, had been pelted with oranges by a rabble of foreign troops in the very heart of his own capital—on the threshold of his own office! Had anyone told him a week ago that such a thing could happen he would have laughed him to scorn. Fuming, he walked and turned on the polished parquet, his curious light, springy step echoing in the high, empty room. Around him were all the evidences of his position—the white-and-gold paneled walls on which hung heavy gilt-framed pictures of kings and queens and patriots of Italy. Umberto I, bearded and grave on a richly caparisoned white horse, Victor Emmanuel I with his huge moustaches, Cavour plump and spectacled, Garibaldi stern and dignified. There in front of him was his great desk, his three telephones, his chair of brocade and gold—the ultimate center of the island's life. And outside—he could still hear them—a lot of shabby, oafish, ignorant soldiers were jeering and booing at him —at him!—at Colonel Lemonfield and all His Works!

He longed to pick up one of those telephones and order his own troops to clear the square. In his mind's eye he saw the rigid columns of huge Negroes advancing inexorably across the Piazza del Re, their bayonets glittering in the hot yellow lamplight, driving those wretched creatures below back to the docks, back to their ships, off the island and out to sea.

If such a course was out of the question—and it clearly was— he could at least have the square cordoned off. Acting on the impulse, he phoned the Casa dei Fiori and, finding Christopher at home, gave the necessary orders.

"From 6 a.m. to 12 p.m., sir?" queried Christopher glumly.

"Yes. And I want to see your men in the Piazza within fifteen minutes—understand?" There was a note in the Colonel's voice that Christopher had never heard before.

"Very good, sir," he said resignedly and the Colonel rang off.

Then he rang Police Headquarters.

"Paige here, sir."

"Have you any idea what's happening in the Piazza del Re?" asked the Colonel coldly.

259

"Well, I have, as a matter of fact." Paige sounded quite unapologetic. "I didn't send any of the men there because the sight of the Carabinieri seems to have an awkward effect on the troops. It seems to make them want to despoil them, if you see what I mean. And we can't have their uniforms ruined just to make a British holiday, can we? I mean, that business of Commino's hat——"

"Confound Commino's hat! Go and find some military police —there must be some around—and bring them to the Piazza with the Carabinieri. The troops won't touch your men if they have redcaps with them. I want that square cleared of British troops in ten minutes—before Kellermann's men arrive, and they'll be there in twelve. Hurry!"

"Yes, sir."

He rang the electric bell on his desk and Fortu entered. "Is the Major in the Palace?"

"Yes, Excellency."

"My compliments, and ask him to come to this office."

"Yes, Excellency."

For a further few minutes he paced up and down and then James came in.

"This is a shocking business, Euan," he remarked with his invariable nonchalance. "Shocking. I'm going to have one of your cigars if I may. I've run out below and I hardly like to send a messenger out for some more at the moment—he might get hung from a lampost or tossed in a blanket or something equally embarrassing from the point of view of the Administration."

"The square will be cleared in a few minutes!" snapped the Colonel. "Some of those wretched fellows threw oranges at me as I came up the steps!"

"So Fortu says. Disgusting! All shore leave should be stopped. Surely they'll stop it now—after this."

"I doubt it. The officers are just as bad as their men. Fortu says he saw some looking on earlier in the evening and they went away without doing anything. No, I don't think they'll stop the shore leave. I've complained continually of the troops' behavior and they've taken no notice—I doubt if they'll take any now. But there's one thing I *can* do and I shall. They're here for two more days and on both those days I'll have every bar closed within the area of the troops' bounds—and every shop, restaurant, and café, too. And I'll have all the streetlights, except for the minimum necessary for police patrolling, cut off. And I'll have all vendors and peddlers off the streets and the public transport services diverted through other roads."

"But Euan!" James was appalled. "What *will* the people say —or the Mayor or the Municipality? Good Lord, you'll be the most execrated man in the town!"

"No, I shan't. I shall tell Belotta that we have discovered that the troops intend to beat the place up on the next two nights. Their recent behavior will lend convincing support to such a suggestion. I shall say that my instructions are for the benefit of the populace. What's more, I'll put that in print in the *Courier* the day after the convoy leaves. The people here know me well enough to take me on trust till then. If we can't stop these beastly creatures coming ashore we can at least see that they have no amusement when they do!"

29

Two evenings later at seven o'clock, Colonel Lemonfield sat in his office studying reports from Paige's agents on the state of popular opinion in the town. On the whole it was satisfactory. The grumbling at the stringent measures he had taken to close down the city's life for two days was considerable, but lacked real anger. The present high temperature forbade serious efforts at work in any case, and once he had circulated the reasons for his drastic action he had little fear that any temporary lapse in popular esteem that he might have suffered could not be made good. For the townsfolk had not enjoyed the week of British Military occupation—Paige's reports proved that. No, they had not enjoyed it at all. But the behavior of the troops and their animosity toward himself had at least served the purpose of showing the townsfolk that their Governor was on their side in the matter and in no way responsible for the conduct of his fellow countrymen.

But Euan's thoughts were not wholly confined to the papers

before him. For twenty-four hours now he had been expecting to hear from the General concerning Captain Pirie's discovery. There was no doubt that Pirie intended to use the information he had acquired to cause as much trouble as he could. But the story must be authoritatively confirmed to be of the smallest use in this respect. If it were not the Colonel would naturally laugh it to scorn, dismiss it as some ridiculous dockside rumor. Euan smiled slightly as he turned over the leaves of Paige's reports. It had been his desire for confirmation from an authoritative quarter that had induced Pirie to make the mistake of going to Christopher. A natural enough mistake, perhaps, for three years ago a simple hint of the Army's displeasure would have hypnotized Christopher into a state of abject fear in which he would have blurted out the whole story, hopelessly compromising everyone, including himself. But in the three years since Pirie had known him, Christopher had acquired a certain amount of self-control —still shaky, but at any rate sufficient in this case to have helped him adopt the right attitude. He had refused to confirm anything and immediately reported the matter to the Palace. He had given the Colonel time to prepare his brief.

And now he waited for General D'Aumont. The convoy was to leave at dawn next day and if any action was to be taken on the information Pirie must have laid before his master it would have to be taken now. Of course, D'Aumont *could* do nothing at present, merely return to the mainland and then arrange for an investigation to be discreetly made. But such a course would be foredoomed to failure in the light of the Colonel's present knowledge and future preparedness. No. From what little he had seen of him Euan guessed that D'Aumont was shrewd enough to come and see him now—hoping, doubtless, to take him by surprise.

Unhurriedly he gathered Paige's reports together, snapped them into a file marked "Secret" and locked them in a small steel safe built into his desk. Then he took out of a drawer a battered and much-thumbed file marked "Police Vehicles—Gasoline Consumption." A flicker of amusement crossed his pale face as he opened it. The old, old story of too much gasoline and too little mileage to be gone into for the hundredth time at this very moment of crisis. He glanced at the battered work tickets and indent forms and the sight of these companionably mundane documents soothed his taut nerves. Here was Mrs. Tamminetto's

262

handwriting, bold, loose and wriggly—like her character, thought Euan, smiling—and Brinsmead's neat meticulous figures in red and green ink and some remarks by Paige in his odd, backward-sloping hand. He picked up a pencil and set to work. The ormolu clock, reflected in the polished glass of the desk top as in a calm pool of lamplit water, ticked primly in the silence. Outside the great square lay hot, dark, still, and empty under the stars.

Footsteps. A knock on the door. Fortu's calm olive face.

"The British General is here, Excellency."

"Show him in."

Euan rose, smiling, as D'Aumont entered, ominously alone. "Good evening, sir."

"Good evening, Lemonfield." The General's voice was grim, his dark face hard and purposeful.

"Will you sit down?"

Without a word D'Aumont took the chair indicated. "You may perhaps think a visit from me at this time rather surprising," he began. But Euan was not to be caught easily. All his long training in the courts came to his assistance. He sat back smiling and attacked at once.

"Perhaps a little, sir, but nonetheless I'm delighted to see you. There are one or two matters arising out of the—ah—shall I say rather uninhibited behavior of the troops who have been ashore here which it would perhaps be best if I discussed with you before forwarding my report to my own Organization's Headquarters. I'm afraid there have been several regrettable occurrences during the last seven days, and I trust you will not think me disrespectful if I remind you that I advised against shore leave for the troops in the first place. I understand from reports recently submitted by my Police Chief that not only have my fears concerning the possibility of severe detriment to the relationship between the Administration and the townspeople here been amply realized, but that the troops appear to have done considerable material damage to public and private property as well. I must, of course, request my Headquarters for permission to compensate, and I fear the figure will not be small. I hope you will not think me lacking in civility toward you yourself, or respect for the rank you hold, if I say that the whole affair takes on a grave aspect in the light of——"

"I've come about this story I've heard concerning a German

officer whom you captured here," said D'Aumont without the smallest recognition of having listened to a word that Euan had been saying. He eyed the Colonel bleakly.

"Yes?" queried Euan calmly.

"You admit that you captured a German officer, then?"

"Admit it, General? Why not? To capture an enemy soldier during hostilities is surely a perfectly legitimate act of war."

D'Aumont looked surprised and a trifle taken aback. "Of course. Did you report the capture?"

"No."

"Why not, may I ask?"

"The man was unconscious and dying—dying rapidly. As the doctor who saw him fully expected him to be dead within twenty-four hours of his discovery I thought it a waste of time to report the capture of a man who would be dead before the report was even dispatched to its destination. It is not, I believe, necessary to report dead enemy—at any rate in such small numbers."

"But he didn't die, did he?"

"No. He lived."

"Yet you never reported him?"

"He was on the point of death for weeks. The doctors despaired of his life again and again. Every time I inquired whether he could live I was told it seemed impossible. Therefore my first reason still held good. I can send for the doctor who attended the man if you wish to question him on that point."

"I don't. I have no doubt that he would corroborate what you have just told me."

"I've no doubt of it either, sir," agreed Euan blandly and with perfect sincerity.

"But still, he lived—this officer. S.S., wasn't he?"

"Yes."

"And very likely an agent of extreme importance. A man whose capture should have yielded the most valuable information had he been interrogated."

"We interrogated him here—when he was sufficiently recovered for that to be practicable. He was evasive and obstinate, and refused to disclose any but the most unimportant facts about himself."

The General grunted. "There are ways of making these fellows talk—of course, you wouldn't know them."

"Well, we cut off one of his legs."

D'Aumont started visibly, but Euan continued at speed. "I intended to send him back to the mainland as soon as he was sufficiently recovered to stand the journey. However, the doctors kept postponing this, for the unfortunate man had several severe relapses. In the end he managed to escape."

"And in doing so killed your Police Officer—another incident you failed to report. In fact, not only did you fail to report it, but you invented a deliberate lying story to conceal it. Some nonsense about a fight with smugglers."

Euan sighed and frowned. "Well, sir, I admit I did wrong in that, but it was with the best of intentions. Captain Baines, the Police Officer, was an excellent young man whose work in every respect came up to a high standard. He rendered me much service in his position and, in fact, I had him promoted. However, in this matter of the German prisoner he completely and inexplicably disobeyed my direct orders. I had given the most stringent instructions that the German was to be closely guarded at all times. Captain Baines not only failed to carry these out, but actually let the man drink at bars and go for short walks—inasmuch as his crippled condition permitted. Not, perhaps, surprisingly, the German—a man of outstanding initiative and resource—took the opportunity to arrange and carry out his escape. Baines discovered this in time to pursue him, and it was when he caught him that we assume he was killed. How, exactly, we don't know, for his body was never recovered. I felt most unwilling to report on this matter, for it would have meant showing Captain Baines in an unhappy light when I had—beyond this one regrettable and totally inexplicable lapse—no fault to find with him. Thus, in view of the pain such a report must inevitably cause his parents, and on the whole the injustice of such a reflection on a good officer, I felt compelled to take the course I did. *De mortuis nil nisi bonum.* It was, strictly speaking, wrong, but humanly speaking, I think, justifiable."

Euan stopped and saw that D'Aumont was looking at him with a certain grudging admiration.

"You're a barrister by profession, Lemonfield, aren't you?"

"Yes, sir."

"A good one, I'll swear, too."

"I took silk in 'thirty-eight."

"Indeed? Well, I can see that it's no use arguing with you about this matter. However, I'm not satisfied—not satisfied at all. If I thought it would serve any useful purpose, disciplinary or otherwise, I'd recommend your court-martial on my return to the mainland. But from what I've just heard I can guess only too well what course such a trial would take. So I shan't do that." He paused and eyed Euan rather as if the Governor were some strange animal, formidable yet unlikable, half impressive, half disgusting. It was much the look that Euan himself was wont to bestow on William's octopus. "I'll say one thing more. I don't like the attitude you appear to have adopted toward this island, its inhabitants, and your position here. It is unhealthy and peculiar, to say the least. Nor, may I add, do I like the undoubted hostility you have displayed toward the troops in the convoy."

"Hostility!" began Euan. "My dear sir, I——" but D'Aumont held up a large hand wearily.

"No, Lemonfield. I haven't finished and I don't want to hear any facile arguments. I'm not arguing—I'm just making statements. I think you're probably good at your job—possibly very good. Your sort generally are. I expect some of the rude comments of the troops did not altogether escape your ears the other evening, and I want you to know that I do not share their sentiments, based, as of course they are, on ignorance and prejudice, concerning your value to Britain. You have done an important and difficult job to the best of your considerable ability and you deserve the gratitude of your country as much as any other member of the Services, and probably more than quite a few." His mouth twisted in a slight, hard smile. "It is one of the injustices of Service life that you O.E.T.A. people have to put up with an unwarrantable amount of careless disparagement, often from people who should know better. There's really only one thing wrong with you, Lemonfield, when all is said and done. It's not organic and it's easily rectified."

Euan smiled. "I'm relieved to hear it, General. What is my mildly distressing complaint?"

The General rose, with about his heavy bull-like frame that indefinable attitude of weariness that Euan had noticed before.

"You've been here far too long—and so have all the other British personnel here. Far too long. The sooner you all leave Baressa the better for everyone—yourselves, perhaps, most of all. I'm not going to do anything about the German prisoner business—the war's nearly over now, so what's the good? But I *am* going to insist on your transfer, and that of all the other Englishmen here. The moment I return to the mainland I shall make a special journey to O.E.T.A. Headquarters and I shall privately inform them—without, as far as possible, doing you or anyone else any harm—of what I conceive to be the situation here. If that is not enough—though I think you must realize that it will be—I shall see the Commander-in-Chief. Good night."

The General walked slowly from the room and out of the door without a single glance behind. Such a glance would have revealed Colonel Lemonfield sitting stiffly in his chair as if turned to stone, his face a pallid mask of shocked surprise which gave way gradually, dreadfully, to bewildered, idiotic despair.

30

THE war was nearly over. Toward dusk a gusty wind laden with thin gray rain drove three of the aircraftmen into the low broken building on the edge of the smashed airfield. Only the Oberfeldwebel who was to pilot the machine remained on the camouflaged bomb-cratered runway, checking his light angular plane. He was nervous and he had a cold. He sniffed and muttered to himself continually, wiping his sore nose on an oil-stained khaki handkerchief. As the light began to leave the high gray sky a formation of Russian fighters roared past high above the field, flying fast toward a yellow streak in the western clouds. The Oberfeldwebel did not look up—Russian fighters had been continuously overhead for days.

Inside the broken concrete building it was almost dark, and very cold. The wind blew through the great gaps in the walls that had once held broad plate-glass windows. The one-legged man in the dirty gray shirt and blue paint-stained workman's overalls shivered as he sat at an iron table with an enamel mug of cognac between his cold, rough hands. The three Fliegers lounged listlessly on a bed against the wall, while another built a fire between two bricks in a corner. Standing opposite the man at the table was a ruddy black-haired officer wearing the silver insignia of a major on the carmine-colored tabs and epaulets of the Luftwaffe General Air Staff. His short tunic was open, disclosing a khaki flannel shirt, and he had his hands in his trouser pockets. He looked with a mixture of interest and perplexity at the cripple in the dirty overalls bowed silently over his cup of brandy.

"I do not like this, Herr Hauptsturmführer," he said, frowning. "I can give you no cover. I do not think you will get in. If what you have is so important why do you not go to Kietel's Headquarters? The air is———"

Stralowski raised his face, gray, lined, and unshaven, from the cup in his hands. "Why do you suppose I have come all this way?" he asked tiredly. "It has not been easy. I *must* get in now that I am so near."

In the dusk the tabs on the Major's collar glimmered pinkly, and Stralowski was reminded momentarily of Colonel Lemonfield's scarlet tabs on the occasion of his one and only interview with him. Nearly two years ago. Two years ago—one year ago—he had been on Baressa. It seemed unbelievably remote now—an island on a distant planet.

"I must get in," he repeated harshly and shivered again. His blood was thin from the constant recurrences of uncured malaria and he was worn with undernourishment and strain. His body contracted inside his clothes every time the gusty wind swept across the room. Guns boomed in the distance. The war was nearly over.

The makeshift plank door swung open and the Oberfeldwebel pilot stood silhouetted against the yellow streak in the western evening clouds. He was thin and young with a pale face and oiled fair hair. He reminded Stralowski of someone—the tired mind groped back wearily—Summerson. Summerson as he had first seen him that time a year ago on the docks. The paling sky, the soft evening over the blue-gray water, sailors shouting cheerily from the dhows. . . .

"We could start now, Herr Major." The Oberfeldwebel went to a cheap fiber suitcase in the corner and, opening it, took out a clean handkerchief. He blew his nose and looked inquiringly at the hunched cripple in the cold gloom. Stralowski reached for his battered crutches and rose wearily, and they went out one by one into the cold windy dusk, leaving the empty room to the encroaching night. On the wall a cheap paper calendar fluttered its leaves and, as the wind dropped, resumed its position giving the date—27th April, 1945.

The journey was like some mad nightmare. Immediately the Fieseler-Storch took the air, clumsily and slowly like a great heron, the flames of the encircled capital were visible to the east, glowing and fading and flaring on the horizon, new fires seeming to spring up out of the growing darkness at every moment. Flying as low as they dared, they twice passed below an air fight where Russian and German planes milled together, slashing the dusky air with lines of fiery bullets and bursting shells. Then they were over territory occupied by the enemy and the slow, cranelike Storch could no longer hug the hostile ground, but must rise higher into the equally hostile air. The plane was struck by incendiary bullets as they flattened out over the rooftops to land, and as they rolled to a lurching halt in the rubble-strewn Charlottenburger Chaussee the engine caught fire and burned fiercely. Heaving himself from the narrow cockpit, Stralowski slithered down the side of the plane and, adjusting his crutches under his armpits, hobbled across the torn, cratered roadway. Out of a doorway stepped a dark figure and swung him around. For the first time in five years Stralowski saw a man in the uniform of the Waffen S.S. "The Reichskanzellerie," he panted weakly. "Take me to the Führerbunker."

An orderly brought some food, canned meat and bread and some black olives on an embossed gold-edged plate, and also a bottle of wine. Stralowski ate slowly. He was no longer hungry, though he had eaten nothing for the past three days and little enough for weeks before that. He answered shortly the questions they asked him—the two S.S. officers with the high-ranking collar badges and Liebstandarte insignia on the forearms of their tunics. He would not say from whence he had come or for what purpose. He wanted time to sit quietly and try to realize that the great and invincible Third Reich he had left five years ago at the height of its most splendid victory was now reduced to a handful

269

of doomed men waiting to use the poison phials in their pockets in an underground warren amidst the burning ruins of an encircled, shell-swept city.

"I had instructions," he said at last, "when I left on my mission, to report only to the Reichsführer S.S. himself. As he is not here I must personally see the Führer."

One of the S.S. officers shrugged resignedly. "Well—we will see." He lifted the telephone from his desk and raised his eyes to Stralowski. "I shall ask the Führer's personal adjutant, Sturmbannführer Guensche. Perhaps——" He was connected and then apparently cut off. A dead silence sealed the underground chamber from which so few would ever emerge. Stralowski felt as if he were trapped in a broken submarine at the bottom of the sea.

Later the Adjutant came in and Stralowski, who had written something on a sheet of paper, folded it and handed it silently to him. Sturmbannführer Guensche read it carefully with a growing look of surprise.

"Ah!" He glanced at the grimy cripple with new interest, but also a certain mocking compassion. "It is a great pity now, is it not? After all that. But you want to tell the Führer yourself, of course. Well—I suppose that's the least we can do for you. I'm afraid you'll find him—changed. When you have seen him come back here and we'll try to find you a job of sorts. Now come with me."

He left the room and passed along a narrow, brightly lit corridor while Stralowski hobbled after him. There was a wait of a few minutes in a small anteroom where Guensche disappeared through another door and two S.S. guards eyed the newcomer without interest.

Stralowski's mind was in a daze; he could only think of one thing, the one thing that had never left his thoughts since he had escaped from Baressa—that now, after long months of perilous travel, he was going to finish his work. Once he had got inside that door his job—the job that had cost him his leg and nearly his life—would be over. Guensche appeared suddenly in the doorway. He nodded and jerked his head, holding the door ajar.

"The Herr Doktor Stralowski of I.G. Farben, *mein Führer,*" he announced respectfully.

Stralowski limped forward into the room.

3 1

I T was after midnight before Major Naughton-Muirhead had finished the letters he was writing in his sitting room on the second story of the Villa. The long windows leading to the balcony were open and when, with a sigh of relief, James closed the blotter on the last of his correspondence, he rose and walked out onto the small balustraded platform. Far below the lights of San Pietro glittered and shone, crowding in gold lines and clusters like miniature constellations around the horseshoe of dark star-lit water that was the harbor. Farther out, sensed rather than seen, the ocean spread vast and calm to the limitless horizon. For years past he had leaned on the marble balustrade and gazed out over the sparkling lights of the town toward the huge panorama of the tropic sea. He would miss this serene view when he left. His mouth tightened a little at the thought of leaving. It was a deep pain, this realization that his days on Baressa were drawing so rapidly—so unexpectedly rapidly—to a close. The convoy had sailed two days ago. Shortly it would be docking and General D'Aumont would step ashore. There would be a journey to O.E.T.A. Headquarters, an interview, consultations, the checking of lists of available personnel—and then Hope would bring the message of recall to the Palace. A week or two later their replacements would arrive. In a month—or six weeks at the latest—Baressa would be staffed by entirely new British personnel. He and Euan would presumably be the first to go. Fortu would drive them down to the docks as he had driven the Giordanos five years before. There would be a rather more ceremonious farewell than on that occasion, perhaps even a guard of honor, but otherwise the heartsick routine would be the same as on that distant day.

Perhaps, when the *Emperor Napoleon* had cast off and rounded the Dhow Control Point with her bows pointing to the open sea, Fortu would sit again on the running board of the car as James had found him on that far-off summer afternoon. With a vivid, nostalgic clarity there passed before his mind's eye scenes from his early days on the island. They had been happy then, and busy—Euan in the Palace, he in the Villa, clearing away the traces of the ridiculous, despised Giordanos. Poor Giordanos! Only now, five years later, did he realize how they must have felt. But surely they could not have known such grief at their departure as the present rulers of Baressa. For the Giordanos—however pathetic their leave-taking might have appeared—had only been on Baressa for three years, each of which had been interrupted by several months' leave in Italy. Then, they had never really liked the place; they had only been there to make what they could out of their position. And even when they left they must have had the consolation of a belief in their eventual return after an Axis victory.

But for us, thought James sadly, there is no hope of return. We shall be exiled, banished for life. Of course, he told himself more practically, they could presumably return later if they wanted to do so, but as mere foreign civilian visitors. It would be more pain than pleasure. Euan, he knew, would never set foot on the island again; for him it would be impossible. For all of them their recall from Baressa would be an inconsolable distress, but for the Governor it was an appalling disaster.

For Euan, as James knew, had hoped to remain on Baressa for several more years—at least another five. He had never dreamed of his replacement by anyone until the island's future had been decided at some still far-distant date. And then, if the handing over would still be sad, it would be performed in a ceremonious and flattering manner. There would be long consultations with whatever new regime was to be installed, during which his advice would be sought and listened to with every token of respect. There would be banquets, laudatory speeches and addresses, and probably orders and decorations from the nations involved, salutes of guns, red carpets, and all the rest of it. Euan had seen himself winding up the British—which in practice would mean the Lemonfield—Administration in a blaze of success and glory. And now he would be hustled out with the minimum of ceremony, with hardly time to say good-bye, before the story had been finished. It would be his successor, or perhaps his successor's successor, who would wind up the British Administration of the island amidst the cheers and flash cameras and saluting cannon. By then Euan would have become a mere memory. If some future historian ever wrote of the war years and their aftermath on Baressa he would say, "Under British Administration the island and its people prospered as never before," rather than, "Under the firm and energetic rule of the British Military Governor, Colonel E. Lemonfield. . . ."

On a sudden impulse James turned back from the balcony. He would go and see Euan—he was almost certainly in the library or in his study. There was little that could be said to console him, but they could at least talk over the past and try for a short time to forget the dark, blank future. In any case, Euan, who had taken the matter about as badly as he could, should not be left alone. In a moment of black despair he might do anything. After his interview with General D'Aumont two evenings ago he had returned at once to the Villa and refused to see anyone. It had not been till the following night, twenty-four hours later, that he had summoned James to his study and informed him fully but briefly of what had taken place in the Palace on the preceding evening. He had seemed anxious to get rid of his friend's presence as soon as possible, for he had confined himself to a few bitter remarks, had told James to impart the information to no one else, and requested that his meals should be brought to him in the study until further notice.

Now, as he approached the semicircular green room in which the Colonel had cloistered himself for the past forty-eight hours, James could hear the restless tread of feet pacing and pacing lightly up and down on the thick carpet. He knocked. The footsteps ceased.

"Who is it?" Euan's voice sounded sharp and exasperated.

"Only me." James opened the door a little apprehensively and entered the softly lit study. Euan, looking ill and paler than James had ever seen him, stood beside his desk. The discolored flesh beneath his eyes told of two weary, sleepless nights. When he spoke his voice was brittle and expressionless.

"You're up late."

"Yes. I didn't feel like sleep. I didn't suppose you'd gone to bed either."

"I haven't slept since that man left." Euan indicated a low

273

round table set with decanters and glasses. "Help yourself to some cognac—it's the best. We might as well drink what we can of it while we still have the chance."

Ever the connoisseur, James poured some of the golden brandy into a great balloon goblet, warmed it between his cupped hands, and sniffed it appreciatively. "We leave behind many friends, many memories, five years of our lives—and at least three dozen more bottles of this."

"Because D'Aumont fancies himself a psychiatrist and reads some mental malady into all of us," said Euan harshly. "Or, as I am beginning to suspect, because he envies me my position and popularity. British Generals—as well as being the stupidest and most hidebound—are surely the vainest, most conceited, and venomous of mortal men. They acquire stomach ulcers when anybody else has any success and they fight more savagely and underhandedly amongst themselves than they ever do against the enemy. This simple-straightforward-soldier stuff they try to put over is nothing but a mask—it's but too cloak their knavery, in the words of Suckling. We'd been here too long, had we? Too long! Is one supposed to master the intricacies of governing a foreign country in weeks or months? There is always something to learn—something to be improved or changed."

"I wonder where we'll go next."

"Some wretched ruined German town, I've no doubt," snarled Euan furiously. "Hamm, I expect. I don't know the Germans and I don't like what I've heard of them. The only one I've ever had any dealings with murdered my best police officer. I'm not interested in them and I don't want to govern them. Give me some more brandy, please, James."

"I wonder *why* we like this place so much," mused the Major while he bent over the decanters. "Because, you know, it's not such a terribly attractive place really—not a Tahiti or anything of that sort. The climate isn't good for Europeans, part of the island's a rocky desert of the most depressing sort, and San Pietro's a dreadfully one-horse town, however one looks at it. Then there's no sport—not that you or I mind that, I know—but shooting's practically nonexistent, except for Saccomani's half-tame pigeons, and our coastal waters hold such extraordinary things that fishing is completely unconventional. The food isn't bad at all, I admit—with, perhaps, the exception of the meat, which can be shockingly tough on occasions. Then there's malaria and sand-fly fever in the north, and snakes and scorpions and Mrs. Tamminetto——"

"It's no use going on like that!" interrupted Euan savagely. "The fact is we *do* like it here. We've done a lot for the place, and however quaint it is we belong here now. It is home to us —to me, at any rate. I still can't believe that we'll be gone this time next month. We've got so used——" He broke off and started to pace up and down. "If only there was some way of explaining to Headquarters that we *hadn't* been here too long—not long enough. That it was only silly little things that D'Aumont noticed—things that weren't in keeping with his idea of British military life. He knew nothing of what we'd done here. There's so much more I could do. But there's no way"—he gazed hopelessly at the curtained windows—"nothing we *can* do."

"Unless we seize the island ourselves and proclaim it an independent state," suggested James with a halfhearted attempt at humor.

Euan laughed shortly. "A delightful idea, indeed! We'd be hustled home and put in a lunatic asylum—quite rightly." He continued his pacing.

James chuckled. "Yes, I suppose so. General D'Aumont would return with some military police and a dozen straitjackets."

"It wouldn't be D'Aumont," corrected the Colonel, with his usual pedantic regard for accuracy. "It would be our old friend Glasscraft—he's G.O.C. on the mainland now. He'd be still more pleased to do it, though—and that frightful follower of his, Pole."

"He couldn't, you know." James smiled. "We'd man his famous fortifications and wave flags and fire guns and he'd be scared off. Don't you remember how he said he thought those wretched casemates would make the place impregnable? He'd hang about on the coast huffing and puffing and writing letters to the Home Government—'Dear Prime Minister, Colonel Lemonfield has announced his personal suzerainty over Baressa and won't come home. I foolishly fortified the island for him and now I can't get it back. What shall I do? Yours uncertainly, H. Glasscraft.'"

To James' pleasure the Colonel stopped his pacing and laughed outright. "And do you know what would happen? The Government would say it was profoundly shocked. That's all the help poor old Glasscraft would get. They'd refer it to the United Nations, and of course *they'd* say—when they got around to it on their agenda in about three years' time—that it was really up to the inhabitants and that if they *liked* being governed by Colonel Lemonfield——" He broke off as a sudden thought seemed to strike him and James at the same time. For a moment they gazed at each other silently and the smiles slowly left their faces, to be replaced by looks of awe and half incredulous speculation. Then Euan said softly, "They *do* like it. I wonder. . . ."

The night wore on and a gibbous moon, rising out of the sea, illumined the island and the sleeping town of San Pietro, where the few lights still burning paled into insignificant yellow dots. In the dining room of the Villa Mrs. Giordano's parrot awoke as a moonbeam moved across its cage. It cocked its balding head at the low continuous murmur of voices that came from the far end of the corridor, swore rapidly but softly, and slept again.

The eastern sky paled slightly to gray-silver, then warmed to yellow. Birds called in the jungle garden of the Casa dei Fiori, and Christopher, lying beside Toki but dreaming of Silvana, tossed uneasily in his sleep.

In Police Headquarters Amerigo, on night duty, saw the dawn sky lightening through the black-barred window of the charge room. He yawned cavernously, rubbed a hand over his bristly chin, and slouched over to the gas ring to make himself some coffee.

In her bungalow beside the slaughterhouse Mrs. Tamminetto woke with a splitting headache and a bad temper. She looked at a little luminous bedside clock at her elbow and nudged the heavy bearded form that snored beside her. "Franz! Franz, it's time for you to go! It's getting light! Franz Ferdinand, *will* you wake up!"

32

THAT morning neither the Colonel nor the Major visited the Palace. Instead Brinsmead and Fortu were summoned to the Villa and kept there until lunchtime. The routine of the Administration was completely disorganized by this unusual occurrence and the clerks and typists sat idly in their offices without work or orders while their departmental chiefs phoned the Villa for instructions, to receive nothing but Fortu's invariable, "I'm sorry, His Excellency is very busy. He can attend to nothing at the moment."

It was approaching the hottest time of the year and no one minded taking things easily—except Maresciallo Riccomini. It was the day of the Major's monthly inspection of Fort Brocca and the Guardie di Finanza were mending pots and kettles in sullen boredom. If the Major didn't come soon they'd be at it the whole day. And if he didn't come today they'd have to continue tinkering tomorrow. The Maresciallo strode up and down his dignified office with his Edwardian brow creased into an angry imperious frown as he reckoned up the money he was losing by the Major's dilatoriness.

"Idle! Slack! Inefficient!" he muttered furiously. "Really, I don't know what things are coming to!"

That night the Colonel gave a dinner party to the English personnel. They were phoned at their offices by Brinsmead, and informed that the Colonel had something extremely important to say to them all and that they must not be late on pain of his severest displeasure. There was something so peculiarly jubilant and excited in Brinsmead's usually somber voice that it at once aroused keen speculation among the recipients of his message. Paige postponed a nocturnal journey around the brothel area in the enlightening company of Brigadiere Rondotto, and Christopher rang Silvana to say that he could not meet her down by the shore as had been arranged. She sounded deeply disappointed, he noted with a sort of painful pleasure, and he consoled her as best he could over the telephone while keeping an eye on the door lest Toki should appear. He felt intuitively that what the Colonel had to say would concern the recent visit of the troop convoy and probably Pirie's discovery. For a moment a cold hand clutched at his heart, but then he remembered Brinsmead's voice. Surely if the Colonel had bad news to announce his Chief Clerk would not have sounded so buoyant. And yet—no one had seen the Colonel for three days. Unable to work, he went back to the Casa dei Fiori, after a halfhearted attempt to check equipment in the company store, and wandered apprehensively about the big shadowy rooms as the long, hot hours dragged slowly past.

At last the fiery sun swooped into the purple western sea, the quick twilight fell, and it was time to go to the Villa. When the guests arrived, carefully dressed in the starched and iron drill uniforms that the occasion necessitated, they found several guards of the Banda in the big hall, but no sign of the Colonel. They were shown into the library, where the Major rose from playing chess with Fortu to greet them with his invariable air of slightly ironic benevolence.

"How nice to see you all here again! Just like last Christmas— only this time please don't corrupt the parrot with alcohol, it's so degrading for the poor thing. It hasn't really got over the last party yet. I think drink brings on a forced molt or something, for it's lost an indecent amount of feathers during the past four months. Of course, it *may* be old age. Yes, Christopher, please help yourself, and then hand them around. The Colonel's still working—you can hear him dictating and Brinsmead typing if you listen, but you're not supposed to, so I think you'd just better make polite conversation with me—unless you find the prospect too boring for words. No, Whyton, those are Turkish. Try one by all means if you like, but you'll find Virginians in that frightful rococo shell affair on top of the radiogram. It was presented to the Colonel on his birthday three years ago by Captain Zvengetzov—malice aforethought we consider. . . ."

Later the Colonel came in, accompanied by Brinsmead. Everyone rose, but, contrary to general expectation, no announcement of any kind was made. Instead William and Paige and Sergeant Hope were taken around the walls to look at the Major's pictures. In a big gilt frame above a low bookcase they examined his portrait of the Colonel—"The Proclamation." Euan, sitting upright and dignified behind his enormous desk, writing by the light of a shaded lamp of carved alabaster. The golden light, the dark shadowy background, the primly studious figure, all blending to form an atmosphere of subtle power and strength that, according to a remark from the artist at the other side of the room, was as good as anything the old Dutch masters had ever done. William knew little of the old Dutch masters—he preferred the weirdly melancholy picture of Christopher leaning against the soaring rose-tinged pillar lit by the weary mauve afterglow of an

278

opal sky. For a time they studied the Major's newest picture. It was of Silvana. In an eighteenth-century pose she stood on a draped balcony in her green-and-white ball dress, holding a rose in one hand while the fingertips of the other lightly caressed the head of the Mayoress' pale cream Pekingese.

"Horrible little thing!" called the Major. "It bit Zubier and he spanked it and it immediately made a mess on the sofa."

"It's a good likeness, isn't it, sir?" said William to the Colonel.

"Yes, very. The Maresciallo's extremely pleased with it—and so's Silvana. The Major wanted to paint her in her dirtiest sailing clothes, lying on her stomach on the stern of your boat. She refused to allow it—very rightly, in my opinion."

"It would have been much better," called James, "more artistically right." He was engaged in showing Brinsmead, Fortu, and Whyton an album full of family snapshots of the Giordanos. Mrs. Giordano had forgotten to take it with her and for five years it had given James constant caustic amusement. He invariably showed it to guests and kept up a witty sarcastic commentary as he turned the heavy pasteboard pages. Christopher had seen it before and privately thought James' remarks to be in the worst of taste. It was rather like reading someone's private diaries or letters aloud, and he could never understand why the normally kind and considerate James indulged in such an unpleasant practice. But the two executive officers, he knew, had some phobia about the Giordanos, whom neither of them was ever able to malign sufficiently.

It was not until dinner—during which the guests were tacitly given the choice between discussing rain erosion with the Colonel or the vagaries of the Port Pilot with the Major—was finished that any hint of the reason for the party was forthcoming. But as Brinsmead, who was extraordinarily partial to port, put down his empty glass and titivated his moustache with his napkin, the Colonel rose.

"Well, if everyone's finished I think we'll have coffee in the study," he announced.

With an audible sigh of relief they pushed back their chairs and trooped after Euan across the hall, through the library, and down the corridor to the study. Here the lights were glowing and the coffee things laid out on a low round table. While his subordinates were seating themselves the Colonel went to a small safe, from which he took a dark-red file, and at the same time James unhurriedly locked the door and put the key in his pocket. As he did so there came the heavy tread of footsteps outside and the unmistakable click and rattle of grounded arms.

"Now," remarked the Colonel as he took his seat at the coffee table, "I think we can get started." He glanced from face to face of his expectant audience. "James, Dawson hasn't got any coffee."

Texas blushed vividly. "I don't drink coffee, sir. Thank you very much."

The Colonel looked amused. "Not drink coffee, Dawson? You surprise me. I thought everyone on this island drank coffee. Considering the excellence of the coffee we import. . . ."

Christopher gritted his teeth, received an ironic glance from James, and flushed. Paige took off his spectacles, breathed on the lenses, and wiped them with a handkerchief.

At last the Colonel finished his discourse on coffee and, demonstrating his own partiality for it by draining his cup, poured himself another with a steady hand. Then he opened his file.

"Now what I have to tell you this evening," he began pleasantly, "will be rather a shock—in fact, rather a series of them. I will only preface my remarks by saying that what I have decided, in consultation with the Major and to a certain degree with Sergeant Brinsmead, has only been resolved upon after the most careful reflection, in which the interests of everybody concerned—and in particular of all of you here tonight—have been fully considered. It is my intention to end the present British Military Administration on Baressa and to make this island a free republic. This is a step which I consider should be taken in view of the past, and particularly the recent, history of the island. Eighty years ago Baressa was sparsely populated by a few indigenous inhabitants, who led an uncertain existence harried by the continual descent of pirates. After Giulio Brocca landed things changed rapidly, and the fact that a very small amount of gold was found in the north caused a good deal of mixed immigration for many years. But the gold soon ran out. The Italians had taken this island primarily under the pleasing but erroneous assumption that it was almost solid gold a few feet under the surface. When this was at last—and they fought against the disappointing fact for an extraordinarily long time—proved not to be the case, they lost interest in Baressa and left it to carry on as best it could under a varied assortment of dishonest officials who sucked the financial blood of the place for years. Under Fascist rule things were, if anything, worse. I really think that right up till 1940 the Italians were still smarting under the disappointment of not finding gold and were determined to get money out of Baressa by hook or by crook. They got it mostly by crook, as we know, and the wretched place was burdened with taxes and tariffs and extraordinary restrictions in the interests of Italian monopolists, many of whom were Fascist party chiefs. Not surprisingly, therefore, Baressa appeared in the eyes of the world—or such of the world that took the trouble to notice it—as a poor and valueless little place, the rather ridiculous island where the Italians had hoped to find gold but had failed. It is in that light that it is still looked on today.

"But when I—we, rather—came to Baressa things altered. It was easy to see why the place was poor and the removal of the excessive taxes, the monopolistic restrictions, and the corrupt officials soon altered the state of things beyond recognition. In two years I proved that Baressa was comfortably off—in five I have proved it to be moderately wealthy. Trade has increased vastly, agriculture—but you know all that, or if you don't you certainly should.

"Now, as you also know, I and my Administration are held in the very highest esteem on Baressa because of the changes that have taken place in the last five years and that are rightly attributed to me. If I were a civilian and this were the early nineteenth century I should probably find myself in the position of the first Rajah Brooke of Sarawak and, in recognition of the benefits I have bestowed on them, the inhabitants of Baressa would make me their king." The Colonel smiled, sipped his cooling coffee, and continued. "Things are different today and kings are out of fashion, but the inhabitants' gratitude remains very real. This gratitude has been earned—I want to point that out clearly—by myself chiefly, perhaps, but also very certainly by you who have assisted me. It has been earned and it is deserving of reward. But of reward we are—or were, I should say now—to have none. At the end of the stay of the troopships that left so recently I was visited by General D'Aumont in my office, told that I—and all of you—had been here too long, and tersely informed that steps would be taken as soon as possible to have us recalled to the mainland and replaced." He paused and there was a gasp of astonishment and anger from his audience.

"Yes, we who have done so much for Baressa were to be ignominiously bundled out with hardly time to say good-bye to our friends. We were to be ejected in precisely the same way that Colonel Giordano and his worthless entourage were ejected five years ago.

"This was to happen to us because of the fearful misdemeanors and extravagances we had perpetrated. Because the Palace footmen called me 'Excellency' instead of 'sir.' Because Major Naughton-Muirhead and myself tried to keep a respectable state of order in the streets during the enforced visits of that shabby rabble of soldiers from the ships. Because Captain Pirie—our old friend Pirie—who happened to be aboard is actuated by motives of hatred and jealousy arising from his regrettable sojourn here. Because Lieutenant Paige and the D.A.P.M. could not agree. Because the General saw you, Summerson, wearing a civilian shirt instead of a khaki one. Yes, those and others of that sort were the heinous offenses that were to cause us to be expelled promptly from Baressa. Needless to say, the real reason was jealousy. Jealousy of how we lived, jealousy of the friendship we had earned and the esteem we had won—above all, jealousy because we had succeeded in doing something really worthwhile.

"I myself am not prepared—nor do I think you are—to tolerate such treatment. We are none of us professional soldiers like General D'Aumont, and we are all perfectly capable of thinking and acting for ourselves. Our impending treatment at the hands of an ungrateful country absolves us utterly, in my opinion, from any duty we might conceivably have owed in that direction. For that matter, Baressa is our adopted country—and the adoption in this case will be completely reciprocal. We are going, in modern parlance, to cash in on the gratitude the islanders feel for us and we are going to do it in this way. We cannot ask Baressa openly how it wants to be governed in future, but we can be morally certain that if among the alternatives offered it was national sovereignty under the present Administration it would unhesitatingly choose that. Fortunately, there are about a dozen rich and influential men on the island who between them own nearly a quarter of Baressa's wealth and who would willingly see the *status quo* maintained. To those men I can discreetly indicate the situation and can acquire their backing. With that backing it will be an easy matter to carry out a simple coup and proclaim the independence of Baressa as a sovereign elected republic, of which I shall be the chosen President. As soon as that is done a plebiscite and elections can be held to confirm it. That they will confirm it there is no reasonable doubt at all.

"Once that is accomplished we shall arrange the position very much as it is today. As President I shall retain much the same amount of power that I exercise at present. To you shall be given senior and well-paid posts. Major Naughton-Muirhead will control foreign diplomacy—should there be any." The Colonel smiled and his audience laughed discreetly. "Captain Kellermann will command whatever armed forces we decide to maintain. Lieutenant Paige will continue as Chief of the Police, Sergeant Brinsmead will become a sort of Secretary of State on the American model—it is a position that he has unofficially held for several years past—and the rest of you will be found appropriate and adequately rewarded positions. None of you, judging from the talks I had with you all last Christmas, seemed either keen to leave the island or at all certain what occupations you would follow when you did so. Now the former event will not take place and your futures will be provided for."

The Colonel paused and turned over a page in his file. He studied it for a few moments and continued. "Fourteen days from tomorrow the *Emperor Napoleon* will be back in harbor, bringing at least some of the men who are to take over from us. We have therefore two weeks to prepare and bring about these—alterations in Baressa's domestic government. It is my intention, immediately a republic is proclaimed, to throw ourselves upon the mercy of the United Nations Organization and to appeal loudly and insistently to the rights of small nations as laid down in the Atlantic Charter. Freedom and self-determination have been so vaunted as part of the allies' war aims that an appeal to the very organization expressly set up to deal in those two commodities can hardly go unheard. Our plea may be embarrassing, but how much more embarrassing—how irredeemably shameful —it would be if this first demand for freedom and self-government were to go unregarded by U.N.O. Needless to say, our demands must be loud as well as ethical. They must be clamorous. Major Naughton-Muirhead is to see to that. He was, as you may know, once a journalist on the staff of a large New York newspaper. He still has connections there and he is going to invite some of his erstwhile colleagues to Baressa with the promise of a world scoop. They will arrive on the eve of the announcement of the Republic and will be carefully briefed. It will be a very fine story for these reporters and we think they will be sufficiently grateful to take our side and help us in our demands. You can imagine the great impression the friendly reception of our action in America would make elsewhere. U.N.O. will not be able to disregard us and will have to give us its blessing or stand condemned as a hypocritical laughingstock, to be ridiculed and disregarded. If we have U.N.O.'s blessing no one will dare to touch us—certainly not the British Government.

"You can, of course, see that we must have time for the Major's friends to publish their version of the position and for the impression thus caused to take effect. Until that has happened we shall be in some peril of the British Army on the mainland acting promptly to subdue and remove us. And if they do we shall never get back again, whatever U.N.O. may say at a later date. A new Governor and new staff will be hurriedly installed and the whole thing will be hushed up as far as possible. It will be put about that our length of service in the hot climate had regrettably deranged our wits and doubtless we shall all be dismissed from the Service—which you may think would be a quick way to get demobilized in such an eventuality.

"But we are not going to let that happen. We shall achieve all the time we need by bluff. The G.O.C. on the mainland is General Glasscraft, the officer who ordered the fortifications to be built here, with the remark that if they were properly manned and held the island would be impregnable. That he was talking nonsense I firmly believe. This island is not, nor ever can be, anything but indefensible, and I personally would not think for one moment of attempting to defend it against anybody. But if General Glasscraft likes to think it is impregnable we will obligingly do all we can to further that belief. We will do everything in our power to give him the impression that not only are the defenses manned by resolute and well-equipped troops, but that we ourselves are determined to fight to the last drop of blood to repel any invasion. If the General believes that he must fight to regain control of Baressa it follows that he must believe he will sustain casualties. If we succeed well with our bluff he may even be dubious of the chances of a successful invasion at all. His career, his reputation—even his pension—will all be at stake, all involved in a tricky politico-military action of the sort British generals dread and hate—doubtless for the best of reasons, for few emerge from them unscathed. He will hesitate. He will request instructions from the Home Government—and his chance will be lost. The matter will pass from the military to the political sphere, and we shall be able to await events with almost certain assurance of success."

Euan closed the file and sat back, smiling. At once a clamor of enthusiastic speech broke loose. He was showered with questions and suggestions, congratulations and promises of support. After a few minutes he held up a hand for silence.

"We must start tonight, and I shall give you all your orders separately. James, take everyone except Paige into the library and give them a drink—but not too much, for I don't want any misunderstanding of instructions. Paige, you stay here."

For the rest of that night the Colonel gave his orders in his study. One by one his officers and men left James' animated group in the library and, passing down the corridor, entered for the second time that night the green and silver semicircular room where, surrounded by files and maps, the Colonel sat at the low round coffee table.

33

ON the morning after his momentous decision Colonel Lemonfield left San Pietro for a rapid tour of the plateau. He was away two days and nights visiting the more important landowners and discreetly sounding their opinions on Baressa's future. He never once admitted his intentions by anything but the vaguest hint, but he returned to the city completely satisfied with the results of his journey.

Meanwhile Major Naughton-Muirhead had dispatched his equally enigmatic telegrams to his American friends and had received satisfactory replies. At least five journalists would fly to Baressa at the agreed time and meanwhile no hint of anything untoward would become known in the outside world. It thus remained to set in motion the necessary preparations in San Pietro itself. The censorship of outgoing mail, which had lapsed since Italy's reentry into the war, was secretly reimposed and all radio traffic was rigorously checked by Hope and Whyton. The garrison company, the Banda, and the native police were all issued with Italian steel helmets and drab but formidable-looking battle uniforms, hurriedly run up by a large-scale Indian tailoring establishment. They were then photographed in a variety of warlike attitudes by Mr. Siropian, the Armenian staff photographer of the *Courier*. Mr. Siropian, fat, tall, and jovial, displayed a surprising flair for complex composite pictures in which, by a cunning use of perspective, squads of soldiers swelled into companies and battalions and Captain Diaz's six old shell-less field guns appeared a whole regiment of artillery. The British armored car which had fallen into the harbor in 1940 and had been subsequently salvaged and forgotten was found rusting under a mass of creeper behind the power station. It would not actually work, but, painted in camouflage colors, manned by Texas in crash helmet and goggles, and sextuplicated by superimposition, it made an impressive photograph and added a startling touch of modernity to Baressa's mainly fictional forces.

The manner in which the American journalists, and through them General Glasscraft, should be deceived about the number of the island's fighting troops had been ingeniously devised by Major Naughton-Muirhead. He planned to fit out every government employee of the lower grades, from the Palace messengers to the municipal street scavengers, with exactly the same somber green-khaki uniform as that recently issued to the troops. These, diversified only by high-numbered but meaningless shoulder numerals, were to be donned on the eve of the *coup d'état,* on which there was to be a general three-day holiday. Thus the streets of the city would at all hours be filled with individuals who reasonably might—and it was hoped would—be taken for soldiers off duty.

Having set their minds as far as possible at rest concerning the military deception so necessary to gain time immediately after the announcement of independence, the two administrative officers and their chief clerk proceeded to the more congenial task of drafting a modern and progressive constitution for the future republic. It took them a great deal of time and trouble, for it was necessary to disguise what would, in fact, be a continuation of the Colonel's dictatorship under the appearance of a free parliamentary democracy. When it was finished it was rapidly garnished with progressive touches calculated to win the approval of the more idealistic and less practical U.N.O. delegates. The Colonel abolished the death penalty and corporal punishment as well as certain barbarous practices—slavery, police torture, judicial mutilation—which, as far as could be ascertained, had never existed on Baressa. He introduced widespread social services and adult education, and it was only in view of the undoubted opposition of the Roman Catholic Church that he regretfully abandoned legalized birth control and euthanasia. The legislature was overhauled to include habeas corpus, trial by jury, and the Scottish verdict of "Not proven." It was, as the Major said, a model constitution unfitted for practical use anywhere—least of all on Baressa, which had thrived as never before under a blatant military dictatorship—but thoroughly high-minded and in advance of the times.

When it was completed Brinsmead printed two dozen copies on the Palace Roneo machine and the Colonel locked them securely in his safe. Looking at his desk calendar as he pocketed the keys, he noted that ten days had passed since the convoy had sailed. In another week the *Napoleon* would dock, bringing the new Governor and his staff. He pressed the electric bell and, on Fortu's appearance, sent him out with messages for Christopher, Paige, and Hope, summoning them to a conference that night. Meanwhile he sent for Brinsmead and together they started to make plans for the plebiscite which was to confirm the new regime as soon as possible after its inception.

"And there's the Proclamation to do this evening, Brinsmead. I have a rough draft already typed, but it needs working on. I think we'll get down to it after the conference. The Major says he'll lend a hand, but I'm afraid it will take us most of the night."

"Well, it's really too hot to sleep, sir, in any case."

To Christopher, as day followed day with ever-increasing heat, the situation became continually more unreal until he seemed to be living in a dream from which he longed and yet dreaded to awake. Exactly a week after the convoy had left, the orders for a general replacement of personnel were received by the Signal Office. General D'Aumont had wasted no time.

It had been with a cold feeling in his stomach that Christopher had received the terse military message, and though Texas, who had brought it to his office, had grinned and said, "Reckon you can put that straight in the wastepaper basket, sir," he could not overcome as quickly as the dispatch rider that heavy innate fear of the Army that had dogged him at a distance through the sleepy sunlit years.

So now, at last, when it was too late, they were trying to get him back. If it *was* too late. Even here on Baressa, hundreds of miles from the mainland, even after five years of isolation, they still could half hypnotize him into clammy fear with a small square of orange paper. "They"—a remote, doom-bearing Kafkaesque "They"—impersonal, omnipotent, and sinister. Once again his old fears that he had thought buried under a mountain of serene island hours fought their way, skeletal and sickening, to the surface. It was only his belief in the Colonel that kept them at bay, that stopped him from acquiescing silently to the signaled orders and going back to "Them" as a rabbit jerks shivering toward a stoat. The fight between "Them" and the Colonel for his possession invaded his dreams. Once more he would wake trembling and sweating in the hot, damp darkness from grotesque fantasies in which hordes of steel-helmeted men invaded the Palazzo Firenze and stormed into Lemonfield's office through doors which, however vainly barricaded by Paige, William, Fortu, himself, slowly bent and heaved apart to reveal the huge form and slavering face of Booker. Then he would turn with a strangled scream to the great desk, to the Colonel—and the Colonel would not be there, but in his place, laughing and jeering, his small gray eyes filled with triumphant hate—Pirie.

He awoke from these dreams to find Toki bending over him, worried and soothing. "Christopher, what is it? What has happened? What is troubling you? Has it come back now—after so long?" And guiltily he would recall that she had been his mistress for four and a half years—long enough to remember the nightmares that had racked him during his first months on Baressa.

And soon Toki must go. Somehow he must dismiss her. For, once established firmly on the island for good, he would be able to marry Silvana. The Army's permission would no longer be needed; all that would be required would be the Colonel's consent, and that consent would only be given if Toki were finally and irrevocably banished from the Casa dei Fiori.

The Colonel's *coup d'état* and the stormy interview that he must have with his pathetically faithful little half-caste were the two barriers separating him from a life that would surely be one of such glorious happiness and secure content that the very thought warmed him to a golden glow and made him for the moment forget his fears. For he feared deeply both these barriers that must be overcome. He was genuinely fond of Toki, and though he had never—could never—feel for her the love she felt for him—the love he could only feel for Silvana—yet he dreaded the pain he must cause her and shied away from the infliction of it like a startled horse.

Of the *coup d'état*, too, he had fears—fears of the consequences of failure. That these were not shared by his compatriots was no consolation, for if ever they considered the probable results of a catastrophic fiasco it was only to shrug their shoulders and say that nothing much would happen. Paige had even, amidst shouts of laughter, invented some long ludicrous speeches to make at his court-martial. But to Christopher the visions of disaster were horribly real. He saw himself, bound and helpless, handed over to the grimly gloating wrath of "Them." He could have felt no more fear of the court which he believed would try him if it had been composed of the savage, black-uniformed Germans who were at this moment being hunted to their deaths in Central Europe.

The very normality of everyday life made it almost impossible to realize that such a wildly improbable occurrence as a *coup d'état* was being planned—much less that it was about to take place. Beyond a quantity of fancy-dress photographs having been taken by a perspiring middle-aged Armenian no preparations of any sort appeared to have been made. The Colonel still entered his office punctually at nine in the mornings, the guard still presented arms as he walked sedately up the steps—and within seven days he intended to rise from his office desk and defy the British Empire. It was difficult not to feel that when he had done so he would sit down again and turn his attention to the police gasoline account.

The growing tension of inactive waiting was felt by all the Englishmen, with the possible exception of the Colonel. It was waiting unrelieved by any form of action. Being already the undisputed rulers of the island, they had no one to overthrow, no power to seize. The usual furtive nocturnal flittings and conspirings, the invariable prelude to a conventional *coup d'état*, were therefore missing. There were no fevered conferences in cellars, no secret passwords or signals, no hidden arsenals of arms. The hot bright days moved infinitely slowly on as the tempo of island life slowed to its most lethargic pace under the glaring sky of early summer.

There was nothing visible to fear, no tangible opposition to be braved. The sun, on the day of destiny, would set over as peaceful and ordered a scene as that over which it had arisen. The Union Jack would no longer fly over the Palace, the Colonel, if he remembered, would have taken the pictures of the King and Queen from the wall behind his desk and put them in a drawer, but his valet would still run his bath to the correct temperature before dinner, Zubier would still see to the proper cooling of the wine, and the Villa's gardeners would take a last chance to mow the lawns before the rains broke. The everyday routine would be as unaffected for those whose lives were lived on a humbler scale.

Yet from this very quietness was born a feeling of growing unease—a tingling of the spine and a slight coldness in the pit of the stomach. Soon, very soon, the step from which there could be no retreat would have to be taken. This growing tension among the Englishmen communicated itself slowly in some subtle way to the townsfolk of San Pietro. Perhaps now that the European war was over they guessed that the near future must hold changes for them and that the calm ordered existence of the last five years might soon give way to another sort of life. Perhaps Giordano would return—nobody wanted him, and a rumor that he was actually to arrive on the next visit of the *Napoleon* caused mild consternation until it was officially contradicted. But that such a rumor should have circulated at all showed the trend of popular feeling. An atmosphere of unrest and expectancy—starting, doubtless, at that fountainhead of all communal mental processes, the native bazaars—spread like a rapidly widening stain through the city, permeating the minds of all races and classes until a sultry atmosphere of tension hung over San Pietro as day followed day and the great sun arched flaming through the white-hot sky to extinguish itself in lurid, bloody light below the rim of the tepid sea.

34

ON the morning of the day before that on which Baressa was to become a free republic Major Naughton-Muirhead slowly mounted the marble stairs of the Palazzo Firenze on his way to the Colonel's office. Slowly, because the day was overpoweringly hot—hotter than he had ever known it in the last five years. The rains would come soon, and older members of the colonial population prophesied that they would be early and torrential. James hoped they were right. The island climate during the rains was humid and sticky, but even so it would offer a welcome change from the glaring furnace of the present weather.

Though the Palace was filled with the whirr and swish of electric ceiling fans the two guards of the Banda who stood, vividly clothed ebony statues, on each side of the tall doors before Euan's office were blinking the sweat out of their eyes, and their faces shone and glittered. Within the office Euan sat at his desk, fully dressed in his pale uniform with its brass buttons and red tabs and looking as cool as ever. James wondered how he managed it, and thought that the answer probably lay in the sea breeze, hot though it was, that blew through the tall open windows, moving the heavy curtains and rustling the leaves of the small notepad that lay at the Colonel's elbow.

"Well, James, how are you feeling now? In just twenty-four hours I shall be reading the Proclamation out there, *coram populo*." Euan indicated with a slight nod of his head the balcony beyond the fourth window.

"Pleased." James sank with a sigh into an armchair beside his friend's desk and placed the briefcase he was carrying on the floor. "Pleased to feel that we're so soon going to get it over. I wish it were this time next month."

Euan smiled. "I thought you were looking forward to it—I mean, to the experience itself. You said it would be the most diverting one you'd ever had."

"I know—but it's too hot. And then there's the uncertainty. At the moment I just feel I'll be glad to get it over and settle down again. I'm looking forward to the results, but not—so much —to the actual performance." He yawned. "Ah, well, I expect I shall enjoy it once we get started. I feel oddly depressed at the moment—it's this infernal temperature. I hope the rains don't break tomorrow—it would be a nuisance if they did."

"They won't. It's still far too early, whatever anybody may say," said Euan assuredly. He paused a moment. "Well, everything's ready. Everybody's briefed and your journalist friends are due this afternoon. I don't mind admitting that I shall be glad when we get started, myself. By the way, you haven't seen this." He opened a drawer and, pulling out a large folded piece of material, shook it open. It was a flag—a tricolor of pale green, purple, and blue. "Our national banner—rather revolting, isn't it?"

"Horrible! Really, Euan, couldn't you have thought of something less—less torrid?"

The Colonel laughed and folded the flag again carefully. "These colors were all we could find in the correct materials to make a sufficiency. One could hardly use *crêpe de Chine* or canvas. Otherwise there were only beige and gray."

"That would have been better—*much* better. Unusual and discreet."

"H'm—perhaps. People would have made rude jokes about our large assortment of half-castes. Mud-color and off-white. You've brought the photographs?"

"Yes."

"Let's see them." Euan's voice quickened with interest as James unclasped his briefcase. From it he took Mr. Siropian's work— piles of big glossy photographs. He dealt them like cards across the glass desk top, commenting on each.

"The Banda in battle dress—you'll notice he makes them look at least a battalion. Then here's the armored car on the move— we pushed it downhill to get this picture. Here are the guns.

More Banda—or Christopher's men, perhaps—one can't tell with those uniforms, but they look very formidable. Here are the strongpoints near Agamo, fully manned. The white officers, as you can see, are Fortu, Summerson, and Dawson. Here they are again with another lot of troops, but their faces are turned away from the camera so that they can't be recognized as the same people in the last picture. This is the stern of the dredger—Zvengetzov in charge—it's supposed to be laying mines. By the way, I've drawn a great shaded belt around the entire island in the big map in my office and marked it 'Minefields (impenetrable)' and I shall be careful to see the Americans notice it. Here are more troops charging with the bayonet and wearing gas masks and being led by Whyton and Dawson—something went wrong with Dawson's mask and he nearly suffocated before Mr. Siropian and I could get it off. These are all much the same—soldiers and officers. Now here are the others. All of us on the balcony waving to the crowds—you alone. These are the crowd scenes—they're excellent. You'll notice the Villa gardeners in front waving the 'Freedom for Baressa' banners. They were taken by themselves in the back garden and superimposed on a crowd scene Siropian took at the opening of the Aquarium. Here's another that he superimposed over an old picture of a Fascist gathering. Giordano is behind the 'Lemonfield for President' banner—you can just see his bandy legs if you look carefully. Here are Zubier's children—he's got eleven—waving 'Vote for Lemonfield and Freedom.' Mr. Siropian's idea, I may say; he prides himself on his ability to get children to pose nicely. I watched him—too coy and avuncular for words—quite sickening. There are a lot more balcony and crowd scenes, but you've seen the best."

"They're very good, James. You and Siropian are to be congratulated. You'll hand them out to your friends tomorrow? And you'd better collect some Roneo'd copies of the Constitution and the Proclamation from Brinsmead as you go past his office. Have you seen to the *Courier*?"

"Yes." James collected the photographs and shuffled them into a neat pile before putting them into his briefcase. "They're all standing by for a special edition, which the printers are setting up under the supervision of the confidential police agents. The Proclamation takes up most of the front page with your leading article and the Mayor's petition to you and your answer—everything that we planned. I wrote a warlike article early this morning—I started it as Mahmud was running my bath and finished it while dressing. It's headed, 'Baressa's Small but Determined Army prepares to defend Islanders' New-found Freedom.' It's all about the fine fighting qualities of the inhabitants. I've made up the most delightful fabrications concerning their fanatical courage and iron endurance and about a frightful knife they always carry and with which they disembowel their enemies with a flick of the wrist."

"Well done!"

"And I did another later, full of imaginary interviews with native notables. I did a lovely description of the Sheikhs of the Sharia Court bowing toward Mecca and praising Allah that they had lived to see the day, etc., etc.—very moving. We'll have to subsidize this edition of the *Courier* because it's twelve pages instead of six and they are giving away a colored print of you with every copy. Mr. Siropian's cashing in on that."

"I'm sure he is. Never mind, he deserves to—he's done very well. Brinsmead's ordered over a hundred pounds' worth of fireworks for tomorrow evening and Christopher says we should double the pay of his men if we want to be certain of their continued assistance. It's lucky we have the money put by. Otherwise I would have had to borrow it from the Municipality, which would have been a nuisance and entailed awkward explanations." He paused and gazed musingly down the long room. Through the wide open windows, borne on the hot sea breeze, came the noises of the docks, the rattle of cranes and winches, the shouts of sailors on the dhows. The day after tomorrow No. 1 berth would be being kept vacant for the *Emperor Napoleon*. "It's odd to think," he said slowly, "that today's the last day in which I sit here as Colonel Lemonfield, the British Military Governor. This time tomorrow I'll be President."

James smiled. "Do you like the idea?"

"Oh, I shall get used to it, I've no doubt. At present I feel, like you, that the weather's too hot to exert one's imagination to believe in any change until it's actually taken place." For a few moments they sat silently together in the hot, bright room while the breeze rustled the heavy curtains and brought the acrid smell of diesel oil from the wharves to their nostrils. Below them in the sun-baked Piazza a heavy truck loaded with salt rumbled noisily past the Palace and as the roar of its engine died away along the Via della Costa James rose with a sigh.

"Well, there's a lot more for me to see to. And I mustn't waste any more of your time. . . ."

That afternoon William could not sleep. He lay in the hot room he shared with Texas, listening to the clank-clank of the old green ceiling fan and watching the dust motes swim lazily in the shafts of light that slanted from the louvers of the closed shutters. Lying in the still heat, he turned over in his mind the events of the morrow—events in which his part was to be small, merely that of a supernumerary secretary to the Colonel. William wondered what the Colonel was feeling like now—what he was doing on this long fiery afternoon.

It was no use trying to rest. Texas snored heavily on the other side of the room, but he could sleep through anything. He had no nerves and in any case looked forward to tomorrow with a childish delight and a firm conviction of success. Getting off his bed, William dressed and walked softly in rubber-soled shoes to the door and out onto the pale, hot concrete of the veranda. Immediately the heat rose and struck him and he half-closed his eyes against the white, penetrating glare. He would go down to the shore, to the high-roofed open shed on the slipway where the *Columbia* lay careened, waiting for some minor adjustment to its cranky engine. An odd nostalgia possessed him, tinged with excitement at the thought of tomorrow. For after that nothing would be the same again. Today was the last day of the old order —the last day of nearly five years.

Trailing slowly down the dry, dusty lane that led to the shore, keeping wherever possible in the shade of a wall or a projecting roof, William reviewed the past years with commingled feelings of pleasure and sadness and affection. There had been good times, serene and happy and free. He forgot now the early months of Hope's nagging and petty tyranny, for even Hope had succumbed to the island at last, had become by degrees less stiff, less efficient, inclined to daydream and be absentminded. Baressa was a good place. He would be content to live his life here. A visit to England occasionally, perhaps, but always to return to this sun-drenched land, the white town circled by the blue-green sea stretching remotely to the far horizon.

He wandered out of the lane on to the rough, cracked blocks of the slipway and picked his way carefully across rusting lengths of chain and twisted red steel hawsers. The breeze struck him, ruffling his hair and billowing his faded blue shirt coolly from his damp skin, and in front of him the sea stretched, a great expanse of glittering wavelets under the high afternoon sky.

It was thus that Silvana saw him as, walking home from particularly late labors at the Police Headquarters, she crossed the Via della Costa to look out over the long peninsular shore of Ras Godron to where, a quarter of a mile away, the high curved roof of the slipway shed reared its rusty surface above the jumble of buoys, winches, and old upturned boats. She saw William, a tiny figure in a blue shirt and khaki shorts with the wind ruffling his fair hair, far down the cluttered shore, picking his way slowly along the white sloping concrete path to the shed, and she stood watching him, a smile on her lips.

In her, too, the mounting tension of the past fortnight, with its troubled air of impending change, had engendered an affectionate nostalgia for the past. And there was William, so much a part of the past five years, a small solitary figure at this improbable, uninhabited time of day, moving far up the shore among the litter of sea-weathered salt-stained marine junk amongst which they had wandered—oh, years ago. Dear William. Her heart went out suddenly to the memory of those early days when, children together, they had idled laughing and learning each other's tongues along this very shore, rambling far down the coast that stretched westward around the curve of the island. Always in her thoughts she would associate William with the jumbled rusting engines and gear, the flaking blistered hulls of this forgotten foreshore, this backwater of the harbor. Always she would see him against a background of bright sky and glittering lapping water, with the smell of tar and brine, the acrid odor of diesel oil mixed with the salty scent of drying seaweed. And suddenly she knew that it was to him she belonged, with him that the future lay and with no one else. Perhaps she had half known it ever since they had first met long ago in Mrs. Tamminetto's office at Police Headquarters, before she had even seen Christopher, before she had been mesmerized by those troubled, slanting green eyes that lit up like a cat's with the heat of his desire.

He was beautiful—as exotic in his way as the place in which he lived—and that queer beauty that changed so quickly from unhappy faraway stillness to excited passion had touched some answering chord within her that thrilled with an equally urgent desire. She had thought she could never live without Christopher and, knowing her love to be returned, had waited, lost in a dream of white and gold. She had tried to disguise her feelings for William by pretending to herself that she looked on him as a childhood friend rather than a prospective husband. Perhaps this had been partly pique, for William had treated her as a companion, a playmate, for so long—until Christopher had shown him that she was something more. And by then she had not wanted to give up her beautiful lover even though William— Poor William! With a stab of warm pity she saw him again as he had been at that first dance in the Municipio, thin and shabby in faded drill, leaning against the wall his face set and unhappy as she danced with Christopher.

She must go to him now and explain. It suddenly became a matter of fearful urgency to see William, to speak to him, to tell him —what, she did not quite know, but catch him she must before he left that magic shore. She jumped down to the beach and started to run over the loose shingle. Sharp pebbles edged between the straps of her light sandals and she slipped and stumbled among the hot rocks, and somewhere she dropped the bright canvas satchel she had been carrying. But on she ran, driven by a vivid glorious happiness, a huge necessity to see William, to tell him that she loved him, that she would marry him, would go to Europe, England, anywhere with him. For where he went there, too, would she go, she would make his people her people and his home hers.

The hard white sunlight flashed on the pale quartz-speckled shingle and the unbearable quicksilver of the dancing sea. Ahead the fox-red iron roof of the tall shed shimmered and shivered in the heat. Was he there still? Had he wandered back another way, hidden from her by the old hulks? No. For now he was coming out of the sharp shadow beside the *Columbia*'s hull. He must have heard the clash of her footsteps on the shingle and left his boat to investigate. For a moment he stood again as she had so often seen him, outlined against the glittering sea, and her heart swelled with love for him as panting, laughing, half crying, she called, "William!"

It was as he had expected—things were not going well. She was taking it badly. Striding unhappily up and down the court-yard in the soft light of late afternoon, Christopher tried hope-lessly to soften the blow which he knew must be so mortal. He had returned from the barracks to find Toki setting out the tea things in the small walled courtyard, and during tea he had steeled himself to cross this first of the two barriers between him and that bliss which was so great that he hardly dared think of it. At first Toki had seemed to think that he was joking. Her small red mouth had parted in peals of childish laughter, but, seeing this angered him, she had abruptly ceased and sat silently watching and listening with an expression of incredulity that slowly gave place to appalled despair.

Christopher, unable to keep still and to look at the small golden face, now shocked and horrified, that had smiled and laughed at him with so much adoring love throughout the last five years, had risen and now walked rapidly up and down the courtyard, his heavy boots ringing on the stones.

"It's not that I *don't* love you anymore, Toki," he said for the fifth time. "It's because of something that's going to happen soon. Something that's going to make a—a difference. Something that will change everything."

"What? What is it that will change so much?" Toki's voice was dulled with despair. "What can change you or my love for you?"

"I can't tell you that now. It's an official secret. But you'll know soon. And it's not a question of not loving you, only—oh, I can't explain it all, but the war's over now, and what was all right then is not the same when peace comes."

"How not the same? Oh, Christopher, my love! We have been happy so long together." Her voice broke into a sob. "I had thought that after the war—I knew you could not while the war went on, but I thought, perhaps, afterward—we might——"

Perspiration broke out on Christopher's forehead. He turned and his arms fell to his sides. "Toki, you *know* I couldn't marry you! You can't say I *ever* pretended I could! I've told you that

298

Colonel Lemonfield would never allow such a thing. He'd have me sent away at once."

"Oh!" sobbed Toki furiously. "It's always Colonel Lemonfield! Is he to ruin our lives? Christopher—is it he—now?"

Christopher seized on this suggestion with avidity. "Yes—I suppose you'd better know—as you've guessed. He says that now the war's over you must leave the Casa dei Fiori and we must stop seeing each other. Apparently the General who was here two weeks ago with the convoy heard something. Anyway, he spoke to the Colonel and the Colonel has told me that it's got to stop—and at once. Oh, Toki, I'm sorry! But what can I do? I've *got* to obey the Colonel. I can't do anything else—you must see that!"

"Oh, I see it! I see it!" Toki burst into passionate weeping, her small face crumpling into a little yellow mask of misery while her two tiny birdlike hands rubbed and wrung each other in her lap.

Christopher stood almost as miserably beside her. He put out one hand to touch her shoulder, but she shook him off.

"Go away! Go away, Christopher! Let me alone! Leave me!" She flung herself facedown on the sofa and abandoned herself to fearful, racking, heartrending sobs. The evening sunlight, filtering through the golden-green leaves of the trees that lifted their branches above the low walls, played softly on her, and as Christopher, half frightened, half ashamed of what he had done, reluctantly withdrew a dove cooed in the flower forest around the house. A long, warm, throaty sound indicative of serene content, it was answered by its mates and all the still gold air was suddenly full of the calls of doves.

Christopher, hurrying down the lane, buttoned his tunic with shaking fingers. His nerves on edge, wondering at his own cruelty, exalted and unhappy by turns, he pushed between the crowding bushes of sweet pink oleander and white jasmine. As he gained the road he heard the faint hum of an airplane and, looking over toward the vast panorama of evening sea that stretched calm and golden to the far horizon, he saw an approaching speck in the eastern sky. High up in that enormous blue empyrean, already turning to the opal tints of oncoming evening, a flying boat appeared and circled over the bay. Lower and lower it came, roaring over the town in long curving sweeps, flashing brilliantly in the orange light of the falling sun. James' friends! They had arrived and now things would start. In the excitement of the moment he temporarily forgot his recent emotion and stared up into the glowing sky. The plane came in from far out to sea, flattening out, roaring low above the bright blue water—sank. A sudden gush of pure white beneath its keel increased to a thick flurry of flying rainbow spray, and out of this, the roar of its engines decreasing quickly, came the slim silver shape. Then it taxied toward the harbor entrance.

35

LATE that afternoon heavy purple storm clouds had swollen suddenly out of the west and the sun had gone down behind them in a lurid glare of sullen crimson flame. There was no wind, but by half past seven the few stars that twinkled after sunset were obscured by the banks of rolling clouds and the night was pitch-black. Pitch-black and moistly hot, with a heavy electric tension in the motionless air that gave a plain indication of the storm to come.

Colonel Lemonfield opened the long windows of the Villa's brightly lit library and walked out onto the loggia. He stared for a moment into the inky blackness of the silent garden and then began to stroll to and fro beside the stone balustrade. He was alone, for James was down in the town entertaining the journalists at dinner. It had been agreed that none of the Englishmen on the island save James and Brinsmead should meet the American newspapermen until the morrow. Euan was therefore intending to have an early night. At half past eight he would eat a light dinner by himself in his study and go to bed at ten. He had not, he reflected, been in bed before half past two—and most nights later than that—for the past fortnight. Tomorrow, too, was bound to be a long, exciting and tiring day.

But as he walked slowly up and down the terrace Euan did not feel excited—only despondent and a little depressed. He wondered why this was. He looked forward to becoming President of Baressa and to freeing himself forever from the galling ties of the mainland. His plans had all been laid with scrupulous exactitude; there was practically nothing that could go wrong, and all the chances of success seemed to be on his side. Of course, there was always the risk of some politicians in England actually taking action, or of the Army taking it first. But then some risks could not be entirely avoided in this sort of situation. Still—one never knew. Would this be his last secure night as generally accepted ruler of Baressa? Would some determined spirit at Command Headquarters—and it would have to be someone quite unlike Glasscraft—start shooting first and asking questions afterward? He pitched a cigarette end—a glowing arc of light—into the dark garden and smiled wryly. He was letting the strain of the last fourteen days play on his nerves. This feeling of gloom—he shrugged his shoulders as if to throw it off. Probably it was due to the electric tension of the oncoming storm, the black, hot, heavy night. Nothing more.

The storm would break as he had seen countless storms break over the island in the past five years, and after crashing thunder and a few hours of cataracting rain it would be over. Tomorrow the sky would be a pale washed-out blue, the air cooler than it had been for days, and the soaked earth steaming gently in the sun.

Tomorrow—five years ago. For nearly five years he had been on the island and for the last two—or perhaps almost subconsciously ever since he had set foot on the docks that August afternoon in 1940—he had known the fear of leaving. Growing through the long, slow seasonal curve of the tropical years, looming behind him, a grim black shadow weakening his will, his power for good. Destroying, too, much of the pleasure he had found in his schemes and plans for the island. "It is no use," it would whisper over his shoulder as he sat at his ornate desk, pen in hand, busy over some new improvement to trade, legislature or the public services. "You may be gone before this idea can come to anything, so why begin it? You cannot finish it and it will remain uncompleted." Or, "It is useless to do that, for if your successor is an Italian he will certainly reject it."

But ever since he and James had concocted their plan for complete independence the dark specter had gone. He had suddenly and with incredulous relief realized its departure on the morning after he had sat up scheming with James. All had seemed sud-

301

denly easy. Decision had returned to him in full force and within two weeks he had completed the intricate machinery that was to turn a colonial possession of Italy occupied by British military forces into a free and independent republic. At the thought of that his gloom lessened and he smiled. This time tomorrow he would be President of the Republic of Baressa. The island would be completely his. No alien generals could invite themselves to his house and air their crass opinions on his work. No foreign troops could brawl and shout insults in the streets of his capital. Tomorrow. . . .

He looked at his watch. Eight o'clock. There was a rumble of thunder, a dull warning roll from the west like the muffled guns of an advancing army. He looked up into the inky, starless sky, but nothing stirred. The impenetrable blackness pressed down, hot and heavy.

It was then that he thought of Christopher. Had he performed his allotted task with the careful regard to detail that was so necessary to the smooth efficiency of the *coup d'état?* One never knew with Christopher—unless he was given fully detailed orders he was inclined to be slipshod and forgetful. It had long been Euan's custom, when he wished the garrison company to perform any novel duty, to draft the orders himself and explain them carefully to Christopher in a personal interview, at the same time pressing him to ask questions concerning any points on which he was uncertain. But he had been too busy recently to do more than explain everyone's role at a general conference. Brinsmead, he remembered, had read out the notes of the part the garrison company were to play—the quick impatient voice moving too fast from point to point to enable Christopher to ask any questions even if he had wanted to. The fact that he had not approached the Palace for any clarifications at a later date pointed to a full understanding of his part, but—Christopher had an important role to play tomorrow, and on the appearance and bearing of his men much depended. The American journalists would form much of their opinion concerning the probable success of the coup on James' military propaganda.

Euan glanced once more at his watch and calculated quickly. If he walked down to the Casa dei Fiori now and talked to Christopher for, say, a quarter of an hour, that would set his mind at rest and he could be back in the Villa soon after half past eight.

If the storm broke before that Christopher could drive him back in his car.

He went quickly into the library and emerged with an electric torch. Its beam cut a yellow path of light through the deep blackness. As he went down the steps of the loggia thunder boomed out again—closer this time. He decided to take the shortcut through the garden, and some birds twittered apprehensively from the bushes of milky frangipani that lined the drive as his footsteps crunched the gravel. Then his torch bobbed away and the loggia was left empty save for a blaze of light from the open library windows.

It was less than ten minutes' walk to the Casa dei Fiori if one went through the Villa's garden. As Euan came out onto the road a jagged streak of lightning gashed the night sky with blue flame and thunder crashed out close behind. He found the narrow path to the Casa with some difficulty and proceeded quickly along it. On either side towering oleanders and hibiscus bushes rattled eerily, though there seemed to be no wind. Birds called fearfully in the undergrowth and a monkey chattered shrilly and was still. When the twisting path eventually emerged from the tangled bushes Euan found himself against the south veranda of the Casa. The undergrowth and creepers pressed so close to this house that they seemed to be trying to squeeze it in upon itself. Euan climbed the grotesquely ornate veranda steps.

"Christopher!" he called. "Christopher!"

There was no answer. He walked through an arched and fretted Moorish doorway, framed by two voluted horns of plenty, and found himself in the circular domed room with the pillars and urns. It was brilliantly lit, but quite empty. At his feet the Sabine maidens writhed bonelessly across the floor in the arms of their equally serpentine abductors.

"Christopher!" he called again. "Are you at home?"

Silence. He opened a further door, passing down a small passage, and found himself in a walled courtyard. A mango tree, bougainvillea purple and crimson, a marble fountain shining white under the torch's beam.

"Is anyone at home? Is anyone in?" he shouted. There was no answer. Thunder crashed closer.

"Hell!" muttered Euan angrily to himself. "Hell and damnation! No Christopher, no servants, nobody! I suppose he's down in the town and the servants are taking the opportunity to have a night out, too." He turned and retraced his steps toward the circular main hall. Then, on the threshold, he stopped with a jerk. Had something moved on the dark veranda beyond the open Moorish door? A shadow? Something flitting past as he entered the other side of this hideous room? He raised his voice. "Is anyone at home? This is Colonel Lemonfield. Is anyone there?"

No answer. Hot, tense, brooding silence pressed heavily down. He flung open a door at random and flashed his torch around a high bedroom with a heavy classical fresco of carved marble. Empty, as he had expected. On a green stone pedestal in a corner Perseus, staring into his mirror shield, struck stiffly at snake-haired Medusa. There was a queer, elusive scent, but nothing else.

Euan, muttering crossly, decided to go home. He might get caught in the storm, but it was better to risk that than to be caught here—Christopher might not be back until very late.

There was a deafening crash of thunder. It started overhead with a cracking, splitting, brittle noise and burst into an echoing roar. Euan felt a heavy drop of rain strike his upturned face as he left the house and, flashing his torch along the path, set off at a fast pace through the tangled garden. Lightning flashed bluely, and he heard a few of the heavy raindrops splash hesitatingly on the leaves at either side. He would get soaked before he got home, he realized angrily. He thought of turning back to the shelter of the house, but decided against it. It wouldn't matter if he did get wet—he could have a hot bath, and, anyway, he was going to bed early.

Suddenly the silent flower forest on either hand seemed to come alive. Birds called, monkeys shrieked, and something barked hoarsely. The storm was about to break. Euan started to run, and in an instant found himself amongst thick pressing bushes and tangled creepers. He pushed his way through them and then hesitated, his torch turning and flashing, probing and peering among the dark boles and thick stems. Was this the way he had come in? Surely the path had not been quite so narrow, the vegetation so rank and stifling? Another vivid flash of lightning, tearing the sky with the noise of ripping silk, showed up the heavy, dank foliage around him. Great creeper-clad trunks loomed upward, bright for a second, and then plunged back into intense pitchy darkness. His eyes were dazzled and he took a few uncertain steps forward, tripped over a root, and fell against a tree, clutching a thorny creeper. Then the sky, out of sight above the treetops, seemed to be rent open by a blinding, deafening clap. The hot darkness was suddenly filled with a crashing, shattering deluge of water that tore through the heavy leafy roof above and sent Euan, blinded and soaked, staggering on through a hissing, roaring wilderness.

Where was the road—had he missed it? He remembered with a peculiar sharp stab of panic that Christopher had once told him that it would be quite easy to lose one's way for days in the impenetrable undergrowth of his horrible garden. A man was supposed to have done so once—lost himself and never come out. No one had looked for him. Somewhere in the middle there was said to be a lake.

Euan pulled himself together, almost smiling. He was not lost —or was he? Well, even if he was so unfortunate as to become benighted here he would only have to shout loudly enough—once the rain had stopped, of course—to be heard and rescued. He mentally resolved to have the whole of this wilderness cleared in the near future, regardless of any wishes of Christopher's.

His torch probed here and there, gleaming on the thick lines of silver rain that fell in almost solid sheets. He plunged on while thorns and creepers tore at his clothes and springy boughs and twigs lashed at his face. He hoped he was turning back toward the house—he didn't know. Something behind him fell with a thump. There was a gasp—an almost human grunt. He turned quickly, flashing his torch, stabbing unavailingly at the torrential blackness. But there was nothing to see—the beam could not cut through the shining walls of falling water.

"I must get back to the house," he muttered, beginning to feel frightened with a curious dull fear that would not be dispelled. This sinister, gloomy forest might be full of noxious things— snakes and reptiles of all sorts. Even as these thoughts crossed his mind something flitted low over his head with a rush of wings, passed him, and hit something behind. Again there was that human-sounding grunt. Euan turned once more, this time really frightened, and again tried to pierce the lashing rain with his torch. But he could see nothing. He turned and blindly—knowing that it was madness—started to run.

Torn by thorns, tripped by roots and creepers, with a thousand invisible hands seeming to pluck to his sodden clothes and his brain a jumble of queer terrified thoughts, he ran. He lost count of the times he stumbled and fell, pitched forward on his face only to get up again and press onward faster than before as if to make up for some urgent lost time. He was no longer the Colonel of the British Army, the Governor and would-be President of Baressa, but only a small and bedraggled human being lost and filled with the age-old instinctive terror of storm and night and things that lurked in the undergrowth.

He had lost one shoe and sharp things cut his foot and his right wrist throbbed and ached as if it had been sprained. He must surely be nearly through this terrible wood—it could not go on forever. Then something struck his kness and down he went, turning over and rolling on soft mud. His torch, which he had clung to grimly until now, was gone, and as he picked himself up, panting, hurt, and filled with a nameless terror; he could not see it. It must have smashed and gone out.

As he stood, shivering and gasping, with his heart hammering against his ribs, another flash of vivid lightning illuminated the jungle. He saw, in that bright moment, that he stood on the edge of a stretch of muddy, stagnant water on which the rain fell in a hissing roar, throwing up spray and rebounding in flurries of silver across the surface. He stood leaning against a tree, holding on to its slippery bole with one arm for support, while he bent forward and felt for an agonizingly broken ankle.

He moaned softly with pain and terror, and as he did so he heard again—this time very close—that half-human grunt, and suddenly something struck him with terrible force on the back of the neck. White and scarlet parabolas of light exploded inside his head, flashing out to an unbelievable clearness of palest blue, and Euan Lemonfield drifted out and away across the water into the storm and blackness, while another flash of lightning revealed Toki bending over a small, crumpled, headless body and glittered on the bloody steel of the samurai sword.

36

NEXT morning at a quarter to eleven, when William, wearing a new civilian suit, entered the anteroom before the Colonel's office, he saw the Major's American journalists. There were six of them, and they looked exactly as he had imagined they would—tough, good-humored, and dressed in a variety of ostentatiously tropical clothing. He smiled at them and they grinned back resignedly. They were still in the dark as to exactly what was going to take place, for it had been decided that everything must remain a secret until the actual public announcement timed for noon. Two of them were rolling dice at a small table, while two more, with cigarettes drooping from their lips, were assembling or testing complicated cameras.

When William entered the Colonel's office he saw at once that something was wrong and his heart missed a beat.

Brinsmead and the Major were facing each other beside the Colonel's great desk, looking pale and unhappy, while Paige, Hope, and Christopher stood anxiously behind them. Beyond a quick glance from Hope no one took any notice of William's entry.

"But he *must* be somewhere!" exclaimed Brinsmead, tugging at his moustache with nervous exasperation. "He can't just disappear like a—like a damned fairy godmother!"

James mopped his forehead with a silk handkerchief; the day was hot and steamy and he had risen several hours earlier than usual.

"Of course not," he said wearily. "But *where* is he? It's so utterly unlike him to be late—at a time like this it's inconceivable!" The knuckles of his hand on the desk showed white and the glass was clouded by the damp heat of his fingers. "I came in late last night. I was tired after the party and went to bed. I thought he'd gone there long before—in fact, I listened outside his room for a moment, but there was no sound, so he must have been asleep.

Everything had gone according to plan, so there was no reason to wake him up. Then this morning at breakfast he wasn't there, so I thought—knowing his habits—that he had got up long before me and, not wanting any breakfast, had come on down here. When I didn't see him here I thought he must be with Keller-mann or Hope or Paige——"

Brinsmead sighed with weary irritation. "We've tried every-where, sir. Where *is* he? Where can he have got to? It's so odd. So unlike him. I've worked with him every day for nearly five years and not once have I known him to be late. Unless something's happened——"

Paige said shortly, "What *can* have happened?"

Brinsmead rubbed his hands together nervously. "I don't know. No—nothing can have *happened* to him, of course. Why should it? But it's so late—and no one knows where. . . ." His voice trailed off, leaving the sentence uncompleted, and for a moment they all stood in anxious silence

Then Paige said, "What *could* have happened, after all, to the Colonel? I mean, he was well enough when you saw him last, James, wasn't he? He couldn't have been taken ill suddenly somewhere, you don't think?"

"Oh, he was well enough. A little tired, perhaps, but that's all." James' voice was unusually strained and high and his black eyes flickered fearfully. "It was about ten past seven last night that I last spoke to him—just before I left for the town. I said, 'I'd go to bed early if I were you,' and he said, 'Yes, perhaps I will.' "

"He *did* go to bed, I suppose?"

"I suppose so. I really don't know. Surely——"

"Didn't you ask the servants, sir?"

"No. You see, I was positive he must be down here. But I told Fortu to ask them. When I got down here I found Fortu already waiting in this office and, not finding Euan, I told him to go back to the Villa just in case he'd returned and we'd missed each other. I told him to find out if the Colonel was there or at your house, Christopher. I thought perhaps he might have dropped in to try to catch you before you left. When Fortu comes back——"

He left the sentence unfinished and Paige said curtly, "If Fortu hasn't found him I'll get all the police and agents out. It's the best thing, you know." He looked apologetically at the others. To speak of a police search seemed somehow morbid. As if one expected to find—well, as if things might be unpleasant.

William joined the group around the desk, but said nothing. No one took any notice of him, but with troubled faces they stared at one another, looking for the signs of fear that might appear at any moment. On the great shining glass desk top Euan's fine ormolu clock ticked gently but inexorably.

Suddenly Christopher said, "Is anyone beside Fortu search—looking for the Colonel?"

"Mr. Lillywhite is." James raised his head and smiled wryly. "I saw him coming along the road as I was talking to Fortu on the steps. He had one of his half-caste children with him—the mad, blind one—and I asked him if by any chance he'd seen the Colonel. He looked at me oddly. I asked him why and he pointed to the child and said it had had bad dreams in the night. It's supposed to be psychic or something——"

"Nonsense!" exclaimed Brinsmead quickly. "It's just because he thinks it attracts attention."

James ignored the interruption. "Anyway, he said he would like to help if he could, and without being invited they got into the car. Lillywhite muttered something to Fortu—I don't know what, but whatever it was Fortu didn't like it—and they drove off."

"Good Lord, what a party to send to look for the Colonel!"

"I *didn't* send them, my good Christopher—they went of their own accord!"

There came the sound of footsteps outside. Everyone looked up. In the doorway stood Fortu, Mr. Lillywhite, and the mad child. At the sight of them there was a gasp from the group around the desk. Fortu's olive face was pale, almost gray, and his eyes dark with fear and horror. The once spotless white uniform in which he was dressed was bedraggled and muddy as if he had been forcing his way through wet undergrowth and in his bloodstained hands he carried a Japanese sword. Mr. Lillywhite was equally disheveled, though as this was his customary state it caused little notice. His complexion was a seasick green and he looked as if he might vomit at any moment. Only the idiot child seemed happy. A foolish grin wreathed its round, coffee-colored, dribbling face and its huge sightless eyes rolled incessantly.

309

Fortu gently closed the door behind them and stepped uncertainly forward toward the desk. "He's dead."

An hour later they were still there. It was noon, and outside the Palace a huge crowd seethed expectantly in the Piazza del Re, the roar of their voices coming muffled to the boom of distant surf through the now shuttered office windows.

Joined by Whyton, Texas, and a silent, somber Captain Zvengetzov, the group still stood around the desk in the greenish gloom that penetrated the long shutters.

With an effort James said, "Christopher—why did she do it? Surely you have some idea?"

"She hated him." Christopher's voice was hollow and toneless, drained of all feeling. "She always had, I suppose. She used to think that he disapproved of our—our relationship and wanted it to stop. She wanted me to marry her, I think. Of course, the Colonel wouldn't have allowed that."

"And you told her so?"

"Yes."

"So," said Brinsmead in a bitter, quiet voice, "she killed him and then killed herself. Because you had to mix up your dirty little affairs with the Colonel you've had him killed. You've as good as——"

"Stop it, Brinsmead!" Paige's voice held a hard note that no one had heard before. He stared angrily at the furious, quivering little clerk. "You know perfectly well that what has happened is not Captain Kellermann's fault. How the devil was he to know that the woman would go stark staring mad in that fashion? Anyway, she'd dead now and so is he, and we can do nothing about it."

"That's true," agreed Brinsmead grudgingly. He crumpled his handkerchief into a ball and rubbed it between his hot, moist hands. "We can't"—pulling himself together with an effort he appealed to all of them—"think about that now. We mustn't—we haven't time. We've got to forget about it till later. We've got to make plans now—and quickly. Those journalists are still waiting. Something's got to be done." There was silence, no one moved, and Brinsmead continued with painful urgency, "We've got to carry on. Major—you must see them. You must make the announcement. You must be the President."

They had all known that this must happen, ever since they had seen Fortu's face when he had entered the room an hour before. And now in the stifling midday heat of the shuttered office all eyes were turned on James—the senior in rank and position of them all, the dead Colonel's closest friend, and a man of culture and worldly experience. But they were doubtful eyes. Was this the man, sitting there at the great desk with his head bowed in his long slim hands, to carry through the coup? The man to bluff the world, to rule the island, to give them all they had been promised? They stared and said nothing, hoping against hope, willing him to look up and make answer.

The bowed figure behind the desk did not raise its head. James felt the eyes upon him and, looking into the future, saw its possibilities and quailed. He could never hope to bring this off successfully. Euan could have done it. Euan could even have risen to this occasion. With quickly thought-out and boldly executed plans he could have explained away a murdered predecessor and taken control himself. But Euan was dead, and the void of his absence deprived his great plan of the possibility of success and even the appearance of sanity. Now that he had gone the scheme that had seemed so brilliantly practical took on the appearance of a sick daydream—the idle, foolish fantasy of lotus eaters exiled on a tropical island too long. During the five years that he had governed the island Euan had made Baressa a part of his own towering, compelling personality. While he had lived he had been the island's greatest son—by self-adoption, perhaps, but all the more attached for that reason. Now that he had gone he had taken with him something that could never be replaced and had left behind only the "rather ridiculous little island where the Italians had hoped to find gold but had failed." To imagine for one moment that anyone, even his greatest friend, could take his place was madness.

Brinsmead was speaking again, speaking urgently. "Sir, you've got to do it—otherwise we're sunk." There was a halfhearted murmur of assent. They knew already what his answer would be.

James looked up slowly and everyone was shocked at the haggard face with despair and defeat so plain to read in the eyes. They had never thought the Major could look like this, the amused, amusing, ironic, kindly James, to whom life had seemed

311

to be a graceful, easy accomplishment never to be taken too seriously.

"I can't," he said finally, sadly, almost musingly, as if he knew he had failed them, albeit through no fault of his own, and was sorry for them. "It would never do. You must see that it would be impossible. I'm not the Colonel. I don't——"

"Captain Kellermann—" suggested Brinsmead doubtfully, but one glance at Christopher's pale, dully suffering face made it evident that such a suggestion bore no trace of reality. He turned back to James. "Sir, you must. I'll help you. I'll tell you what to do."

"I can't! I tell you I can't—and I won't!"

"Think what will happen if you don't."

"Nothing!" cried James almost furiously. "Nothing will happen. We'll go home. We'll clear up this mess and hand over. The sooner we get out of here the better! That General was right— we've been here too long!" His voice was beginning to rise hysterically. The hideous death of his friend and the terror of the colossal burden they were trying to lay upon his shoulders unnerved him. "We've just got time to put things right—or as nearly so as will satisfy the people who come on the *Napoleon* tomorrow. Euan's death will explain any confusion there may be. We must undo everything—put everything back as it was before. I'll somehow get rid of these Americans. It's not too late if——"

Brinsmead, Paige, and Hope turned on him furiously. Until he had spoken of abandoning the great plan they had still, somehow, been clinging to the hope that by some collective superhuman effort disaster might yet be averted. But, except for the Major, none of the others save Brinsmead had sufficient knowledge to become ruler of Baressa, and in any case the indispensable backing of the wealthy landowners, so essential to success, would be given, now that the Colonel was dead, only to his known friend and close companion. So they must fail. So all would come to nothing. All their individual plans and prospects were to disappear as if they had never been. The golden future promised them by the Colonel was a mirage that glittered and faded irrecoverably beyond the hot horizon.

"It's all very well for you!" snarled Brinsmead, banging the desk with his fist and glaring down, white-faced with fury, at

312

James. "You've got plenty of money—you're all right. What about *us*, though? What about the positions we were going to have? The salaries we were going to draw? What have *we* got to go back to? What about Hope, or Whyton, or Dawson? Sir"— he flung suddenly around and faced Christopher, the second most senior officer present—"what do *you* say to this?"

Christopher leaned against the wall, his face looking ghastly in the suffused greenish light. "The Major's right," he said with cold finality. "We must do what he says—there is nothing else." On the mainland "They" waited for him—Pirie, Glasscraft, D'Aumont. His regiment was fighting heavily with the 14th Army somewhere in Burma, crying out for reinforcements. They would send him there. The black mad horror of 1940 had not been banished after all. A grinning, ineffably disgusting ghoul, it had only hidden, biding its time, for the last five calm years and now it rose once more, huge and ominous, blotting out the future as last evening's towering thunderclouds had obscured the fading sky. The cold-eyed judges were arrayed and waiting, the torturers were coming out from behind the trees with newly sharpened knives. But with one last triumphant flicker of revolt he would thwart them. He would go back to the Casa dei Fiori, his last refuge, in which lay the bodies of the Colonel and Toki and from which the servants, fearful of the dead, would have absconded. There, alone, in the quiet of the golden evening, he would die—peacefully and unmutilated. He had enough of Dr. Valdonetti's sleeping tablets to ensure an easy, painless escape from the intolerable future, and when at last the sun sank over the calm sea he would be out of reach of "Them"—of everyone— for all time.

William stood farthest from the group around the desk. He was torn between deep sympathy for James, who had lost his friend and been placed, at this fearful moment, at the head of Baressa's Administration, and a realization of the bitter disappointment the others were feeling. For himself he cared little. A few short hours ago he had been planning to spend his life on this island. But now the blazing sunshine, the brilliant sea, and the bright variegated tropical colors had lost their allure. They seemed hard and sinister, brutal and somehow redolent of death. The roar of the restless crowd surged up into the hot, airless room, full of trapped, exasperated people, leaning motionless against the wall, gazing unseeingly over their heads with a curious, almost exalted expression on his upturned face, seemed wearily indifferent. A feeling of sorrowful pity filled William as he looked at that calm, scarred face—Christopher, too, had loved Silvana. At the thought of Silvana he smiled and his heart lifted and sang within him. Whatever happened now she was his. He would leave the island, but before that he would marry her, and soon he would be free and she would come to him. Secure and full of the confidence of youth and love, he viewed the future with unmixed happiness. He would return to his home, to the quiet of the cathedral town, the English countryside of hedgerows and spinneys and windy downs, and soon Silvana would be with him. Suddenly this long, hot room and its occupants took on an air of complete unreality, became a fevered nightmare from which he could awake at will. He must get away, he must free himself from this place of tottering dreams and escape into the daylight. He would find Silvana and together they would walk once more along the sunlit shore and plan their future. Muttering some unintelligible excuse to Hope, he turned away. He heard Brinsmead's voice raised again in vehement expostulation as he went out.

As William closed the door behind him the door of the other end of the anteroom opened and a man came in. It was Signor Balla, and he was followed by two natives carrying polished cedar boxes. There was something triumphant, jubilant, in his bearing as he looked around the room. The journalists noticed it. Bored and annoyed at being kept waiting so long, one of them turned half jokingly to him.

"Well, brother, are you the guy that's bringing us the glad tidings?"

Balla looked at him inquiringly and another journalist sidled up, grinning, and translated the question into Italian.

"Glad tidings?" Balla's chest swelled and his eyes sparkled with triumph. "You want good news—yes?"

"Sure we do! That's what we been waiting for, isn't it?"

"Then I, Giacomo Balla, shall give you good news! Good news for this island—for the world! I have myself—myself alone, you understand—discovered on this island what I believe to be one of the biggest deposits of uranium ore in the world!"

There was an electric silence. The journalists ceased smiling.

"Say that again!"

"Ha! You think I joke? No, no, *signori,* Balla is not joking! Everyone for years think that there is some mineral on this island. One finds a little gold—another finds a little nickel—someone else finds some tin. But it is I, Balla, who find the *real* mineral wealth of Baressa. It is uranium and I have found it!"

The journalists crowded around him, snapping questions, hardly waiting for answers, scribbling madly. "Please, *signore!*" A flash bulb exploded in a burst of magnesium white, then another. Balla smiled, posing feet astride and hands on hips—his day had come at last. Then, "I'm for the radio!" exclaimed one journalist, snapping shut his notebook and making for the door. The others dashed after him and the room was empty save for Balla and his men, the guards of the Banda, statuesque at the office door, and William.

The whole thing had taken less than five minutes.

37

THE hard, hot light of a late afternoon at the end of August 1950 glared on the great white concrete road that sloped in carefully graded turns down the escarpment and through the far-reaching new suburbs of San Pietro. It glittered blindingly on the huge, shiny enameled signs and advertisement hoardings —"Mobilgas," "Dubonnet," "Goodyear Tires"—that filled the dusty vacant lots between the unending rows of raw concrete buildings. Up and down the road moved continual crowded traffic, a never-ending double train of heavy, snorting diesel trucks, jeeps of drably uniformed Control Commission police, vast earth-moving machines, angular and sinister as prehistoric monsters despite their vivid paint, on their way to the great craters of wealth on the plateau—craters that had once been plantations of tangerines and fields of flowering beans.

Jostling each other for room, the traffic hooted and ground its way to the town or tableland. Small English runabouts, Austins and Morrises, full of shirt-sleeved, hard-faced foremen, engineers, and mining mechanics, big glossy American Cadillacs, Packards, and Pontiacs in which the new aristocracy of the island, the United States senior executives, scientists, and managing directors reclined behind blue glass windows.

One of these—a great shining black automobile like a flattened whale, opulent with chromium fittings, nosed carefully in and out of the traffic on its way through the long straight streets of hastily erected houses down toward the town. From time to time, when their great vehicle was held up, throbbing gently in the pale dust and blue exhaust gas of the thick traffic, the two occupants might catch a glimpse of the town below them. Of tall, smoke-belching chimneys whose tops shivered in unbearably heated air, of great new concrete jetties dwarfing the old harbor, of the dog-tooth corrugated iron roofs of acres of factories and machine shops ablaze beneath the pitiless sun. Raw yellow earth, white ferro-concrete, harsh black iron, and always still more strident hoardings against the tropical sky—"Johnnie Walker," "Socony Vacuum," "Pabst Blue Label Lager."

The long car rolled up to the high, many-windowed modernistic front of the new hotel as the sun was falling into the west. The door opened and a big elderly American in a pale-gray tropical suit of expensive cloth got out and turned to the driver.

"Well," he said, smiling, "we certainly did that run quickly. That road to Dinghité is the goods, all right. What did we make it in?"

"Two hours and forty-five minutes."

"That's swell! We'll do it in less tomorrow, eh?"

"I hope so, *signore*."

"Sure we will! Right, Fortu, you can get along now. Come for me at seven thirty tomorrow."

"Very well, Signor Direttore. Good night."

"G'night, Fortu." The Director turned and mounted the stone steps of the hotel and a tall, thin doorman with reddish hair and watery blue eyes behind his steel-rimmed glasses solicitously swung the revolving glass doors for him. Mr. Lilly-white had found steady employment at last.

Fortu drove away through the long dull roads of the new town and at last into the shabby streets and squares of the old. He was held up by a train of heavy trucks in the Piazza President Wilson and drew into the side near the clanking, grinding terminus of the overhead railway to the escarpment that stood on the site of the long-since demolished Aquarium. Then he drove on through the crowded, clanging streets to the comparative quiet of the Daldacara shore. It had not changed much in the past five years, and after he had put the car away in the Company's garage, he walked to his own house next door—the wooden bungalow that had been occupied in turn by Captain Pirie and Major Sherwood years ago.

He went in and changed out of the khaki uniform with the Company's collar badges that he wore when driving for the Director into a blue shirt and trousers. There would be time to sail around the harbor before dusk, and it was cooler out there in the bay.

As he was about to go out he caught sight of a calendar beside the wide, cracked mirror. The twenty-ninth of August. He stopped suddenly and remained motionless, staring into the mirror at the dark, somber face that stared back. The house was silent with an evening calm. Then a truck started up in the garage and the rhythmic roar of its engine filled the hot air. The twenty-ninth of August. Ten years ago today the British cruiser had steamed over the horizon and the British rule on Baressa had started. Ten years—a decade. He had been sixteen then, and now he was twenty-six. He felt somehow much older. Ten years. . . .

The truck's engine stuttered and halted and the spell was broken. Fortu sighed abruptly and went out at the back of the house on to the long slope of rank-smelling mud, flashing gold in the falling sun. He pushed his old silver seaplane float into the still, evening-calm water, got in, and raised the sail. A faint, almost imperceptible breeze bent the white canvas and slowly, gently, he glided out into the harbor. Glided out past the beached hulk of William's old motorboat, the paint blistering and peeling off its rotten sides, and the *Italia* that now lay beside the new oil installation at her weedy moorings. Glided faster as the breeze became stronger farther out in the harbor and bellied out the white canvas now tinged with orange from the setting sun. There was the *Bina* against the commercial docks—Rossi would be sailing tomorrow for *bêche-de-mer*. He had failed to find a cargo again, for there was not much work for little free-lance freighters these days. Past the Dhow Control Point with the khaki-clad figures of the Commission's police on the little jetty whose white stone was washed with gold in the evening light. And now he was outside, and the breeze stiffened and the silver boat leaped forward across the shining sea.

"Once again," thought Fortu, "and I'll go back." He lounged idly in the stern, whistling gently as he gripped the tiller. Around went the boat, close under the stern of the British cruiser. A few sailors shouted to him and waved from the deck and he raised a bronzed arm in reply. Then out past the Dutch destroyer, and it was time to turn and go back. He looked across at the island a mile away. The sun was just disappearing below the hills to the west and San Pietro was already in shadow—a long mass of irregular buildings sprawling up the hill. Ten years ago. He sighed and shifted the tiller and the little boat turned back toward the shore. A last ray from the setting sun flashed a myriad colors from the curve of spray at the bow.